DATE DUE			

Edinburgh Bilingual Library (10)

Edinburgh Bilingual Library (10)

RAMÓN DEL VALLE-INCLÁN

Luces de Bohemia

ESPERPENTO

BOHEMIAN LIGHTS

Translated by
ANTHONY N. ZAHAREAS
University of Minnesota and
GERALD GILLESPIE
Stanford University
Introduction and Commentary by
ANTHONY N. ZAHAREAS

University of Texas Press
Austin

International Standard Book Number
0–292–74609–1 (cloth)
0–292–74610–5 (paper)
Library of Congress Catalog Card Number 75–36215

Set in 10/11 'Monotype' Barbou
and printed in Great Britain by
W & J Mackay Limited, Chatham

Edinburgh Bilingual Library

FOREWORD

An imperfect knowledge of a language need be no bar to reading a work written in it if there is a good translation to help. This Library may aid those who have a wide-ranging and adventurous interest in literature to jump the hurdles of language and thus do something to help break down the barriers of specialization. That it may be helpful for courses in Comparative Literature is our hope, but not our main aim. We wish to appeal to a wider audience: first to the cultivated, serious reader of literature who is not content to remain within the English language, secondly to university students and teachers of English and of Modern Languages by inviting them to throw from outside some new light on, perhaps even discover different values in, their particular fields of specialization.

The languages represented will be French (with Provençal), German, Italian, Portuguese, Spanish (with Catalan), and Medieval and Renaissance Latin. The translations will not be 'cribs' but good literature worth publishing in its own right. Verse will generally be translated into verse, except where the unfamiliarity of the language for most readers (Provençal, Catalan, Old French, Old High German) may make a more literal prose rendering advisable. In the majority of cases the Introductions will present up-to-date assessments of each author or work, or original interpretations on a scholarly level. Works already accessible in translation will be included only when we think we can offer a new translation of special excellence or when we wish to relate it to another volume in the series.

Contents

Bohemian Lights

Ramón del Valle-Inclán

PREFACE

The Spanish text of *Luces de Bohemia, Esperpento* is based on the most recent second edition of Espasa-Calpe, Colección Austral No. 1307 and has been prepared with the aid of the author's son, Dr Carlos Valle-Inclán. The Espasa-Calpe version had already been collated with two previous editions, the first complete version of *Bohemian Lights* in the 'Opera Omnia' series of Editorial Rua Nueva (Madrid 1924) and the version included in the second edition of the complete works of Valle-Inclán (*Obras completas*, Vols. I–II) published by Editorial Plenitud (Madrid 1952).

I have collated the two versions of 1920 and 1924 and have used the variants in establishing an accurate text, in providing a historical background to the episodic action, in assessing the author's intentions, and in interpreting the work. This is, hopefully, a full-dress treatment of all the textual aspects of Valle-Inclán's first *esperpento*.

The original version of *Luces* appeared in serial form in the weekly *España* between 31 July and 23 October 1920. It had twelve scenes, one for each weekly issue. In 1924 a newer, longer version appeared in book form with fifteen scenes. Valle-Inclán added three new scenes, II, VI, and XI, integrated the new material into the old plot, elaborated some of the older 1920 material and, finally, made some important stylistic changes. The three new scenes contain mainly historical material; since all three precede the famous scene XII where the blind hero, as he is dying, defines the *esperpento*, the additional scenes lead directly to that climactic moment and thus determine the final method and vision of Valle-Inclán's new theatrical genre. In short, to a highly stylized perspective of the grotesque in 1920, Valle-Inclán added in 1924 the immediate impact of the disquieting features of the Spanish situation: even the series of small but telling changes or some interpolations throughout the play are strategically placed so that everything in the plot, characters and setting point neatly to a more historical orientation of the *esperpento.*

Despite successful theatrical productions in Paris and Buenos Aires and despite constant demands by various theatrical producers (at least two to three Valle-Inclán plays are being produced each year in Madrid), *Lights* was never allowed to be performed in Spain until 1972. Official censorship found too many offensive elements and would grant permission for a theatrical production only if they were deleted. It is therefore significant that most of the passages crossed out by the Spanish censor (and which I was able to examine carefully thanks to Dr Carlos Valle-Inclán who provided me with the same marked text which government officials returned to the Teatro de Bellas Artes) were precisely the ones Valle-Inclán interpolated in 1924. Such censorship, though narrowminded, was understandable: Valle-Inclán's final version of his pioneering *esperpento* contains some of the most immediate, harsh, painful, most brutal and sarcastic, most unsettling comments on Spaniards and the Spanish establishment.

Extensive notes with elaborate cross-references are required by the fact that Valle-Inclán used a cinematic sort of technique to give the reader a panoramic sense of early twentieth-century Madrid. Trying to identify and recover the post World War I Bohemian and political background from *Lights* was often like drawing the shape of a tree's roots from the appearance of its branches. But where historical evidence exists Valle-Inclán's picture of Bohemian Madrid is largely corroborated, while most of the historical content of the 1924 additions can be documented. In short, *Lights* is an accurate documentary, and the historical or cultural background is indispensable in framing a theory of the *esperpento* and in clarifying what is puzzling in this form of the drama of the Grotesque. Valle-Inclán strove to include the smallest details of happenings, meetings, newspaper headlines, popular topics, political debates, common phrases, clichés, current slang, and, above all, of the physical aspects of the city. The first *esper-*

pento is a rich and persuasive picture of life in a specific community at a specific time.

I have tried to sketch a meaningful version of the 1900–1920 background. The notes identify real characters (writers, journalists, politicians), make connections with others (poets, anarchists, government officials), locate places (especially Old Madrid, the hubbub of night life), trace colloquial and slang expressions, explain the popular literature of the times (especially the popular musical comedies and satirical, burlesque reviews), describe political debates and, finally, seek to capture the complex relationship between the night life of artists or Bohemians and the government bureaucracy. Documenting *Lights* in *its* historical, contemporary terms is a way of elucidating the *esperpento* aesthetically and of penetrating its meaning.

The notes which give this information apply both to the Spanish and to the English text. I have consulted standard histories of the period, but also contemporary magazines of Spanish, European and American newspapers which kept close to the events. I have extensively used Alonso Zamora Vicente's detailed reconstruction of the background of *Lights*, first in his inaugural address to the Royal Spanish Academy and later in the published version, *La realidad esperpéntica* (*Aproximación a 'Luces de Bohemia'*), Gredos (Madrid 1969). I also interviewed several residents of Madrid and natives of Galicia who either lived through the period of *Lights* and still remember the particular expressions or allusions of the time, or who still today use the same forms of speech that Valle-Inclán recreated for some of his characters. I am especially grateful to the historian Luis Vázquez de Parga and to the most remarkable inhabitant of Madrid I know, Ignacio Montoya, who reproduced for me Valle-Inclán's speech patterns and slang; finally, I owe much to Dr Carlos Valle-Inclán who spent several days with me clarifying obscure allusions and letting me consult Don Ramón's private library.

Bohemian Lights was produced in Paris by Georges Wilson; it was performed at the Edinburgh Festival in August 1968 by the Oxford Theatre Group under the direction of Nic Renton and has at last made its appearance in Madrid under the direction of José Tamayo. Professionals and amateurs who wish to acquire the performing rights of this translation should contact the publisher or write to me.

I dedicate this volume to *ἀγαπητὸς Ἀλέξανδρος* not only for encouraging me but also for being so tolerant and so patient. ¡Lo que ha tardado esto!

Anthony N. Zahareas

Introduction

BOHEMIAN LIGHTS AND VALLE-INCLÁN'S THEATRE

Great Britain. When Valle-Inclán's 'grotesque' play *Bohemian Lights* was chosen by the Oxford Theatre group as their opening Fringe production at the 1968 Edinburgh Arts Festival, drama critics remarked that the production was 'shooting at difficult game' and most confessed that they were very little prepared for such a play.[1] Some viewed this piece as a black carnival set in a surrealist limbo, others were puzzled by its episodic form, similar to the epic, satirical plays of Brecht; two or three suspected that the spirit of Peter Brook was brooding over the producer's adaptation of it; many were stunned by the masked characters, most of them partially deformed or entirely grotesque; and all commented on the inertia, the cruelty and the sentimentality of Valle-Inclán's painful Bohemian underworld of Madrid in the early 1900s.

Bohemian Lights was 'unknown' to the British public yet it got a good reception from many of the critics and from an audience that grew and became more appreciative day by day. One critic even called the playwright 'the still extraordinarily avant-garde Valle-Inclán',[2] while in an assortment of reviews *Lights* was called 'controversial', 'stunning', 'theatre of the minority', 'harsh', a 'tremendous exhibition', 'truly haunting', full of 'Valle-Inclán's exquisite poetry', 'brilliant, absurd, confusing', and a 'tragedy-travesty'.

Spanish literature in general, unlike that of France, Italy, Russia, or Germany, is at times remote from the taste and artistic conventions of England and America. It has had very little influence on writers or playwrights. Yet occasionally a writer in Spanish does impose himself and leaves a lasting impression on certain thinkers. Unamuno with his 'tragic sense of life' and Ortega y Gasset with his 'rebellion of the masses' or 'dehumanization of art' were two of these; Federico García Lorca with his surrealist tendencies was probably another. More recently, the influence of the Argentinian Borges on American writers has been greater than that of most French and German authors. I believe that Valle-Inclán's influence on the theatre and cinema, like that of Fernando Arrabal or Luis Buñuel, could well prove as powerful as that of Lorca on poetry and Borges on prose.

The Oxford group's production of *Bohemian Lights* was the first time a major work by Valle-Inclán had been staged before English-speaking audiences. Although *Lights* was published as early as 1920 it had never been allowed production in Spain because of the persistent censorship. Yet Ramón del Valle-Inclán, who died in 1936, was both a novelist and dramatist of international stature, and it is now conceded that without him the Spanish theatre would not be what it is today. Martin Esslin, drama critic and Brecht scholar, has drawn attention to Valle-Inclán's style of writing, called *esperpento* (the grotesque or ridiculous), in which the world is depicted as inhabited by tragicomic, almost mechanically actuated marionettes, and has classed him and Lorca as Spain's 'two important dramatists' and has commented favourably on his Brecht-like theory of drama.[3]

Valle-Inclán's plays have not been easily accessible. This has led the American critic George Wellwarth to complain: '[The fact] that these [Valle-Inclán's] plays—among the best of the modern theatre—are only just becoming partially available in English is a commentary on our disgraceful publishing practices.'[4] The drama critics at the Edinburgh Festival anticipated Wellwarth's complaint and reviewed the première of *Lights* by observing that it was 'recalled from obscurity', by agreeing that *Lights* 'stands out clearly as something of a discovery', by arguing that the play 'shouldn't have had to wait 48 years for its British première', and by suggesting that this and other Valle-Inclán plays 'deserve a long overdue revival'.

The present bilingual version of *Lights* (the same translation that the Oxford group adapted at Edinburgh) coincided with a partial revival of Valle-Inclán's theatre in Europe and the

Americas; so partial, however, that one cannot yet take any biographical or bibliographical facts for granted.

I propose here to raise certain problems and to ask certain questions about the 'practical' aspects of Valle-Inclán's plays. I shall refer to recent productions in Edinburgh, Paris, Madrid and New York because they happen to embody the crucial confrontation between dramatic literature and theatrical production. Few playwrights have meditated so thoroughly and so intelligently as Valle-Inclán on all the relationships between script, stage direction, performance, dramatic crisis, the reader's mind and the observer's eye, scenario, the actual and the imagined actors. And in *Bohemian Lights* we have the case of a script meant to be staged as spectacle, but which has instead been only read and taught as literature or which has led to papers, articles, monographs, theses, books and, ironically, even to an inaugural address.[5] Valle-Inclán would be the first to suspect a judicious, balanced and essentially academic critique of his theatre, since he functioned as an iconoclast, a dramatist who felt that the Spanish literary establishment, especially the Academy, had to be lashed into awareness. A brief consideration of some theatrical aspects of Valle-Inclán's works can illuminate the text and complement the purely academic fate of his plays; these aspects can also provide a more accurate background to the standard presentation of his life and works.

There is the question whether this 'grotesque' play is complete without performance. The Edinburgh production was a reminder that *Lights* as Valle-Inclán conceived it, has a double existence: it is a literary work, an 'unaided' script, but it is practical theatre. The play lends itself to the theatre and when it is staged by a firm-minded producer who has the necessary theatrical experience, it can be very uncompromisingly antagonistic to traditional theatrical responses. Many of the critics at Edinburgh realized the difficulties of such a production, especially the efforts to achieve on the stage Valle-Inclán's attempt simultaneously to delight and to alienate his audiences. *Bohemian Lights* is a dynamic script which forces a producer to distinguish between the differing moods of its fifteen scenes; its production lends itself to trickery from the Theatre of the Absurd, to visual effects from Expressionism or from the clever stagings of Peter Brook, to choreographic techniques from the French school of mime. There are no less than fifteen episodes that mingle reality and fantasy, in which the producer must draw a picture of Spanish society with a blind Bohemian (a poet-genius for some or a drunkard nuisance for others) wandering through it, having to come to terms with himself and the world. The difficulties of staging so many tableaux are great: we witness a few compressed hours in the death of the Bohemian Max Estrella wandering drunkenly but full of wit into a series of improbable confrontations with the law and the Establishment, its victims, a smooth civil servant and his unlikely Minister; an incredible band of Modernist poets, drunks, street-walkers, policemen and even various animals. The blind poet, recalling various traditional figures of the prophet or seer (Homer? Oedipus? Teiresias? Belisarius?), is guided on his last hellish journey by a parasite, symbolically called Don Latino de Hispalis.

The difficulty that faces the producer in staging this episodic play is to achieve a rhythmic flow between the many diverse scenes. A succession of static scenes, even if they occasionally form brilliant grotesque tableaux, could minimize or destroy the effect of a spectacular, dynamic montage. The fact that Valle-Inclán constructed this grotesque play in the episodic form which Brecht was later to tailor so expertly to his satirical ends makes the play even more challenging for theatrical producers. One perceives in the script an intensely compassionate writer protesting angrily, but above all eloquently, against political and literary humbug. The producer of the Oxford Theatre group staged *Lights* in a surrealist, avant-garde manner, utilizing masks, lights, colour and sounds. He wanted to tackle the grotesque play with originality without undercutting its central meaning or obscuring its tragicomic vision.[6] The problem was to juxtapose incongruous elements effectively.

The producer followed Valle-Inclán's composition closely by concentrating the whole piece on Max; he showed to the audience a blind poet, who cannot earn a living, put in very difficult personal and social circumstances and evolving a theory of *esperpento* by 'sensing', 'imagining' and 'feeling' the existence around him, and by being prompted at last by incidents with a personal relevance, i.e., meeting the 'nymph-whore' Lunares, hearing the mother with the dead child in her arms, and learning about the murder of a prisoner, to shrug off the inertia and pathos of blindness and helplessness. But focusing mainly on the starving Bohemian meant not emphasizing the historical background of Spain that lurks in every single scene, and not stressing the full brutality of the strikes and social misery. Much of the grotesque mosaic of historical details had to be eliminated, avoided or merely suggested. Every producer must take up such practical positions as are based on his particular reading of the *Lights*' scenario; and each stage decision of this kind, no less valid than a scholarly one, will follow a close reading of the play. Renton, the Oxford producer, was fascinated to find that *Bohemian Lights* could hold so much in historical and social detail and was still able to exist theatrically. He thus tried to solve the dilemma between foreground and background by replacing the facts of political brutality with a mood of starkness based on the spiritual deadness and inertia that falls on a decadent society. The players used masks and spoke with pitched voices that were almost sexless in their intonation. They created ambiguity between person and mask and tried to capture the effects that are usually associated with *Lights*—absurdity, travesty, mechanization, silhouettes, marionettes, the uncanny, carnival. For the central scene, the producer chose not the 'discovery' scene, scene XII (where Max hits on the *esperpento*) but scene XIV between old Bradomín[7] and the modernist poet Rubén Darío in the cemetery following Max's burial. Correctly perhaps. Bradomín's opinions on life and drama and his gentle mockery both of the Spanish popular theatre and of the sophisticated modernist literature summarize the standpoints from which Max Estrella had forged his *esperpento*. This is a new, different way of interpreting Valle-Inclán's view of the artist within the play: a chance to give and to help (especially face to face with the indifference of the establishment) is the supreme gift of the artist, who finally refuses to bury himself in egocentricity and sentiment.

America. Bohemian Lights has not reached New York yet, but two short plays composed after *Lights* and which elaborate further its grotesque theatricality were performed in 1970 as part of the La Mama Experimental Theater Club. A quick look at them and at the production provides further insights into Valle-Inclán. The plays, *The Head of John the Baptist* and *Paper Rose* (or *Cheap Token*), were selected as innovating drama that would be interesting to Americans unfamiliar with Spanish culture, yet relevant enough to the theatrical problems of the New York community. Valle-Inclán was introduced and advertised as Spain's best modern playwright and its great theatrical innovator. Soon afterwards *Paper Rose* was adapted in a dazzling exhibition of Hieronymus Bosch-like technicolour by TV's CBS Camera 2 and was shown twice to American audiences.

The arrival of Valle-Inclán's theatre in America inevitably led to further inquiries about his work, his theories, his potential for theatrical productions and also pointed to a need for reappraising his work in the literature departments of universities. Valle-Inclán is above all known for inventing a grotesque type of drama called *esperpento* in which the tragic sense of life is, metaphorically speaking, acted out by classical heroes reflected in distorting, concave mirrors. His theory was that in the past a dramatist had looked up, as if on his knees, at reality and presented a reverent picture of it, like the Greek tragedians, or else he had confronted it standing on the same level, somewhat like Shakespeare, and this had led to more realistic visions of life. Not so in our days. The dramatist can see the world from above like a puppeteer, and from this vantage point it would appear ridiculous and absurd, for it would be seen as if through the eyes of an unconcerned dead man looking back on life.

The implications of this approach for the theatre are many. The company at La Mama followed closely Valle-Inclán's theory of theatrical distance in staging *John the Baptist's Head* and *Paper Rose*. So did the producer of the TV spectacle. We must imagine a puppet theatre about to perform a heroic drama or a shattering tragedy, when the puppets are suddenly abandoned by the puppet master and left alone to perform the great tragic moments of life.[8] Naturally the result is ludicrous, jerky gestures in the midst of authentic tragic moments. The cliché 'when the cat's away the mice will play' becomes no less than the guiding aesthetic for staging these playlets. In *John the Baptist's Head*, a dashing foreigner blackmails an avaricious inn-keeper who long ago had murdered his own wife. The old man will not give up his hard earned money and appeals for help to his young mistress, who traps the youth into an embrace while the inn-keeper knifes him in the back. But stunned by the stranger's lustful kiss as he meets his death, she cannot remove her lips from his cold mouth and, clinging desperately and absurdly to the corpse, she realizes too late that she had killed what was life-giving. In *Paper Rose* a proletarian blacksmith shows indifference to the suffering of his dying wife until he realizes that 'this heroine' has been hoarding money for years. Mourning in rural Galicia with its Irish-like superstitions turns out to be a Buñuelistic nightmare, especially when in a moment of drunken passion the husband is attracted by the corpse's beautiful whiteness (the superstitious gossiping neighbours had spruced her up for the funeral as if for a wedding). Shouting that he is within his rights, he tries to get under the covers watched by the scandalized villagers.

These two plays are farcical versions of religious morality plays staged on Corpus Christi day (the same *autos* so brilliantly composed by the great Calderón in the 17th century) and are part of a series of five one-act plays with the title *Puppet Altar-Piece of Avarice, Lust and Death.*[9] With the same exquisite language and the same lively sacrilegious sense he displays in *Bohemian Lights*, Valle-Inclán embodies the moral problems of evil, lust, death in living farce. But in contrast to traditional farce, the *Baptist's Head* and *Paper Rose*, like the earlier *Bohemian Lights*, are no simple laughing matters. The dramatist's harsh, cold perspective exposes human helplessness to derision: man's frailties are bared and his vices flayed; silhouette-like simpletons such as Max's companion Latino, the proletarian blacksmith, the modernist poet Dario de Gadex, or the avaricious inn-keeper are savaged for being the ridiculous creatures they are. The characters with which Valle-Inclán populates his puppet melodramas in part account for this. They are a congregation of dupes, fops, braggards, bullies, Bohemians, loud-mouths, whores, bureaucrats, bitches and dirty old men. No one seems to give a damn about anyone. If we are shown perversity in love, it is perversity not love that matters. And all this is done with an incredible, stupendous force of style. It is like putting the grotesque canvases of Bosch, Goya, or Solana on the stage and animating all their bizarre figures.

This is very difficult theatre. The La Mama group concentrated on a Brechtian kind of alienation by capturing the strange combination of hilarity and hideousness. Valle-Inclán's puppet plays, like much of modern theatre, establish the reality of illusion and instead of offering only good material with a social treatise they create a tangible nightmare. For example, the sensation of the wife's grotesque triumph as she lies in cadaverous glory amid the squalor of a poor house becomes overwhelming. And right there the theatrical evening ends spectacularly as actors begin moving about like frantic puppets trying to reach the strings which at the start of the play had directed all their movements. But the puppeteer, as Valle-Inclán would want it, is not there. The point is that God's head is turned away; left alone to play, the puppets make a complete mess of the situation just as human beings disfigure the most sublime tragic moments of the human condition.

The New York production was a worthy follow-up to the première of *Lights* at Edinburgh. This was the first time New York was seeing Valle-Inclán staged professionally, yet he was and is the strongest influence making for the resurrection of a Spanish-speaking theatre.

Spain. It may not be Britain's or New York's fault that Valle-Inclán has not arrived at his position of rightful eminence earlier, since in Spain the theatrical establishment is, aesthetically speaking, reactionary, afraid of new experiments and has never quite known what to do with Valle-Inclán's daring innovations. Besides, there has always been censorship, and even after a lapse of some 50 years several of his plays remain proscribed because of their satirical irreverence. Yet it is difficult to imagine a more meaningful display of theatrical pyrotechnics than those provided by him. Figures emerge out of the most unexpected places, they enter through space, the scenery flies up and down in full view, ropes and puppet strings are outlined against the sky as actors run across the stage; in short, every conceivable trick of the trade of the theatre, of the cabaret, of the burlesque, and the cinema can be applied to *Lights* or other plays with a lusty abandon and a Grotowski-like control. It was ironical that after some four decades his grotesque plays should be performed first as a

Fringe event in Scotland and then by the vanguard community of New York in Off-Off Broadway.[10]

All his life Valle-Inclán had to fight against conservative theatrical producers in Spain and unimaginative critics steeped in the traditions of social drama with naturalistic staging. They were intimidated by his ribald humour, sardonic tone and lusty vulgarity. They were antagonized by his new techniques and frightened by his iconoclastic anarchism. In this sense Valle-Inclán represents everything that is best in and everything that is wrong with the Spanish theatre. Spain has often had great drama and there are distinguished modern playwrights. Yet the practical side of play production is wretched: actors still declaim, and producers still give shape to middle-class naturalistic drama. They cater to the audience and have refused to experiment. Valle-Inclán, however, and many of his followers today, do not compromise. The result is excellent 'underground' theatre or reliance on productions abroad.

We see in *Bohemian Lights* how Valle-Inclán mastered two styles of theatre rather than one, being equally adept in the contrasting styles of realism and expressionism; he was equally effective in short one-act plays, in long episodic dramas (sometimes twice the normal length of modern plays), and even in trilogies or quartets or quintets. His search for expressive form and spectacle, due to the aesthetic urge to integrate old and new ideas about dramatic art, led him to experiment with archetypal figures, masks, elaborate impressionistic stage directions, low-class choruses, verse, scenic and rhythmic effects, carnival-like movements, choreography and schematizations. He exemplifies the modern theatre's aspirations and achievements as well as its more or less inevitable limitations and even failures. It is largely this multifarious engagement with the possibilities of dramatic art and the sharpening of techniques, combined with their application to a significant subject-matter and even to straight history, that makes Valle-Inclán a playwright of international importance, of the stature of Brecht, Pirandello, O'Neill, Beckett, or the latter's possible heir-apparent, Fernando Arrabal.

Valle-Inclán is a modern dramatist in that he was searching for an aesthetic and ethical centre. This search was frustrated because he was read and praised but not produced. He was certain that he had found his own way to drama and was confident that the result was worth the labour involved. Like Cervantes, long before him, he kept on repeating that his time would come.[11] His plays embodied the ideas and conflicts of the first three decades of our century, assimilating their advances in theatrical technique, incorporating cinematic montage, and expressing all the unease and anxiety of our tragic and absurd horror of life. His impressiveness as a dramatist results, moreover, from his determined effort to extract a detached, and lucid vision from Spanish history, virtually emptied of meaning by centuries of lies, presumptuousness, helplessness and, above all, bombast and rhetoric. He did not find many comforting assurances in the state of Spain, it is true, but he had the integrity to acknowledge his country's failures and the skill to dramatize perspicaciously the absurdities of Spanish life as he saw them.

Valle-Inclán was the first modern dramatist of the Spanish malady, the first to dramatize the tragicomic fact that the consciousness of modern Spain is so sensitive to failure, so blunted by rhetoric, so overladen with the tragic sense, that it has stifled all its humorous qualities and lost the ironic touch. In *Bohemian Lights*, as in all the *esperpentos* and the puppet melodramas or silhouetted *autos*, Valle-Inclán's characters are often like loud-mouthed automata filling the centre of the stage with a prolonged, self-generated chatter. He is a puppeteer whose plays show us how cells behave in mechanized organisms. But because he is a great dramatist these organisms are not only Spanish figures in a Spanish society prior to its dissolution in civil war; they are figures in the more universal society of modern Western man. The paralysis of will and the numbing of the mind which he ruthlessly diagnosed and coldly dramatized must be one of the most profound and disturbing perceptions of our own condition that any artist has had. He understood how disquietingly we are compounded of the tragic, the farcical, the sad, the pathetic, the uncanny, yet somehow remaining all too real and human. He understood how absurd we are when called upon to play 'the big roles of life', and he saw the uncanny results of a tragic destiny enacted only by gesticulating automata. Valle-Inclán's experiments were not undertaken to suit the whims of an aesthete, or the calculations of a theatrical opportunist bent on following the latest fashion: they manifest, rather, a unity of high purpose rarely found in modern playwrights.

THE WRITER AND HIS WORK

The Writer. His real name was Ramón José Simón, later changed to Ramón Valle Peña. Born in 1866, he was the son of Ramón Valle Bermúdez, a restless seaman and amateur writer who had a considerable influence on young Ramón. Ramón was to become the first, and so far the last, professional writer in his family. Writing for a living has been a particularly hazardous occupation in Spain, especially for those who have no independent income. Valle-Inclán was harassed by economic stringencies throughout his career. With modest, irregular earnings, he barely managed to get by, raising a large family and living in Madrid. Persistent creativity in spite of constant insecurity was Valle-Inclán's experience for almost all his 45–50 years as a professional writer. He thus came to understand that the political, religious and legal institutions of Spain, as well as the literature by means of which Spaniards represented the world in which they lived, their place within it, and themselves—all these were not independent from but reflections of the political structure and economic basis of Spanish society. All too aware of the terms on which an author had to struggle to live, he followed his own vision of art with the tenacious integrity of one totally committed to a life of creative writing.

Famous contemporaries like Unamuno, Baroja, Azorín, Machado, Galdós or Benavente became independent enough to be able to afford to live and work in or near Madrid. Others, like Azorín, compromised their values and standards.[12] Valle-Inclán rarely managed to work on his own terms; he was never successful enough in Madrid to be free from financial worries. Even around 1910–12, the stage in his career when he was concentrating on the theatre and had had some successes, most of his letters are concerned with the delays in receiving payments from his publishers or the difficulty of obtaining advances. He even asked Rubén Darío several times to intervene on his behalf and, in the elegiacal scene of the graveyard in *Lights* (XIV) he makes the Marquis of Bradomín say to the poet Darío, 'let's climb into the coach for we've still got to visit a bandit. I want you to help me sell the manuscript of my *Memoirs* to a publisher. I need the money, I'm completely ruined . . .' It so happened that in 1911 Valle-Inclán had written to Darío, 'You're familiar with the financial situation of the *Review* and what it usually pays. I rely on your intervention.' Or, 'I'd appreciate your intervention since at the present I'm broke. . . .'[13] At the same time his letters show how he refused to compromise with producers who wanted to change scenes they thought would be disagreeable to the audience; or how upset he was that a play might be dropped from the repertoire and his income suddenly stop.

Valle-Inclán had to accept any way of selling his writings short of compromising his principles. Financial need was probably the main reason why most of his important works, including *Bohemian Lights*, first appeared serialized, often in cheap magazines, and then were reworked and republished. Several other works were later collected and rearranged as parts of trilogies and in other groupings. Times were difficult for writers of fiction, and Valle-Inclán must often have been faced with the need to fill pages in order to complete an instalment and so make more money. During the early part of his career he even translated novels from Portuguese and French, although he disliked translation because it was time-consuming and, in any case, he knew he was not very good at it.[14] And in 1900, before he had become famous, he was desperate enough to convert a popular, sentimental play by Arniches into a long novel because the publisher wanted to take advantage of its box-office success. This notorious example of adaptation, *The Face of God* (*Cara de Dios*), was never reissued; only one copy has been preserved, in the possession of his friend, doctor García-Sabell.[15]

It's not improbable then that Valle-Inclán converted his own economic vicissitudes into the literary theme of the artist humiliated by modern society. The blind poet of *Bohemian Lights*, for example, is treated like a 'poor annoying wretch' by his old friend the Minister when all he wants is 'bread in my house'. The artist here is forced to accept a small handout because, as he confesses, 'I've no alternative' and like the rest, 'I myself am riffraff'. Valle-Inclán was not only concerned, as were others, with Spain's notorious incapacity to appreciate her intellectual minority (a commonplace since Ortega y Gasset's writings),[16] or with the Romantic motif of the isolated, misunderstood artist, or with the notion of the artist's disillusionment with contemporary reality; he was indignant at Spain's disregard for or indifference towards her artists and furious at his own economic humiliations. For example, an exaggerated helplessness and frustration grips his blind Bohemian who sarcastically claims to be the first poet of Spain yet is now ignored and starving. The embittered Max Estrella, like other characters, is in many ways the expression of deep-seated anarchical tendencies in Valle-Inclán. The discussion between the Minister and the poet on this matter of making a livelihood through literature is revealing of the times (see p.153). The writer in Valle-Inclán's fiction becomes an outcast, facing humiliation, yet with enough pride to strike out blindly at the society in which he lives, where he has no means of livelihood.

The fictional situations in which Valle-Inclán placed his artists are portrayed within the range of social typology. They are not buco-romantic figures, thrown-into-the-world without purpose. He stresses the historical and economic forces which determine the literary personality of Spain and he selects those life situations and human experiences which determine specific types of artists—like himself. Max Estrella is what he is, in part because of the nature of his economic difficulties, and those difficulties—that inter-relation between artist and society—are as much a part of this Bohemian figure as are the individual traits of genius which distinguish him from other Bohemians. Valle-Inclán does not portray the Bohemians favourably or pejoratively; he looks at them from a historical perspective, as those persons involved with some aspect of the arts who have broken with their social class and hence have no social roots. Old ideologies are rejected and no new ideologies have taken their place. The Bohemian was not one who lived in the Puerta del Sol and got drunk every night; he was an intellectual vagabond with a sense of rebelliousness who, as a rule, sought refuge as a hanger-on of the art world. He was in literature a symbol of the polarizing process which divided the arts from the establishment. The socio-political system is challenged by two enclaves of rebellion, that of Bohemians and Anarchists. This picture of Bohemia has a great deal in common with the sombre canvas of Bertold Brecht later. Valle-Inclán had seen the rebel's personal anarchism or iconoclasm as a product of existing political and economic circumstances. Max's criticism of the shoddy treatment of artists in Spain sprung from an extreme sensitivity to the disparity between ideals and practices, but it reflects above all the hostility of the artist to a bureaucratic world that holds his values in contempt and mocks his ambitions. Valle-Inclán's personal attacks against the establishment are now proverbial. In a lecture in Argentina in 1907 (he agreed to the lecture tour because he needed the money), he remarked caustically that 'when the music of verses and the music of rattling bells are not enough to fill pocketbooks, then we buffoons and poets start giving lectures in the Americas'. He also remarked that the one thing writers had in common with gypsies was the fact that both were persecuted by the civil guards.

Bohemian Lights opens with a desperate economic situation in a professional writer's home and with the improbable proposal of an inexpensive, collective suicide; the evening is spent attempting either to recover some miserly pesetas from a bookseller or to find money for drinks, but it does not end with Max's death, which is the result of under-nourishment, alcohol and despair: Max has left a winning lottery ticket with his companion Don Latino, who kept the money for himself while Max's wife and daughter were committing suicide. The graveyard scene sums up the world of a writer like the Bohemian Max (see p.201).

With Valle-Inclán, of course, we must be careful to distinguish between the writer and his creations. He was careful to raise the problem of an author's relation (likes or dislikes) to an important protagonist—analogous, say, to Cervantes's attitude toward Don Quixote.[17] *Bohemian Lights* leaves open the question whether the author shares his Bohemian's grotesque vision of life or not. But that Max is a wholly fictitious character—a 'puppet'—is something I think few would maintain: he clearly projects Valle-Inclán's own situation as a struggling writer. *Lights* remains the great tragic-farce of the economic plight and humiliation of Bohemian and artist. It reveals Valle-Inclán's life-long preoccupation with his own economic insecurity.

Valle-Inclán's economic struggles point to his commitment to literature, for he bore poverty and misfortune with more dogged persistence than any Spanish writer since Cervantes.

Yet, despite his productiveness and the wide variety of its forms and themes, there is little in Valle-Inclán that can be considered hack-work. He used to claim that a work of art owes its allegiance to itself and that it must maintain its integrity as art if it is to function as a valid commentary on our world and on ourselves.

Thus while giving free reign to his creative powers Valle-Inclán simultaneously exercised strict discipline over his form and style, by discipline and strenuous contemplation. His only work with an autobiographical structure, *The Wondrous Lamp*, is an aesthetic theology, for it deals with the craft of writing as a mystical experience. He felt an intense drive to write and publish, and never stopped struggling to perfect his means of expression. The poet Antonio Machado was aware of Valle-Inclán's struggle and called him 'the saint of Spanish letters'.

On several occasions Valle-Inclán claimed that he had not been tempted only by literary fame but also by the glory that rewards adventures. He bragged all his life of having been a man of action. His claims to adventure are misleading, however, and the account of his life impresses one as a rather ordinary story, conspicuous for its aspirations and its extravagant staging but also for the absence of any spectacular activity or unusual accomplishment. Except for some travelling (not nearly as exotic as some anecdotes claim), Valle-Inclán did not in fact lead a very active life. He was not a good actor, he failed in business, and he never realized his ambition to attain to the title of Marquis. He was a bad political campaigner and lost two elections, one as a Carlist and another, some years later as the opposite, a Progressive. He even had less luck as a land speculator in real estate. He was successful only as a writer.

Valle-Inclán was, like his contemporary Thomas Mann, a skilful imitator who could turn to a variety of classical and popular styles. He was a master of literary 'pastiche' and a study of his art raises the question of imitation as burlesque or parody, and as original fiction.[18] He was a versatile craftsman who could adapt any style from any source, even to the extent of cultivating the two extremes of pure aestheticism and of popular or folk literature. He readily accepted the challenge of a different style or another view or another perspective and used it to get the best from his own talent. Far from bordering on plagiarism as some critics have suggested his adaptation of others reveals great resourcefulness in varying his methods of satirical writing.

His methods of parody resemble the later practices ot Bertold Brecht. He based various stories, novels and plays on fragments of existing works, on documents, chronicles, musical reviews, legends and even hearsay. Pseudo-literature, ballads, parliamentary rhetoric, popular songs old and new, bullfighting or sports news, puppet shows, all were at his command, to be drawn into a play wherever needed. Again and again he drew on motifs from the Bible, from the classics, from Shakespeare and especially Cervantes. Few models are treated respectfully, many are ruthlessly parodied. He parodies classical tragedy in *Bohemian Lights*, Shakespeare and Calderón in *The Horns of Don Friolera*, and the Bible, especially the parables of Christ, in *Divine Words*; as with all great ironists, Valle-Inclán's parody is double-edged and we are not always sure who is the butt of his mockery. The best proof of his variety is the persistence of his own earlier styles, not because he could not bear to discard them but rather because he was one more writer to be adapted and parodied.

In some ways Valle-Inclán is a writer's writer, often an intellectual, in spite of his intention to write for everybody. There are countless concealed quotations, echoes, pastiche and parody of past literature in almost all his works. Yet within this 'bookishness' there is a lively clarity of expression that gives his plays, for all his allusions and interest in styles, a down-to-earth quality that is rare among sophisticated stylists. It was always the unpretentious readers who interested Valle-Inclán. And the use of parody, very much like that of Cervantes, reveals his ambivalent attitude towards traditional models; the same ambiguity surrounds the iconoclasm of Max Estrella as surrounds the obsessions of Don Quixote.

For Valle-Inclán there is no parthenogenesis in literature. The way to originality was imitation. Like Brecht later, he was not afraid to ransack the work of his predecessors and contemporaries. He rejected the romantic view of the poet as the purveyor of divinely inspired intuitions and conceived the creator as a craftsman and inventor. And this may explain why he never hesitated to elaborate or alter his own work, according to the circumstances of the moment: he did not consider his works 'sentimental attachments', or 'somewhat inspired'; works of art were artifacts, the products of men for other men. He was by no means a 'humble' writer. He thought, as Cervantes did, that he was the most inventive and most skilful writer of his time. To invent one had to master the skills of imitation. A demiurge is for Valle-Inclán a skilful craftsman, one who debases himself only when he becomes too attached to his own creations.

Valle-Inclán has been considered a liberator of Spanish prose, and his elegant command of language is the one factor hailed in all histories of Spanish literature. His volatile, sometimes surrealist but controlled, musical prose boldly crossed the well-defined frontiers and freed the Spanish language from dross and clichés, investing it with a new intensity and colour. His sharp style in the grotesque manner has exerted a great influence on such modern writers as García Lorca, Camilo José Cela and, in Latin America, José Donoso, Carlos Fuentes and Miguel Asturias. He is considered a goldsmith of modern Spanish and a prodigy of verbal musicality. His prose is shaped with the eye of a sculptor and the ear of a composer, yet it is interspersed with the telling irony and malicious wit of a penetrating commentator on the human condition and historical reality. Valle-Inclán has, above all, an extraordinarily precise and tactile sense of the power of words, and he is a master of tone and impression. His style is decidedly anti-rhetorical; each sentence is obviously the result of careful craftsmanship of a process of refining almost word-by-word. So much so that many critics have analyzed his plays or judged his vision strictly on aesthetic grounds. His stylizations and incredibly rich vocabulary make heavy demands on the reader. In fact, the mingling of poetry and slang with an amazing synthesis of several Hispanic dialects place his later works in the same category as Quevedo's *Visions*, as the most difficult in Spanish literature. His linguistic virtuosity is especially evident in his capacity to coin and compound new words. His language oscillates from poetry and aristocratic elegance to the grotesque slang of the Madrid underworld, but in every case it is meticulously orchestrated.

The reputation of Valle-Inclán as an author of linguistic complexity (even to the point of his stylistic manipulations being compared to those of his contemporary James Joyce), has not been always to his advantage. At times he has been facetiously praised for his purely aesthetic stylization and detrimentally pigeon-holed as the brilliant 'innovator' of Spanish prose. *Bohemian Lights*, for example, was for long examined mainly as a stylistic *tour-de-force*, while the other grotesque dramas were studied for their artful contrivances; even theatre critics had until recently treated his *esperpentos* as if they were brilliant aesthetic exercises and not committed literature or social theatre. The question his critics raised was how far a great writer could deal with history without doing violence to his talent. Valle-Inclán's case shows that pure style need not be divorced from the realities of human and national experience.

As far as the content of his works is concerned, he is the most committed (and perhaps the most ethical) writer of his time. Yet there are many who still argue that while his plays may be of some interest as vehicles for the problems and anxieties of the age or as political satire, none-the-less their chief distinction lies in their being memorable language. This implies reading some of the most immediate, painful, most brutal, most unsettling pages of modern literature without really being moved. It is true that Valle-Inclán—like Brecht—was a thorough craftsman, but his grotesque dramas do not stand simply for an aesthetic doctrine but above all for a sense of life surrounded by and lived in history. In short, Valle-Inclán's aesthetic talents were not injured by his commitments; on the contrary, historical interests provided a remedy for the nihilism of pure aesthetics and even determined the shape of his later style.

In Valle-Inclán grotesque vision and pure style are separate but intertwining threads. His language plays with the distorted, the absurd, the tragicomic. He achieved the rare feat of creating in his novels and dramas a language all his own, which suggests the rhythms and gives the feeling of real speech in Madrid, Galicia or Mexico without being tied to any particular regional dialect. My linguist colleague Larry

Grimes has demonstrated to me that the language of *Bohemian Lights* or that of the brilliant novel *Tyrant Flag* (*Tirano Banderas*)[19] is not in reality the speech of any Spaniard or Spanish American but a conglomeration of the Spanish spoken or written at every social, literary, and regional level. All these elements are combined around the core of a popular vernacular but, here too, art intervenes to cut this vernacular down to its essentials, leaving only a crystallization. This is such a vital and original linguistic synthesis, so well composed, so deeply rooted in a number of oral and literary traditions, that it succeeds in creating the illusion of real speech.

A Valle-Inclán work once read will not easily be forgotten. His grotesque humour, his parody of Spanish bombast, his plastic buffoonery, the precision of his verbal energy, the excesses of his parody and his controlled irony, all stick as pictures and sounds in the memory. One has to read all his late works to be aware how brilliantly he tested the frontiers of incongruity or how effectively he exploited the borderline of farce and tragedy by forcing the gates of the absurd, while retaining unsullied his view of his stylistic craft and his control of his imagination. It's as if he saw himself by turns as a cold anatomist of Spanish reality, a passionate destroyer of myths, an oblique moralist, an ironic clown, and a pure stylist who learned to test the Spanish language so that, as he scornfully said, words would be seen and felt pulsating rather than declaiming or reasoning. He is a mystic of hilarity and rage, holding up the concave mirror of modern Spanish absurdity. He stands next to authors like Céline as the painter of a moribund society and next to stylists like Joyce as a liberator of language. As a comic genius, a master of irony, verbal slapstick and the grotesque, he may perhaps have no peer.

Life and Legend. Valle-Inclán's biography would be simple enough but for the fascinating legend of the *persona* whose apocryphal name and assumed aristocratic title have become proverbial: Don Ramón María del Valle-Inclán y Montenegro, Marqués del Valle y Vizconde de Viexin. So much attention has been paid to the anecdotal aspects of his life that the legend has coloured each factual detail. His biography has been pieced together like a patchwork quilt from scattered anecdotes supplemented by recollections on the part of his many friends, admirers and enemies. Valle-Inclán worked tirelessly to overcome inactivity through a well disciplined 'mythomania', for, to compensate for uneventfulness and boredom, he invented an existence that was out of the ordinary. Whatever effect his frustrations and disappointments may have had on his character, they by no means broke his spirit. Perhaps no biographer can deal justly and fully with such a man. For a good part of his true life was the apocryphal one, the passions, fantasies and sense of humour, the yearnings, self-reproaches and indignations that lay behind the surface of the public writer. Such a life could be revealed only in an autobiography, and an unusually frank one. Yet people like Valle-Inclán—hard working, witty, imaginative, unsuccessful—do not usually write their lives. But if he could not experience real adventures, he could stage them:

> The one you see here, with a Spanish face like that of Quevedo, with a black mane and a long beard, that's me: don Ramón María del Valle-Inclán . . . I barely reached the age called youth when, because of the end of an unfortunate love affair, I embarked for Mexico in 'La Dalila', a frigate that on its next trip was shipwrecked on the coast of Yucatan . . . On board of 'La Dalila'—and I recall this with pride—I assassinated Sir Robert Jones. It was a vengeance worthy of Benvenuto Cellini.

Such passages which are scattered in a series of self-portraits, do much to confirm the legendary picture of Valle-Inclán, a picture which we might imagine subtitled 'The Writer as a Child of His Own Invention'. As Unamuno observed, with amazement and irritation, Don Ramón created a stage for himself, a vaudeville; that is, he tried to transform facts into anecdotes while life was yet being lived. He took his surname, for example, out of his family's history, but the overall effect of the combination *Don Ramón María del Valle-Inclán*—a perfect hendecasyllabic line of verse, strikingly sonorous and rhythmical—was his own creation. He claimed, tongue in cheek, that such a name should serve as a refrain in some poem. His admiring friend and fellow modernist Rubén Darío obliged in his 'Balada laudatoria' where each stanza repeats the name as if in a refrain.[20]

The legend of Don Ramón usually begins with his notoriously extravagant appearance—long beard, heavy-rimmed glasses, purple cape, and elegant high hat. Tall and thin, a combination of sinful sage, decadent aristocrat, and absurd pilgrim, he used to walk with arrogance and talk with a deliberate, thick lisp. As though acting out Goethe's observation that literature lurks in the shadows of good conversation, he talked continuously and always attracted an audience. In fact, Valle-Inclán's public appearance, i.e., his utterances, costume and physiognomy, were deliberately calculated to make an impression. His success with these affectations is attested to by the fact that he ranks with Don Quixote and Sancho Panza as a prominent literary subject in modern Spanish painting and graphics. It is said that besides inventing extravaganzas and pontificating on almost everything, he used to insult many and outshout all. He was probably the most accomplished public performer in Spanish letters since Lope de Vega, while the anecdotes, incidents and dirty jokes are matched only by the other legendary figure, the great satirist Quevedo. Among the more memorable anecdotes are the following: how he visited Mexico because there is no other country with the letter *x*; how he led uprisings there and was named '*coronel general de los Ejércitos de Tierra Caliente*'; how he interrupted an Echegaray play to point out indignantly that a female covered with silk but with iron veins underneath is not a brave woman but an umbrella.

Yet this extravagant personality, no matter how boastful, was also conscientious and even humble, with an instinctive dislike for pedantry and pretentiousness. We are faced with a baffling paradox in trying to reconcile, first, the public clown with the serious writer and, secondly, the pure aesthete with the committed satirist. It is Valle-Inclán himself who, like the astute Velázquez of *Las meninas*, creates an imaginary self-image which he then proceeds to incorporate into his real life as if the invention were fact, so that lived experience and invented experience are interwoven in a work of art. It all seems a delightful contrivance. And if contrivance does not make an authentic biography, the boundary of legend-life does dramatize effectively a valid predicament. Valle-Inclán reminds us of the clown who walks the tightrope and fails to reach the opposite post. He falls off the rope and executes a grotesquely confused double somersault in mid-air. We laugh as if we had never seen anything so ludicrous. But the clown knows that what he did required more skill and more imagination than merely to walk the tightrope from post to post. That makes all the difference, and we can understand why the clown is often a man with a special brand of dignity, as well as with a grudge.

The dictator Primo de Rivera had a taste of the clown's grudge when Valle-Inclán in his *esperpentos* began mingling his witticisms and jokes with devastating criticism and invective. The dictator imprisoned him supposedly for being a 'distinguished writer but an extravagant citizen,' whereupon Valle-Inclán retorted:[21]

> What this character Primo de Rivera says is okay; because he doesn't know Spanish. He meant to say that I'm an 'eccentric' citizen, and has said instead 'extravagant'. I certainly am extravagant because I always tend to travel away from the road where other people go.

This is an aspect of Valle-Inclán's life that counters the legend of the clown because, for all his playfulness, Don Ramón kept his dignity, his sharp critical sense, and, above all, his deep scepticism. His involvement with the issues of his day often led to harassment, and on more than one occasion he was arrested for his open criticism. In short, he experienced all the frustration and disillusionment of his fellow Spaniards. He was strange, complex, unpredictable, but this is sometimes the way with genius.

Valle-Inclán was born at Villanueva de Arosa, a coastal town in the province of Pontevedra in Galicia on 26 October 1866 and spent his childhood speaking the regional language of the Galicians. He was exposed to ancient traditions and local superstitions and, as a child, he listened to innumerable local legends, many of which he later incorporated in his works.[22] Galicia is often compared to Ireland. With its rough peasants and strange folk tales, its primitive passions and lyrical softness, Galicia became a strong influence on the works of Valle-Inclán—from the evocative mists of the *Autumn Sonata* and the violent world of the *Barbaric Comedies*, to the moral grotesqueness of *Divine Words*. In fact, Valle-Inclán's appeal lies in great part in his lifelong concern with Galicia, a kind of regionalism that recalls Synge's view of Ireland and William Faulkner's commitment to the Deep South.

He started publishing stories, anecdotes and articles in local reviews while studying law in Santiago de Compostela. He was not an avid student. When his father died in 1890 he left school, went to Madrid, travelled to Mexico in 1891–92 where he published some items, and returned to Madrid where he started his career as a professional writer. He supplied stories, translations, sketches, critical and literary articles, for a variety of publications. It was here that he exhibited new extravagant clothing and assumed his elongated name. He spent a lot of time in the cafés of Madrid, became immersed in the city's intellectual and artistic activities, and led a mainly Bohemian life.

The big city exerted a magnetic attraction for the young writer. It seemed a place not only of chaos, decadence and impending danger but also, at least at first, of opportunity and renewal, of a richer and freer existence. Much of the attraction of Madrid could be attributed to the new experimentation in literature, the arts, and education, and to the perpetual battle between progressives and conservatives. Among the contending radical philosophies, anarchism and syndicalism appealed more to young artist-rebels than the more staid versions of socialism, and the activists in various movements seemed close to the spirit of artistic rebellion. Madrid was a great cultural centre, and Valle-Inclán met playwrights, musicians, actors, writers and painters. Above all, he closely observed every facet of the Bohemia of Old Madrid. The genesis of *Bohemian Lights* is in this early period of his life. On the one hand, he understood the philistines' resentment at the Bohemian scale of values that was not based on money; yet, on the other hand, he also understood how often Bohemians were poseurs, not responsible for the tradition of intellectual life, talking endlessly but never writing. These contradictions are seen in Max Estrella, Rubén Darío, Don Latino and the Modernists of *Bohemian Lights*. In Madrid, Bohemia was a way of life full of extravagance and ingenuity, but also of weakness and ineptitude.

Here in Madrid, young Valle-Inclán displayed his brilliant wit and sarcasm. He had a great sense of humour but was by no means an easy man to get on with. Temperamental and impatient, he appeared unstable and irascible, and his mythomania called his sincerity in question; yet he was a budding genius. Between 1899–1912 he composed several plays, became involved with theatre people, did some acting and, in 1907 married the actress Josephine Blanco. He helped with the artistic direction of the theatre company where she was working. They had six children. Economic pressures increased, his health deteriorated, he underwent operations which required long periods of convalescence. He learned to write in bed. His politics, especially early in the century, are an enigma. He was an anarchist, a socialist and an admirer of their leader Pablo Iglesias; yet he even joined the conservative Carlists, although his famous character Bradomín announced that he defended their traditionalist views only for 'aesthetic' reasons.[23]

Valle-Inclán showed more obvious concern for historical issues and more responsibility toward social problems during and immediately after the First World War. He visited France and the Allied war fronts in 1916 and later published his impressions of the conflict.[24] Some critics claim that this war experience made him face up to integrity and responsibility. Certainly after the war political comments pervade his speeches and writings. In the late twenties the *Esperpento of the Captain's Daughter* was confiscated because it was considered insulting to the military regime. Later the Republican government honoured him in his last years, by appointing him director of the Spanish Academy of Fine Arts in Rome.

When he reached his sixties, and after this radical change of perspective, Valle-Inclán continued writing with amazing vitality and was, in the words of one critic, 'young among the old and even among the young themselves'.[25] He seemed during his last years to be engaged, at least verbally, on every front: literary, political, social, intellectual. His health, however, was failing rapidly, and he returned to Galicia. There, according to a recent biographer, he seemed to relive his youth: 'He visited the cafés . . . talked incessantly, to the amazement and wonder of his captivated audiences. His gift for words and stories had never been better.'[26] He died of cancer on 5 January 1936, some six months before the outbreak of the Spanish Civil War. It was reported in the newspapers that he said of his imminent death: 'I'm dying! . . .

But . . . it's really taking a long time!'[27] Whether true or not, it was characteristic that Valle-Inclán should on the verge of death joke about it with the same peculiar mixture of dread and humour that was the trademark of his life and works.

Valle-Inclán had travelled three times to Latin America. His first visit was to Mexico in 1892 and to Cuba in the following year. Spanish America projected itself into some of his early works and eventually became the central preoccupation of his brilliant novel, *Passionate Lands: Tyrant Flag* (*Tirano Banderas*, 1926). In 1910 he accompanied his wife to Latin America as the artistic director of her theatrical company. Wherever he went he launched attacks against the Spanish theatre and the Spanish-speaking public, scandalizing audiences and even causing riots that interrupted performances. He had become humorously arrogant about the successful contemporary playwrights, reacting violently and sardonically against the rhetorical clichés, the commonplace social melodramas, the conventional naturalistic scenery, the stage tricks and mechanical precision which characterized most of the contemporary theatre. In *Lights*, scene XIV, a character ridicules the Spanish variety of bourgeois morality and facile characterization: 'In our Spanish theatre . . . Hamlet and Ophelia would become two highly amusing characters: a timid youth and a silly girl! Think what our glorious Quintero Brothers would have done with them!' His attacks were part of his effort to renovate the Spanish theatre and salvage it from the quagmire of countless 'well-made' but routine plays. Of one of the public scandals he caused he wrote:

> What I did, really, was to anticipate what the public was going to do a little later: reject the play. I said aloud what many others thought and what afterwards everybody in one way or another ended up by saying. I, because I was more intelligent, or more experienced, or more truthful, already saw in the second act what the public came to admit at the end of the work.[28]

In Buenos Aires he lectured on modern art and on the craft of writing, and toured most of the other South American capitals. In 1921 he returned to Mexico as the special guest of honour of President Obregón. While there he documented his novel on dictators and on his return to Spain started his famous insults against the Spanish settlers in America (*gachupines*).

His personality was one of contradictions and paradoxes, and his divided nature, in its alternation between imagination and discipline, may be the key also to his art, with its paradox of total commitment to writing and total restlessness. No full-scale study of Valle-Inclán's life and times, and artistic personality yet exists. Perhaps the time is ripe for one now because his importance may transcend his significance as a writer, and as a picturesque personality. He may be an epitome of his times. Most of the cross-currents and contradictions, the moral and political dilemmas, the economic, artistic, and literary trends of modern Spain are focused and exemplified in the life of Valle-Inclán.

Although most of the biographical documents are not yet accessible and although the views of the people who knew him are contradictory, yet enough is known about Valle-Inclán and his various masks for the preparation of a fairly circumstantial picture of his character and a reliable account of the main events and decisions of his life.

What we do know is that he was unusually dedicated to his craft, that he never had economic security, that he nevertheless acted with all the arrogance of an aristocrat, that he protested with the passion of an anarchist, and that on the whole he was as deeply involved in the conflicts of Spain as any of his contemporaries. We can see what must have led him to the literary grotesque: his reaction to the collapse of Spain in the disaster of 1898; his dilemma as a sensitive and passionate artist in a country where the majority of the reading public did not know what good literature was; the necessary choice between opportunism and freedom to create; his indignation at the social evils of Spanish society; the theoretical and practical difficulties he encountered in an inflexible establishment.

Dramatic Works. Valle-Inclán's dramatic works are an especially difficult subject for his critics and his biographers. With the exception of Sumner Greenfield's recent literary interpretation there are no thorough studies of his plays as theatre and there has been no attempt to provide a guide to the understanding of the key plays.[29] There is nothing on

Valle-Inclán for example even approaching M. Esslin's *Brecht: The Man and His Work* or Phillipe Thody's *Jean Genet.* Valle-Inclán worked in so many forms and on so many subjects that he is certainly one of the most varied dramatists in the history of world theatre.

Unlike Benavente and most of his contemporaries, Valle-Inclán was a 'radical' as far as his approach to the drama was concerned: he rebelled against every aspect of the theatre that was being produced in Spain. He did not write 'for' but rather 'against' the Spanish public. Hence according to José Ruibal, one of the so-called 'underground' playwrights of present day Spain, 'the ethical value of his dramatic works. Valle-Inclán, keeping a close watch over the artistic quality of his plays and over his independence as a dramatist, found himself surrounded by obstacles. But today, more than thirty years after his death, who has given us more than he?'[30]

Valle-Inclán started his career in the theatre by adapting some of his own prose works and by doing some acting himself until he lost his arm in 1899. He wrote directly for the stage between 1905 and 1912, toured with theatrical companies, theorized about the stage and, in general, made a real attempt to succeed as a man of the theatre. After several battles with theatrical companies, a serious altercation with Spain's most eminent novelist and man of letters, Pérez Galdós, who rejected one of his plays, Valle-Inclán stopped writing for the theatre.[31] None-the-less, he continued to write plays; in 1920 alone he published four major plays, among them the first *esperpento, Bohemian Lights*, and the tragicomedy of rural Galicia, *Divine Words*. The next six years were very productive: not only did new plays appear, but old ones were reused and collected together for republication. His production faltered after 1927 and his last plays, a trilogy appeared in 1930.

Valle-Inclán never felt the need to repudiate his first plays, for in them there already appear seminal motifs and novel stage techniques which are later systematically defined. For this reason his dramatic work, despite the variety of genres, has an impressive unity. His first important play, which deals with the amorous recollections of the Marquis of Bradomín, for example, cannot be isolated from contemporary Modernism yet it is here that the playwright disengages himself from the idealism of Modernist poets and undercuts the subjectivity of his protagonist. At the same time many of the grotesque characters of the *Barbaric Comedies*, especially the servant Don Galán, the crazy Fuso Negro and the chorus of Villagers, already show the background of horror and farce essential for the understanding of Valle-Inclán's later grotesque techniques and political orientation.

His approach to the theatre is unorthodox and almost precludes the use of such traditional terms as play and playwright. Rarely does he submit to the conventional concept of the stage as a static frame for the unfolding of a dramatic situation. A play becomes a visual experience so that the traditional dramatic content is usually subordinated to spectacle or in the case of the *esperpentos* to the grotesque pictures which give concrete form to its conception. Valle-Inclán structured his plays as 'works in dialogue', that is, as both drama and plastic art. He accomplished this by concentrating a variety of complex visual elements in highly elaborate stage directions (*acotaciones*) which were complementary to the dialogue.

These stage directions posed an almost insurmountable obstacle for the resources of the orthodox stage of that time, for they involve a basically cinematographic technique: close-ups, panoramic 'sweeps', surprise appearances, shapes moving in the dark, kaleidoscopic effects achieved through the mounting of scenes in rapid succession, variation in the angle of viewer vision, physical metamorphosis, and, of course, all sorts of visual distortion. Valle-Inclán is probably unsurpassed in the composition of stage directions. Many of the plays described in the survey, for example, have not been easy to mount on the stage because of casting problems (there is a galaxy of peculiar characters in each play); because of unusual demands on actors (they are instructed to exaggerate physical traits, to follow technical acting for marionettes, to perform grimaces, to do pantomime or to vary their dialogue). There is also the difficulty of complex settings and costumes (rapidly shifting scenes, crowd movements, simultaneous time shifts). Moreover, a wide variety of non-human acts and sounds such as the zig-zagging of dogs, squeaking boots, the gallop of horses, background noises, animals etc., are incorporated into these stage directions. In fact, there were critics who once argued that while his major plays, especially the *Barbaric Comedies* and the *Esperpentos*, made good 'reading theatre', they were not really performable theatre because they stand in some no-man's land between the novel and the drama. Such a view ignored Valle-Inclán's expressed intentions and overlooked the advances made in stage production. A Valle-Inclán drama is meant to be a self-contained visual as well as an auditory work. Theatre and novel were deliberately fused through the art of what today is known as 'cinematic cutting' and thus achieved a plastic fluency through simultaneity and montage.

Valle-Inclán was one of the first dramatists to create what the French have called 'literarization of the theatre'. While a dramatic script is by tradition incomplete and brings the reader-spectator towards it, the plays of Valle-Inclán, especially his grotesque ones, are deliberately auto-suggestive and complete, projecting themselves into the reader-spectator. In many ways Valle-Inclán anticipated what André Malraux had called the 'theatricalization of the cinema': 'The main problem for the author of talking films is to know "when" his characters ought to talk. Let's not forget, however, that on the theatrical stage characters talk all the time.'[32]

Valle-Inclán was aware of the problems of printed dialogue, since words in a dramatic script are not devised to be read but to fall on the ear with the accents of a living voice. The dialogue of most of his plays tends accordingly to become ancillary to stage spectacle and to grow directly out of the immediate situation or action. The dialogue, as J. E. Lyon correctly analyses, 'does not reason, argue, describe, analyse or relate; it alternates between the expression of spontaneous emotion and ageless choral feeling: *gritos* and *sentencias*'.[33]

The dazzling verbal fireworks and devastating commentary are part of a series of dialogue techniques which, on the one hand, make use of metrical forms, repetitions, Galician rhythms etc. and, on the other, are integrated into Valle-Inclán's conception of the theatre as spectacle.

Most of the plays are divided into many scenes. Each brief scene opens with an elaborate stage direction, and when the action begins, the dialogue itself is constantly interrupted (or rather, 'surprised' as if by a camera) by descriptive comments. Because these cover everything from sound to movement to characterization, they are not marginal but as dramatically essential as the dialogue. For example, verbs of motion like go, run and walk are accompanied by sounds and echoes or colours and smells. In their interacting movements and speech, in the grotesque spectacle of the *esperpentos*, the characters bring about their own distortion. This is what Valle-Inclán meant when he explained the difficulties of his drama:

> I write in theatrical form, almost always. I am not concerned whether or not my works can be produced later. . . . . I want my characters to present themselves alone without commentary, without an author's explanation. Let the action itself be everything.

The printed directions, therefore, influenced by the special devices of cinema, aim at enhancing the image so that it makes an impact that the traditional theatrical script cannot produce.

The primary object of each play is not a psychological study, but the spectacle put on by the characters. Most of Valle-Inclán's plays are realistic despite the witty style or the later grotesque, representation. In the later *esperpentos*, especially, each character is a Spaniard with a historical dimension; no matter how deformed he may appear, he is not, like the fictional characters of Unamuno or Baroja, broadened into symbols or individualized within the limits of personal experience (psychology); instead he is intimately bound beyond his own self to a social reality which acts upon him or is acted upon by him. Valle-Inclán portrays all his characters as typical representatives of their social classes—a poet, a bohemian, a police officer, a prostitute, a landowner, a nobleman, an editor, a minister, a mason, a gravedigger, a priest, a soldier, a man of the circus, an intellectual, a puppeteer, a lieutenant, a smuggler, a gossiper, a gambler, a general, a monarch. Each one of the characters has a unique, colourful, individuality but is simultaneously a 'Spanish archetype' in that his values, attitudes and even language are those of the social classes from which he emerges. Each character is trapped in what the historian Américo Castro was later to call his 'Spanishness'.

Even though Valle-Inclán did not write extensively about his dramatic theories and techniques, we know that by 1920 he had at his disposal the same technique of artistic distance which Brecht later called *Verfremdung*. His own wording leaves no doubts about his mastery of the technique and his awareness of the artistic implications:

> This theory or sensation of the centre leads me to think that the artist ought to look at the landscape or a scene with 'eyes of loftiness' so that he can grasp the whole (ensemble) and not only the variable details. When art keeps the feeling of collective observation that popular literature has, things acquire the beauty of distance. . . .[34]

Collective observation was for Valle-Inclán a way to spectacle. 'Spectacle', as later the 'epic' for Brecht, was for Valle-Inclán the theatre of destroyed illusions and demanded a wide-awake audience. When attacking the 'conventional' theatre of his own time he claimed that Spanish drama did not have the thrill of a spectacle—like bullfighting. He saw audiences victimized by sentimentality, emotional empathy, dogma or theatrical illusion. Empathy, dogma and illusion were harmful because they made the spectator irrational, took away his critical abilities, and clouded his judgment with wishful thinking and with dreams of harmony founded on ignorance of history. Paradoxically, spectacle was for Valle-Inclán the stage where pure theatrical technique and history correspond. Spectacle strives to keep the audience sober and critical.

Valle-Inclán's aesthetic of drama makes it clear that his plays, though full of historical material, are not merely non-didactic but, by stylistic conviction and conception, anti-didactic. The spectacle of an *esperpento* on the stage relies on various angles of visual distortion to plunge the audience into the grotesque immediacy of contemporary history. The destruction of stage illusion is of course a positive undertaking; it creates a distance between the spectator and the actors, a distance which enables the audience to look at the action in a detached and critical spirit. Thus familiar Spanish attitudes and situations appear in a new and strange light and create, through alienation, an uncanny sense of wonder, a new view of Spain and a more stark vision of the human condition. To paraphrase don Estrafalario in the prologue of *The Horns of Don Friolera*, when plays can convey aesthetic violence they become heroic drama, like the *Iliad.* That is what Valle-Inclán strove to compose.

The result is spectacle and entertainment but always with special, political or historical concern. His plays are about institutions like the government, the army, the Academy, the Church. Each play is structured so carefully that it could be justified simply as entertainment, but Valle-Inclán chose to wed entertainment to a series of synthetic presentations of the Spanish crises that go back to the early nineteenth century and of the frightening conjunction of domestic economic problems with world unrest, revolutions and war. I cannot think of another playwright, with the possible exception of Brecht, who has integrated so successfully pure entertainment with pure commitment to history. Generally several of the characters are led by their sense of values to accept Spanish society pretty much as it is, but these values are parodied so effectively that the society, and its myths, are totally condemned for their inherent contradictions.

Literary Works. Valle-Inclán conceived his first novels as *sonatas* characterized by musical motifs and a refined but decadent sensibility.[35] They made him appear an aesthete, a typical 'disengaged' writer. Despite the novel musicality and polished style of those works, the nostalgic world of Bradomín and his sensual 'princesses' did not seem sober enough for an authentic literary undertaking. The philosopher Ortega y Gasset was among the first to praise Valle-Inclán's style but to complain about his 'blonde princesses' and 'useless incests', while others accused him of ideological insincerity and frivolity.[36] Yet even Valle-Inclán's exaltation of an archaic concept of aristocracy was mocking and insolent. It was not a question of 'escapism', because the theme of decadence overshadowed everything from the start; and so did a strong vein of irony and self-mockery, of which the Marquis of Bradomín (a grotesque version of Don Juan, 'ugly, Catholic and sentimental') is the personification. Bradomín later appears in *Lights* and even reappears in Valle-Inclán's last historical novels.[37]

After the *Sonatas* and the Galician stories of *Shadowy Garden* (*Jardín umbrío*), Valle-Inclán dealt more explicitly with the problems of Spain but without giving up his overwhelming stylistic preoccupations. The sense of tragedy and the problems of social injustice in the *Barbaric Comedies* (*Comedias bárbaras*), the historicity of the trilogy *The Carlist War* (*La guerra carlista*), and the satirical elements in his first farces signalled a more historical orientation. Above all, his fictional aristocracy was sneeringly offensive to all middle class ideals and values. An expressed loathing of the vulgarity of Restoration Spain is found in the early *Barbaric Comedies*. And the protagonist Montenegro is one of the best examples since *Don Quixote*, of the social reality of anachronism. Valle-Inclán's shift to the aesthetics of commitment is thus neither 'definitive' nor 'the return of the prodigal son', but a development of his art forms.

Many contemporaries, notably Ortega, Baroja and Unamuno, were hard put to it to explain Valle-Inclán's apparent lack of interest in Spanish problems during the years 1895–1908. The period of the *Sonatas*, *Flor de santidad*, and the *Comedias bárbaras* was, after all, a time of great national and intellectual ferment, but Valle-Inclán's serious thinking was on aesthetic rather than national or ideological lines. In their objections to Valle-Inclán there was a common air of regret that a great talent had not as yet found its direction or purpose, that it was too self-indulgent, too determined to follow the 'blind alley' of aestheticism. Many felt that his art was indeed an admirable search for a pure aesthetic emotion, but that it lacked 'seriousness' and 'authenticity'. Valle-Inclán seemed alone among the writers of his generation in lacking explicit philosophical ideas. These contemporaries have of course been proved wrong. For while the emphasis on aesthetic mechanisms may indeed have carried with it too great a sacrifice in terms of themes and ideology, the brilliant stylizations in which Valle-Inclán was continually wrapping his penetration of the national realities were by no means created in a vacuum. We see now that they were, rather, the culminating point in the development of a style which from the beginning apotheosized the plastic values of the human figure.

Valle-Inclán toyed with the grotesque from the start of his career, even when he was creating the exotic worlds of Bradomín and his erotic ladies.[38] When it subsequently became the keystone of his art of critical deformation, it brought with it not a rejection but a subversion of the rich modernistic world that had preceded it. His postwar orientation represents only a more radical refocusing of a lens that has become optically 'defective'. The disconcerting implications of the state of Spain and the hard realities of the human condition turn out to be all the more distressing for their deformed exteriors.

The final period of Valle-Inclán's creative activity, with one or two exceptions, was devoted almost exclusively to historical narratives. He had not written a novel since the end of the Carlist trilogy in 1909. None of his works was greeted with greater attention than *Tyrant Flag* in 1926. The synthetic approach to language, history and geography have made it Valle-Inclán's acknowledged masterpiece. The return to the novel was part of a long-range plan; it was also perhaps due to his deep disillusionment with the unfavourable reception of his plays. Following *Tyrant*, Valle-Inclán started publishing the most ambitious literary undertaking in Spain since the *National Episodes* (*Episodios nacionales*) of Benito Pérez Galdós:[39] the *Iberian Arena* was planned as nine very long novels divided into three series and was intended to paint a very broad and all-inclusive picture of Isabella II's reign. He was able to complete almost a third of this ambitious work, yet this one third is so voluminous that it represents about a quarter of his total output.

Not surprisingly, his last historical novels have the same rigorous detailed organization as *Tyrant Flag* and the *esperpentos*. They have a tight circular plan, a part-within-part pattern and a masterly handling of the related problems of narrative, chronology, and history. These last works sum up and intensify all his preceding techniques and preoccupations: a controlled, refined style; 'aesthetic distance', to such an extent that the narrator becomes a movie camera; Spanish history as novelistic content. There is little difference in this respect between the *esperpentos* and the last historical novels.

Valle-Inclán's characters, without being his mouthpieces, do criticize Spanish values and attack the prevailing myths about tradition, government, justice, middle-class, the Church, the military, heroism, the tragic sense. Thus Valle-Inclán, at any rate in his maturity, had sympathies at least as wide as other contemporaries, and was troubled by questionings that ran very deep. He never echoed Unamuno's 'me duele España' ('I ache with Spain'). He is the least anguished, the least suicidal, the least 'despairing' of his contemporaries. Yet, all his major works are almost exclusively concerned with 'the problem of Spain'.

No Spanish writer of that period was more intensely aware of the abyss between the apologists of Spanish tradition and Spain's dismal present than Valle-Inclán. He refused to say yes to official Spain and its version of the past, but he was also very sceptical about such '98 ideological attitudes as *agonía, intra-historia, abulia,* and *españolismo.*[40] This is why Pedro Salinas' conception of him 'as the prodigal son' of the generation of '98 falls somewhat short of the mark. Valle-Inclán did not adhere to the 'tragedy of Spain' approach. He felt that the values on which the anguished attitude of others rested had become idle rituals, if indeed not mere window dressing, and he never participated in the obsessive process of soul-searching which, with Unamuno and others, tended toward a national introversion. His grotesque vision of Spain focuses on the direct experience of the Spanish condition. Dramatic immediacy, in short, is what distinguishes him as a writer of the generation of '98, not meditative anguish. If he came to stress the absurd instead of the tragic, it was because to him there were few parts of Spanish history, past or present, at which a Spaniard could look without seeing not tragic images but grotesque realities. Valle-Inclán's purpose was not to diagnose the 'Spanish problem' but to re-create it as an anomalous deformity in the context of the modern world.

Valle-Inclán was alive to most of the cross-currents of modern literature and many works, especially the *esperpentos* have been compared to the theatre of the absurd or to existentialist writings in general. He believed that 'literature marches in step with history and with political movements';[41] he felt that a standpoint, no matter how stylized, if it is to be valid, must not be divorced from the historical matter of everyday experience; on the other hand, when Ionesco later explained that the puppet-like bourgeois he ridicules is not to be found in a determined society but in all societies of all times, he, like many of his contemporaries, was questioning the historical orientation of the literary absurd.[42] In short, the ground in the theatre of the absurd is antihistorical and universal while in the *esperpento* it is historical and circumstantial. Unlimited by history the avantgarde theatre concentrates on man's general predicament or on the 'tragi-comic' plight of the human condition. Becket and Ionesco, with their so-called anti-theatre in particular, have brought about a disintegration of language with which they successfully undermine the so-called 'sickness of being', and sabotage the heaviness of 'Angst' with paroxysms of laughter. Yet this theatre often lacks the urgency and immediate impact of the *esperpento* precisely because it is too general and not historically oriented. The advantage of 'universality' becomes a drawback when ideas of grotesqueness hold a priority over things grotesque. What in the tragic farces of Ionesco and Becket, for example, is often a matter of sophisticated games, abstractions and conscious stylization becomes in the *esperpento* a concrete, authentic case of grotesque experience. The very idea of the absurd as independent of history can become, as Sartre has warned us, a metaphysical deviation. The grotesque becomes a game or begins to be formalized into a code, it loses its vitality; when it is entirely formalized, as Ionesco's own theories (in *Notes and Counternotes*) would indicate, it is dead —it becomes pseudo-grotesque, metaphysical and abstract. Because the grotesque plays of Valle-Inclán deal with the so-called No-Exit, meaningless and alienated condition of man, they need a sense of concreteness and urgency in order to be convincing, and I personally find that by eliminating abstraction, and integrating abstract symbols into concrete history, Valle-Inclán achieves vital authenticity.

The *esperpentos* share with much of modern literature a serious existential concern for man's meaningless existence as summed up in Yeats' well-known image that things fall apart and the centre cannot hold.[43] We begin with man-in-the-world, abandoned and aimless since science, reason or morality do not have enough hold over man's will to dictate a way or pattern of life. Man is, in the words of Sartre, condemned to be free because he cannot know if what he does is the right thing. Such a burden leads to anxiety and despair, but it also accounts for uneasiness, and laughter.[44] Unamuno, Heidegger and Sartre, among others, are serious about this condition. Sartre in fact polemically asserts that it is bad faith to pretend that man is not free and absurd. Man is not a 'thing', but he becomes a thing when he yields his responsibility to others. When men live in a state of bad faith, they distort the world and render it grotesque. To be authentic, man must accept his awareness and his freedom no matter how unbearable they may be.

I have deliberately paraphrased some of the commonplaces of Existentialism (and I am stressing not the word but the phenomenon) in order to create a better background for Valle-Inclán's particular version of the absurd and the grotesque, and to point out some parallels and differences. He would agree with Sartre that man has his salvation and his authenticity in his own hands as long as he acknowledges that he is responsible. He can be the painter of his own condition, as it were. Both Valle-Inclán and Sartre, for example, point to a lack of authenticity as the reason for the degeneration and distortion of man. Yet both dramatize this basic problem differently: while Sartre balances absurdity with responsibility, Valle-Inclán balances the grotesque with uncanny laughter.

I do not mean to pass a comparative judgment on the work of Sartre and Valle-Inclán but rather to distinguish the French literature of the absurd from the Spanish literature of the grotesque. The absurd points to a disparity which can be laughed at and 'taken seriously' at the same time. Nothing would be more dreary and more purely academic than an absurd situation read with tears and no laughter. *Nausea* for example is full of viscous images and also full of jokes as Sartre effectively unites the oddly humorous with the deformed in portraying society.

Sartre observed that existentialism is, of all doctrines, the least scandalous and the most austere. Sartre's basic stand that man finds his salvation in his capacity for commitment to decisions, or that morality arises as an answer to social and political oppression and is therefore a serious matter, is admirable. Yet one is sometimes vexed with writers like Sartre, Unamuno, Kafka and Camus because there is often too much 'commitment'; we are put off by bleakness and conceptual heaviness. With few exceptions, there is so little amusement or authentic laughter in the world that such authors, devoid of playfulness, seem completely consumed by theory, argument, logic and the blaze of militant action or passionate anguish. Valle-Inclán, on the other hand, always brings his absurd vision down to the concreteness of humour and grotesquerie so that real circumstances never become abstract in the name of the 'absurd', 'human solidarity', or 'the tragic sense of life'. The vision of many existentialists is at times too austere, too bleak and too 'authentic' to play with the uncanny, and this refusal to play and ironize often excludes them from the real grotesque. Hence the importance of the *Esperpentos*.

THE ESPERPENTOS

Valle-Inclán once explained that the one factor which led him to change some of his ideas about theatre and create the new dramatic genre of *esperpento* was the view of the playwright not as an artist who either admires the deeds of his heroic characters or is moved by their afflictions, but as a totally ironic creator—a puppeteer. The puppeteer never looks up to his puppets nor does he become emotional over them but, rather, he looks down at them, from a distance, as if they were performing at his feet. If the playwright arranged characters and scenes as the puppeteer arranges his puppets, the created situations would be characterized by distortions or striking incongruities in the appearance, shape and manner of the fictional characters. The term *esperpento* in Spanish refers to things or people who are grotesque, bizarre, ludicrously eccentric, absurd. Valle-Inclán uses *esperpento* strictly in aesthetic terms: it's a style of writing, a manner of representing, a way of portraying. It is a principle of art not necessarily a fact of experience.

Esperpento, moreover, is used to designate a distinct type or category of drama into which plays can be grouped according to their structure, their approach and their technique of the grotesque. It is, no less than tragedy or comedy or tragicomedy, a genre; it is supported by an aesthetic theory, by a stylistic technique, by dramatic principles and by a vision of the human condition. The *esperpentos* have not been created out of a vacuum; they are the result of a search within a long tradition. We can briefly schematize the *esperpento* as follows: in style, a systematic deformation of things described to the point of grotesquerie; in literary tradition, a devaluation of tragic view of life and a new version of classical, Elizabethan or Golden Age tragedies, a tragedy 'in modern dress'; in perspective, alienation, estrangement, distance, the breaking of illusion which detaches and reorients the spectator; in content, episodes from the life of Spaniards and scenes from the history of Spain.

Valle-Inclán labelled *esperpentos* four dramatic works published during the last decade of his career: *Bohemian*

Lights in 1920; *The Horns of Don Friolera* in 1921; *The Regalia of the Deceased* in 1926; and *The Captain's Daughter* in 1927. In 1930 he reworked the last three into a trilogy, *Shrove Tuesday Carnival*. In seeking to understand the type of drama Valle-Inclán conceived the *esperpentos* to be and what their relevance is to the modern Spanish and European stage, we should examine them, like the works of Brecht and the theatre of the absurd, both as literature and as theatre. I shall stress the theatricality of the *esperpento* and will rely both on some comments by Valle-Inclán on the art of the theatre and on dramatic principles elaborated within the first two *esperpentos*.

The esperpento and the tragicomic. The first *esperpento, Bohemian Lights*, is a revaluation of the function of tragedy on modern times. It is a modern, nocturnal odyssey about the frustration, death and burial of a blind poet, Max Estrella. The setting is 'a Madrid that is absurd, brilliant and starving'. The characters are either Bohemians or figures of the Establishment putting on an inconsolable yet histrionic exhibition of misery against a historical background of contemporary political chaos. Just before he dies, Max reappraises his own role as an artist on the Spanish stage in a half-jesting, half-serious conversation with his grotesque companion, Don Latino, and proposes to dramatize reality as if in a 'concave mirror' which distorts and ridicules appearance.

The difference between traditional and modern versions of the tragic acts on the stage are crucial. At the beginning of Act v, Scene I in *Hamlet*, for example, two rustic gravediggers enter, carry on a discussion of suicide and Christian burial, and follow this with a series of jokes. Their comments are funny, but the occasion is after all Ophelia's burial and this concerns Hamlet's response. Shakespeare's Hamlet is a tragic figure and his mental torture is more significant than the gravedigger's remarks; in fact, such comic relief in traditional tragedy stresses the difference between one type of action and another.[45] But a tragic burial scene can be presented in a different light, as is the case at the end of Scene XIV in *Bohemian Lights*. Here the two gravediggers, after burying Max Estrella, carry on a conversation about death and burials with a poet and an old nobleman who are, significantly, discussing

Shakespeare's tragedy. Prince Hamlet is here looked upon as a young simpleton because he could not understand or handle a female like Ophelia 'in the age of the peacock'. And the same ludicrous gravediggers who provided comic relief in *Hamlet* are here called 'stoical philosophers' because of their brutal naturalistic truths about death, and their earthy discourse on the travails of the gravedigging profession. They are even wished good luck so that they may yet witness many more funerals in the future.

If Shakespeare's juxtaposition of tragic and comic provides comic relief within the tragic, Valle-Inclán's mixture gives tragic relief within the farcical and the grotesque. That is, the very life blood of farce can be tragic. The tragic elevation of the traditional graveyard scene is in *Lights* deliberately mocked; by extension, the possibilities of tragic experience on the stage seem topsy-turvy. The new theatrical version of the traditional gravedigging event here stands for a mixture of cross purposes, for an inextricable union of solemnity and triviality that in drama constitutes the essence of the tragicomic. The dramatist can tease or unsettle the spectator by mingling the dread of death with bizarre amusement. The situation on the stage is now radically different from what we are accustomed to: there is nothing simply comic, or satiric or tragic about such goings on and the way they tantalize viewers; for we are dealing not simply with the absurd but with a peculiar, uncanny play on the absurd.

One would suspect that Valle-Inclán had already by 1920 anticipated in both theory and practice the observation made much later by Dürrenmatt that the closest we come to the tragic is by way of the grotesque, that strange borderland phenomenon related to the tragicomic. 'But the tragic is still possible even if pure tragedy is not. We can achieve the tragic out of comedy. We can bring it forth as a frightening moment, as an abyss that opens suddenly.'[46] Such a borderland is staged in Max Estrella's garret after the evening of misadventures which led to his death. The wake is staged by fusing diverse elements. His despairing widow and daughter lament while a group of friends, neighbours and acquaintances come to pay their last respects and, in the process, exchange some jokes, assume comic poses of sympathy, smile indulgently, argue, drink or get bored. There is much play-acting and histrionic affectation. A death scene is a painful sight, one friend observes melodramatically; therefore it should not be prolonged, suggests another, matter-of-factly. But this one is prolonged. Suddenly the situation gains speed as if the performers had no control over their acts. Someone comes to cart the body away when, unexpectedly, a so-called 'scientist' raises the question of whether Max, given his illness, is really dead or in a cataleptic state, and it is even proposed to burn the corpse's thumb as a test. Incredible doubts set in. A combination of a wife's anxiety, irresponsible opinions, foolish misunderstandings and futile gesticulations, leads to a state of chaos and mad confusion. 'Not dead?' shouts an indignant concierge. 'Why, dead and stinking!' And the zany expert retorts: 'You, madam, not having studied in a University, cannot dispute about such things with me. Democracy does not exclude technical categories, you at least know *that*, Madame Concierge.'

Here the spectator laughs instinctively at this ridiculous argument, but soon laughter is harnessed and, mingled with awe, changes into an embarrassed grimace. It's a slapstick side-show calculated to make one more and more uneasy: for the traditional and familiar wake scene outlandish and alien in its hilarity, and all the while Max lies dead on centre stage while his widow and orphaned daughter are perplexed and in anguish. The scene is composed so that the tempo increases with confusion piled upon confusion generating absurdity in the midst of tragic loss. The stark silence for the macabre test is suddenly interrupted by the strident shriek of the daughter 'My father! My father! My beloved father!' who crazily rolls her eyes and grotesquely begins to beat her head against the floor. It is as if we look on with horror and pity at a profound tragedy, shaking with laughter all the time at an irresistible burlesque. We are before an estranged world in a funeral situation which, as such, we thought a recognizable and natural experience; suddenly it turns out to be ominous and ludicrous. Valle-Inclán stages a grotesque funeral, where the intermingling of the laughable and the frightening precludes the more conventional and unequivocal response that we associate with pure comedy or traditional tragedy. For when we think of a grotesque play or *esperpento* we do not refer simply to a specific dramatic form but to some mingled quality of harlequinade which can lead to a variety of theatrical effects—comic and pathetic, frightening and tragic, monstrous and absurd.

The dramatist as puppeteer. Valle-Inclán's grotesque vision as illustrated in *Bohemian Lights* depends on a rigorous application of artistic distance. Valle-Inclán did not bother to write at length on his practices in the theatre, as other playwrights like Brecht, Lorca, Pirandello or Ionesco did. He did, however, in an interview give brief explanations about the intentions of his *esperpentos*. Many of these off-the-cuff remarks do contain a single, homogeneous body of theory concerning the proximity or distance between dramatist and character, or between spectator and spectacle.

The dramatist can avoid the epic and tragic manners of Homer or Shakespeare, and instead observe the world from a detached, higher plane; from this vantage point the world may appear ridiculous and absurd—this is the difference between tragedy proper and tragic farce. The implication here is that an uninvolved 'outsider', something like a mathematician playing with numbers, becomes for Valle-Inclán the symbol of the detached artist as an objective viewer of reality, virtually a disinterested 'stranger'. Such a dramatist is an authentic creator, a *demiurgo*, and resembles James Joyce's artist who like an invisible god indifferently manipulates everything while paring his fingernails. A key expression in his comments is 'farce' (*sainete*): this is tantamount to replacing the God of Creation, traditional symbol of the artist, with a puppeteer and the traditional theatre of the world with a puppet stage. The artist's new position—what Valle-Inclán calls the 'third way'—necessarily entails a revision, or even inversion, of values: if a playwright looks at his heroes as a puppeteer looks at his marionettes, these heroes suddenly seem grotesque and disturbingly amusing. It is as if the playwright has usurped from God the right to have a good last laugh at his own creation.

The guiding principle of art upon which the *esperpentos* are based is further formulated and illustrated in the second *esperpento*, *The Horns of Don Friolera*. This work attempts a revaluation of the problem of mimesis in the light of man's tragic predicament and aesthetic alienation. The hero is a middle-aged lieutenant of the guards who must kill his wife because he suspects her of infidelity. Friolera is modelled on classical heroes of honour—Orestes, Horace, Othello and Don Gutierre—and his portrayal raises many questions about the so-called theatrical or aesthetic 'perspective'. Valle-Inclán presents one basic archetypal situation—a man trapped by his duty and passion and bent on revenge—viewed from at least seven different perspectives each one with its tradition and its *raison d'être*. He suggests that the puppeteer's manner is the most successfully estranged or distanced and consequently the one most appropriate for a portrayal of tragic man in modern times. An antisentimental aesthetic must be forged that reaches beyond tears and laughter to concentrate on the aesthetic emotion of a precarious situation. Valle-Inclán's strong objection to sentimentality, empathy or even catharsis comes in the prologue to *Don Friolera* and is crystallized in one of the wittiest remarks ever made on the relation between bullfights and the spectator:

> The sentimental people who feel the agony of the horses at bullfights are incapable of experiencing the aesthetic emotion of the spectacular struggle itself. Their sensitivity turns out to be similar to an equine sensitivity, and through unconscious cerebration, they come to suppose their own luck to be that of those gutted nags.[47]

The danger of identification (something akin to the 'affective fallacy') is that it discourages a critical frame of mind, and the beauty of the spectacle is thereby lost. Sentimentality destroys art. An 'honour' play, for example, is like a bullfight: if the audience is drawn into the 'predicament' of the hero and made to identify with the character, the idea of theatrical—that is fictional—reality is falsified. The hero and his problem may be interesting, but if the spectator is not put at a distance, he will be in an uncritical frame of mind.

Most of these points are debated by two roving 'intellectuals' in a prologue which contains a puppet-show; they are also reiterated in the epilogue. In this sense, the drama proper of the modern hero, Friolera, is a puppet show, that is, the action is a duplication of the debate. After watching a traditional 'honour' play (*Othello* or *The Surgeon of his Honour*) represented by puppets, the liberal don Estrafalario raises the question with the conservative don Manolito of whether the present world can be represented authentically on the stage by the older traditional art forms, striving to formulate for his stubborn friend the concept of a fictional world in which we no longer have tragic heroes but only vast tragedies staged by puppeteers and produced for the amusement of onlookers. In such a world where the individual cannot have the dignity and courage of being responsible and guilty, man, no matter how vociferously he proclaims his honour and nobility, is simply not a suitable subject for pure tragedy.

Perhaps the puppet show would seem to be more suitable for modern man's gestures because, as Estrafalario argues, 'It has more possibilities', that is to say the rogue's puppet theatre conveys the power and meaning of man's plight more effectively than traditional drama. Although it is Estrafalario rather than Valle-Inclán who proclaims the ideas of distance and alienation, and although there is always considerable psychic distance between Valle-Inclán and his characters, here as in the case of the blind poet Máximo Estrella, author and character seem to speak with one voice. Valle-Inclán's explanation of the three ways, and Estrafalario's defence of the puppet show, follow closely the arguments of classical aesthetics: the concern to make art both an authentic creation, a world in itself, and simultaneously an authentic representation of our world.

Implicit in the most traditional art forms are moral, ethical and rational criteria according to which man's actions and reactions are measured; they are placed into perspective so as to arouse moral and rational reaction and are to be judged as good or bad, and even to be approved or disapproved. The puppet-show on the other hand is not bound by pre-existing norms, and need make no moral statement whatever: it simply allows the absurd to reveal itself. Because of his irony and indifference the puppeteer need not create characters but only telling gestures; he need not create human relationships between people but only sharp, nervous moments of collision. Let a man cease to be a hero-worshipper or humanist, make him stop viewing himself and others in an epic, tragic and romantic light or even make him stop taking himself seriously; let him stand back from the performance and look at himself, let him see himself and others as the puppet he really is.

The actor as puppet. Because of distance, one of the salient characteristics of an *esperpento* production is the deformed appearance and ludicrous traits of the human figures, often represented on the stage by actors who are puppet-like. Puppets, mannequins or marionettes are grotesque figures par excellence because they suggest, ludicrously, a radical and disturbing departure from figures that are familiar to the audience. Stunted in physique, awkward in movements and mechanized in gestures, the puppet is a telling symbol of man's stunted spirit; the actor must suggest through diction and movements the absence of authentic being or sense of creativity, the incongruity between what a character is said to be and what in fact he is. It is nevertheless a question of how an author handles the puppet figure that determines its grotesque impact.

As a preliminary illustration of the technical aspects of grotesque puppetry let us picture first a mountebank away in a corner, bent, worn out, decrepit, a ruin of a man whose shanty is more wretched than that of the most brutelike savage. This hapless creature might be one of Baudelaire's famous hump-backed cronies trotting around like humanized marionettes.[48] Or else let us recall the clowns who represent a distortion or aberration or deformity of the human norm. What Baudelaire called the dizzy height of hyperbole and all the trappings of mockery, carnavalesque, grotesque clumsiness, anomaly and dehumanization are there. So with the clown of Chaplin. Now, if the creator, besides being able to distort, were also detached, if he had a wicked or malicious nature and, to paraphrase Valle-Inclán, if he refused to consider author and character of the same human clay, such an awkward marionette or clumsy clown would seem histrionic and laughable. And this is the point: Baudelaire or Chaplin are neither detached nor malicious enough and do not always laugh as if they were superior to and amused by the figures they have created; instead, Baudelaire explains away this puppet's stunted condition as that of the old poet now without friends and degraded by public ingratitude while Chaplin's tramp in his ridiculous and pathetic failure to adjust, conform, or succeed, becomes the secret hero of the spectator's heart. Baudelaire opens to the suffering of this pitiful old buffoon and thus dignifies the grotesque figure with pathos.

Chaplin turns around the shafts of ridicule against the tramp and strikes at the absurdities or tyrannies of society itself. The spectator applauds the puppet or the clown. The horrific and laughable potential of the marionette or clown figure is undermined as we react movingly to its heart-beats. A sort of romantic dualism is maintained alongside the puppet's grotesque antics: even the puppet or the clown have a dimension of tragic isolation or dignity, and the grotesque of the dehumanized condition is finally undermined, loses its force and is finally absorbed by sentimentality. The grotesque in both cases is only a means to description or acting, it is not an end.

Let us view another puppet, but this time follow its contours along ruthlessly logical lines to their absurd extreme, pitilessly, as if the author would never stop considering himself superior by nature to his puppet. This is the way Valle-Inclán conceives some figures in his graphic, detailed stage directions. The parts of such a figure in the *esperpentos* are so exaggerated with respect to the whole that it is a caricature. The lines of the figure's profile are distorted to disproprotionate degrees. Valle-Inclán draws a hump, makes his arms gnarled and elongated, his hands bony and shrivelled, wraps his shapeless legs in rags, hunches his body and renders his face grisly. He places a scarf, which looks like a green snake, around his neck and gives him the slow unsteady gait of a puppet. To paraphrase Quevedo, whom Valle-Inclán admired, the creator sticks a human figure on to its anatomical parts.[49]

This figure is the miserly, opportunistic, banal book-dealer in *Lights* (11), always ready for a deal, always complaining about hard times, always ready with stock, meaningless platitudes; a prisoner of worn-out clichés. Valle-Inclán intensifies the incongruity of this puppet by naming him Zarathustra and calling his bookstore, frequented by artists, a cave; he thus alludes simultaneously to Plato's cave and to Nietzsche's hero.[50] The name Zarathustra stands for Nietzsche's ideas on the power of the will to overcome obstacles, on how the most powerful man wins and has the right to win. Nietzsche suggested that if others are weak, it is their fault, and they must therefore make room for the willing and the strong. Valle-Inclán's Zarathustra emulates his namesake by cheating the blind helpless poet of some books. That is, the superman's amorality becomes in the *esperpento* an exploitation of the miserable and helpless. This Zarathustra has the 'will' to be 'amoral' over a few pesetas. The cave-bookstore recalls the Platonic image of prisoners in a cave (in *The Republic*) who, limited to the material world, mistake appearances for realities. The cave has thus become the traditional symbol of the ambivalent nature of knowledge. Zarathustra is the handler of books in a cave, that is, the superman of stored knowledge. He comes up to three 'intellectual' visitors and resolves their argument concerning the import of religion by delivering a banality with a pretentious solemnity: 'Without religion there cannot be good faith in business dealings.' This cliché is a travesty of Plato's idea of a thinker. The puppet Zarathustra and his cave make this grotesque world totally estranged from the traditional models of Plato and Nietzsche.

Baudelaire's marionette and Chaplin's tramp illustrate the loneliness of man and are indictments of the world's indifference and cruelty. Valle-Inclán's puppet becomes an accusation against man and his myths much more than or complaint against the world. In this sense his perspective is basically anti-romantic. There is no sentimentality, as in Baudelaire or Chaplin; Valle-Inclán plays havoc with the idea of dualism (think of Hugo's hunchback or Chaplin's tragic tramp) which salvages man and puppet: what is absurd in puppet-like Zarathustra, implies his creator, will not become 'rational', 'meaningful', 'sentimental' or 'noble' simply because we associate it with 'other' 'traditional' figures and other situations. Nor is Zarathustra merely a parody of standard philosophical positions like Plato's 'essential' realities or Nietzsche's existential precepts. In the case of Valle-Inclán's grotesque puppets, it is man throwing doubt on the possibility of being a man. The genius of Valle-Inclán is that he perceived in our awkward moments and in our puppet-like behaviour something mechanical and dehumanized grafted upon life.

The question is, how can a puppet be on the one hand sufficiently mechanical to be removed from our situation and on the other hand be intimately related to the world we inhabit. Or to put it in terms of perspective, how is one to reconcile a playwright's irony, which creates a distance from immediate reality, and the same playwright's committed position, which stands for proximity? The paradox is solved with another paradox: a dramatist becomes distant ('removes' himself, 'disappears', becomes 'indifferent') at least temporarily in order to take a better look at his own invented situation—in the words of don Estrafalario, one observes the human predicament as through the eyes of a dead man (*difunto*) looking back on life.

Zarathustra is mechanical, but he is also a Spaniard who unnerves us because he is recognizable through his Spanish pretentions. The key to Valle-Inclán's brand of artistic distance is a seemingly endless shuffling of a mechanical world and a historical one, the precarious borderline between Zarathustra as an invented puppet and Zarathustra as a real or potential Spaniard. The puppets of Valle-Inclán like Zarathustra are dehumanized, and dehumanization presupposes that puppets are human after all. Their absurdity causes laughter. But more than the element of amusing parody, it is the 'mechanicalness' of puppets like Zarathustra which produces a disconcerting effect on our laughter. The components of this grotesque puppet are not removed from us, they are simply estranged. The difference is crucial: estrangement implies divorce but also a former belonging. We feel that we are not at home in the cave of Zarathustra because we are uneasy, and yet we are uneasy because the cave and its puppet are recognizable, as if they belonged to us. Estrangement destroys the facile dualities of traditional puppets and is consequently the pivotal ingredient of the *esperpento*.

The tragic predicament of puppets. After the debate of the roving intellectuals in *The Horns of Don Friolera*, the drama that follows, about the tragicomic predicament of don Friolera, is an elaborate dramatization of Estrafalario's arguments concerning artistic distance. The actor who plays Friolera must appear confused as he balances his wife's guilt and innocence and as he ponders his course of action: 'And if this infamy were true? . . . For the woman who turns out bad, capital punishment . . . And even then I couldn't forgive her. I'm on active duty.' The suspicious hero acts tragically and yet hilariously when, in the attempt to cleanse his honour and therefore live up to the well-known tradition that 'in the Customs Guards there is no room for cuckolds', he accidentally kills his own daughter while aiming at his wife. At the end the spectator faces two sets of inevitability in Friolera: he is on the one hand the picture of a man who had to perform terrible things, like a traditional hero; he is on the other hand the silhouette of a disoriented figure who had to perform foolish things, like a common marionette. The tragic and the burlesque remain in balance: Friolera assumes a dual perspective, so that it is no longer possible to see him purely as a tragic hero like Othello or purely as a comic but like the figures of traditional farce; for Friolera is ambivalent, somewhere between an avenger of his dishonour and a consenting cuckold.

Valle-Inclán's conception of the character is entirely modern in its insistence on representing on the stage the ambiguity of man's lot: the borderline between a wronged man and a cuckold is as valid and as unsettling as the thin line that separates tragic action from foolish action. If the passion of Othello and the honour of Don Gutierre can lead to terrible yet moving or honourable acts, they can also control and direct man's actions and thus reduce man to a thing, to something mechanical—like a puppet. It is all a question of how a dramatist looks at a man's predicament. Friolera is Othello looked at by a puppeteer, according to Estrafalario 'from the other shore'. It is as if on stage a trapdoor opened under Othello's feet with absurd suddenness or a gust of wind swept him and then comically sent him bumping on his bottom.[51]

The case of Friolera, however, is not simply quaint or comic or parodic. Friolera, conceived ambivalently like Don Quixote, has as many shades and degrees of the tragic as Othello or Don Gutierre and for all his absurdity he constantly skirts tragedy. A skilful performer would make us laugh at what, under different circumstances, would produce in us pain and even a sense of horror. The hero of the *esperpento* loses his orientation and is like a puppet in the hands of an alien force, divorced from the tragic world of Shakespeare and the moral world of Calderón. Tradition can teach Friolera no profound lesson, conventional reasoning and morality teach him nothing. His attempts at rational deductions are thwarted and with them his attempt at sanity; Friolera is destined, finally, to degenerate into a puppet, waving his hand like a pistol and pretending to shoot, '¡Pim! ¡Pam! ¡Pum!', but Valle-Inclán exploits in Friolera what Calderón, Shakespeare and popular farces fail to consider: the obvious fact that the situation on stage of a character trapped by passion and duty has, along with the tragic or moral lessons, many inherently amusing moments and disturbing intimations.

Friolera is an amazing figure because he is so unamazing. As he goes through his monologues we see the tortures inside his mind. He does not wish to be violent or unreasonable: 'I won't get divorced because of an anonymous accusation. I despise it! Loreta will remain as my companion, the angel of my home.' He cannot kill because he is a loving man ('We were in love when we got married and that can never be forgotten') yet he must kill because traditionally 'A dignified officer never pardons his unfaithful wife'. Friolera would like to get hold of himself and rationalize the situation ('The wife goes one way, the husband another, the children without warmth or protection, unsheltered') but he is after all what he is: 'I'm a Spanish soldier and I have no right to philosophize as they do in France.' Thus the audience watches a fundamental predicament—to kill or not to kill—but in a rather ordinary Spanish mind, by turns wary and gullible, emotional and naive, filled with trivial considerations, framed by military clichés, and laced with a standard assortment of commonplaces on Spanish honour.

How then can Estrafalario and Valle-Inclán dare suggest that this puppet of compadre Fidel is a protagonist in any sense of the word, particularly within the honour tradition? Friolera is after all supposed to be the modern Othello! Is Friolera simply a parody of Greek, Shakespearean and Calderonian heroes, the falling off, say, from glory to the inglorious? We cannot dismiss Friolera simply as a clown capering in the footsteps of traditional heroes. For Valle-Inclán, he qualifies as a legitimate modern hero (or anti-hero) because he is desperately trying to define not the norm but himself, and to find by himself his own solution to marriage and honour. Friolera, unlike his traditional counterparts who at least have their author's sympathy or hate, must tramp a relativistic and alien world on his own: down go the moral signposts, yet man-actor has the disconcerting task of making crucial judgments and taking accountable action, but without any guidance from his 'author' and before an 'audience' which makes his predicament an occasion for an entertaining spectacle.

The spectacle of the *esperpento* on the stage is for this reason disturbing: what is ludicrous in a character will not through association with heroic passion and honour become something worthy but rather more ludicrous. If this is true, if man is like a puppet, then his author could take delight in poking fun at his heroic pretensions and in deflating him. From the estranged viewpoint of a puppeteer-author, the comic destiny of the cuckold and the tragic destiny of the dishonoured hero converge and fuse in an absurd destiny. Friolera is to be acted in a half-serious manner: to be taken seriously in his predicament but to be laughed at in his posturings and helplessness. The situation of Friolera is incongruous, and as in the case of Don Quixote incongruity is as potentially tragic as it is ridiculous; the pattern of his predicament fulfills the condition of farce and tragedy. Inevitably Friolera's gestures, his ¡pim! ¡pam! ¡pum!, are both hilarious and pathetic, sad and silly. For in the grotesque play of our times, incongruity is a fundamental part of honour codes; it stands for the disparity between Friolera's limitations as a hero and his wish to be one.

This *esperpento* then is the tragi-comic expression of a would-be hero who cannot transcend the crippling biological, social, psychological and accidental banality of life in general and his present predicament in particular. Valle-Inclán perfects in this *esperpento* the perspective of estrangement as we examined it in the case of Zarathustra: the prime point with Friolera is the intimate fusion of two opposed forms of situation, painful and amusing, dreary and ludicrous, into a single mixed situation. But concern for this mixed situation exists here in depth, and it is this engagement with man's absurd lot that makes Valle-Inclán's 'third manner' a viable theatrical expression and a significant view of drama as life: tragedy needs heroes and this is an unheroic age; tragedy takes the nobility of man for granted and is essentially uplifting. Such faith in the nobility of man is gone now. Inevitably, man's honour appears meaningless or insignificant and there is—*but for the grace of artistic spectacle*—no salvation. But for the grace of artistic spectacle: if man's lot be absurd, make the best show of it. Be like a puppeteer for it is he who has 'a demiurgic dignity'.

And as with the puppet Zarathustra—or more important with Don Quixote—Friolera too, no matter how much of a puppet he is on the stage, is completely recognizable. Valle-Inclán grasps, like Cervantes earlier or Brecht and Pirandello later, the perplexing interplay between illusion and reality. A subtle parallel is drawn, in Valle-Inclán's concave mirror, between the observed reality of Spain and the imaginative reality of his *esperpento* about Spaniards. The transfer from one level of reality to another, that is, from real grotesque to invented grotesque, is captured by the formal perspective of the *esperpentos*. In fact, Friolera's predicament as I examined it above is actually a duplication within the play itself. For in it, two intellectuals are watching a puppet-show about a military suitor who suspects his fiancée of shenanigans while the 'play' about the horns of Don Friolera that follows is an elaborate dramatization of this same puppet show. Valle-Inclán consciously patterns this scene after the famous puppet-show episode in Cervantes' *Don Quixote* (Part II, chap. 26) and forces the spectator to distinguish between two kinds of reality, a distinction which is crucial for the theatrical illusion as applied to all the *esperpentos*. One is the reality of the fair where a Spanish audience watches a play without flesh-and-blood players, a marionette show; these Spaniards live, however, in a world of concrete reality in which the marionette show's phenomena are verifiable. Within their real world is encapsuled an absurd puppet world, fabricated in the mind of a puppeteer. To the Spanish audience, the puppet version of Friolera's predicament is not 'real' in the sense that the world they live in is real. But from another point of view, the puppet world represents a reality in which the marionettes are real people, any traditional Spanish couple with the traditional problem of honour. They are absurd—for Don Estrafalario at least—as are real Spaniards in real Spain. The key to this seemingly endless shuffling of worlds is the precarious borderline between puppets as invented Spaniards and puppets as real Spaniards. Thus grotesque drama overflows its theatrical framework into the reality outside.

To sum up: the absurd conception of life and the grotesque picture of the Spanish world, which Valle-Inclán dramatizes in his second *esperpento, Don Friolera,* are a product of two factors: one, inherited aesthetic views of puppetry and traditional archetypes; the other, the sort of realism which may be called 'historical', using this word in its broadest sense. Individual critics may differ widely in regard to the proportions in which these two factors enter into Valle-Inclán's theatre but it is the presence of both, fictional technique and historical matter, which characterizes the dramatic situation of *Don Friolera* or *Lights* or any of the *esperpentos.*

Principles of the Esperpento. Based on the above, we can now venture some preliminary generalizations about the *esperpento* as it is formulated in *Lights* and *Don Friolera.* In the *esperpento* there is no distinction between comedy and tragedy; these genres have been discarded, violated, reworked. Comic elements recur at the most tragic moments; tragic strains recur throughout comic situations. The dissolving of the barriers between comedy and tragedy in the *esperpento* makes possible the intensification of life at these extremes, for it is on extremes, especially when he protests or gesticulates, that modern man reveals himself. The *esperpento* is consequently an aesthetic doctrine, but it is also a vision. The so-called puppet-stage of the world, for example, only heightens the grotesque elements of modern life and discovers through them new depths in modern times; for the *esperpento* is a spectacle that can only draw out possibilities that belong essentially to life in general and to the Spanish situation in particular. The deformed style which portrays the human and Iberian elements by turning them into grotesque deformations is not only artifice but simultaneously a grotesque situation. With the comment 'The tragic sense of Spanish life can be rendered only through an aesthetic that is systematically deformed', Max Estrella implies that in order to be valid and profound, the grotesque cannot be only pure style but must be related to the historical reality outside the fictional creation.

Aesthetically, the *esperpento* dramatizes the contrast between traditional tragedy and tragedy 'in modern dress' and, specifically underscores the disparity between the tragic Spain of the generation of '98 and Spain as a 'grotesque deformation of European civilization'. More than a parody, the *esperpento* questions the tragic sense of life itself and, like the later theatre of the absurd, reelaborates it to fit better the temper of modern times. The central feature of the *esperpento* is theatricality, but in the full sense of the word. Drama is spectacle, and the manipulation of action on the stage brings about the unmasking of appearances. The stage projects 'the whole miserable life of Spain' like a spectacle, as if it were an arena observed by the multitude, mingling effectively the grotesque plasticities of Goya, the farcical tone of the puppet-show, the ritual of traditional theatre or bull-fights, and the fragmented montage of cinematography.

The catalyst of performance is usually alienation. There are no easy equivalents for this much-abused term; for modern dramatists it refers to the distance needed to break the illusion of the performance yet without however alienating the spectator in the sense of creating hostility;[52] it is a matter of reorienting him toward critical detachment. Conceptually, Valle-Inclán focuses on the human condition in existentialist terms, that is, he envisions man's existence as absurd and pictures life not as a meaningful established order but as a precarious adventure. Such a situation, full of immediacies, puts great pressures on man. On stage, the *esperpentos* formulate implicitly, without ever once being didactic, the great moral problem of the twentieth century: the anguished perplexity brought about by man's predicament in the absence of valid restraints and the abundance of freedom. As with the later theatre of the absurd, the *esperpento* undermines with paroxysms of laughter the weight of anguish it presents. The key to the salient features of the *esperpento*—its perspective, distortion, puppetry, realism, tragicomedy, theatricality and existentialism—is estrangement as explained by Valle-Inclán, as debated by don Estrafalario and as illustrated by Max Estrella and don Friolera.

The reasons for labelling a drama, 'comedy', 'tragedy' or 'esperpento' are of course historical or personal or both. Were Büchner's *Wozzeck* to be written today, for example, it probably would have been called something like a tragicomedy. Brecht called his theatre 'epic' but avoided any designation altogether when it came to individual plays, while Ionesco called *The Chairs* a tragic farce and Dürrenmatt called *The Visit* first a 'bullish comedy' and next a 'tragicomedy'. Valle-Inclán composed his plays before and after World War I, a time when both in Europe and in America the framework of the drama became largely diffused, the genres began merging and the stage was in full flight from reality in form or content or both. The *esperpentos* are part of this restless stage in the history of modern drama. Valle-Inclán's one contribution to the theory and practice of drama was to undo the myth, propagated in Spain by Unamuno and in Italy by Pirandello, of the so-called 'autonomy' of created characters in novels or plays.[53] Such an approach was a way, according to Valle-Inclán, of encouraging a crude identification with the characters on the stage. The spectator must be discouraged from losing his critical detachment if he is to have an aesthetic capacity. He blamed the English and the French for this development of theatrical events and he defended the Spanish practice whereby the author feels himself superior to the drama.

The Esperpento and the Tradition of the Grotesque. Valle-Inclán's four grotesque plays might be considered the culmination of the tradition of the grotesque in literature because he attempted to convert what was a loose assortment of grotesque mannerisms into an autonomous literary or theatrical genre. Because the grotesque does not depend on a specific structural plan it has been easily adaptable and has been realized in varying ways through the centuries: in the Middle Ages, for example, the grotesque took the form of demonic possession of the body (a situation that could be both horrific and riotously funny), while later in a poet like François Villon it became a combination of horror and almost hysterically ribald mockery; in Quevedo's nightmarish visions, as earlier with Hieronymus Bosch, the grotesque became an aesthetic of bodily distortion, violence and humour giving rise simultaneously to an ethical vision of man; in Swift's satirical spectrum, it is a method of sarcasm with an uncompromising indictment of socio-moral conditions; in Goya's etching, grotesque fantasy symbolizes the intangible power that can capriciously drive men to adopt fantastic attitudes and carry out ludicrous actions; in Victor Hugo, the grotesque is a catalyst of contrast, a mingling of unequal worlds that gives rise to the sublime; in Nietzsche's discourses on tragedy, the grotesque image is a comic release from the nausea of the absurd, while in Baudelaire's discussion of 'Laughter' it stands for the 'absolute comic'. In our century, the grotesque is often equated with the quality of chaos and absurdity which we attribute to all art that expresses the modern dilemma, that is, it deals with what is alienated, meaningless and gratuitous in life. For some, like Kenneth Burke, the grotesque is incongruity without laughter unless we are out of sympathy with it,[54] while for Dürrenmatt the grotesque is a way of expressing in a tangible manner 'the form of the unformed', of making us physically perceive the paradoxical.[55]

Valle-Inclán's grotesque manner belongs to modern art as Thomas Mann later defined it:

> The striking feature of modern art is that it has ceased to recognize the categories of tragic and comic, or the dramatic classifications, tragedy and comedy. It sees life as tragicomedy, with the result that the grotesque is its most genuine style—to the extent, indeed, that today that is the only guise in which the sublime may appear. . . . The grotesque is the anti-bourgeois style.[56]

The grotesque is the visitation upon us of the uncanny and irrational; although its effect may range from loathing to dread, from terror to laughter, it presents a monstrous and mysterious world which withstands any attempt on our part to arrange its components according to a rational scheme. In his study of the history of the grotesque, Wolfgang Kayser concludes that inherent in its structure is the collapse of the categories whereby we systematize our world; we find in their stead 'the fusion of realms which we know to be separated, the abolition of the law of statics, the loss of identity, the distortion of "natural" size and shape, the suspension of the category of objects, the destruction of personality, and the fragmentation of the historical order.'[57] In short, the grotesque shatters the world order as we know it, or at least the illusion of that order.

Valle-Inclán took the grotesque manner and adapted it to the drama by making the producer stage a situation as if he were putting a concave mirror before the actors thus catching, distorting and ridiculing their appearance. He deforms their gestures systematically in order to capture the essence of pretentiousness. The result is surrealist movements, fantastic impressions, absurd aspects of human conduct. Moreover, the producer must transform visual or acoustic deformations into a pattern, metaphorically speaking, like the mathematician who converts loose numbers into a formula; the producer stages distortions through an acting and pace that are rigidly controlled so as to have order and harmony. Grotesque deformations seen on the stage could be perturbing, psychologically speaking, but from the theatrical aspect, they are beautiful if successfully choreographed. As Max explains in *Lights*: 'Deformation stops being deformation when subjected to a perfect mathematic'. Every thing in an *esperpento* is so well conceived that the grotesque is no longer only a manner, as in most traditional grotesque works, but a particular category or form; the grotesque here does not only treat values as does grotesque satire but reveals them, since its purpose is not only analytical but also critical. Valle-Inclán's grotesque conveys an impact but also embodies a world view. It's a vision. It may not teach or purge but it can serve a function in reality for it can lead to recognition and even to responsibility. This is so because by handling historical subject matters Valle-Inclán's grotesque dramatizes before our eyes how inapplicable are the categories or the ideas which supposedly apply to our world view. The *esperpentos* are thus analogous to creations like Picasso's *Guernica*, some of Giacometti's desiccated figures, Solana's mannequins, perhaps Bartok's quartets, some of the Dada humour, Ghelderode's masks, Ionesco's early farces and some Buñuel films such as *Viridiana*.

The Vision of Esperpentos. More important, however, the *esperpentos* raise the question of what is authentic in the world, which values are real, which are without foundation and which therefore are false. In this sense, the grotesque setting of the *esperpento* is not only theatrical deformation but it also contains satirical and ethical preoccupations. Valle-Inclán's deformations recall some of Quevedo's portrayals in satirical poems where a woman, for example, may be totally transformed—she is a monstrous elaboration of the idealized mistress in love sonnets (similar to those he himself composed).[58] There seems to be no intervening reflection in either Valle-

Inclán or Quevedo, no compromising irony as in the more ambiguous caricatures of a Shakespeare or a Cervantes. Their distortions do not cause total disintegration or destroy all proposition. Quevedo's satirical sonnets, like all the *esperpentos*, are funny and at times hilarious because, as later with Valle-Inclán, there seems to be a malicious sense of superiority over the butt of ridicule.

The issue of Quevedo's distorting manner is mentioned only because of Valle-Inclán's own views on Quevedo. He once explained that he would not like to live the life of his own characters because as an author he felt vastly superior to his creation. And he singled out Quevedo precisely as the one Spanish author who considered his characters inferior to him.[59] Quevedo's satiric manner is for Valle-Inclán an example of estrangement, which converts ordinary satire into the grotesque. Unlike satire, the grotesque need not relate the object of mockery to some social or cosmic order of things; the grotesque points out the inescapable disintegration and loss of everything distorted—face, eyes, mouth, hair, body, movement and virtue. Because if we were to look from a distance at a number of elements laden with false decoration, beauty would lose the strands of significance that constitute a woman's world.

Whether Quevedo's known moral commitments and stoical views finally absorb the grotesque element (the fact that 'mi lengua pecadora',—'my sinful tongue'—is the cause of distortion should not be overlooked) is not at issue here. What matters is Valle-Inclán's attempt to explain the unsettling effect of his *esperpentos* by referring to Quevedo's satiric visions. This raises another problem about the *esperpento*: how to suspend accepted conventions and still preserve some sense of proportion, some semblance of realism, some kind of defence against the chaotic; how to pluck some sort of meaning out of distortion or disintegration. First of all, what is shocking and unsettling about Quevedo's and Valle-Inclán's grotesque satire is that the clearing away of deceptive appearances does not seem at first glance to result in the celebration of reality as with Cervantes or Shakespeare, nor in an implied view of another 'better' reality as with most satirists, but results often in simply nothing at all, other than the brilliant art. When appearances are demolished in Quevedo's sonnet, nothing seems to remain. There is nowhere the underlying teasing irony of Shakespeare, nowhere the implied corrections of the satirist; reality is no more and no less than the sum of silly pretensions. If such a view appears disengaged, wit for wit's sake, distortion for art's sake, as various Hispanists believe, it is very misleading.

It happens that the distance achieved in Quevedo's grotesque satire (and this cannot be stressed enough in Valle-Inclán) is obviously the result of a profound concern for the absurdities of the human condition and a committed stand against the abuses of contemporary artists. His grotesque reaches beyond its most immediate satiric objects and embodies the state of man. For there is a point at which distortion ceases to be a corrective, humanistic undertaking. This point is reached when the grotesque satirist potentially loses his sovereign position and finds himself in the midst of the things he repudiates, and his mockery of contemporary absurdities changes to resentment and dissatisfaction with regard to existence itself. In the less grotesque satire of Shakespeare the disturbed structure of woman's reality springs back into place and the rents in the fabric of her beauty can be mended. But in Quevedo the order is irreparably destroyed and the supposed order or meaning of things continually collapses. This mingled state of alienation and disillusionment is the setting for Quevedo's and Valle-Inclán's satires in a grotesque environment.

That the grotesque has been dominant in the literature of our century goes without saying, but there are theoretical and technical developments in the *esperpentos* of Valle-Inclán which are unique and call for a careful revaluation. It may be a little misleading to relate the *esperpentos* only to the traditions of the grotesque or to compare them to European counterparts, such as the elements of the absurd in existentialist literature and avantgarde theatre. The relationships are there and the comparisons do make Valle-Inclán's grotesque plays more meaningful and more accessible. Yet despite such obvious parallels these plays embody that special Spanish vision which has a keen sense for deformation, for nonsense and for playful irony. Valle-Inclán did not need naturalism in order to portray harsh, sordid realities because Quevedo and the picaresque novel had already existed, not to mention

Galdós; he did not need European romanticism to reveal the sense of horror and capriciousness because, as he himself said, they had been depicted effectively by Goya; he did not need to coincide with Pirandello in order to stage the mysterious interplay of fantasy and arbitrary fact for he was steeped in Cervantes. It so happens that the Spanish brand of grotesque expression has much in common with the agony or absurdity of modern consciousness—witness alone either Quevedo or Cervantes. Behind every grotesque situation in the *esperpento* the spectator senses a protest, some sort of wounded sense crying for justice, throbbing with needs, questing for grace. Through a spokesman like the blind poet Max Estrella who becomes the first theorist of the *esperpento*, the protest of Valle-Inclán—(to paraphrase Thomas Mann)—rises through grotesque fiction to sublimity.

We need to take a new look at Valle-Inclán and his times. Every artistic revolution creates new worlds. The Modernists and the generation of '98 created a whole new vocabulary, to which Valle-Inclán's *esperpento* was an important contribution. To Spanish readers it meant taking a hard look at appearances, throwing off the tragic yoke, creating distance, gaining a perspective of history, ceasing to escape from reality beneath surfaces of social life. But *esperpento* implied much more than this: it meant throwing off superstition and social myths, analysing history and not idealizing it, abolishing 'word blindness' and analysing things not only for what they mean but as they are: our normal vision of Spanish reality is distorted, suggests Valle-Inclán, precisely because we Spaniards ignore surface reality and try to get beneath or beyond it, because we try to explain and interpret Spanish history by means of fictions or myths which endeavour to bring dignity, depth, substance and significance to what is really brutish, hollow and absurd. *Esperpento* meant to enter into a new, grotesque literary world.

BOHEMIAN LIGHTS

Bohemian Lights is the *esperpento* within an *esperpento* because it includes in the action a complete theory of the new genre which it has been simultaneously putting into practice. All the experiences of the fifteen scenes are integrated into the blind poet's formulation of grotesque fiction just as he is dying. This first *esperpento* is the record of a single evening (late sunset to early dawn), sometime between 1917 and 1920 in a Madrid bustling with activity. Although marked by skirmishes between the police and workers on strike or by patrols and by arrests, that day is none-the-less very much like any other. In the early evening a Barcelona striker is carried to prison; a little later the blind poet is arrested for disturbing the peace; sometime before midnight a child is shot accidentally and a Barcelona striker is deliberately shot in the back while trying to escape. Mobs, violence, screams, *la ley de fuga* (i.e., the law that allowed prisoners to be shot while 'trying to escape'), syndicalism, governmental upheavals. At about the same hour the weather breaks and the biting Madrid wind begins numbing the weak body of the blind poet. He dies as people begin their daily chores. A woman neighbour complains upon seeing the dead body: 'I simply can't wait around anymore! I've already lost half a day.'[60]

In the intervals the inhabitants of Madrid have discoursed with animation on Spanish politics, religion, anarchism and literature. The structure of this *esperpento* is episodic: the action takes place in a garret, a bookstore, a tavern, the streets, a prison, newspaper offices, the Minister's office, a café frequented by poets, a park where prostitutes roam, street corners, a threshold, a cemetery. An ordinary 'travelogue' of Madrid during a perfectly ordinary day because, given the prolonged strikes and the political upheaval, the violence of the streets had become commonplace. Yet this evening is not quite ordinary because everything is based upon the bizarre experiences of the bizarre blind poet, Máximo Estrella. He is the king of Bohemians. A Minister of the Interior recalls that 'He had everything: demeanour, eloquence, wit' and that without question this poet 'was worth more than anyone else of my generation'. *Lights*, of course, is about more than the final hours of this witty Bohemian; it's how Max came to be 'this phantom of Bohemia' according to an old friend but, in the words of a young bureaucrat, 'now deep in the gutter, reeking of alcohol and greeting all the old bawds in French'. What gives an organic unity to Valle-Inclán's first *esperpento* is the blind poet's progressive insight into himself as a degenerate Bohemian and into a new understanding of Spanish history and human suffering.

As Max deals with the problem of feeding his impoverished family, encounters representatives of the decadent avantgarde and Bohemia, walks through streets torn with revolutionary and reactionary violence, is manhandled by the police, cheated by his crony, and left finally to die in a doorway, he not only undergoes debasing disillusionment but captures the grotesque images of modern humanity for us in the 'concave mirror' of his mind. As a sufferer, Max experiences, but as an artist he studies the shift from noble, hence tragic, values—arriving at the previously cited formula that the tragedy of Spain can be rendered only through an aesthetic that is systematically deformed. Of course, the transmutation of man's dignity and sentiments into the grotesque gestures of puppets asserts the rejection of the tragic attitude as sham—both on the personal and the national level. In the first place he converts himself into a puzzling exemplar of modern consciousness, and refuses to be just another imitation of the classical hero. His inwardness does not protect him from the ugliness of the world; rather, it debunks everything, including itself. When Max discovers he must play out his part as a blind, starving Bohemian before an insensitive audience of fellow puppets, his objectivity reveals the inexorable absurdity of even this role.

It is significant that Max is a poet, a Bohemian and, in general, a modern artist, a radical thinker, a member of the avantgarde with a strong dislike for orthodox literature. His grotesque vision before he dies is pure art, it offers a reappraisal of modern fiction and deals with certain ideas on the absurd which have been the common property of a good many European writers. Yet his new grotesque manner no matter how visionary or fictional, no matter how witty or existentially oriented, acquires its true value when understood as reflecting limited, circumstantial, historical conditions in Spain. Max's deforming aesthetic of the concave mirror is rooted in contemporary historical events—witness his involvement with street disturbances, police brutality, strikes, syndicalist terrorism, government instability, etc. Whatever he says about art therefore derives from and applies directly to the Spanish situation. *Lights* is in fact structured in such a way that specific events of history (like the violent strikes and political arrests of 1917 and 1919) and the stuff of fiction (like the nocturnal odyssey of Max) are juxtaposed so that they make their own comment on one another. The Bohemian life of Madrid, everywhere articulated in minute detail, is grafted effectively onto several archetypal myths.[61] Yet the entire mythical grotesque vision stands on a solid historical footing. There is no allusion to a person, no reference to a strike, no description of an event in *Lights* that was not reported and analysed and commented upon often in the very same reviews where Valle-Inclán was publishing his *esperpentos*.

The Historical Background of Bohemian Lights. A good deal of the content has been documented: the proletarian-like exhortations, roaming-mobs, glass-strewn streets, skirmishes, patrols, arrests, beatings, killings, or the discussions about property and labour, revolutions and anarchism, or the severe criticism of the press, the military, the government and its ministers, and, finally the lurking shadow of violence. I myself have related all these elements to historical events and have shown how these vignettes, reflect the labour crisis which turned Spain into an arena of assassinations, terror and instability.[62] In short, I have demonstrated that Valle-Inclán composed a miniature tableau of the times, stressing the most horrible and preposterous aspects of national calamities, integrating them into the myth-like odyssey of the blind poet's last day, and, based on these findings, I have argued that the grotesque situation of *Lights* was a map of Spanish life, that *Lights* is tied to the historical realities of its own time and place and that Valle-Inclán's stylistic virtuosity and invented myths were, more than aesthetic exercises, aesthetics of commitment.

He touches in fact upon the problem of Spain's political and social failures within the narrow angle of the death of one Bohemian. He did not simply describe the historical realities of his time but instead carefully worked out a general relationship between the episodic structure of the Bohemian's last journey through Madrid and the fragmentary structure of Spanish society where the action was staged. The history of early twentieth-century Spain is a culmination of calamities and chaos; and the portrayal of Bohemian life in Madrid criticizes the artists' lack of realism or sense of responsibility before such chaos. Valle-Inclán could hardly exaggerate the grotesqueness of historical facts. The shooting of the Catalan prisoner, for example, could have been any one of many political assassinations which, according to statistics, totalled over 700.[63] Max Estrella's great moment of exasperation when he hears of the shooting is understandable precisely because it is a combination of personal crisis, national tragedy and a sense of futility (see p. 181).

The connection between the story of Max and contemporary history is a masterful example of dense dramatic synthesis. Valle-Inclán crowds into one section of Madrid and into a few hours a series of strikes that took place over a spell of two years in many different regions. The strike crisis therefore seems prolonged and endless. Valle-Inclán attempted, as he put it to 'fill time the same way that El Greco used to fill space',[64] that is, to reassemble several events and place them together in order to create a composite mosaic of historical bits and pieces. Each allusion to patrols, clashes, arrests, shootings, to the government and the press stands in some relation to everything else. Thus, while the actual events are rearranged and compressed, the strike picture as a whole is historically valid. Valle-Inclán merges history and fiction by perfecting the difficult technique of the montage, that is, he captures the news-like material in a succession of fragmentary shots which immediately create a synthetic canvas. The technique is that of viewing an action from several angles as with a movie camera: every episode of the central action contains at the same time a glimpse of the strikes and thus the foreground of the national calamities. The historical matter, fragmentary and disparate as it might appear in *Lights*, is unified by the common denominator of Max's 'tragic clowning', which enables us to place the various items in some causal relationship to each other. The clowning is topical, limited to a historical situation, but it is at the same time a grotesque, shambling carnival of Spanish history. Valle-Inclán's elaboration of the political disturbances is generated in *Lights* as an oyster creates a pearl, around an irritant; the 'concave mirror' offers a faithful reflection of grotesque historical situations.

It is difficult to make an absolute distinction, in Max's mirror, between what belongs to the historical reality of Madrid and what belongs to the imaginative reality of Max's grotesque vision of the city. Valle-Inclán squeezes the utmost out of the frontier between history and fiction: in the stylized world of the *esperpento*, the strikes, as tragic and ludicrous events, are a painful masquerade; in the real world of Spain, the strikes as an artistic elaboration of history are only a shadow of reality, pure fiction; but also in the real world of Spain, the strikes exist—they endure beyond the aesthetic world of the *esperpento* and are, in fact, a part of the world in which Spaniards such as Valle-Inclán exist. Max, the Catalan prisoner, Latino, Maura, the Bohemians, the Minister, 'the Spaniards', they are all such stuff as the grotesque is made of. Tragic carnival is, in fact, the bridge that Valle-Inclán constructs between pure aesthetics and commitment to history.

Textual History of Lights. The question of Valle-Inclán's intentions in rooting his new grotesque vision in his country's history has led to many polemics. An author's intentions are of course almost always elusive, especially when we deal with ironists like Valle-Inclán.[65] My main objective here is to answer the question by ascertaining just what happens in *Bohemian Lights*, a task which is in this case indispensable for any large-scale interpretation of the first *esperpento*. To understand exactly what Valle-Inclán's purposes were, we must start with the convenient clues provided by the textual foundations of the play: it is necessary to know, for example, the exact nature of all the additions and interpolations between the first and second versions, 1920 and 1924.

Besides various timely stylistic changes, the final version in 1924 has three added scenes and some key adjustments to smooth the integration of the new added material. The new scenes are: Scene II, the dialogue about Spanish realities and absurdities at Zarathustra's bookstore: Scene VI, the prison scene where Max discusses politics with a young Catalan prisoner who is taken away to be shot, supposedly while trying to escape; and Scene XI, the street gathering where a mother screams hysterically because her child has been shot, where some shots were explained as the killing of Max's cellmate and in which, finally, Max lets out his exasperated cry about Spain's 'tragic clowning'. The additions and changes are crucial because they amplify the character of the protagonist Max, add a new dimension to his nocturnal voyage through Bohemia and, most important, give a new historical orientation to the blind poet's definition and vision of the *esperpento*.

The background of strikes and disturbances gains coherence through the narrative of the Catalan prisoner. This setting of national calamities begins subtly in the first added scene, Scene II, in front of Zarathustra's bookstore when a striker is carried to prison: 'A small squad of policemen passes by with a man in handcuffs.' Both the background of strikes and the prisoner's fate are next focused in the second added scene, Scene VI, in a prison cell. The national calamities are focused on the Catalan's tragic fate and link up with the world of art and Bohemian decadent life through Max's absurd arrest (see p. 121). Henceforth Max's nocturnal odyssey, i.e., the fictional part of *Lights*, is an integral part of the recorded historical events in general and of the prisoner's fate in particular; he will be shot and no one, least of all the impotent intellectuals and the lackey press, can do anything about it. And it is in the third added scene, Scene XI, where significantly, Max disparages the hypocrisy of artists ('Scum! All of them! We the poets more than anybody'). After hearing the mother's harrowing screams over her child accidentally shot and after realizing that the Barcelona striker, his cell-mate, was shot in the back deliberately, Max sums up in a tortured frenzy the harrowing and ludicrous effects of the political calamities by calling the entire situation, in disgust, a 'tragic clowning'.

The loose references of the 1920s version to mobs in the streets, shouts, smashed store windows, shots and troops, become integrated into the plot in the 1924 version: the added scenes form a secondary plot by focusing on the Catalan prisoner (his arrest, imprisonment and execution); this plot gives a more ordered sequence to the historical background and intensifies the climax of the dramatic action: the poet's death and his definition of a new, deformed way to look at and capture reality. Because Max is associated, as a poet, with the imagination, he helps define the art of the grotesque but because he is touched, as a Spaniard, by the harsh reality of the Catalan victim, he makes the grotesque aesthetic depend utterly on contemporary history. The changes affect the very conception of the new genre: Max's definition of the *esper-*

pento in the first version is not as effective as in the final one. The most famous and oft-quoted chilling observation, for example, that 'Spain is a grotesque deformation of European civilization' had little really that led up to it in the shorter 1920 version of *Lights* without Scenes II, VI and XI. Very little and nothing concrete. The three added scenes prepare the stage so that everything leads precisely to this remark about Spain and thus amplifies the definition of the grotesque. In the first added scene, Scene II, at Zarathustra's, Max elaborates upon his first comments on Spain: 'It is a miserable spot', a 'terrón nublado'. In fact, Max's observations about leftist demagogues, Spanish metaphysics and superstitions, Spain's intellectual limitations and her foolish pretensions, are a miniature *esperpento*; to paraphrase his words, he deliberately deforms his comments in order to capture 'the entire miserable life of Spain'. Thus the historical consciousness of Max, coming early in the action, at the start of his journey through the hell of Madrid as he calls it, intensifies all his subsequent barbs about Spaniards and Spanish institutions. After Scene II, everything that Max says about Spain becomes more immediate, loses its facile cleverness and achieves vital authenticity.

The second added scene, Scene VI, provides precisely the experience needed to render Max's remarks more responsible. For in the prison Max discusses many of the political problems of Spain and the world, among them, anarchism, revolution, law-of-escape (*ley de fugas*), Lenin, Russia, the war, strikes, syndicates, the press. An analysis of the added material tells us much about *Lights* and the orientation of the *esperpento.*

The arrests, beatings and killings of strikers that appear in the added scenes, all amply documented, correspond with historical reality. The fate of the young striker from Barcelona, to take a key example, closely parallels a famous practice by General Anido known as *ley de fuga* which shocked the world press: 'The police arrested syndicalists and shot them as they were being conducted to the police station: they were reported as shot trying to escape.'[66] There is nothing to be done: an artist like Max can only expand his indignation in useless adjectives like 'barbarians', while the press, clearly unfavourable to labour and its demands, will only report, in Max's words, 'Whatever they're told to print'. And the guard who removes the prisoner, cynically tells him how he is about to go on a 'nice vacation'. The guard's chilling euphemism gives rise to an ambivalent feeling of hilarity and despair. Helplessness, indifference and cynicism render death not pathetic or tragic but common, absurd and estranged.

During the climax of the strike crisis, Max and Latino walk in a street where a scuffle has taken place and hear a woman holding her dead child screaming 'Killers of children'. A crowd gathers, begins to argue loudly while some advise the screaming mother to be more prudent. Historical events are reduced to the still warm corpse in the arms of a grief-stricken mother who subconsciously holds it close to her upon hearing shots nearby (see p. 179).

It is amidst this general confusion and indifference, appropriately, that a night-watchman discloses how the shots just heard were for 'a prisoner attempting to escape'. The esperpentic potential of the strikes is further realized as Valle-Inclán skilfully stages the shooting of the Catalan striker together with the murder of an innocent child. And Max crystallizes the harrowing and ludicrous effects of these events when in tortured frenzy he calls the entire situation, disgustingly, a 'tragic clowning'. Max's exasperated oxymoron captures the tragic dimensions of a travesty. And the integration between grotesque history and grotesque fiction is completed as Max, immediately after defining the *esperpento*, reviews the national situation with, 'And what will those scum newspapers report tomorrow? That's what the Catalan outcast was asking himself'. It is important that Max's crucial words were interpolated by Valle-Inclán in the 1924 version.

Max's repetition of the bitter, sarcastic words of his fellow prisoner is of course a very significant addition; it tells much about Valle-Inclán's intentions concerning his new genre. For whatever polemics there may be about the *esperpento*, he at least, here in its final formulation, has Max explain it as directly related to the historical situation of the years 1917 to 1919. Max's ironic query is placed exactly after his definition of the *esperpento* and immediately before his tragic farcical death. It thus brings everything together: the tragic story of the Catalan prisoner, the tragic national conditions, the callous way they are reported and Max's awareness of his and Spain's miserable situation. And the integration between grotesque history and grotesque fiction is neat, for Max reviews the national situation as he explains that the best fictional way to capture reality is to distort it. Thus the *esperpento*, a new manner of fiction in 1920, becomes deliberately topical in 1924.[67]

Obviously Valle-Inclán in 1924 develops in *Lights* all the historical elements that were embryonic in his first version of the *esperpento*. The definition of the *esperpento*, full of artificial gimmicks such as concave mirrors, symmetrically executed deformations or aesthetically pleasing distortions (not unknown in the tradition of aesthetics), becomes an authentic vision; the concave mirror is, more than an aesthetic manner, a faithful reflection of historical situations. This is the meaning of Max's suggestion: 'let's deform style in the same mirror that distorts our faces and contorts the whole miserable life of Spain'. Max's definition of the *esperpento* is now directly related to his evolution from a disengaged Bohemian to a committed artist.

There were hints of this state of mind in the first edition; for example, Max's obvious impatience with the young Modernists who called him their 'maestro'. Their cleverness irritates him and he often insults them outright. None of their quips and criticism contain, for Max, an ounce of truth or sympathy or insight; they are excessively talkative, indulging in wisecracks and lies, certainly quite irresponsible compared to Max's rudimentary truths. Their very Bohemian condition—the avantgarde's aesthetic orientation itself—is the harbinger of Bohemian chaos and decadence. After calling their leader, Dorio de Gadex, 'an ass', he spells out the difference between them and him:

> I feel like one of the people. I was born to be tribune of the Plebs, but I mixed with scum and became a bastard perpetrating translations and hammering out verses. Even so, better ones than you Modernists make.

In the final 1924 version, to Max, the Bohemian intellectual, pretences and aesthetic preoccupations are a meaningless rigmarole. For here, Max is directly involved with the pain of historical realities. Hence his rejection of the avantgarde literary movements as he launches his new vision: 'The avantgarde are foolish humbugs. It was Goya who invented the grotesque.' Modernists are criticized for lacking concreteness and for being remote from the daily struggles of humanity. And the plot of *Bohemian Lights* is precisely about how a Bohemian poet in early twentieth-century Madrid came to see himself and his role in society.

The Bohemian Poet and the degeneration of the tragic role. An essential part of the first *esperpento* remains tragic, or rather it becomes a devaluation of the tragic sense. What is essential in *Lights*, then, is to see by what means an inherently tragic puppet can become liberated from his puppet condition and assume an authentic dimension. Now the concept of the tragic hero has never been explained to everyone's satisfaction, for even in antiquity there were divergencies among the various approaches of the tragic poets. What makes possible, for example, the greatness of Sophoclean heroes is that the source of their action lies in them alone, nowhere else. The tragic hero (Oedipus or Ajax) was a man who, unsupported by the gods and in the face of human opposition, makes a critical decision which springs from the deepest layer of his individual nature and then blindly, ferociously, heroically maintains that decision even to the point of self-destruction. Dürrenmatt, speaking about modern attitudes to life, explained that such a tragic hero was no longer possible in our times. On the one hand, tragedy presupposes guilt, despair, moderation, lucidity, vision, a sense of responsibility; on the other hand, 'In the Punch-and-Judy show of our century . . . there are no more guilty and also, no responsible men.'[68] Dürrenmatt, Valle-Inclán and others have actually carried to a logical conclusion the concept which Euripides developed: the hero, suffering rather than acting, was unlike the responsible, fully guilty heroes of his predecessors, Aeschylus and Sophocles. In Euripides many characters are victims rather than heroes because disaster usually strikes capriciously and blindly; it often comes not from the hero's stubbornness but from outside forces, from the gods themselves. In the tragedies of Euripides man is once more in a world where the autonomy of his action or any responsibility are in doubt. This is precisely the point that both Valle-Inclán and Dürrenmatt have developed and intensified for our times:

> And indeed, things happen without anyone in particular being responsible for them. Everything is dragged along and everyone gets caught somewhere in the sweep of events. We are all collectively guilty, collectively bogged down . . . That is our misfortune, but not our guilt: guilt can exist only as a personal achievement, as a religious deed. Comedy alone is suitable for us.[69]

I quote Dürrenmatt because he has managed to sum up well many of the anti-tragic views of our century. Valle-Inclán has stated almost the exact concept of the lack of tragedy of the modern hero when he argued that man's destiny, fatality, pain or haughtiness may be the same as always, but that the heroes who act out such big roles have changed radically: they are too apologetic, too tiny and unimportant to be able to live up to the big roles in life. The disparity between actor and role and the sense of the absurd are inevitable, and also funny. Yet Valle-Inclán, at least in *Bohemian Lights* closely follows the human predicament as postulated by Euripides in his tragedies, where the only consolation that can be offered the broken victims of this unfeeling universe is the advice to suffer with dignity. Max is a broken victim too and within his unfeeling surroundings learns to suffer with humour. Charting the way to a position of laughter in the midst of calamities is one example of modern attempts to devalue classical tragedy and simultaneously to capture the tragic sense. Naturally, classical heroes and traditional values are diminished in such a modern grotesque environment; if anything, they too become puppet-like and distorted. These precepts of the *esperpento* are inextricably connected to the life and death of the blind poet, that is, Valle-Inclán's grotesque manner is grafted on to the absurd situation of Max and how he reacts to it.

At the beginning of the play, Max is still prepared to carry on somehow his struggle as a true protagonist. ('I see, and I see magnificently' he protests to others). He identifies his responsibility as poet with his dignity as man. Thus the vicissitudes of being blind, out of work, forgotten, cause tragic pain to which he reacts proudly. But this noble disposition leads, ironically, only to severer humiliations and his awareness of ridiculous impotence. He must submit to a series of degradations—being cheated of money, hearing the mumbo-jumbo of the cafés, witnessing police barbarity—until his patience is exhausted and his endeavours begin to resemble the gestures of a frustrated marionette. When Max demands justice for the police beating from the Minister of the Interior, who was a boyhood friend, he is offered a hand-out instead; he admits his failure to obtain redress of his injured dignity, accepting the debasement as fact—'because I too am a swine'. He can now distinguish between the absurd way things are and how noble we would like them to be. As his quite real disgrace evolves into a sad farce, the illusion of tragic sentiment is dispelled. Max's paralysis of will introduces a second stage of crisis in the degeneration of the classical hero. He turns inward and, by poeticizing reality, attempts to transcend his present tribulations and limitations. His gift of creative imagination outlasts by a little the urge to assert human dignity. He accepts being 'a spectre of the past' who lives with memories and dreams.

But reality batters down even this defence. It is impossible for him to be seduced again by the need for, or charm of, illusory worlds. Max no longer sees things in his head 'magnificently', and to the suggestion, 'Gentlemen, we must think of tomorrow,' replies drily, 'Let's not!' In a final guttering of his sensibilities, even the zeal for beauty is dampened. Just before his death, while Max is transforming the vulgar whore Lunares into a poetic nymph—much as Don Quixote embellished Maritornes[70]—she responds to his tenderness with lascivious sensuality: 'Don't feel my face any more. Feel my body.' Max's dreams matter nothing to her, and he is performing mere verbal exercises. Lacking a genuinely sympathetic audience, imaginative vitality does not achieve meaning but becomes absurd. In the process of being reduced to the truth of everyday reality, Max at first poeticizes his own agony, then dramatizes his condition, later grows bitter, and finally ridicules his own sentiments with trenchant sarcasm. His attitude toward the suffering of others follows the same course from sympathy toward caricature. The world's apathy invades him, or he discovers that there is no genuine compassion—in either case, he cannot feel for the wretches who inhabit a country in which admiration for the tragic no longer has a place.

In feeling the pain of others, Max had expected reciprocal

affection. But the opposite occurred. Both his talent and misfortune are viewed distantly, with insensibility, until he is reduced to nothing and feels only exasperation. Yet, for this very reason, he too can finally view his own misery with detachment and indifference. Unlike the classical hero, Max neither accepts his fate with dignified resignation, nor fights against destiny. Rather, he becomes fed up with his tragedy; sometimes it nauseates him, sometimes it amuses him. The ultimate step toward artistic intuition of existence as an *esperpento* is Max's total divorce from his role. The incongruity of playing a tragic part under carnival conditions prompts a real or feigned apathy, but this incongruity in itself is the source of a new aesthetic pleasure. Such at least is the daring perception of a classical hero become grotesque, who chooses to salvage whatever form may remain. The state of the *esperpento* is attained in Max's last moments when, interpreting his own and Spain's story, he alternates between seriousness and frivolity. This wry depersonalization in extreme agony removes the last vestige of classical heroism: not dignity, but the self-pity on which it rests. Max is simultaneously the ridiculous, gesticulating, suffering puppet and the genial puppet-master laughing at the show.

Max is of course one of 'The classical heroes . . . gone to take a stroll in Cat alley', that is, the proud poet is forced to act out his tragic role before an indifferent or insensitive public that has no values. The absurd circumstances and his own failings conspire to make his lofty visions mere hallucinations. But he does persist for a while, and in his persistence he appears stubbornly unyielding, foolishly blind, nobly enduring, arrogantly joking (or rather a combination of all four). He finally mocks his own tragedy and rejects it as a complete absurdity. For Max is the classic hero reflected mockingly in a concave mirror and at the same time the artist who envisions his own deformed mockery in the mirror of his mind. He is the tragic hero gesticulating like a puppet, and the classic artist converted into an indifferent puppeteer who sets down the grotesque formula of the *esperpento*. Simultaneously character and author, Max becomes the objective painter of his own ridiculous destiny.

Inevitably, Max is amused by his own performance. He perceives clearly the ludicrous and pathetic plight of himself being entrapped by a foolish pretention and useless hope, but he also comes to realize that he must nevertheless either adjust to his absurd situation or clamour against it—but above all in some way endure it. Endure it, but not accept it. Man is like a puppet with enough human traits to make a fool of himself even during the most anguishing moments of life. Max is convinced of this when he looks at his own agony as if he were a stranger. He refuses to substitute for grotesque realities the illusions of tragic grandeur. He may be a marionette at the end, pained and ridiculous, but he is also the puppet master, impersonal and ingenious, who has enough irony left to laugh maliciously and enough wit to enjoy the grotesque gestures of the ludicrous show that he and Spain are putting on.

Max frees himself from the shackles of an inept tragedy through laughter and art, that is, he looks down at himself from above. This is in many ways an affirmative step on the part of Valle-Inclán. By rejecting the tragic mantle and ridiculing his own condition, Max is at least regenerated as an artist. He is again sharp and funny and even confident, for he refuses to be one more gesticulator in this tragic clowning. And his jesting mood while dying is, ironically, the only authentic release from the grotesque. Max laughs at himself not only because he behaves like a puppet that puts on tragic airs, but also because he is vitally alive in the pursuit of freeing himself from his absurd predicament; he may not succeed totally but he discloses his humanity in the very process of mocking it.

In this respect, Valle-Inclán's first *esperpento* has many significant parallels with Sartre's *Nausea*, if we discount the formal and theoretical differences in each work: both put a man in a crucial situation by confronting him with the absurdity of his life (a state of 'nausea' in one, of 'grotesquerie' in the other), and both heroes solve their predicament through the power of creation, through art. *Nausea* is the diary of an isolated, 20-year-old, weary historian, Roquentin, who records his experiences of recurring nausea, the mental disorientation wherein man cannot find a meaning for existence, because 'the world of explanations is not the world of existence'. Like Max before him, Roquentin accepts his immediate experience and rejects humanistic explanations. As Max finally laughs at his own tragic role as poet, so Roquentin laughs at his humanist role as historian; both reject their roles as absurd, and both are regenerated when they accept their role as artists. *Nausea* and *Lights* distort external reality and stress the absurd condition of man; above all, they dramatize art and estrangement as the decisive focus of the liberation of man from the nausea of the absurd or from the grotesque condition of puppetlike behaviour. One resource at least left to man is the artistic creation by which man tries to make possible a living stance face to face with a 'nauseous' or 'grotesque' reality.

I point out the parallels between Sartre's *Nausea* and Valle-Inclán's *Lights* in order to stress the fact that the grotesque filter of the *esperpento* is not merely technique, but a problematic situation; and that the *esperpentos* are not only related to the tradition of caricature but are, like the works of Brecht, Pirandello, Sartre and Ionesco, part of our own times. The impact of Valle-Inclán's play, its catharsis if any, is achieved precisely by its expansion into the ludicrous grotesque. The grotesque then makes good sense in *Bohemian Lights*: the difference between man and puppet is that man feels responsible for his lot while a puppet is controlled and predetermined. A tragic role is one made by others and for others, and therefore to live as a tragic character, man becomes a thing of others, a puppet. This warning about tragic roles may be the key message of the first *esperpento*. Max's unwillingness to continue the tragic formula releases him from the absurd and gives him authenticity. The revelation of his insignificance and absurdity is accompanied by anguish in Max, the anguish of man's lost dignity and that of man's responsibility. But as Max goes further in the experience of absurdity, he becomes progressively so unimportant to others that his tragedy turns into farce, and an absurd laughter bursts forth. This is why Max jokes as he is dying. He sees clearly what his 'tragedy' is all about.

In fact, we are bothered or at least puzzled by the seeming gaiety of his last moments because Max converts the traditional death scene into something altogether estranged and hilarious (see p.187). The brutal naturalistic truth, coupled with Max's stacatto, matter-of-fact delivery, jars our sensibilities. Although he may not eliminate or even alleviate the grotesque, he at least faces it and, unlike the other Spanish puppets, grapples with it. Laughter is one way to freedom.

NOTES

1 I was able to read the opinions which appeared in *Sunday Times*, *Scotsman*, *Times Educational Supplement*, *Observer*, *Edinburgh Evening News*, *Glasgow Herald*, *Guardian*, *Scottish Daily Express*, *Cumberland News*, *Daily Telegraph* and *Sunday Telegraph*.

2 In 'Controversial "*Lights* . . ." Opens Cottage Season', signed only R.J., in *Cumberland News*.

3 *The Theater of the Absurd* (New York 1961) 286–7.

4 In his review of *Ramón del Valle-Inclán: an Appraisal of his Life and Works*, in *Modern Drama* (February 1970) 434.

5 By Alonso Zamora Vicente, 'Asedio a *Luces de Bohemia*, primer esperpento de Ramón del Valle-Inclán'. The talk was published by the Real Academia Española in 1967. The Academy had denied membership to Valle-Inclán on personal and moral grounds yet, ironically, his *esperpento*, which harshly mocks the Academy (scenes IV, V, VIII), became the subject for an inaugural address by a newly elected member.

6 The producer, Nic Renton, was kind enough to carry on a detailed correspondence with me concerning his ideas and plans for the translation and production of *Lights*.

7 The Marquis of Bradomín, hero of the four novels called *Sonatas*, was Valle-Inclán's first important creation, his first archetype who also reappears in later works. See R. Salper de Tortella, 'Valle-Inclán and the Marqués de Bradomín', in *Ramón del Valle-Inclán: an Appraisal of his Life and Works*, ed. by A.N.Zahareas (New York 1968) 230–40. Henceforth the vol. referred to as *Appraisal*.

8 This crucial point will be explained with more detail in the section on the *Esperpentos*.

9 For an interpretation of the *autos sacramentales*, see A.A. Parker, *The Allegorical Drama of Calderón*, (Oxford London 1947); and Bruce Wardropper, *Introducción al Teatro Religioso del Siglo de Oro* (Salamanca 1966).

10 France has actually been the clearing house through which Britain and America have obtained access to much of continental literature, and *Bohemian Lights* was first performed in Paris in 1963 by the theatrical company of Jean Vilar in a production by Georges Wilson.

11 Compare the irony of Cervantes's title, *Eight Plays and Eight Interludes Never Performed* (1615).

12 Cf. the interesting chapter on Azorín in Carlos Blanco-Aguinaga's *La juventud del '98*, Siglo XXI (Madrid 1968).

13 Most of the relevant letters between Darío and Valle-Inclán are quoted or paraphrased by Robert Lima, 'Valle-Inclán: The man and his Early Plays', *Drama Critique*, IX, 2 (1966) 69–78.

14 See Alice Clemente, 'Valle-Inclán, Translator', in *Appraisal*, 241–7.

15 See D. García-Sabell, '*La cara de Dios*', tr. by M. Mandel and A. N. Zahareas, in *Appraisal*, 813–18.

16 Developed especially in *Invertebrate Spain* (*España invertebrada*) 1921, translated into English in 1937.

17 The question of 'aesthetic distance' is discussed more fully in the sections on the *Esperpentos* and *Bohemian Lights*.

18 See the various studies by Sumner Greenfield in *Appraisal*.

19 Cf. E. Susana Speratti Piñero, *La elaboración artística en 'Tirano Banderas'* (Mexico 1957). Now a part of a longer collection of studies, *De 'Sonata de otoño' al Esperpento (Aspectos del arte de Valle-Inclán)* (London 1968).

20 Reproduced in volume I of *Obras Completas* (Madrid 1954) p. xxiv.

21 Primo de Rivera published his opinion in one of his notorious 'notas oficiosas', a series of paragraph-long news items which he used to deliver to the press.

22 Especially true of his collection of stories and novelettes, *Shadowy Garden*, 1902–5.

23 In *Winter Sonata* 1905. Complete Works (1954) 237.

24 Published under the title of *Midnight: Stellar Vision of a Moment of War*.

25 César Barja, 'Ramón del Valle-Inclán', in *Libros de autores contemporáneos* (New York 1935) 362.

26 José Rubia Barcia, 'A Synoptic View of Valle-Inclán's Life and Works', in *Appraisal*, 25. The study first appeared as Part I of *A Bio-bibliography and Iconography of Valle-Inclán* (1866–1936) (Berkeley and Los Angeles 1960).

27 Reported in *La Voz*, a Madrid daily, on January 5 and 6 of 1936.

28 In Francisco Madrid, *La vida altiva de Valle-Inclán* (Buenos Aires 1943) 365.

29 *Valle-Inclán: Anatomía de un teatro problemático*, Fundamentos (Madrid 1972). The only drama critic to relate Valle-Inclán to European trends is Juan Guerrero Zamora, 'Ramón del Valle-Inclán', Chapter VII of

Historia del teatro contemporáneo, I (Barcelona 1961) 153–216.

30 'Escribir contra el público', *ABC* Madrid (February 1969).

31 Galdós was then the artistic director of the 'Teatro Español' and turned down *The One Bewitched* for production whereupon Valle-Inclán gave a public reading of it in the Ateneo in February 1913.

32 Quoted from his 'Bréviaire du cinéma', in Henri Agel's *Esthétique du Cinéma*, 'Que sais-je?' No. 751 (Paris 1962) 122.

33 'Valle-Inclán and the Art of the Theater', *BHS*, XLVI, 2 (1969) 132–52.

34 From an interview with José Montero Alonso, reproduced in *La Novela Semanal*, VI (Madrid 1926). My translation.

35 Amado Alonso's doctoral thesis was on the musicality of Valle-Inclán's early prose, published later in *Materia y forma en poesía* (Madrid 1955) 257–369.

36 '*Sonata de estío* de Don Ramón del Valle-Inclán', *La Lectura*, I (1904).

37 Cf. R. Salper de Tortella, in *Appraisal*.

38 See the chapter on the *esperpento* in Speratti Piñero's *Tirano Banderas*, 85–122.

39 The *Episodios nacionales* consist of 46 volumes and describe the important events of Spanish history from *Trafalgar*, 1873, to the Restoration.

40 The Generation of 1898 was a loose-knit group of modern Spanish writers who were deeply concerned with the calamities of Spanish history and who explored the nature of the so-called 'Spanish Problem' in a passionate process of self-examination. Among the early accepted members were Angel Ganivet, Miguel de Unamuno, 'Azorín' Antonio Machado, Ramiro de Maeztu, Pío Baroja and, on and off, Valle-Inclán and the playwright J. Benavente. They were 'engaged' writers and are identified with a variety of motifs such as 'the tragic sense of life', self-absorption (ensimismamiento), historicity, 'intra-history'.

41 In an interview with Gregorio Martínez Sierra, *ABC* (Dec. 1928), reproduced several times since then in various critical works. For a synthesis of Valle-Inclán's comments on his art, see R. Cardona and A. N. Zahareas, 'Apéndice Documental: Valle-Inclán como teórico de la creación literaria', *Visión del Esperpento* (Madrid 1970) 233–45.

42 '. . . La petite bourgeoisie à laquelle je pensais, n'était pas une classe liée à telle ou telle société car le petit

bourgeois était pour moi un être se trouvant dans toutes les sociétés. . . .' Eugene Ionesco, *Notes et Contre-notes* (Paris 1962) 49. This collection throws much light on Ionesco's and the Avantgarde's detestation of commitment in general and dislike for writers such as Brecht in particular. The doctrine of art for art's sake and a distrust of circumstantiality filter through in arguments that cathedrals exist simply to assert the laws of architecture, and symphonies to assert those of musical form.

43 W.B.Yeats, 'The Second Coming'.

44 Most of Sartre's early views have been summed up neatly and simply in 'Existentialism is a Humanism', in *Existentialism from Dostoyevski to Sartre*, ed. Walter Kaufmann (New York 1956) 289.

45 For a penetrating discussion of some of these problems, see Albert Hofstadter, 'The Tragicomic: Concern in Depth', *Journal of Aesthetics and Art Criticism* (1966) 290–302.

46 Friedrich Dürrenmatt, 'Problems of the Theater', in R.W. Corrigan, *Theater in the Twentieth Century* (New York 1963). Earlier in *Tulane Drama Review* (October 1958) 3–26. (Originally, *Theaterprobleme*, 1955). It was mainly a justification of new dramatic techniques for what Dürrenmatt considers an apocalyptically absurd age.

47 From Bryan Creel's unpublished English translation with some minor adjustments. (M.A. Thesis, University of California at Davis).

48 Charles Baudelaire, 'Le vieux saltimbanque', in *Petits Poëmes en Prose* (1850–1864).

49 'Érase un hombre a una nariz pegado' ('There was once a man stuck to a nose'), an oft-quoted caricaturesque sonnet, no.522 in the edition of *Obras Completas, Poesía Original* by José Manuel Blecua (Barcelona 1963).

50 F.W.Nietzsche, *Thus Spake Zarathustra*, tr. R.J.Hollingdale (1961).

51 Cf. Vladimir Nabokov's comments in *Gogol* (Connecticut 1949).

52 For two excellent discussions of the problem of distance and alienation, see John Willett, *The Theater of Bertolt Brecht* (London and New York 1959) 168–90, and Martin Esslin, *Brecht: The Man and His Work* (New York 1961) 120–49.

53 For a study of the history of this problem, see J.Gillet, 'The Autonomous Character in Spanish and European Literature', *HR*, XXIV (1956) 179–90, and L.Livingston,

'Interior Duplication and the Problem of Form in the modern Spanish novel', *PMLA*, 73 (1958) 393–406.

54 'The Grotesque', in *Attitudes Toward History* (Boston 1961) 57–69.

55 Dürrenmatt, op. cit., 69.

56 In his essay on Joseph Conrad, *Past Masters and Other Papers* (New York 1933).

57 *The Grotesque in Art and Literature*, Indiana Univ. Press (Bloomington 1963) 17; also the chapter 'An Attempt to Define the Nature of the Grotesque', ibid., 179–89.

58 Sonnet no. 568 in Blecua, op. cit., 'Sol os llamô mi lengua pecadora' (sun was what my sinning tongue called you).

59 'The truth of the matter is that I wouldn't have liked to live the life of any of my characters. . . . Goya painted his figures as beings that were inferior to him. Just like Quevedo. . . . like the authors of these [picaresque] novels who went to great pains so that no one confused them with their characters whom they considered inferior to them [the authors] . . . I too consider my characters inferior to me.' In Madrid, *Vida*, 104.

60 For a long interpretation of the first esperpento, see 'Sentido y forma de *Luces de Bohemia*', and 'La construcción crítica de *Luces de Bohemia*', in Cardona-Zahareas, *Visión*, 69–115 and 163–78.

61 The outlines of Max's nocturnal 'odyssey' spring from the tradition of familiar myth. Like Adonis and Osiris, Odysseus and Aeneas, the hero of Bohemia enters the country of lower depths, undergoes experiences which equip him with new insights, and emerges into the sphere of light and, as a writer, tells about it. To die and to be reborn; to plunge in the dark and to see the light: these are old stories, endlessly repeated in legend and endlessly elaborated by writers, ranging from Homer to Joyce in different periods.

62 'The Esperpento and Aesthetics of Commitment', *MLN*, 81 (March 1966) 159–73. Among the various documents, I referred to several issues of the *New York Times* which often reported the very same events and sense of chaos represented later by Valle-Inclán in *Lights*.

63 Most of the pertinent documentation is available in Gerald Brenan's *The Spanish Labyrinth* (Cambridge 1960) and in Raymond Carr, *Spain: 1808–1939* (Oxford 1966).

64 A comment which appeared in his 'Self-Criticism' ('Autocrítica'), *España*, August 8, 1924.

65 José F. Montesinos first asks 'what is it really that Valle-

Inclán wants?' and next answers his own question as if the Valle-Inclán of the 1920s should have been a novelist of the 1870s. 'Modernismo, esperpentismo o las dos evasiones', *Revista de Occidente,* XV, 44–5 (Nov.–Dec. 1966) 146–65. This is a very disappointing study.

66 Brenan, op. cit., 73.

67 This topicality is true of all the *esperpentos*; the wedding of pure fiction and historical realities is documented and appraised in Cardona-Zahareas, *Visión*, 186–228.

68 Dürrenmatt, op. cit., 69.

69 Ibid.

70 Cf. Chapters XVII–XVIII of the First Part of *Don Quixote*.

Ramón del Valle-Inclán

LUCES DE BOHEMIA
Esperpento

BOHEMIAN LIGHTS[1]
Esperpento[2]

PERSONAJES[3]	DRAMATIS PERSONAE[3]
Max Estrella	Max Estrella,
Su mujer Madama Collet	His wife Madame Collet and
y su hija Claudinita	his daughter Claudinita
Don Latino de Hispalis	Don Latino de Hispalis
Zaratustra	Zarathustra
Don Gay	Don [Pilgrim] Gay
Un pelón	A dimwitted urchin
La chica de la portera	The concierge's little girl
Pica Lagartos	Lizard-chopper
Un coime de taberna	The bar boy
Enriqueta la Pisa-Bien	Henrietta Tread-well
El Rey de Portugal	The King of Portugal
Un borracho	A drunk
Jóvenes Modernistas	*The Modernists*
Dorio de Gadex	Dorio de Gadex
Rafael de los Vélez	Rafael de los Vélez
Lucio Vero	Lucio Vero
Mínguez	Mínguez
Gálvez	Gálvez
Clarinito	Clarinito
Pérez	Pérez
Pitito, capitán de los équites municipales	Pitito, captain of municipal cavalry
Un sereno	A night watchman
La voz de un vecino	The voice of a neighbour
Dos guardias del orden	Two officers of the law
Serafín el Bonito	Serafin-the-dandy
Un celador	A bailiff
Un preso	A prisoner

El portero de una redacción	Newspaper office porter
Don Filiberto, redacción en jefe	Don Philbert, Editor-in-Chief
El Ministro de la Gobernación	[H. E.] the Minister of the Interior
Dieguito, secretario de su Excelencia	Dieguito Garcia, secretary of his Excellency
Un ujier	A ministry usher
Una vieja pintada y la Lunares	An old hag and Beauty Spot
Un joven desconocido	An unknown youth
La madre del niño muerto	The mother of the dead child
El empeñista	The pawnbroker
El guardia	The policeman
La portera	The concierge
Un albañil	A mason
Una vieja	An old woman
La trapera	The rag-woman
El retirado	The retired officer
Todos del barrio	People of the district
Otra portera	Another concierge
Una vecina	[Cuca] a neighbour
Basilio Soulinake	Basilio Soulinake
Un cochero de la funeraria	A hearse coachman
Dos sepultureros	Two gravediggers
Rubén Darío	Rubén Darío
El Marqués de Bradomín	The Marquis of Bradomín
El pollo del Pay-Pay	The fop, Fan-Fan
La periodista	[Pacona] old newsvendor
Turbas	Crowds
Guardias	Police
Perros	Dogs
Gatos	Cats
Un loro	A parrot
La acción en un Madrid absurdo, brillante y hambriento[4]	The action takes place in an absurd, brilliant, and starving Madrid[4]

ESCENA PRIMERA

(Hora crepuscular. Un guardillón con ventano angosto, lleno de sol. Retratos, grabados, autógrafos, repartidos por las paredes, sujetos con chinches de dibujante. Conversación lánguida de un hombre ciego y una mujer pelirrubia, triste y fatigada. El hombre ciego es un hiperbólico andaluz, poeta de odas y madrigales, MÁXIMO ESTRELLA.[5] *A la pelirrubia, por ser francesa, le dicen en la vecindad* MADAMA COLLET.[6]*)*

MAX. Vuelve a leerme la carta del Buey Apis.[7]

MADAMA COLLET. Ten paciencia, Max.

MAX. Pudo esperar que me enterrasen.

MADAMA COLLET. Le toca ir delante.

MAX. ¡Collet, mal vamos a vernos sin esas cuatro crónicas! ¿Dónde gano yo veinte duros, Collet?[8]

MADAMA COLLET. Otra puerta se abrirá.

MAX. La de la muerte. Podemos suicidarnos colectivamente.

MADAMA COLLET. A mí la muerte no me asusta. ¡Pero tenemos una hija, Max!

MAX. ¿Y si Claudinita estuviese conforme con mi proyecto de suicidio colectivo?

MADAMA COLLET. ¡Es muy joven!

MAX. También se matan los jóvenes, Collet.

MADAMA COLLET. No por cansancio de la vida. Los jóvenes se matan por romanticismo.

MAX. Entonces, se matan por amar demasiado la vida. Es una lástima la obcecación de Claudinita. Con cuatro perras de carbón, podíamos hacer el viaje eterno.[9]

MADAMA COLLET. No desesperes. Otra puerta se abrirá.

MAX. ¿En qué redacción me admiten ciego?

SCENE ONE

(Dusk. A garret with narrow windows, full of sun. Portraits, engravings and autographs are scattered over the walls and held by drawing-pins. Languid conversation between a blind man and a fair-haired woman, now sad and worn-out. The blind man is a hyperbolical Andalusian, poet of odes and madrigals, MAXIMO ESTRELLA.[5] *Because the blonde woman is French, everyone in the neighbourhood calls her* MADAME COLLET.[6]*)*

MAX. Read me the letter from that Big Sacred Bull once more.[7]

Mme COLLET. Be patient, Max.

MAX. He could have waited till I was dead.

Mme COLLET. He'll go first.

MAX. Collet, without the money for that article we're in a fine mess. How else can I earn those pesetas, Collet?[8]

Mme COLLET. Some other door will open.

MAX. Death's! We can all commit collective suicide.

Mme COLLET. I'm not afraid of death myself. But we have a daughter, Max!

MAX. And what if Claudinita subscribed to my formula of collective suicide?

Mme COLLET. She's too young, Max.

MAX. Young people kill themselves too, Collet.

Mme COLLET. But not because they're disgusted with life. Young people kill themselves for romantic reasons.

MAX. Then they kill themselves because they love life a little too much. What a shame Claudinita is so blind. Fourpennyworth of coal and we could all journey into eternity.[9]

Mme COLLET. Don't despair. Another door will open.

MAX. What other newspaper office will employ me, a blind man?

MADAMA COLLET. Escribes una novela.

MAX. Y no hallo editor.

MADAMA COLLET. ¡Oh! No te pongas a gatas, Max. Todos reconocen tu talento.

MAX. ¡Estoy olvidado! Léeme la carta del Buey Apis.

MADAMA COLLET. No tomes ese caso por ejemplo.

MAX. Lee.

MADAMA COLLET. Es un infierno de letra.

MAX. Lee despacio.

(MADAMA COLLET, *el gesto abatido y resignado, deletrea en voz baja la carta. Se oye fuera una escoba retozona. Suena la campanilla de la escalera.*)

MADAMA COLLET. Claudinita, deja quieta la escoba, y mira quién ha llamado.

LA VOZ DE CLAUDINITA. Siempre será Don Latino.

MADAMA COLLET. ¡Válgame Dios!

LA VOZ DE CLAUDINITA. ¿Le doy con la puerta en las narices?

MADAMA COLLET. A tu padre le distrae.

LA VOZ DE CLAUDINITA. ¡Ya se siente el olor del aguardiente!

(MÁXIMO ESTRELLA *se incorpora con un gesto animoso, esparcida sobre el pecho la hermosa barba con mechones de canas. Su cabeza rizada y ciega, de un gran carácter clásicoarcaico, recuerda los Hermes.*[10])

MAX. ¡Espera, Collet! ¡He recobrado la vista! ¡Veo! ¡Oh, cómo veo! ¡Magníficamente! ¡Está hermosa la Moncloa![11] ¡El único rincón francés en este páramo madrileño! ¡Hay que volver a París, Collet! ¡Hay que volver allá, Collet! ¡Hay que renovar aquellos tiempos!

MADAMA COLLET. Estás alucinado, Max.

MAX. ¡Veo, y veo magníficamente!

MADAMA COLLET. ¿Pero qué ves?

MAX. ¡El mundo!

MADAMA COLLET. ¿A mí me ves?

MAX. ¡Las cosas que toco, para qué necesito verlas!

MADAMA COLLET. Siéntate. Voy a cerrar la ventana. Procura adormecerte.

MAX. ¡No puedo!

MADAMA COLLET. ¡Pobre cabeza!

MAX. ¡Estoy muerto! Otra vez de noche.

(*Se reclina en el respaldo del sillón. La mujer cierra la ventana, y la guardilla queda en una penumbra rayada de sol poniente. El*

Mme COLLET. Then write a novel.

MAX. And not find a publisher.

Mme COLLET. Oh! Don't crawl on all fours, Max. Everybody respects your talent.

MAX. I'm forgotten! Read me that Sacred Bull's letter.

Mme COLLET. You can't take this particular case as an example.

MAX. Read.

Mme COLLET. It's hard to read through, like Dante's *Inferno*.

MAX. Read slowly.

(MADAME COLLET, *her features downcast and resigned, spells out the letter in a low voice. Outside, a clattering broom is heard. The doorbell rings.*)

Mme COLLET. Claudinita, put the broom down and see who's calling.

VOICE OF CLAUDINITA. It must be Don Latino, as usual.

Mme COLLET. Good God!

VOICE OF CLAUDINITA. Do I slam the door in his face?

Mme COLLET. He amuses your father.

VOICE OF CLAUDINITA. You can already smell the alcohol.

(MAXIMO ESTRELLA *suddenly jumps up with animated gestures, his beautiful beard, with tufts of grey, spread out on his chest. His blind, tousled head has a strong classic-archaic character and recalls the statues of Hermes.*[10])

MAX. Wait, Collet! I've recovered my sight! I see! Oh how well I see! Magnificently! How beautiful Moncloa is![11] The only French touch in this bleak spot of Madrid! We must return to Paris, Collet! Collet, we have to go back there! We must relive those times!

Mme COLLET. You're having hallucinations, Max.

MAX. I see, I tell you, and I see magnificently!

Mme COLLET. But what is it you see?

MAX. The world!

Mme COLLET. And me, do you see me?

MAX. Things that I touch, what do I need to see them for!

Mme COLLET. Sit down, I'll close the window. Try and get some sleep.

MAX. I can't.

Mme COLLET. Poor wretch!

MAX. I'm dead! It's night again.

(*He falls back into the armchair. The woman shuts the window, and the garret is plunged into semi-darkness streaked a little by the*

ciego se adormece, y la mujer, sombra triste, se sienta en una silleta, haciendo pliegues a la carta del Buey Apis. Una mano cautelosa empuja la puerta, que se abre con largo chirrido. Entra un vejete asmático, quepis, anteojos, un perrillo y una cartera con revistas ilustradas. Es DON LATINO DE HISPALIS.[12] *Detrás, despeinada, en chancletas, la falda pingona, aparece una mozuela:* CLAUDINITA.*)*

DON LATINO. ¿Cómo están los ánimos del genio?

CLAUDINITA. Esperando los cuartos de unos libros que se ha llevado un vivales para vender.

DON LATINO. ¿Niña, no conoces otro vocabulario más escogido para referirte al compañero fraternal de tu padre, de ese hombre grande que me llama hermano? ¡Qué lenguaje, Claudinita!

MADAMA COLLET. ¿Trae usted el dinero, Don Latino?

DON LATINO. Madama Collet, la desconozco, porque siempre ha sido usted una inteligencia razonadora. Max había dispuesto noblemente de ese dinero.

MADAMA COLLET. ¿Es verdad, Max? ¿Es posible?

DON LATINO. ¡No le saque usted de los brazos de Morfeo![13]

CLAUDINITA. Papá, ¿tú qué dices?

MAX. ¡Idos todos al diablo!

MADAMA COLLET. ¡Oh, querido, con tus generosidades nos has dejado sin cena!

MAX. Latino, eres un cínico.

CLAUDINITA. Don Latino, si usted no apoquina, le araño.[14]

DON LATINO. Córtate las uñas, Claudinita.

CLAUDINITA. Le arranco los ojos.

DON LATINO. ¡Claudinita!

CLAUDINITA. ¡Golfo!

DON LATINO. Max, interpón tu autoridad.

MAX. ¿Qué sacaste por los libros, Latino?

DON LATINO. ¡Tres pesetas, Max! ¡Tres cochinas pesetas! ¡Una indignidad! ¡Un robo!

CLAUDINITA. ¡No haberlos dejado!

DON LATINO. Claudinita, en ese respecto te concedo toda la razón. Me han cogido de pipi.[15] Pero aún se puede deshacer el trato.

setting sun. The blind man falls asleep and the woman, a sad shadow, sits down in a small chair while folding the letter from the Sacred Bull. A sneaky hand gives a push to the door and it opens with prolonged squeaking. An asthmatic little old fellow enters, peak-cap, glasses, a small dog, and a portfolio with illustrated reviews. He is DON LATINO DE HISPALIS.[12] *Behind him, dishevelled, in slippers, her skirt dirty, a young girl appears:* CLAUDINITA.*)*

DON LATINO. In what sort of spirits is our genius?

CLAUDINITA. The genius is waiting for the cash from some old books that an old rascal was supposed to sell.

DON LATINO. My dear girl, can't you select more fitting language when you address a fraternal companion of your father, of that great man who calls me 'brother?' What language, Claudinita!

Mme COLLET. Did you bring the money, Don Latino?

DON LATINO. Madame Collet, you surprise me, because I have always admired your rationality and understanding. Max has already disposed of the money in the noblest manner possible.

Mme COLLET. Is this true, Max? Is it possible?

DON LATINO. Don't tear him away from the arms of Morpheus.[13]

CLAUDINITA. Papa, what do you have to say?

MAX. You can all go to Hell!

Mme COLLET. Oh, my dear, with your generosity you've left us without supper again.

MAX. Latino, you are a cynic.

CLAUDINITA. Don Latino, if you don't come across with the cash,[14] I'll scratch you.

DON LATINO. Trim your claws, Claudinita.

CLAUDINITA. I'll tear your eyes out.

DON LATINO. Claudinita!

CLAUDINITA. Tramp!

DON LATINO. Exercise your authority, Max.

MAX. How much did you get for the books, Latino?

DON LATINO. Three pesetas, Max! Only three filthy pesetas! A scandal! A larceny!

CLAUDINITA. You shouldn't have left them!

DON LATINO. Claudinita, dear child, in this case I concede that what you claim is perfectly correct. I was caught with my trousers down.[15] But we can still cancel the deal.

MADAMA COLLET. ¡Oh, sería bien!

DON LATINO. Max, si te presentas ahora conmigo en la tienda de ese granuja y le armas un escándalo, le sacas hasta dos duros.[16] Tú tienes otro empaque.

MAX. Habría que devolver el dinero recibido.

DON LATINO. Basta con hacer el ademán. Se juega de boquilla, maestro.

MAX. ¿Tú crees? . . .

DON LATINO. ¡Naturalmente!

MADAMA COLLET. Max, no debes salir.

MAX. El aire me refrescará. Aquí hace un calor de horno.

DON LATINO. Pues en la calle corre fresco.

MADAMA COLLET. ¡Vas a tomarte un disgusto sin conseguir nada, Max!

CLAUDINITA. ¡Papá, no salgas!

MADAMA COLLET. Max, yo buscaré alguna cosa que empeñar.

MAX. No quiero tolerar ese robo. ¿A quién le has llevado los libros, Latino?

DON LATINO. A Zaratustra.

MAX. ¡Claudinita, mi palo y mi sombrero!

CLAUDINITA. ¿Se los doy, mamá?

MADAMA COLLET. ¡Dáselos!

DON LATINO. Madama Collet, verá usted qué faena.[17]

CLAUDINITA. ¡Golfo!

DON LATINO. ¡Todo en tu boca es canción, Claudinita!

(MÁXIMO ESTRELLA *sale apoyado en el hombro de* DON LATINO.[18] MADAMA COLLET *suspira apocada, y la hija, toda nerviosa, comienza a quitarse las horquillas del pelo.)*

CLAUDINITA. ¿Sabes cómo acaba todo esto? ¡En la taberna de Pica Lagartos!

Mme COLLET. Oh Max, that would be great!

DON LATINO. If you come with me now to that scoundrel's bookstore, Max, and kick up a row, you can get as much as two *duros*.[16] You make a better impression.

MAX. Yes, but we'd have to return the money he gave us.

DON LATINO. A mere gesture will suffice. You can promise without forking up, maestro.

MAX. You think so?

DON LATINO. Naturally!

Mme COLLET. Max, you shouldn't go out.

MAX. The air will refresh me. It's as hot as an oven in here.

DON LATINO. Well, there's a cool breeze in the streets.

Mme COLLET. You'll only get upset and you won't gain a thing.

CLAUDINITA. Father, don't go outside!

Mme COLLET. Max, I'll find something to pawn.

MAX. I won't stand for this robbery. Whom did you sell the old books to, Latino?

DON LATINO. To Zarathustra.

MAX. Claudinita, my cane and my hat!

CLAUDINITA. Do I give them, mother?

Mme COLLET. Let him have them!

DON LATINO. Madame Collet, you're going to see some real cape work.[17]

CLAUDINITA. Old tramp!

DON LATINO. My word, Claudinita, everything turns to song in your mouth!

(MAXIMO ESTRELLA *goes out, leaning on the shoulder of* DON LATINO.[18] MADAME COLLET *heaves a deep sigh, completely overcome, and the daughter, all nerves, begins to pull pins from her hair.)*

CLAUDINITA. You know how this is going to wind up, don't you? In Lizard-Chopper's tavern.

ESCENA SEGUNDA[19]

(La cueva de ZARATUSTRA[20] *en el Pretil de los Consejos.*[21] *Rimeros de libros hacen escombro y cubren las paredes. Empapelan los cuatro vidrios de una puerta cuatro cromos espeluznantes de un novelón por entregas.*[22] *En la cueva hacen tertulia el gato, el loro, el can y el librero.* ZARATUSTRA, *abichado y giboso – la cara de tocino rancio y la bufanda de verde serpiente –, promueve, con su caracterización de fantoche, una aguda y dolorosa disonancia muy emotiva y muy moderna. Encogido en el roto pelote de una silla enana, con los pies entrapados y cepones en la tarima del brasero, guarda la tienda. Un ratón saca el hocico intrigante por un agujero.)*

ZARATUSTRA. ¡No pienses que no te veo, ladrón!

EL GATO. ¡Fu! ¡Fu! ¡Fu!

EL CAN. ¡Guau!

EL LORO. ¡Viva España!

(Están en la puerta MAX ESTRELLA *y* DON LATINO DE HISPALIS. *El poeta saca el brazo por entre los pliegues de su capa, y lo alza majestuoso, en un ritmo con su clásica cabeza ciega.)*

MAX. ¡Mal Polonia recibe a un extranjero![23]

ZARATUSTRA. ¿Qué se ofrece?

MAX. Saludarte, y decirte que tus tratos no me convienen.

ZARATUSTRA. Yo nada he tratado con usted.

MAX. Cierto. Pero has tratado con mi intendente, Don Latino de Hispalis.[24]

ZARATUSTRA. ¿Y ese sujeto de qué se queja? ¿Era mala la moneda?

*(*DON LATINO *interviene con ese matiz del perro cobarde, que da su ladrido entre las piernas del dueño.)*

DON LATINO. El maestro no está conforme con la tasa, y deshace el trato.

ZARATUSTRA. El trato no puede deshacerse. Un momento antes que hubieran llegado . . . Pero ahora es imposible: Todo el atadijo, conforme estaba, acabo de venderlo ganando dos perras. Salir el comprador, y entrar ustedes.

(El librero, al tiempo que habla, recoge el atadijo que aún está encima del mostrador, y penetra en la lóbrega trastienda, cambiando una seña con DON LATINO. *Reaparece.)*

SCENE TWO[19]

*(*ZARATHUSTRA'S *cave*[20] *on the lower level of Consejos Street.*[21] *Untidy piles of books cover the walls. Four hair-raising pictures from a serialized magazine story*[22] *are pasted on the four window panes of a door. Within the cave, the cat, the parrot, the dog and the bookseller sit around and have their daily session. Beetle-like and humped, with a snake-green scarf around his wornout, greasy face,* ZARATHUSTRA, *with a puppet's features, evokes a sharp and painful dissonance, very moving and quite modern. Curled up in the ragged stuffing of a dwarfish chair, with his feet wrapped in rags and twined round the brazier stand, he minds the shop. A mouse sticks out his inquisitive snout through a hole.)*

ZARATHUSTRA. Don't think I can't see you, you thief!

CAT. Ssss . . .! Ssss . . .! Ssss . . .!

DOG. Woof! Woof!

THE PARROT. Long live Spain!

*(*MAX ESTRELLA *and* DON LATINO DE HISPALIS *stand at the door. The poet takes his arm out from under the folds of his cape and raises it majestically in time with his classical, blind head.)*

MAX. You do not, oh Poland, receive a foreigner with courtesy![23]

ZARATHUSTRA. What can I do for you?

MAX. I'm here, first, to greet you, and next to tell you that I don't like the way you do business.

ZARATHUSTRA. Why, I've had no dealings with you.

MAX. Not with me, to be sure, but with my agent, Don Latino de Hispalis.[24]

ZARATHUSTRA. And this character, what's he complaining about? Was it phony money?

(DON LATINO *intervenes with that special trait of a cowardly dog which barks from between his master's legs.*)

DON LATINO. The maestro is not satisfied with your price and is breaking the deal.

ZARATHUSTRA. Too late to break the deal. If you'd only arrived a minute sooner . . . But it's impossible now; the whole loose bundle intact–I just sold it, making only two pence profit. The buyer leaves, and you enter.

(The bookseller, keeping up his chatter, picks up the bundle of books which is still on top of the counter, and enters the dark back room, exchanging signs with DON LATINO. *He then reappears.)*

DON LATINO. Hemos perdido el viaje. Este zorro sabe más que nosotros, maestro.

MAX. Zaratustra, eres un bandido.

ZARATUSTRA. Ésas, Don Max, no son apreciaciones convenientes.

MAX. Voy a romperte la cabeza.

ZARATUSTRA. Don Max, respete usted sus laureles.

MAX. ¡Majadero!

(Ha entrado en la cueva un hombre alto, flaco, tostado del sol. Viste un traje de antiguo voluntario cubano,[25] *calza alpargates abiertos de caminante, y se cubre con una gorra inglesa. Es el extraño* DON PEREGRINO GAY,[26] *que ha escrito la crónica de su vida andariega en un rancio y animado castellano, trastrocándose el nombre en* DON GAY PEREGRINO.– *Sin pasar de la puerta, saluda jovial y circunspecto.)*

DON GAY. ¡Salutem plúrimam![27]

ZARATUSTRA. ¿Cómo le ha ido por esos mundos, Don Gay?

DON GAY. Tan guapamente.

DON LATINO. ¿Por dónde has andado?

DON GAY. De Londres vengo.

MAX. ¿Y viene usted de tan lejos a que lo desuelle Zaratustra?

DON GAY. Zaratustra es buen amigo.

ZARATUSTRA. ¿Ha podido usted hacer el trabajo que deseaba?

DON GAY. Cumplidamente. Ilustres amigos, en dos meses me he copiado en la Biblioteca Real el único ejemplar existente del *Parmerín de Constantinopla.*[28]

MAX. ¿Pero, ciertamente, viene usted de Londres?

DON GAY. Allí estuve dos meses.

DON LATINO. ¿Cómo queda la familia Real?

DON GAY. No los he visto en el muelle.[29] Maestro, ¿usted conoce la Babilonia Londinense?

MAX. Sí, Don Gay.

*(*ZARATUSTRA *entra y sale en la trastienda, con una vela encendida. La palmatoria pringosa tiembla en la mano del fantoche. Camina sin ruido, con andar entrapado. La mano, calzada con mitón negro, pasea la luz por los estantes de libros. Media cara en reflejo y media en sombra. Parece que la nariz se le dobla sobre una oreja. El loro ha puesto el pico bajo el ala. Un retén de polizontes pasa con un hombre maniatado.*[30] *Sale alborotando el barrio un chico pelón montado en una caña, con una bandera.)*

DON LATINO. We've wasted this trip. The old fox is shrewder than we are, maestro.

MAX. Zarathustra, you're a crook!

ZARATHUSTRA. These are not becoming epithets, Don Max.

MAX. I'm going to crack your skull.

ZARATHUSTRA. Don Max, remember, you're a poet.

MAX. Baboon!

(A tall, skinny sun-tanned man has entered the cave. He is dressed as an old Cuban volunteer,[25] *wears hemp-sandals for travelling, and on his head, an English cap. He is the strange* DON PILGRIM GAY[26] *who has written a chronicle of his roving life in a lively yet musty Castilian, transposing his name into that of* DON GAY PEARL GRIM. *Without coming further than the door, he greets everyone jovially and circumspectly.)*

DON GAY. *Salutem plurimam!*[27]

ZARATHUSTRA. How did you get on travelling the wide world, Don Gay?

DON GAY. Rather handsomely.

DON LATINO. And whereabouts have you been?

DON GAY. I've arrived from London.

MAX. And you come from such far-away places just so that Zarathustra can fleece you?

DON GAY. Zarathustra is a good friend.

ZARATHUSTRA. Were you able to do the work you had in mind?

DON GAY. Thoroughly. In just two months in the Royal Library, my illustrious friends, I've copied the only existing manuscript of *The Knight Palmerin of Byzantium.*[28]

MAX. But were you really in London?

DON GAY. I was there two months.

DON LATINO. And how's the Royal Family getting on?

DON GAY. I didn't notice them on the quay.[29] Maestro, you must be acquainted with the Babel of London?

MAX. Yes I am, Don Gay.

(ZARATHUSTRA *comes and goes in the back room, with a lighted candle. The greasy candlestick trembles in the puppet's hand. He walks noiselessly, his feet bound in old rags. His hand, gloved with a black mitten, moves the candle light over the book shelves. Half of the face reflected, and half in shadow. It seems as if his nose is bent sideways over one ear. The parrot has tucked his beak under his wing. A small squad of policemen passes by with a man in handcuffs.*[30] *Raising havoc around the district, a boy with a shaven head comes out riding a cane like a hobby-horse and holding a flag.)*

EL PELON. ¡Vi-va-Es-pa-ña!

EL CAN. ¡Guau! ¡Guau!

ZARATUSTRA. ¡Está buena España!

(Ante el mostrador, los tres visitantes, reunidos como tres pájaros en una rama, ilusionados y tristes, divierten sus penas en un coloquio de motivos literarios. Divagan ajenos al tropel de polizontes, al viva del pelón, al gañido del perro, y al comentario apesadumbrado del fantoche que los explota. Eran intelectuales sin dos pesetas.)

DON GAY. Es preciso reconocerlo. No hay país comparable a Inglaterra. Allí el sentimiento religioso tiene tal decoro, tal dignidad, que indudablemente las más honorables familias son las más religiosas. Si España alcanzase un más alto concepto religioso, se salvaba.

MAX. ¡Recémosle un Réquiem! Aquí los puritanos de conducta son los demagogos de la extrema izquierda. Acaso nuevos cristianos, pero todavía sin saberlo.

DON GAY. Señores míos, en Inglaterra me he convertido al dogma iconoclasta,[31] al cristianismo de oraciones y cánticos, limpio de imágenes milagreras. ¡Y ver la idolatría de este pueblo!

MAX. España, en su concepción religiosa, es una tribu del Centro de África.

DON GAY. Maestro, tenemos que rehacer el concepto religioso, en el arquetipo del Hombre-Dios. Hacer la Revolución Cristiana, con todas las exageraciones del Evangelio.[32]

DON LATINO. Son más que las del compañero Lenin.[33]

ZARATUSTRA. Sin religión no puede haber buena fe en el comercio.

DON GAY. Maestro, hay que fundar la Iglesia Española Independiente.

MAX. Y la Sede Vaticana, El Escorial.[34]

DON GAY. ¡Magnífica Sede!

MAX. Berroqueña.[35]

DON LATINO. Ustedes acabarán profesando en la Gran Secta Teosófica. Haciéndose iniciados de la sublime doctrina.[36]

MAX. Hay que resucitar a Cristo.[37]

DON GAY. He caminado por todos los caminos del mundo, y he aprendido que los pueblos más grandes no se constitu-

THE KID. Long live Spain!

THE DOG. Woof! Woof!

ZARATHUSTRA. Spain is in great shape!

(In front of the counter, the three visitors, hovering like three birds on a branch, visionary and sad, forget their troubles by continuing their literary discussion. They ramble on, indifferent to the squad of policemen, to the 'hurrahs' of the noisy urchin, to the yelpings of the dog, and to the whining chatter of the puppet who is exploiting them. These were intellectuals without a penny.)

DON GAY. You have to admit it. There's no country comparable to England. Over there, religious feeling is expressed with such decorum and such dignity that undoubtedly the most respectable families are also the most religious. If Spain could attain to a higher idea of religion, she'd be saved.

MAX. Let's have a Requiem Mass said for her! Over here those who are puritans in behaviour are the demagogues of the extreme left. New sort of Christians, I suppose, but they don't know it yet.

DON GAY. In England, my dear friends, I became a convert to the iconoclastic dogma[31] . . . to a Christianity of prayers and hymns, purified of miracle-working images. And to see the idolatry of our people!

MAX. When it comes to religious ideas, Spain is a tribe from the heart of Africa.

DON GAY. Maestro, we have to refashion our idea of religion after the archetype of the Man-God. It's our duty to bring about the Christian Revolution with all the exaggerations of the Gospel.[32]

DON LATINO. Which are more than those of comrade Lenin.[33]

ZARATHUSTRA. Without religion there can't be good faith in business dealings.

DON GAY. Maestro, we must establish an Independent Spanish Church.

MAX. With the Escorial for its Holy See.[34]

DON GAY. A magnificent Holy See!

MAX. Hard as granite.[35]

DON LATINO. You'll end up professing the Grand Sect of Theosophy, becoming initiates in its sublime doctrine.[36]

MAX. I say let's resurrect Christ.[37]

DON GAY. I've travelled the four corners of this earth and I've learned that the greatest people never got anywhere without a

yeron sin una Iglesia Nacional. La creación política es ineficaz si falta una conciencia religiosa con su ética superior a las leyes que escriben los hombres.

MAX. Ilustre Don Gay, de acuerdo. La miseria del pueblo español,[38] la gran miseria moral, está en su chabacana sensibilidad ante los enigmas de la vida y de la muerte. La Vida es un magro puchero; la Muerte, una carantoña ensabanada que enseña los dientes; el Infierno, un calderón de aceite albando donde los pecadores se achicharran como boquerones; el Cielo, una kermés sin obscenidades, a donde, con permiso del párroco, pueden asistir las Hijas de María.[39] Este pueblo miserable transforma todos los grandes conceptos en un cuento de beatas costureras. Su religión es una chochez de viejas que disecan al gato cuando se les muere.[40]

ZARATUSTRA. Don Gay, y qué nos cuenta usted de estos marimachos que llaman sufragistas.[41]

DON GAY. Que no todas son marimachos. Ilustres amigos, ¿saben ustedes cuánto me costaba la vida en Londres? Tres peniques, una equivalencia de cuatro perras. Y estaba muy bien, mejor que aquí en una casa de tres pesetas.

DON LATINO. Max, vámonos a morir a Inglaterra. Apúnteme usted las señas de ese Gran Hotel, Don Gay.

DON GAY. Saint James Square. ¿No caen ustedes? El Asilo de Reina Elisabeth. Muy decente. Ya digo, mejor que aquí una casa de tres pesetas. Por la mañana té con leche, pan untado de mantequilla. El azúcar, algo escaso. Después, en la comida, un potaje de carne. Alguna vez arenques. Queso, té . . . Yo solía pedir un boc de cerveza, y me costaba diez céntimos. Todo muy limpio. Jabón y agua caliente para lavatorios, sin tasa.[42]

ZARATUSTRA. Es verdad que se lavan mucho los ingleses. Lo tengo advertido. Por aquí entran algunos, y se les ve muy refregados. Gente de otros países, que no sienten el frío, como los naturales de España.

DON LATINO. Lo dicho. Me traslado a Inglaterra. Don Gay, ¿cómo no te has quedado tú en ese Paraíso?

DON GAY. Porque soy reumático, y me hace falta el sol de España.

ZARATUSTRA. Nuestro sol es la envidia de los extranjeros.

National Church. Real political creation is ineffectual if it lacks a religious conscience with an ethic superior to the laws which mere men write.

MAX. Agreed, illustrious Don Gay. The wretchedness of the Spanish people,[38] their great moral misery resides in the cheap sensibility with which they face the enigmas of life and death. For Spaniards, *Life* is a meagre stew; *Death*, an ugly old woman wrapped in sheets with bared teeth; *Hell*, a large kettle of seething oil where sinners are fried like anchovies; *Heaven* a church bazaar free from obscenities which, with the priest's permission, the children of Mary can attend.[39] These miserable people have been transforming every great idea into a fairy tale told by devoutly bigoted charwomen. Its religion is the twaddle of old crones who dissect their cats when they fall down dead.[40]

ZARATHUSTRA. And what can you tell us, Don Gay, about these viragos called suffragettes?[41]

DON GAY. That they're not all of them mannish. My distinguished friends, do you know how much it cost me to live in London? Three pence, which comes to almost forty céntimos. And I was well off, better than here in a house that charges three pesetas.

DON LATINO. Max, let's go die in England. Just show me the way to that Grand Hotel, Don Gay.

DON GAY. Saint James' Square. Don't you get it? The Queen Elizabeth Home. Quite decent. As I said, better than it is here in a three peseta house. In the morning, tea with milk, bread with real butter. Sugar's a little scarce. Afterwards, for dinner, beef stew. At times, herrings. Cheese, tea . . . I used to ask for a glass of beer which cost me three farthings. Everything very clean. Soap and hot water for washing, at no extra charge.[42]

ZARATHUSTRA. It's true that the English wash a lot. I've noticed that. Some of them drop in here sometimes and they always look very scrubbed. People from other countries don't feel the cold the way we native-born Spaniards do.

DON LATINO. Just so. As for me, I'm moving to England. How come *you* didn't stay in that paradise, Don Gay?

DON GAY. Because I suffer from rheumatism and I need the Spanish sun.

ZARATHUSTRA. Our sun is the envy of all foreigners.

MAX. ¿Qué sería de este corral nublado? ¿Qué seríamos los españoles? Acaso más tristes y menos coléricos . . .[43] Quizá un poco más tontos . . . Aunque no lo creo.
(Asoma la chica de una portera.–Trenza en perico, caídas calcetas, cara de hambre.)

LA CHICA. ¿Ha salido esta semana entrega d'El Hijo de la Difunta?[44]

ZARATUSTRA. Se está repartiendo.

LA CHICA. ¿Sabe usted si al fin se casa Alfredo?

DON GAY. ¿Tú qué deseas, pimpollo?

LA CHICA. A mí, plin. Es Doña Loreta la del coronel quien lo pregunta.[45]

ZARATUSTRA. Niña, dile a esa señora que es un secreto lo que hacen los personajes de las novelas. Sobre todo en punto de muertes y casamientos.

MAX. Zaratustra, ándate con cuidado, que te lo van a preguntar de Real Orden.[46]

ZARATUSTRA. Estaría bueno que se divulgase el misterio. Pues no habría novela.
(Escapa la chica salvando los charcos con sus patas de caña. EL PEREGRINO ILUSIONADO *en un rincón conferencia con* ZARATUSTRA. MÁXIMO ESTRELLA *y* DON LATINO *se orientan a la taberna de Pica Lagartos, que tiene su clásico laurel en la calle de la Montera.[47])*

ESCENA TERCERA

*(La Taberna de Pica Lagartos: Luz de acetileno, mostrador de cinc, zaguán oscuro con mesas y banquillos, jugadores de mus,[48] borrosos diálogos.–*MÁXIMO ESTRELLA *y* DON LATINO DE HISPALIS, *sombras en las sombras de un rincón se regalan con sendos quinces de morapio.[49])*

EL CHICO. Don Max, ha venido buscándole la Marquesa del Tango.[50]

UN BORRACHO. ¡Miau!

MAX. No conozco a esa dama.[51]

EL CHICO. Enriqueta la Pisa-Bien.

DON LATINO. ¿Y desde cuándo titula esa golfa?

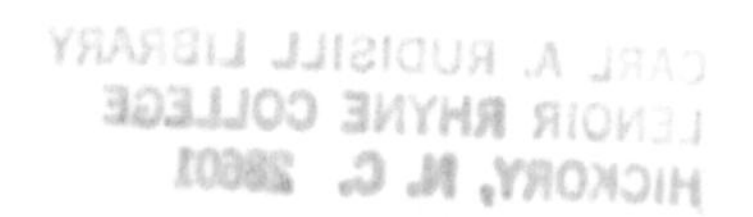

MAX. What would become of this barnyard if it were clouded over? And what would we Spaniards be like? A little sadder, perhaps, and not so choleric . . .[43] Perhaps a little more stupid . . . though I doubt it.

(A concierge's little girl sticks her head out of a door. Pigtail, stockings falling down, famished face.)

THE GIRL. Has the latest instalment of the *Dead Woman's Son*[44] come out this week?

ZARATHUSTRA. It's just being distributed.

THE GIRL. Do you know if Alfredo gets married at the end?

DON GAY. And why do you want to know, my little rosebud?

THE GIRL. Me? Don't care a hoot! It's Doña Loreta the Colonel's wife who's asking.[45]

ZARATHUSTRA. Girl, you tell the lady that whatever the characters do in the novels is a secret. Above all, when it's a question of death and marriage.

MAX. You'd better watch out, Zarathustra, they're liable to ask you about it by Royal decree.[46]

ZARATHUSTRA. It'd be a fine thing indeed if you divulged the mystery. Why there wouldn't be a novel!

(The little girl runs off jumping over the puddles with her cane-like legs. The chimerical PEARL-GRIM *is discussing something with* ZARATHUSTRA. MAXIMO ESTRELLA *and* DON LATINO *head toward the Lizard-Chopper tavern which hoists its classical laurels on Montera Street.*[47]*)*

SCENE THREE

(The tavern of Lizard-Chopper: Acetylene burners, zinc-topped counter, dark lobby with tables and little benches, card players,[48] *and hazy dialogues.* MAXIMO ESTRELLA *and* DON LATINO DE HISPALIS, *shadows among the shades in a corner, toast each other with gill glasses of red wine.*[49]*)*

THE BAR BOY. Don Max, The Marchioness of Tango[50] was here looking for you.

A DRUNK. Crap!

MAX. I'm not acquainted with that lady.[51]

THE BAR BOY. Henrietta Tread-Well.

DON LATINO. And since when does that trollop go around with a title?

EL CHICO. Desde que heredó del finado difunto de su papá, que entodavía vive.[52]

DON LATINO. ¡Mala sombra![53]

MAX. ¿Ha dicho si volvería?

EL CHICO. Entró, miró, preguntó y se fue rebotada, torciendo la gaita.[54] ¡Ya la tiene usted en la puerta!

*(*ENRIQUETA LA PISA-BIEN, *una mozuela golfa, revenida de un ojo,[55] periodista y florista, levantaba el cortinillo de verde sarga, sobre su endrina cabeza, adornada de peines gitanos.)*

LA PISA-BIEN. ¡La vara de nardos! ¡La vara de nardos! Don Max, traigo para usted un memorial de mi mamá: Está enferma y necesita la luz del décimo que le ha fiado.

MAX. Le devuelves el décimo y le dices que se vaya al infierno.

LA PISA-BIEN. De su parte, caballero.[56] ¿Manda usted algo más?

(El ciego saca una vieja cartera, y tanteando los papeles con aire vago, extrae el décimo de la lotería[57] y lo arroja sobre la mesa: Queda abierto entre los vasos de vino, mostrando el número bajo el parpadeo azul del acetileno. LA PISA-BIEN *se apresura a echarle la zarpa.)*

DON LATINO. ¡Ese número sale premiado!

LA PISA-BIEN. Don Max desprecia el dinero.

EL CHICO. No le deje usted irse, Don Max.

MAX. Niño, yo hago lo que me da la gana. Pídele para mí la petaca al amo.

EL CHICO. Don Max, es un capicúa de sietes y cincos.[58]

LA PISA-BIEN. ¡Que tiene premio, no falla! Pero es menester apoquinar tres melopeas, y este caballero está afónico. Caballero, me retiro saludándole. Si quiere usted un nardo, se lo regalo.

MAX. Estate ahí.

LA PISA-BIEN. Me espera un cabrito viudo.[59]

MAX. Que se aguante. Niño, ve a colgarme la capa.

LA PISA-BIEN. Por esa pañosa no dan ni los buenos días. Pídale usted las tres beatas a Pica Lagartos.

THE BAR BOY. Since she came into some of her deceased late father's estate, who isn't dead yet.[52]

DON LATINO. Deadly joke![53]

MAX. Did she say if she'd return?

THE BAR BOY. She entered, took a look around, asked for you and then went bouncing off, twisting her bagpipe.[54] But look! There she is at the door.

*(*HENRIETTA TREAD-WELL, *quite young for a street-walker, squint-eyed,*[55] *vendor of newspapers and flower girl, was raising the small curtain of green serge over her raven head, adorned with gypsy combs.)*

TREAD-WELL. Get your lottery ticket! Lottery tickets! Don Max, I'm bringing you a small reminder from my mother: she's sick and needs the dough for the lucky lottery ticket she trusted you to pay for.

MAX. You give her back the lottery ticket and tell her to go to Hell.

TREAD-WELL. You're welcome, I'm sure![56] Any other favour I can do for you?

(The blind man takes out an old wallet and groping through the papers rather indifferently, he pulls out the lottery ticket[57] *and throws it on the table: it stays there exposed, between the wine glasses, showing its number under the blue blinking of the acetylene. The* TREAD-WELL *hurries to put her claws on it.)*

DON LATINO. This number is going to be a winner!

TREAD-WELL. Don Max scorns money.

THE BAR BOY. Don't let her off the hook, Don Max.

MAX. Boy, I do as I damn well please. Go and ask your boss for the cigar box.

THE BAR BOY. Don Max, it's a lucky number, symmetrical of sevens and fives.[58]

TREAD-WELL. It'll get a prize, can't miss. But you've got to speak out with the dough, and this gentleman stays mum. Sir, I take my leave, your humble servant. If you want a white carnation, I'll give it to you free.

MAX. Stay where you are.

TREAD-WELL. Sorry, Don Max, but my little old billy-goat is waiting for me.[59]

MAX. Let him stew. Boy, go and pawn my cloak.

TREAD-WELL. You won't even get a good-morning for such rags. Better ask Lizard-Chopper for the three blessings.

EL CHICO. Si usted le da coba, las tiene en la mano. Dice que es usted segundo Castelar.[60]

MAX. Dobla la capa, y ahueca.

EL CHICO. ¿Qué pido?

MAX. Toma lo que quieran darte.

LA PISA-BIEN. ¡Si no la reciben!

DON LATINO. Calla, mala sombra.

MAX. Niño, huye veloz.

EL CHICO. Como la corza herida,[61] Don Max.

MAX. Eres un clásico.

LA PISA-BIEN. Si no te admiten la prenda, dices que es de un poeta.

DON LATINO. El primer poeta de España.

EL BORRACHO. ¡Cráneo privilegiado!

MAX. Yo nunca tuve talento. ¡He vivido siempre de un modo absurdo![62]

DON LATINO. No has tenido el talento de saber vivir.

MAX. Mañana me muero, y mi mujer y mi hija se quedan haciendo cruces en la boca.[63]

(Tosió cavernoso, con las barbas estremecidas, y en los ojos ciegos un vidriado triste, de alcohol y de fiebre.)

DON LATINO. No has debido quedarte sin capa.

LA PISA-BIEN. Y ese trasto ya no parece. Siquiera, convide usted, Don Max.

MAX. Tome usted lo que guste, Marquesa.

LA PISA-BIEN. Una copa de Rute.[64]

DON LATINO. Es la bebida elegante.

LA PISA-BIEN. ¡Ay! Don Latino, por algo es una la morganática del Rey de Portugal.[65] Don Max, no puedo detenerme, que mi esposo me hace señas desde la acera.

MAX. Invítale a pasar.

(Un golfo largo y astroso, que vende periódicos, ríe asomado a la puerta, y como perro que se espulga, se sacude con jaleo los hombros, la cara es una gran risa de viruelas.[66] Es el REY DE PORTUGAL, *que hace las bellaquerías[67] con Enriqueta* LA PISA-BIEN, MARQUESA DEL TANGO.*)*

LA PISA-BIEN. ¡Pasa, Manolo![68]

EL REY DE PORTUGAL. Sal tú fuera.

LA PISA-BIEN. ¿Es que temes perder la corona? ¡Entra de incógnito, so pelma![69]

THE BAR BOY. Feed him a good line and the money's in your hand. He says you're a second Cicero, like Castelar.[60]

MAX. Fold the cloak and get going.

THE BAR BOY. How much do I ask?

MAX. Take whatever they give you.

TREAD-WELL. Why they won't even touch it!

DON LATINO. Keep quiet, you jinx.

MAX. Boy, run swiftly.

THE BAR BOY. Just like a wounded deer,[61] Don Max.

MAX. You are indeed classical.

TREAD-WELL. If they don't accept the cloak as security, tell them it belongs to a poet.

DON LATINO. The first poet of Spain.

A DRUNK. Phenomenal brain-pan!

MAX. I never had any talent. I've always lived absurdly.[62]

DON LATINO. You never had the talent of learning how to live, Max.

MAX. And so I die tomorrow, and my wife and daughter do nothing but make the sign of the cross on their lips.[63]

*(*MAX *emits a hollow cough, his beard shaking, and in his blind eyes a sad glassy look from alcohol and fever.)*

DON LATINO. You shouldn't have pawned your cloak.

TREAD-WELL. And that little loafer is not back yet. Anyway, why don't you buy us a drink, Don Max?

MAX. Order what you like, Marchioness.

TREAD-WELL. A glass of anisette: Rute.[64]

DON LATINO. That's a high-class drink.

TREAD-WELL. Ah, but after all, Don Latino, I'm not the morganatic wife of the King of Portugal for nothing.[65] Don Max, I can't wait around any longer; my husband is beckoning to me from the outside.

MAX. Tell him to come in.

(An elongated and dirty tramp, newspaper vendor, smiles as he comes to the doorway, and like a dog in the act of delousing itself, shakes his shoulders jerkily, showing a great pock-marked smile.[66] *He is the* KING OF PORTUGAL *who makes all sorts of shoddy deals*[67] *with* HENRIETTA TREAD-WELL, MARCHIONESS OF TANGO.*)*

TREAD-WELL. Come right in, Manolo![68]

KING OF PORTUGAL. No, you step outside.

TREAD-WELL. What's the matter, are you afraid of losing your crown? So enter incognito, you big oaf.[69]

EL REY DE PORTUGAL. Enriqueta, a ver si te despeino.

LA PISA-BIEN. ¡Filfa!

EL REY DE PORTUGAL. ¡Consideren ustedes que me llama Rey de Portugal para significar que no valgo un chavo! Argumentos de esta golfa desde que fue a Lisboa, y se ha enterado del valor de la moneda.[70] Yo, para servir a ustedes, soy Gorito, y no está medio bien que mi morganática me señale por el alias.

LA PISA-BIEN. ¡Calla, chalado!

EL REY DE PORTUGAL. ¿Te caminas?

LA PISA-BIEN. Aguarda que me beba una copa de Rute. Don Max me la paga.

EL REY DE PORTUGAL. ¿Y qué tienes que ver con ese poeta?

LA PISA-BIEN. Colaboramos.

EL REY DE PORTUGAL. Pues despacha.

LA PISA-BIEN. En cuanto me la mida Pica Lagartos.[71]

PICA LAGARTOS. ¿Que has dicho tú, so golfa?

LA PISA-BIEN. ¡Perdona, rico!

PICA LAGARTOS. Venancio me llamo.

LA PISA-BIEN. ¡Tienes un nombre de novela! Anda, mídeme una copa de Rute, y dale a mi esposo un vaso de agua, que está muy acalorado.

MAX. Venancio, no vuelvas a compararme con Castelar. ¡Castelar era un idiota![72] Dame otro quince.

DON LATINO. Me adhiero a lo del quince y a lo de Castelar.

PICA LAGARTOS. Son ustedes unos doctrinarios. Castelar representa una gloria nacional de España. Ustedes acaso no sepan que mi padre lo sacaba diputado.[73]

LA PISA-BIEN. ¡Hay que ver!

PICA LAGARTOS. Mi padre era el barbero de Don Manuel Camo.[74] ¡Una gloria nacional de Huesca!

EL BORRACHO. ¡Cráneo privilegiado!

PICA LAGARTOS. Cállate la boca, Zacarías.

EL BORRACHO. ¿Acaso falto?

PICA LAGARTOS. ¡Pudieras!

EL BORRACHO. Tiene mucha educación servidorcito.

LA PISA-BIEN. ¡Como que ha salido usted del Colegio de los Escolapios![75] ¡Se educó usted con mi papá!

EL BORRACHO. ¿Quién es tu papá?

KING OF PORTUGAL. Henrietta, watch out I don't muss your hair for you.

TREAD-WELL. Just try, you phony!

KING OF PORTUGAL. Look how she calls me the King of Portugal to make out I'm not worth a farthing. The remarks this whore makes since she went to work and found out the value of money.[70] As for me, I'm little Gregory at your service, and it's just not quite right that my morganatic wife pins this alias on me.

TREAD-WELL. Keep quiet, addlebrained!

KING OF PORTUGAL. Are you moving?

TREAD-WELL. Wait till I drink my glass of Rute. Don Max is treating me.

KING OF PORTUGAL. And what's going on between you and that poet?

TREAD-WELL. We collaborate.

KING OF PORTUGAL. Well get done with it.

TREAD-WELL. As soon as Lizard-Chopper pours it for me.[71]

LIZARD-CHOPPER. My name is Venancio.

TREAD-WELL. Your name is from a story book! Come on, pour me a glass of Pernod and give my husband a glass of water; he's hot under the collar.

MAX. Venancio, don't ever compare me to Castelar. Castelar was an idiot![72] Another round.

DON LATINO. I'm in favour both of the second round and of orators like Castelar.

LIZARD-CHOPPER. You blokes are too dogmatic. Castelar is one of Spain's national glories. I'm sure you don't know my father helped elect him.[73]

TREAD-WELL. How about that!

LIZARD-CHOPPER. My father was barber to Don Manuel Camo.[74] Aragon's national glory!

THE DRUNK. Phenomenal brain-pan!

LIZARD-CHOPPER. Shut your trap, Zachary.

THE DRUNK. Am I perhaps offending?

LIZARD-CHOPPER. You might be!

THE DRUNK. Yours truly had a solid upbringing.

TREAD-WELL. Why then you are a product of the Christian Brothers' College.[75] You were a classmate of my dad.

THE DRUNK. Who's your dad?

LA PISA-BIEN. Un diputado.

EL BORRACHO. Yo he recibido educación en el extranjero.

LA PISA-BIEN. ¿Viaja usted de incógnito? ¿Por un casual, será usted Don Jaime?[76]

EL BORRACHO. ¡Me has sacado por la fotografía!

LA PISA-BIEN. ¡Naturaca! ¿Y va usted sin una flor en la solapa?

EL BORRACHO. Ven tú a ponérmela.

LA PISA-BIEN. Se la pongo a usted y le obsequio con ella.

EL REY DE PORTUGAL. ¡Hay que ser caballero, Zacarías! ¡Y hay que mirarse mucho, soleche, antes de meter mano! La Enriqueta es cosa mía.

LA PISA-BIEN. ¡Calla, bocón!

EL REY DE PORTUGAL. ¡Soleche, no seas tú provocativa!

LA PISA-BIEN. No introduzcas tú la pata, pelmazo.

*(*EL CHICO DE LA TABERNA *entra con azorado sofoco, atado a la frente un pañuelo con roeles de sangre. Una ráfaga de emoción mueve caras y actitudes; todas las figuras, en su diversidad, pautan una misma norma.)*

EL CHICO. ¡Hay carreras por las calles![77]

EL REY DE PORTUGAL. ¡Viva la huelga de proletarios![78]

EL BORRACHO. ¡Chócala! Anoche lo hemos decidido por votación en la Casa del Pueblo.[79]

LA PISA-BIEN. ¡Crispín, te alcanzó un cate!

EL CHICO. ¡Un marica de la Acción Ciudadana![80]

PICA LAGARTOS. ¡Niño, sé bien hablado! El propio republicanismo reconoce que la propiedad es sagrada. La Acción Ciudadana está integrada por patronos de todas circunstancias, y por los miembros varones de sus familias.[81] ¡Hay que saber lo que se dice!

(Grupos vocingleros corren por el centro de la calle, con banderas enarboladas. Entran en la taberna obreros golfantes–blusa, bufanda y alpargatas–, y mujeres encendidas, de arañada greña.)

EL REY DE PORTUGAL. ¡Enriqueta, me hierve la sangre! Si tú no sientes la política, puedes quedarte.

LA PISA-BIEN. So pelma, yo te sigo a todas partes. ¡Enfermera Honoraria de la Cruz Colorada![82]

PICA LAGARTOS. ¡Chico, baja el cierre! Se invita a salir, al que quiera jaleo.

TREAD-WELL. A member of Parliament.

THE DRUNK. I got my education abroad.

TREAD-WELL. Do you travel incognito? You wouldn't by chance be the royal prince Don Jaime?[76]

THE DRUNK. You recognized me by my picture.

TREAD-WELL. Sure thing. And you're going around with no flower in your lapel?

THE DRUNK. Come on and stick one in yourself.

TREAD-WELL. I'll put it on you and you can have it as a gift.

KING OF PORTUGAL. Better be a gentleman, Zachary! And you'd damn well better look out before you lay a hand on her. Henrietta is my property.

TREAD-WELL. Shut up, big mouth.

KING OF PORTUGAL. You little slut, don't you provoke me!

TREAD-WELL. So don't stick your big nose in, you oaf.

*(*THE BAR BOY *suddenly bursts in, breathless and excited, a handkerchief tied on his forehead with spots of blood. A strong gust of emotion sweeps over faces and postures. All the figures, for all their diversity, indicate the same pattern.)*

THE BAR BOY. There's a rumble in the streets.[77]

KING OF PORTUGAL. Long live the proletarian strike![78]

THE DRUNK. I'll shake on that! We voted last night at the Union Hall.[79]

TREAD-WELL. Crispín, you really caught a blow.

THE BAR BOY. From a damn queer from the Committee for Civic Action.[80]

LIZARD-CHOPPER. Speak with more respect, boy. Even the Republicans recognize that property is sacred. The Committee is composed of managers from every walk of life. These men come from decent families.[81] Let's be sure we know what we're talking about, eh?

(Shouting groups run along the centre of the street with raised flags. Some raggedy workers rush in to the tavern—blouse, muffler and sandals—and with them excited women with dishevelled mops of hair.)

KING OF PORTUGAL. Henrietta, my blood's boiling! If you don't feel politics, just stay behind.

TREAD-WELL. I can follow you anywhere, you oaf, I'm an Honorary Red Cross Nurse![82]

LIZARD-CHOPPER. Boy, lower the shutters! Anybody looking for trouble is asked to leave.

(La florista y el coime salen empujándose, revueltos con otros parroquianos. Corren por la calle tropeles de obreros. Resuena el golpe de muchos cierres metálicos.[83]*)*

EL BORRACHO. ¡Vivan los héroes del Dos de Mayo![84]

DON LATINO. Niño, ¿qué dinero te han dado?

EL CHICO. ¡Nueve pesetas!

MAX. Cóbrate, Venancio. ¡Y tú, trae el décimo, Marquesa!

DON LATINO. ¡Voló esa pájara!

MAX. ¡Se lleva el sueño de mi fortuna! ¿Dónde daríamos con esa golfa?

PICA LAGARTOS. Ésa ya no se aparta del tumulto.

EL CHICO. Recala en la Modernista.

MAX. Latino, préstame tus ojos para buscar a la Marquesa del Tango.[85]

DON LATINO. Max, dame la mano.

EL BORRACHO. ¡Cráneo privilegiado!

UNA VOZ. ¡Mueran los maricas de la Acción Ciudadana! ¡Abajo los ladrones!

ESCENA CUARTA

(Noche. MÁXIMO ESTRELLA *y* DON LATINO DE HISPALIS *se tambalean asidos del brazo por una calle enarenada y solitaria.*[86] *Faroles rotos, cerradas todas, ventanas y puertas.*[87] *En la llama de los faroles un igual temblor verde y macilento. La luna sobre el alero de las casas, partiendo la calle por medio.*[88] *De tarde en tarde, el asfalto sonoro. Un trote épico. Soldados romanos.*[89] *Sombras de Guardias.–Se extingue el eco de la patrulla. La Buñolería Modernista*[90] *entreabre su puerta, y una banda de luz parte la acera.* MAX *y* DON LATINO, *borrachos lunáticos, filósofos peripatéticos,*[91] *bajo la línea luminosa de los faroles, caminan y tambalean.)*

MAX. ¿Dónde estamos?

DON LATINO. Esta calle no tiene letrero.

MAX. Yo estoy pisando vidrios rotos.[92]

DON LATINO. No ha hecho mala cachiza el honrado pueblo.

MAX. ¿Qué rumbo consagramos?[93]

(The flower girl and her pimp depart pushing each other, scrambled with all the other customers. A hodgepodge of workers runs through the streets. The crashing sound of metal shutters is heard.[83]*)*

THE DRUNK. Long live the heroes of the Second of May![84]

DON LATINO. Boy, how much did you get for the cloak?

THE BAR BOY. Nine pesetas!

MAX. Collect your dues, Venancio. And you Marchioness, hand over the lottery ticket.

DON LATINO. That hen's flown the coop!

MAX. She's carrying off the dream of my fortune! Where could we run into that tramp?

LIZARD-CHOPPER. That female won't stay away from the riot.

THE BAR BOY. Her headquarters are at the Modernist Café.

MAX. Lend me your eyes Latino and let's look for the Marchioness of Tango.[85]

DON LATINO. Give me your hand, Max.

THE DRUNK. Phenomenal brain-pan!

A VOICE. Death to the queers of the Citizen's Committee. Down with the crooks!

SCENE FOUR

(Night. In a solitary and gravelled street,[86] MÁXIMO ESTRELLA *and* DON LATINO DE HISPALIS *stagger arm in arm. Broken street lamps; all doors and windows closed.*[87] *A continuous, green, pale quivering in the glow of the street lamps. The moon above the eaves, cutting the street in two.*[88] *From time to time, the asphalt resounds. An epic trot. Some Roman soldiers.*[89] *Shadows of policemen. The echo of the patrol dies away. The Modernist Cake Shop*[90] *half-opens its door, and a ray of light parts the sidewalk in two.* MAX *and* DON LATINO, *lunatic drunkards, peripatetic philosophers,*[91] *walk and stagger under the luminous beam of the street lamps.)*

MAX. Where are we?

DON LATINO. The street has no sign.

MAX. I keep stepping on broken glass.[92]

DON LATINO. Our noble people haven't done such a bad wrecking job.

MAX. What direction of the compass shall we honour?[93]

DON LATINO. Déjate guiar.

MAX. Condúceme a casa.

DON LATINO. Tenemos abierta La Buñolería Modernista.

MAX. De rodar y de beber estoy muerto.[94]

DON LATINO. Un café de recuelo te integra.[95]

MAX. Hace frío, Latino.

DON LATINO. ¡Corre un cierto gris! . . .

MAX. Préstame tu macferlán.

DON LATINO. ¡Te ha dado el delirio poético!

MAX. ¡Me quedé sin capa, sin dinero y sin lotería!

DON LATINO. Aquí hacemos la captura de la niña Pisa-Bien.

*(*LA NIÑA PISA-BIEN, *despintada, pingona, marchita, se materializa bajo un farol con su pregón de golfa madrileña.*[96]*)*

LA PISA-BIEN. ¡5775! ¡El número de la suerte! ¡Mañana sale! ¡Lo vendo! ¡Lo vendo! ¡5775!

DON LATINO. ¡Acudes al reclamo!

LA PISA-BIEN. Y le convido a usted a un café de recuelo.

DON LATINO. Gracias, preciosidad.

LA PISA-BIEN. Y a Don Max, a lo que guste. ¡Ya nos ajuntamos los tres tristes trogloditas![97] Don Max, yo por usted hago la jarra, y muy honrada.[98]

MAX. Dame el décimo y vete al infierno.

LA PISA-BIEN. Don Max, por adelantado decláreme en secreto si cameló las tres beatas y si las lleva en el portamonedas.[99]

MAX. ¡Pareces hermana de Romanones![100]

LA PISA-BIEN. ¡Quién tuviera los miles de ese pirante!

DON LATINO. ¡Con sólo la renta de un día, yo me contentaba!

MAX. La Revolución es aquí tan fatal como en Rusia.[101]

DON LATINO. ¡Nos moriremos sin verla!

MAX. Pues viviremos muy poco.

LA PISA-BIEN. ¿Ustedes bajaron la Cibeles?[102] Allí ha sido la faena entre los manifestantes, y los Polis Honorarios.[103] A alguno le hemos dado mulé.

DON LATINO. Todos los amarillos[104] debían ser arrastrados.

LA PISA-BIEN. ¡Conforme! Y aquel momento que usted no tenga ocupaciones urgentes, nos ponemos a ello, Don Latino.

DON LATINO. Just follow.

MAX. Just lead me home.

DON LATINO. Oh, look, the Modernist Headquarters is open.

MAX. I'm dead from drinking and running in circles.[94]

DON LATINO. A stiff coffee will buck you up.[95]

MAX. It's cold, Latino.

DON LATINO. Yes, it's a rather chilly breeze.

MAX. Lend me your mackintosh.

DON LATINO. Poetic delirium has struck again.

MAX. I'm left without a cloak, without any money and without the lottery ticket!

DON LATINO. We'll capture the nymph Tread-Well around here.

(The Nymph TREAD-WELL, *without her paint, slovenly, withered, takes shape and form under a street lamp with her Madrid hussy's cry.*[96] *)*

TREAD-WELL. 5775! Lucky number! Drawing tomorrow! Up for sale! Up for sale! 5775!

DON LATINO. You sure know how to advertise.

TREAD-WELL. And I invite you to a stiff coffee.

DON LATINO. Thank you, precious.

TREAD-WELL. And for Don Max, anything he likes. How nice that we got together, we three sad troglodytes.[97] Don Max, just for you I'll assume a sexy pose, and I'm honoured to do it.[98]

MAX. Just give me that ticket and go to Hell.

TREAD-WELL. Don Max, first of all tell me in all confidence if you conjured up the dough,[99] and if you're carrying it in your wallet.

MAX. You sound like a sister of Romanones.[100]

TREAD-WELL. If I only had that shark's millions!

DON LATINO. Just a day's interest would make me happy.

MAX. The Revolution is as unavoidable here as in Russia.[101]

DON LATINO. We'll die before we see it!

MAX. Well then, we'll scarcely live at all.

TREAD-WELL. Did you go down to Cibeles Square?[102] There was a real scuffle between the demonstrators and the honorary guards of the Citizen's Committee.[103] Boy, we really let one of them have it.

DON LATINO. All yellow scabs[104] should be made to crawl.

TREAD-WELL. Right! And when you can spare a moment from urgent business you and I will get down to it, Don Latino.

MAX. Dame ese capicúa, Enriqueta.

LA PISA-BIEN. Venga el parné, y tenga usted su suerte.

MAX. La propina, cuando cobre el premio.

LA PISA-BIEN. ¡No mira eso la Enriqueta!

(La Buñolería entreabre su puerta, y del antro apestoso de aceite van saliendo deshilados, uno a uno, en fila india, los Epígonos del Parnaso Modernista.[105] RAFAEL DE LOS VÉLEZ, DORIO DE GADEX, LUCIO VERO, MÍNGUEZ, GÁLVEZ, CLARINITO *y* PÉREZ.[106] *Unos son largos, tristes y flacos, otros vivaces, chaparros y carillenos.* DORIO DE GADEX,[107] *jovial como un trasgo, irónico como un ateniense, ceceoso como un cañí,*[108] *mima su saludo versallesco y grotesco.)*

DORIO DE GADEX. ¡Padre y Maestro Mágico, salud![109]

MAX. ¡Salud, Don Dorio!

DORIO. ¡Maestro, usted no ha temido el rebuzno libertario del honrado pueblo!

MAX. ¡El épico rugido del mar! ¡Yo me siento pueblo!

DORIO. ¡Yo, no!

MAX. ¡Porque eres un botarate![110]

DORIO. ¡Maestro, pongámonos el traje de luces de la cortesía![111] ¡Maestro, usted tampoco se siente pueblo! Usted es un poeta, y los poetas somos aristocracia. Como dice Ibsen, las multitudes y las montañas se unen siempre por la base.[112]

MAX. ¡No me aburran con Ibsen!

PÉREZ. ¿Se ha hecho usted crítico de teatro, Don Max?

DORIO. ¡Calla, Pérez!

DON LATINO. Aquí sólo hablan los genios.

MAX. Yo me siento pueblo.[113] Yo había nacido para ser tribuno de la plebe, y me acanallé perpetrando traducciones y haciendo versos. ¡Eso sí, mejores que los que hacéis los modernistas![114]

DORIO. Maestro, preséntese usted a un sillón de la Academia.[115]

MAX. No lo digas en burla, idiota. ¡Me sobran méritos! Pero esa prensa miserable me boicotea. Odian mi rebeldía y odian mi talento. Para medrar hay que ser agradador de todos los Segismundos.[116] ¡El Buey Apis me despide como a un criado![117] ¡La Academia me ignora! ¡Y soy el primer poeta

MAX. Hand over that symmetrical, lucky number, Henrietta.

TREAD-WELL. Let's have the dough first, and you'll get your lucky ticket.

MAX. Your tip when I collect the prize.

TREAD-WELL. The Marchioness of Tango doesn't see it that way!

(The cake-shop half opens its door and from inside the cavern, which stinks with oil, there file out like Indians one by one, the champions of the Modernist Parnassus:[105] RAFAEL DE LOS VELEZ, DORIO DE GADEX, LUCIO VERO, MÍNGUEZ, GÁLVEZ, CLARINITO *and* PÉREZ.[106] *Some are slow, thin and sad, the others are vigorous, jolly and chubby-cheeked.* DORIO DE GADEX,[107] *jovial as a goblin, ironical as an old Athenian, lisping like a gypsy,*[108] *stages his Versaillesque and grotesque greeting.)*

DORIO DE GADEX. 'Sublime and Masterful Magus', hail![109]

MAX. Greetings, Don Dorio!

DORIO. Maestro, you've never trembled before the anarchistic braying of the honourable masses.

MAX. The epic roar of the sea! I feel like one of the people!

DORIO. Not me!

MAX. Because you're an ass.[110]

DORIO. Maestro, let's don the shining garb of courtesy![111] Maestro, you don't feel like one of the people any more than I do. You're a poet, and we poets are the aristocracy. Multitudes and mountains are always joined at their base, as Ibsen said.[112]

MAX. Don't bore me with Ibsen.

PÉREZ. So you've now become a drama critic, Don Max?

DORIO. Shut up, Pérez.

DON LATINO. Only geniuses speak here.

MAX. I feel like one of the people.[113] I was born to be tribune of the Plebs, but I mixed with scum and became a bastard perpetrating translations and hammering out verses. Even so, better ones than you modernists compose.[114]

DORIO. Why don't you solicit a seat in the Academy.[115]

MAX. Don't joke about it, idiot. My credentials are more than enough! But that miserable press boycotts me. They hate my defiance and detest my talent. To succeed, you have to gratify everybody with the same old do-re-mi-fa-so-la.[116] Our Sacred Bull dismisses my petition as if I were a servant![117]

de España! ¡El primero! ¡El primero! ¡Y ayuno! ¡Y no me humillo pidiendo limosna! ¡Y no me parte un rayo! ¡Yo soy el verdadero inmortal, y no esos cabrones del cotarro académico![118] ¡Muera Maura![119]

LOS MODERNISTAS. ¡Muera! ¡Muera! ¡Muera!

CLARINITO. Maestro, nosotros los jóvenes impondremos la candidatura de usted para un sillón de la Academia.

DORIO. Precisamente ahora está vacante el sillón de Don Benito el Garbancero.[120]

MAX. Nombrarán al Sargento Basallo.[121]

DORIO. Maestro, ¿usted conoce los Nuevos Gozos del Enano de la Venta?[122] ¡Un Jefe de Obra![123] Ayer de madrugada los cantamos en la Puerta del Sol.[124] ¡El éxito de la temporada!

CLARINITO. ¡Con decir que salió el retén de Gobernación![125]

LA PISA-BIEN. ¡Ni Rafael el Gallo![126]

DON LATINO. Deben ustedes ofrecerle una audición al Maestro.

DORIO. Don Latino, ni una palabra más.

PÉREZ. Usted cantará con nosotros, Don Latino.

DON LATINO. Yo doy una nota más baja que el cerdo.

DORIO. Usted es un clásico.

DON LATINO. ¿Y qué hace un clásico en el tropel de ruiseñores modernistas? Niños, ¡a ello!

(DORIO DE GADEX, *feo burlesco y chepudo, abre los brazos. que son como alones sin pluma, en el claro lunero.)*

DORIO. El Enano de la Venta.[127]

CORO DE MODERNISTAS. ¡Cuenta! ¡Cuenta! ¡Cuenta!

DORIO. Con bravatas de valiente.

CORO DE MODERNISTAS. ¡Miente! ¡Miente! ¡Miente!

DORIO. Quiere gobernar la Harca.[128]

CORO DE MODERNISTAS. ¡Charca! ¡Charca! ¡Charca!

DORIO. Y es un Tartufo[129] Malsín.

CORO DE MODERNISTAS. ¡Sin! ¡Sin! ¡Sin!

The Academy ignores me! And I'm the first poet of Spain! The first! I say the first! And starving! But I don't lower myself begging for alms. And no bolt of lightning strikes me down. I'm the true immortal, and not those cuckolds from the Academic Almshouse.[118] Maura to the scaffold![119]

THE MODERNISTS. To the scaffold! To the scaffold! To the scaffold!

CLARINITO. We of the younger generation, maestro, we'll press your candidacy for a seat in the Academy.

DORIO. It so happens that at this moment the seat of Don Benito the Bean-Seller[120] is vacant.

MAX. They'll probably elect Sergeant Basallo for his heroic memoirs.[121]

DORIO. Maestro, are you acquainted with the New Couplets about the Dwarf at the Roadside Hotel?[122] A masterpiece![123] We warbled it at dawn yesterday at the Puerta del Sol.[124] The hit of the season!

CLARINITO. Not to mention that even the police came to break us up.[125]

TREAD-WELL. Not even Rafael el Gallo in the arena was in better form.[126]

DON LATINO. You should offer the maestro an audition.

DORIO. Don Latino, your wish is our command.

PÉREZ. And you'll sing with us, Don Latino.

DON LATINO. I can reach a note as low as a hog.

DORIO. You are a classic.

DON LATINO. And what's a classic doing amidst a troop of modernist nightingales? Come on boys, get on with it!

*(*DORIO DE GADEX, *ugly burlesque and hunchbacked, opens his arms which, in the moonlight, look like plucked pinions.)*

DORIO. The Dwarf at the Roadside Hotel.[127]

MODERNIST CHORUS. Tell! Tell! Tell!

DORIO. He had the bravado of all rakes.

MODERNIST CHORUS. Prevaricates! Prevaricates! Prevaricates!

DORIO. He wants to govern a big tribe.[128]

MODERNIST CHORUS. We subscribe! We subscribe! We subscribe!

DORIO. And he's a rogue, like Tartuffe Malsín.[129]

MODERNIST CHORUS. Ting-a-ling! Ting-a-ling! Ting-a-ling!

DORIO. Sin un adarme de seso.

CORO DE MODERNISTAS. ¡Eso! ¡Eso! ¡Eso!

DORIO. Pues tiene hueca la bola.

CORO DE MODERNISTAS. ¡Chola! ¡Chola! ¡Chola![130]

DORIO. Pues tiene la chola hueca.

CORO DE MODERNISTAS. ¡Eureka! ¡Eureka! ¡Eureka![131]

(Gran interrupción. Un trote épico, y la patrulla de soldados romanos desemboca por una calle traviesa. Traen la luna sobre los cascos y en los charrascos. Suena un toque de atención, y se cierra con golpe pronto la puerta de la Buñolería. PITITO, *capitán de los équites municipales,*[132] *se levanta sobre los estribos.)*

EL CAPITÁN PITITO. ¡Mentira parece que sean ustedes intelectuales y que promuevan estos escándalos! ¿Qué dejan ustedes para los analfabetos?

MAX. ¡Eureka! ¡Eureka! ¡Eureka! ¡Pico de Oro! En griego, para mayor claridad, Crisóstomo.[133] Señor Centurión, ¡usted hablará el griego en sus cuatro dialectos![134]

PITITO. ¡Por borrachín, a la Delega![135]

MAX. ¡Y más chulo que un ocho! Señor Centurión, ¡yo también chanelo el sermo vulgaris![136]

PITITO. ¡Serenooo! . . . ¡Serenooo! . . .

EL SERENO. ¡Vaaa! . . .

PITITO. ¡Encárguese usted de este curda!

(Llega EL SERENO, *meciendo a compás el farol y el chuzo. Jadeos y vahos de aguardiente.* EL CAPITÁN PITITO *revuelve el caballo. Vuelan chispas de las herraduras. Resuena el trote sonoro de la patrulla que se aleja.)*

PITITO. ¡Me responde usted de ese hombre, Sereno!

EL SERENO. ¿Habrá que darle amoniaco?

PITITO. Habrá que darle para el pelo.

EL SERENO. ¡Está bien!

DON LATINO. Max, convídale a una copa. Hay que domesticar a este troglodita asturiano.[137]

MAX. Estoy apré.

DON LATINO. ¿No te queda nada?

MAX. ¡Ni una perra!

EL SERENO. Camine usted.

MAX. Soy ciego.

EL SERENO. ¿Quiere usted que un servidor le vuelva la vista?

DORIO. He has the brain of a nitwit.

MODERNIST CHORUS. That's it! That's it! That's it!

DORIO. And he's a hollow libertine.

MODERNIST CHORUS. Pumpkin! Pumpkin! Pumpkin![130]

DORIO. But his arse is full of paprika.[131]

MODERNIST CHORUS. Eureka! Eureka! Eureka!

(Big interruption. An epic trot and the patrol of Roman soldiers comes out of a side street. They seem to carry the moon on their helmets and swords. A bugle calls attention and immediately the cake-shop's door closes with a sudden thud. PITITO (LITTLE WHISTLE), *captain of municipal cavalry,*[132] *stands up in his stirrups.)*

PITITO. It's incredible that you, the intellectuals, should be the ones making such a racket. You leave nothing for the illiterates to do.

MAX. Eureka! Eureka! Eureka! Beak of Gold! And in Greek, for greater clarity, Chrysostom.[133] Mr Centurion Sir, you undoubtedly speak Greek in all its four dialects![134]

PITITO. Take that drunkard to the Police Station.[135]

MAX. And outtrumping any joker. Mr Centurion, Sir, I, too, can dish out your lingo.[136]

PITITO. Watchmaan! Watchmaaan!

NIGHT-WATCHMAN. Comiiing! . . .

PITITO. Take charge of this drunken bum!

(The NIGHT-WATCHMAN *arrives, rhythmically balancing his lantern and staff. Panting and smelling of brandy.* CAPTAIN PITITO *turns his horse around. Sparks fly from the horseshoes. The noisy trot of the patrol is heard going away.)*

PITITO. Watchman, you're responsible for this man!

NIGHT-WATCHMAN. Should we give him a powder?

PITITO. Better still, give him a thrashing.

NIGHT-WATCHMAN. Right-oh!

DON LATINO. Buy him a drink, Max. You have to domesticate this Asturian troglodyte.[137]

MAX. I'm completely broke.

DON LATINO. you've got nothing left?

MAX. Not a farthing.

NIGHT-WATCHMAN. Start walking.

MAX. I'm blind.

NIGHT-WATCHMAN. Do you expect me to restore your sight?

MAX. ¿ Eres Santa Lucía ?[138]

EL SERENO. ¡ Soy autoridad !

MAX. No es lo mismo.

EL SERENO. Pudiera serlo. Camine usted.

MAX. Ya he dicho que soy ciego.

EL SERENO. Usted es un anárquico y estos sujetos de las melenas.[139] ¡ Viento ! ¡ Viento ! ¡ Mucho viento !

DON LATINO. ¡ Una galerna !

EL SERENO. ¡ Atrás !

VOCES DE LOS MODERNISTAS. ¡ Acompañamos al Maestro ! ¡ Acompañamos al Maestro !

UN VECINO. ¡ Pepeee ! ¡ Pepeee !

EL SERENO. ¡ Vaaa ! Retírense ustedes sin manifestación. *(Golpea con el chuzo en la puerta de la Buñolería. Asoma el buñolero, un hombre gordo con delantal blanco. Se informa, se retira musitando, y a poco salen adormilados, ciñéndose el correaje, dos guardias municipales.)*

UN GUARDIA. ¿ Qué hay ?

EL SERENO. Este punto para la Delega.[140]

EL OTRO GUARDIA. Nosotros vamos al relevo. Lo entregaremos en Gobernación.[141]

EL SERENO. Donde la duerma.[142]

EL VECINO. ¡ Pepeee ! ¡ Pepeee !

EL SERENO. ¡ Otro curda ! ¡ Vaaa ! Sus lo entrego.[143]

LOS DOS GUARDIAS. Ustedes, caballeros, retírense.

DORIO. Acompañamos al Maestro.

UN GUARDIA. ¡ Ni que se llamase este curda Don Mariano de Cavia ![144] ¡ Ése sí que es cabeza ! ¡ Y cuanto más curda, mejor lo saca !

EL OTRO GUARDIA. ¡ Por veces también se pone pelma !

DON LATINO. ¡ Y faltón !

UN GUARDIA. Usted, por lo que habla, ¿ le conoce ?

DON LATINO. Y le tuteo.

EL OTRO GUARDIA. ¿ Son ustedes periodistas ?

DORIO. ¡ Lagarto ! ¡ Lagarto ![145]

LA PISA-BIEN. Son banqueros.

MAX. Do you think you're St Lucy?[138]

NIGHT-WATCHMAN. I am Authority.

MAX. It's not quite the same.

NIGHT-WATCHMAN. But it could be. Get going.

MAX. I've told you I'm blind.

NIGHT-WATCHMAN. You're an anarchist, and so are these chaps with the long hair.[139] Make a stir!

DON LATINO. I'll blow a gale!

NIGHT-WATCHMAN. Get back!

MODERNIST CHORUS. Let's accompany the maestro! We'll accompany the maestro!

A NEIGHBOUR. Pepeee! Pepeee!

NIGHT WATCHMAN. Move along! Keep back all of you and don't make trouble.

(He knocks at the door of the cake-shop with his staff: the Baker, a fat man with a white apron leans out. He asks what's the matter and withdraws muttering something; and soon two city policemen come out sleepy-eyed, fastening their belts.)

A POLICEMAN. What's up?

NIGHT WATCHMAN. This character[140] here goes to the police station.

THE OTHER POLICEMAN. We're doing relief duty. We'll drop him at Headquarters.[141]

NIGHT WATCHMAN. It doesn't matter, just so as he can sleep it off.[142]

NEIGHBOUR. Pepeee! Pepeee!

NIGHT WATCHMAN. Another sot! All right! I'm handing him over to you.[143]

TWO POLICEMEN. And you, gentlemen, stand back.

DORIO. We'll accompany the maestro.

A POLICEMAN. I don't care if this drunk's name is Don Mariano de Cavia, the famous journalist.[144] That guy really has a head on his shoulders. And the drunker he gets, the better he writes.

THE OTHER POLICEMAN. At times he even becomes a bore.

DON LATINO. And impertinent!

A POLICEMAN. You, the way you talk, do you know him?

DON LATINO. We're on familiar terms.

THE OTHER POLICEMAN. Are you by chance newspaper people?

DORIO. Knock on wood! Knock on wood![145]

TREAD-WELL. They're all bankers.

UN GUARDIA. Si quieren acompañar a su amigo, no se oponen las leyes, y hasta lo permiten; pero deberán guardar moderación ustedes. Yo respeto mucho el talento.

EL OTRO GUARDIA. Caminemos.

MAX. Latino, dame la mano. Señores guardias, ¡ustedes me perdonarán que sea ciego!

UN GUARDIA. Sobra tanta política.

DON LATINO. ¿Qué ruta consagramos?[146]

UN GUARDIA. Al Ministerio de la Gobernación.[147]

EL OTRO GUARDIA. ¡Vivo! ¡Vivo!

MAX. ¡Muera Maura! ¡Muera el Gran Fariseo![148]

CORO DE MODERNISTAS. ¡Muera! ¡Muera! ¡Muera!

MAX. Muera el judío y toda su execrable parentela.[149]

UN GUARDIA. ¡Basta de voces! ¡Cuidado con el poeta curda! ¡Se la está ganando, me caso en Sevilla![150]

EL OTRO GUARDIA. A éste habrá que darle para el pelo. Lo cual que sería lástima, porque debe ser hombre de mérito.

ESCENA QUINTA

(Zaguán en el Ministerio de la Gobernación. Estantería con legajos. Bancos al filo de la pared. Mesa con carpetas de badana mugrienta. Aire de cueva y olor frío de tabaco rancio. Guardias soñolientos. Policías de la Secreta. Hongos, garrotes, cuellos de celuloide, grandes sortijas, lunares rizosos y flamencos. Hay un viejo chabacano–bisoñé y manguitos de percalina–, que escribe, y un pollo chulapón de peinado reluciente, con brisas de perfumería, que se pasea y dicta humeando un veguero. DON SERAFÍN *le dicen sus obligados, y la voz de la calle,* SERAFÍN EL BONITO.[151] *Leve tumulto. Dando voces, la cabeza desnuda, humorista y lunático, irrumpe* MAX ESTRELLA. DON LATINO *le guía por la manga, implorante y suspirante. Detrás asoman los cascos de los guardias. Y en el corredor se agrupan, bajo la luz de una candileja, pipas, chalinas y melenas del modernismo.)*

MAX. ¡Traigo detenida una pareja de guindillas! Estaban emborrachándose en una tasca y los hice salir a darme escolta.

A POLICEMAN. If you want to accompany your friend, there's no law against it and it's even allowed; but you'll have to behave. I've great respect for talent.

THE OTHER POLICEMAN. Let's start walking.

MAX. Latino, give me your hand. Officers, gentlemen: perhaps you'll forgive me for being blind!

A POLICEMAN. That's enough of politics.

DON LATINO. What direction of the compass shall we honour?[146]

A POLICEMAN. Straight to Police Headquarters.[147]

THE OTHER POLICEMAN. Lively there, lively!

MAX. Maura to the scaffold! Death to the great Pharisee![148]

MODERNIST CHORUS. Death! Death! Death!

MAX. Death to the Jew and to his execrable kin.[149]

A POLICEMAN. Enough shouting! And be careful with the drunken poet! He's asking for it, damn it.[150]

THE OTHER POLICEMAN. They'll knock the hide off the old goat. And that'd really be a pity, because he seems to be a person of distinction.

SCENE FIVE

(Anteroom at Police Headquarters. Set of shelves covered with dossiers. Benches all along the wall. On a table, some dirty leather portfolios. The airlessness of a cave and the cold smell of stale tobacco. Sleepy policemen. Detectives in plain clothes. Bowler hats, clubs, celluloid collars, large finger-rings, flashy hairy skin moles. There's a clumsy old man–a wig on his head and shiny sleeve cuffs–who writes; and a sporty coxcomb–with a glittering hair-do, reeking of perfume–who paces to and fro and dictates something while inhaling American tobacco. Those under his command call him DON SERAFIN, *but he is popularly known as* SERAFIN-THE-DANDY.[151] *Slight tumult. Shouting, his head bare, humorous and lunatic,* MAX ESTRELLA *bursts in.* DON LATINO *guides him by the sleeve, imploring and sighing. Behind them appear the helmets of the policemen. And in the corridor, under the light of an oil lamp there gather the pipes, the scarves, and the long manes of modernism.)*

MAX. I've brought with me a pair of cops I had to stop. They were getting drunk in an old dive and I made them come out and escort me here.

SERAFÍN. Corrección, señor mío.

MAX. No falto a ella, señor Delegado.

SERAFÍN. Inspector.

MAX. Todo es uno y lo mismo.

SERAFÍN. ¿Cómo se llama usted?

MAX. Mi nombre es Máximo Estrella. Mi seudónimo, Mala Estrella.[152] Tengo el honor de no ser académico.[153]

SERAFÍN. Está usted propasándose. Guardias, ¿por qué viene detenido?

UN GUARDIA. Por escándalo en la vía pública y gritos internacionales. ¡Está algo briago!

SERAFÍN. ¿Su profesión?

MAX. Cesante.[154]

SERAFÍN. ¿En qué oficina ha servido usted?

MAX. En ninguna.

SERAFÍN. ¿No ha dicho usted que cesante?

MAX. Cesante de hombre libre y pájaro cantor. ¿No me veo vejado, vilipendiado, encarcelado, cacheado e interrogado?

SERAFÍN. ¿Dónde vive usted?

MAX. Bastardillos. Esquina a San Cosme.[155] Palacio.

UN GUINDILLA. Diga usted casa de vecinos. Mi señora, cuando aún no lo era, habitó un sotabanco de esa susodicha finca.

MAX. Donde yo vivo siempre es un palacio.

EL GUINDILLA. No lo sabía.

MAX. Porque tú, gusano burocrático, no sabes nada. ¡Ni soñar!

SERAFÍN. ¡Queda usted detenido!

MAX. ¡Bueno! Latino, ¿hay algún banco donde pueda echarme a dormir?

SERAFÍN. Aquí no se viene a dormir.

MAX. ¡Pues yo tengo sueño!

SERAFÍN. ¡Está usted desacatando mi autoridad! ¿Sabe usted quién soy yo?

MAX. ¡Serafín el Bonito!

SERAFÍN. ¡Como usted repita esa gracia, de una bofetada le doblo!

MAX. ¡Ya se guardará usted del intento! ¡Soy el primer poeta de

SERAFIN. Watch your behaviour, my dear Sir.
MAX. I don't lack manners, Mr Commissioner.
SERAFIN. Inspector.
MAX. It's all one and the same.
SERAFIN. What's your name?
MAX. My name is Máximo Estrella. My pseudonym, Ill-Starred.[152] I have the honour of not being an Academician.[153]
SERAFIN. You're overreaching yourself. Constables, why was he arrested?
A POLICEMAN. For causing disturbance in the public streets, and for shouting internationalist slogans. He's a bit under the weather.
SERAFIN. Your profession?
MAX. Temporarily out of work.[154]
SERAFIN. In what office have you worked?
MAX. Nowhere.
SERAFIN. But didn't you just say you were now unemployed?
MAX. A free man and singing bird is not employed. Besides, don't I find myself vexed, vilified, imprisoned, searched and interrogated?
SERAFIN. Where do you live?
MAX. Put it in capitals: Corner of St Cosmos.[155] A Palace.
A BAILIFF. Say rather tenement house. My wife, before we got married, used to live in the garrett of the aforementioned property.
MAX. Wherever I live, it's always a palace.
THE BAILIFF. I wouldn't know.
MAX. Because you bureaucratic worms know nothing. Not even how to dream!
SERAFIN. You're under arrest.
MAX. All right! Latino, is there a bench around here where I can lie down and sleep.
SERAFIN. You don't come here to sleep.
MAX. But I'm really sleepy!
SERAFIN. You're insulting my authority! Do you know who I am?
MAX. Serafin-the-Dandy.
SERAFIN. Just repeat that joke once more and I'll knock you down flat.
MAX. I'm sure you'll control yourself! I am after all the first poet of Spain! I have influence in all the newspapers! And

España! ¡Tengo influencia en todos los periódicos! ¡Conozco al Ministro! ¡Hemos sido compañeros!

SERAFÍN. El Señor Ministro no es un golfo.

MAX. Usted desconoce la Historia Moderna.

SERAFÍN. ¡En mi presencia no se ofende a Don Paco! Eso no lo tolero. ¡Sepa usted que Don Paco es mi padre!

MAX. No lo creo. Permítame usted que se lo pregunte por teléfono.

SERAFÍN. Se lo va usted a preguntar desde el calabozo.

DON LATINO. Señor Inspector, ¡tenga usted alguna consideración! ¡Se trata de una gloria nacional! ¡El Víctor Hugo de España![156]

SERAFÍN. Cállese usted.

DON LATINO. Perdone usted mi entrometimiento.

SERAFÍN. ¡Si usted quiere acompañarle, también hay para usted alojamiento!

DON LATINO. ¡Gracias, Señor Inspector!

SERAFÍN. Guardias, conduzcan ustedes ese curda al número dos.

UN GUARDIA. ¡Camine usted!

MAX. No quiero.

SERAFÍN. Llévenle ustedes a rastras.

OTRO GUARDIA. ¡So golfo!

MAX. ¡Que me asesinan! ¡Que me asesinan!

UNA VOZ MODERNISTA. ¡Bárbaros!

DON LATINO. ¡Que es una gloria nacional!

SERAFÍN. Aquí no se protesta. Retírense ustedes.

OTRA VOZ MODERNISTA. ¡Viva la Inquisición![157]

SERAFÍN. ¡Silencio, o todos quedan detenidos!

MAX. ¡Que me asesinan! ¡Que me asesinan!

LOS GUARDIAS. ¡Borracho! ¡Golfo!

EL GRUPO MODERNISTA. ¡Hay que visitar las Redacciones! *(Sale en tropel el grupo. Chalinas flotantes, pipas apagadas, románticas greñas. Se oyen estallar las bofetadas y las voces tras la puerta del calabozo.)*

SERAFÍN. ¡Creerán esos niños modernistas que aquí se reparten caramelos!

I know the Minister of Internal Affairs! We used to be schoolmates.

SERAFIN. His Excellency the Minister is not a tramp.

MAX. You're unacquainted with Modern History.

SERAFIN. In my presence no one insults Don Paco. That I don't tolerate. I'll have you know that Don Paco is like a father to me!

MAX. I don't believe it. Permit me to verify that by telephone.

SERAFIN. You can phone him from the dungeon.

DON LATINO. Mr Inspector Sir, please be a little more considerate! This is a matter touching our National Glory! The Victor Hugo of Spain![156]

SERAFIN. You hold your tongue!

DON LATINO. Pardon my intrusion.

SERAFIN. If you want to keep him company we have lodging for you too.

DON LATINO. Thank you, Inspector.

SERAFIN. Constables, take this drunk to number two.

A POLICEMAN. Walk, you.

MAX. I won't budge.

SERAFIN. Drag him then.

ANOTHER POLICEMAN. Come on, you tramp.

MAX. They're killing me! They're killing me!

A MODERNIST VOICE. Barbarians!

DON LATINO. And to think he's a National Glory.

SERAFIN. I don't allow protest in here! You'd better get out.

ANOTHER MODERNIST VOICE. Long live the Inquisition![157]

SERAFIN. Silence! Or you'll all be under arrest.

MAX. They're killing me! They're killing me!

THE POLICE. Drunk! Tramp!

MODERNIST GROUP. We must get to the newspaper offices!

(The entire group rushes out. Floating scarves, extinguished pipes, romantic mops of hair. One can hear the blows and cries from behind the prison doors.)

SERAFIN. These arty greenhorns must think that we're giving out sweets around here!

ESCENA SEXTA[158]

(El calabozo. Sótano mal alumbrado por una candileja. En la sombra se mueve el bulto de un hombre. Blusa, tapabocas y alpargatas. Pasea hablando solo. Repentinamente se abre la puerta. MAX ESTRELLA, *empujando y trompicando, rueda al fondo del calabozo. Se cierra de golpe la puerta.)*

MAX. ¡Canallas! ¡Asalariados! ¡Cobardes!

VOZ DE FUERA. ¡Aún vas a llevar mancuerna!

MAX. ¡Esbirro!

(Sale de la tiniebla el bulto del hombre morador del calabozo. Bajo la luz se le ve esposado, con la cara llena de sangre.)

EL PRESO. ¡Buenas noches!

MAX. ¿No estoy solo?

EL PRESO. Así parece.

MAX. ¿Quién eres, compañero?

EL PRESO. Un paria.

MAX. ¿Catalán?

EL PRESO. De todas partes.

MAX. ¡Paria! . . . Solamente los obreros catalanes aguijan su rebeldía con ese denigrante epíteto. Paria, en bocas como la tuya, es una espuela. Pronto llegará vuestra hora.

EL PRESO. Tiene usted luces que no todos tienen. Barcelona alimenta una hoguera de odio,[159] soy obrero barcelonés, y a orgullo lo tengo.

MAX. ¿Eres anarquista?

EL PRESO. Soy lo que han hecho las Leyes.[160]

MAX. Pertenecemos a la misma Iglesia.

EL PRESO. Usted lleva chalina.

MAX. ¡El dogal de la más horrible sevidumbre! Me lo arrancaré para que hablemos.

EL PRESO. Usted no es proletario.

MAX. Yo soy el dolor de un mal sueño.

EL PRESO. Parece usted hombre de luces. Su hablar es como de otros tiempos.

MAX. Yo soy un poeta ciego.

EL PRESO. ¡No es pequeña desgracia! . . . En España el trabajo y la inteligencia siempre se han visto despreciados. Aquí todo lo manda el dinero.

SCENE SIX[158]

(The dungeon. A cellar, lighted badly by a small oil lamp. The form of a man stirs in the shadow. Blouse, muffler and hemp sandals. He paces the floor talking alone. Suddenly the door bangs open. MAX ESTRELLA, *pushing and stumbling, rolls to the back of the cell. The door slams to.)*

MAX. Scum! Hirelings! Cowards!

VOICE FROM OUTSIDE. You're going to get it yet! Just keep it up!

MAX. Lackey!

(The figure of the cell's inmate emerges from the darkness. Under the light, he is seen handcuffed, with his face bloodstained.)

PRISONER. Good evening!

MAX. I'm not alone then?

PRISONER. It doesn't seem so.

MAX. Who are you, mate?

PRISONER. An outcast.

MAX. From Catalonia then?

PRISONER. From all over.

MAX. Outcast! Only the Catalan workers punctuate their rebellion with that disparaging epithet. 'Outcast', coming out from mouths such as yours, is an incitement. The hour will soon strike for all of you.

PRISONER. You have eyes that few people have. Barcelona nurtures a blaze of hate:[159] I'm a Barcelona worker and I'm proud of it.

MAX. Are you an anarchist?

PRISONER. I am whatever the law has made me.[160]

MAX. We belong to the same church.

PRISONER. But you wear an artist's muffler.

MAX. The noose of the most horrible servility! I'll put it off so we can talk.

PRISONER. You're not a proletarian.

MAX. I am the pain of a bad dream.

PRISONER. You seem an enlightened man. You talk like the good old days.

MAX. I am a blind poet.

PRISONER. That's no slight disaster! In Spain, work and intelligence are always sneered at. Everything is ruled by money here.

MAX. Hay que establecer la guillotina eléctrica en la Puerta del Sol.[161]

EL PRESO. No basta. El ideal revolucionario tiene que ser la destrucción de la riqueza, como en Rusia.[162] No es suficiente la degollación de todos los ricos. Siempre aparecerá algún heredero, y aun cuando se suprima la herencia, no podrá evitarse que los despojados conspiren para recobrarla. Hay que hacer imposible el orden anterior, y eso sólo se consigue destruyendo la riqueza. Barcelona industrial tiene que hundirse para renacer de sus escombros con otro concepto de la propiedad y del trabajo.[163] En Europa, el patrono de más negra entraña es el catalán, y no digo del mundo porque existen las Colonias Españolas de América.[164] ¡Barcelona solamente se salva pereciendo!

MAX. ¡Barcelona es cara a mi corazón!

EL PRESO. ¡Yo también la recuerdo!

MAX. Yo le debo los únicos goces en la lobreguez de mi ceguera. Todos los días, un patrono muerto; algunas veces, dos . . .[165] Eso consuela.

EL PRESO. No cuenta usted los obreros que caen . . .

MAX. Los obreros se reproducen populosamente, de un modo comparable a las moscas. En cambio, los patronos, como los elefantes, como todas las bestias poderosas y prehistóricas, procrean lentamente. Saulo, hay que difundir por el mundo la religión nueva.

EL PRESO. Mi nombre es Mateo.[166]

MAX. Yo te bautizo Saulo. Soy poeta y tengo derecho al alfabeto. Escucha para cuando seas libre, Saulo. Una buena cacería puede encarecer la piel de patrono catalán por encima del marfil de Calcuta.

EL PRESO. En ello laboramos.[167]

MAX. Y en último consuelo, aun cabe pensar que exterminando al proletario también se extermina al patrón.

EL PRESO. Acabando con la ciudad, acabaremos con el judaísmo barcelonés.[168]

MAX. No me opongo. Barcelona semita sea destruida, como Cartago[169] y Jerusalén. ¡Alea jacta est![170] Dame la mano.

EL PRESO. Estoy esposado.

MAX. We should install an electric guillotine in the Puerta del Sol.[161]

PRISONER. It's not enough. The revolutionary objective has to be the destruction of wealth, as in Russia.[162] Beheading all the rich is not enough. There'll always be some heir apparent; even when you do away with inheritance you won't stop all the dispossessed from conspiring to get it back. We must never allow the return of the old order, and you can only bring this about by destroying all wealth. Industrial Barcelona must collapse in order to be reborn from its ruins with a new conception of property and labour.[163] In Europe, there's no employer with a blacker heart than the Catalan boss, and I'm only referring to Europe because there are still the Spanish colonies in America.[164] Barcelona can't be saved unless it's wrecked first.

MAX. Yet Barcelona's dear to my heart!

PRISONER. I am always a part of her!

MAX. I owe her the only joys I have felt during the blankness of my blind hours. Every day, a dead boss; sometimes, two . . .[165] That's comforting.

PRISONER. But you say nothing about the workers that keep on falling . . .

MAX. Workers multiply prolifically, rather like flies. On the other hand, bosses are just like elephants, and like all powerful and prehistoric beasts, they procreate slowly. Saul, we have to spread our new religion to the entire world.

PRISONER. My name is Matthew.[166]

MAX. But I baptize you Saul. I'm a poet and I've a copyright on the alphabet. Listen and remember, Saul, for when you're free again. A good hunt can put up the price of Catalan employers' scalps, even higher than that of Calcutta ivory.

PRISONER. That's what we're working for.[167]

MAX. And then again, as a last consolation, consider that by doing away with the proletariat, we get rid of the employers as well.

PRISONER. If we destroy the city, we'll exterminate the Pharisees of Barcelona.[168]

MAX. I won't object. Let Pharisaic Barcelona be destroyed, just like Carthage[169] and Jerusalem. *Alea jacta est.*[170] Here, give me your hand.

PRISONER. I am in irons.

MAX. ¿Eres joven? No puedo verte.

EL PRESO. Soy joven. Treinta años.

MAX. ¿De qué te acusan?

EL PRESO. Es cuento largo. Soy tachado de rebelde . . . No quise dejar el telar por ir a la guerra y levanté un motín en la fábrica.[171] Me denunció el patrón, cumplí condena, recorrí el mundo buscando trabajo, y ahora voy por tránsitos, reclamado de no sé qué jueces. Conozco la suerte que me espera: Cuatro tiros por intento de fuga.[172] Bueno. Si no es más que eso . . .

MAX. ¿Pues qué temes?

EL PRESO. Que se diviertan dándome tormento.

MAX. ¡Bárbaros!

EL PRESO. Hay que conocerlos.

MAX. Canallas. ¡Y ésos son los que protestan de la leyenda negra![173]

EL PRESO. Por siete pesetas, al cruzar un lugar solitario, me sacarán la vida los que tienen a su cargo la defensa del pueblo. ¡Y a esto llaman justicia los ricos canallas!

MAX. Los ricos y los pobres; la barbarie ibérica es unánime.

EL PRESO. ¡Todos!

MAX. ¡Todos! Mateo, ¿dónde está la bomba que destripe el terrón maldito de España?

EL PRESO. Señor poeta que tanto adivina, ¿no ha visto usted una mano levantada?

(Se abre la puerta del calabozo, y EL LLAVERO, *con jactancia de rufo, ordena al preso maniatado que le acompañe.)*

EL LLAVERO. Tú, catalán, ¡disponte!

EL PRESO. Estoy dispuesto.

EL LLAVERO. Pues andando. Gachó, vas a salir en viaje de recreo.

(El esposado, con resignada entereza, se acerca al ciego y le toca el hombro con la barba. Se despide hablando a media voz.)

EL PRESO. Llegó la mía . . . Creo que no volveremos a vernos . . .

MAX. ¡Es horrible!

MAX. Are you young? I can't see you.

PRISONER. I'm young. Thirty years old.

MAX. What are you accused of?

PRISONER. It's a long story. I am charged with rebellion . . . I refused to abandon my job and go to war, and I even started a riot in the factory.[171] The boss denounced me, I had to serve a sentence, travelled all over the place looking for work; I'm still going from court to court, always summoned back by some judge or other. But I know the fate that's waiting for me: four gunshots, for allegedly attempting to escape.[172] Well and good . . . if it's only that and nothing else . . .

MAX. Why, what are you afraid of?

PRISONER. That they might enjoy torturing me.

MAX. Barbarians!

PRISONER. You've got to know them.

MAX. Vermin! And they're the ones who protest indignantly about the 'Black Legend'.[173]

PRISONER. For some miserly pesetas, in some solitary city-corner, I'll be passing and they'll put an end to me . . . and they're paid to protect human lives! This is what the rich scum proclaim as justice.

MAX. Rich and poor alike; Iberian savagery is common to them all.

PRISONER. All of them.

MAX. All of them! Matthew, where is there a bomb to tear the guts out of this cursed Spanish plot of ground?

PRISONER. You're a poet, Sir, and you can foresee so many things, but haven't you noticed a raised hand?

(The prison door opens, and a JAILER, *with the arrogance of a bully, motions to the handcuffed prisoner to follow him.)*

JAILER. You there, Catalan, line up!

PRISONER. I'm ready.

JAILER. So get going. You're going to take a nice vacation, pimp.

(With resigned firmness, the prisoner approaches the blind man and touches his shoulder with his chin. He utters his goodbye in a low voice.)

PRISONER. My turn has come . . . I don't think we'll see each other again . . .

MAX. This is horrible!

EL PRESO. Van a matarme . . . ¿ Qué dirá mañana esa Presna canalla ?

MAX. Lo que le manden.

EL PRESO. ¿ Está usted llorando ?

MAX. De impotencia y de rabia. Abracémonos, hermano.

(Se abrazan. EL CARCELERO *y el esposado salen. Vuelve a cerrarse la puerta.* MAX ESTRELLA *tantea buscando la pared, y se sienta con las piernas cruzadas, en una actitud religiosa, de meditación asiática. Exprime un gran dolor taciturno el bulto del poeta ciego. Llega de fuera tumulto de voces y galopar de caballos.)*

ESCENA SÉPTIMA

(La Redacción de «El Popular». Sala baja con piso de baldosas. En el centro, una mesa larga y negra, rodeada de sillas vacías, que marcan los puestos, ante roídas carpetas y rimeros de cuartillas, que destacan su blancura en el círculo luminoso y verdoso de una lámpara con enagüillas. Al extremo, fuma y escribe un hombre calvo, el eterno redactor del perfil triste, el gabán con flecos, los dedos de gancho y las uñas entintadas. El hombre lógico y mítico enciende el cigarro apagado. Se abre la mampara, y el grillo de un timbre rasga el silencio.[174] *Asoma* EL CONSERJE, *vejete renegado, bigotudo, tripón, parejo de aquellos bizarros coroneles que en las procesiones se caen del caballo. Un enorme parecido que extravaga.)*

EL CONSERJE. Ahí está Don Latino de Hispalis, con otros capitalistas de su cuerda.[175] Vienen preguntando por el Señor Director. Les he dicho que solamente estaba usted en la casa. ¿ Los recibe usted, Don Filiberto ?

DON FILIBERTO. Que pasen.

(Sigue escribiendo. EL CONSERJE *sale, y queda batiente la verde mampara, que proyecta un recuerdo de garitos y naipes. Entra el cotarro modernista, greñas, pipas, gabanes repelados, y alguna capa. El periodista calvo levanta los anteojos a la frente, requiere el cigarro y se da importancia.)*

DON FILIBERTO. ¡ Caballeros y hombres buenos, adelante ! ¿ Ustedes me dirán lo que desean de mí y del Journal ?[176]

PRISONER. They're just going to kill me. And what will those scum newspapers report tomorrow?

MAX. Whatever they're told to print.

PRISONER. Are you crying?

MAX. From impotence and rage. Let's embrace, brother.

(They embrace. The JAILER *and the handcuffed man depart. The door slams shut again.* MAX ESTRELLA *gropes, searching for the wall, and sits down against it, his legs crossed as in a religious pose of Oriental meditation. The blind poet's form conveys a painful and silent grief. From the outside comes a clamour and shouts and the gallop of horses.)*

SCENE SEVEN

(The Editorial Offices of the People's Gazette. *A low hall with tiled floor. In the middle, a big, black table, surrounded by empty chairs which mark the places, in front of faded portfolios and piles of papers whose whiteness is accentuated in the luminous and greenish circle of a lamp with a frilled shade. At one end a bald man is smoking and writing, the perennial editor of sad profile, with braided overcoat, hook-like fingers and inkstained fingernails. This mythical and logical man is relighting a cigar butt. The screen opens and the shrill sound of an electric bell rends the dead silence.*[174] *The* PORTER *appears suddenly, a little old grubby man, mustachioed, potbellied, just like those gallant colonels who fall off their horses while on procession. An extraordinary resemblance that seems incredible.)*

PORTER. Don Latino de Hispalis is here with some other capitalists of the same cloth.[175] They're asking for the Director himself. I told them that you're the only one in the place. Will you see them, Don Philbert?

DON PHILBERT. Let them in.

(He keeps on writing. The PORTER *goes out and the little green screen door keeps swinging, calling to mind old gambling dens. There enters the modernist tribe, long hair, pipes, threadbare overcoats, an occasional cloak. The bald newspaper man pushes his glasses onto his forehead, examines his cigar and puts on an air of importance.)*

DON PHILBERT. Gentlemen and good people, come in! Tell me, please, what can I and the *journal*[176] do for you!

DON LATINO. ¡Venimos a protestar contra un indigno atropello de la Policía! Max Estrella, el gran poeta, aun cuando algunos se niegan a reconocerlo, acaba de ser detenido y maltratado brutalmente en un sótano del Ministerio de la Desgobernación.

DORIO. En España sigue reinando Carlos II.[177]

DON FILIBERTO. ¡Válgame un santo de palo![178] ¿Nuestro gran poeta estaría curda?

DON LATINO. Una copa de más no justifica esa violación de los derechos individuales.

DON FILIBERTO. Max Estrella también es amigo nuestro. ¡Válgame un santo de palo! El Señor Director, cuando a esta hora falta, ya no viene . . . Ustedes conocen cómo se hace un periódico. ¡El Director es siempre un tirano! . . . Yo, sin consultarle, no me decido a recoger en nuestras columnas la protesta de ustedes. Desconozco la política del periódico con la Dirección de Seguridad . . .[179] Y el relato de ustedes, francamente, me parece un poco exagerado.

DORIO. ¡Es pálido, Don Filiberto!

CLARINITO. ¡Una cobardía!

PÉREZ. ¡Una vergüenza!

DON LATINO. ¡Una canallada!

DORIO. ¡En España reina siempre Felipe II![180]

DON LATINO. ¡Dorio, hijo mío, no nos anonades!

DON FILIBERTO. ¡Juventud! ¡Noble apasionamiento! ¡Divino tesoro, como dijo el vate de Nicaragua![181] ¡Juventud, divino tesoro![182] Yo también leo, y algunas veces admiro a los genios del modernismo. El Director bromea que estoy contagiado. ¿Alguno de ustedes ha leído el cuento que publiqué en *Los Orbes*?

CLARINITO. ¡Yo, Don Filiberto! Leído y admirado.

DON FILIBERTO. ¿Y usted, amigo Dorio?

DORIO. Yo nunca leo a mis contemporáneos, Don Filiberto.[183]

DON FILIBERTO. ¡Amigo Dorio, no quiero replicarle que también ignora a los clásicos!

DORIO. A usted y a mí nos rezuma el ingenio, Don Filiberto. En el cuello del gabán llevamos las señales.[184]

DON FILIBERTO. Con esa alusión a la estética de mi indumentaria, se me ha revelado usted como un joven esteta.

DORIO. ¡Es usted corrosivo, Don Filiberto!

DON FILIBERTO. ¡Usted me ha buscado la lengua!

DON LATINO. We're here to protest against a contemptible outrage on the part of the Police! Max Estrella, the great poet, even if there are some who refuse to recognize that he is one, has just been arrested and brutally mistreated in the basement of the Ministry of Misgovernment.

DORIO. In Spain it's forever the reign of Charles II.[177]

DON PHILBERT. Holy Mackerel.[178] Could our great poet be a drunk?

DON LATINO. One glass too many does not justify this outrageous violation of individual rights.

DON PHILBERT. Max Estrella happens to be our friend as well. Holy Mackerel! If the Director isn't here at this hour, it means he won't return. Well you know how a newspaper is produced. The Director is always a tyrant! Without consulting him, I can't decide to print your protests in our column. I don't know what policy the newspaper follows as regards the Police Department.[179] And as for your tale, quite frankly, it sounds a bit exaggerated.

DORIO. It's ghastly, Don Philbert.

CLARINITO. Out and out cowardice!

PÉREZ. A damn shame!

DON LATINO. An outrage!

DORIO. In Spain it's forever the reign of Philip II.[180]

DON LATINO. Dorio my boy, don't humiliate us!

DON PHILBERT. Youth! Noble passion! 'Divine Treasure' as Rubén the bard from Nicaragua called it![181] 'Youth, Divine Treasure! You go never to return'.[182] I read too, you know, and sometimes I even admire the geniuses of modernism. The Director even jokes that I'm infected. Have any of you read the story I published in *Cosmos*?

CLARINITO. I have, Don Philbert! I've read it and admired it.

DON PHILBERT. How about you, Dorio my friend?

DORIO. I never read my contemporaries, Don Philbert.[183]

DON PHILBERT. Dorio my friend, I wouldn't want to suggest that you don't read the classics either.

DORIO. Your brain and mine exude cleverness, Don Philbert. You can see the marks on our coat collars.[184]

DON PHILBERT. With such an allusion to the aesthetic of my clothing, you've exposed yourself as a young aesthete.

DORIO. You are indeed caustic, Don Philbert!

DON PHILBERT. It is you who egged on my tongue!

DORIO. ¡A eso no llego![185]

CLARINITO. Dorio, no hagas chistes de primero de latín.

DON FILIBERTO. Amigo Dorio, tengo alguna costumbre de estas cañas y lanzas del ingenio. Son las justas del periodismo. No me refiero al periodismo de ahora. Con Silvela[186] he discreteado en un banquete, cuando me premiaron en los Juegos Florales de Málaga la Bella. Narciso Díaz[187] aún recordaba poco hace aquel torneo en una crónica suya de *El Heraldo*. Una crónica deliciosa como todas las suyas, y reconocía que no había yo llevado la peor parte. Citaba mi definición del periodismo. ¿Ustedes la conocen? Se la diré, sin embargo. El periodista es el plumífero parlamentario. El Congreso es una gran redacción, y cada redacción, un pequeño Congreso. El periodismo es travesura, lo mismo que la política. Son el mismo círculo en diferentes espacios. Teosóficamente podría explicársela a ustedes, si estuviesen ustedes iniciados en la noble Doctrina del Karma.[188]

DORIO. Nosotros no estamos iniciados, pero quien chanela algo es Don Latino.

DON LATINO. ¡Más que algo, niño, más que algo! Ustedes no conocen la cabalatrina de mi seudónimo:[189] Soy Latino por las aguas del bautismo, soy Latino por mi nacimiento en la bética Hispalis, y Latino por dar mis murgas en el Barrio Latino de París. Latino, en lectura cabalística, se resuelve en una de las palabras mágicas: Onital.[190] Usted, Don Filiberto, también toca algo en el magismo y la cábala.

DON FILIBERTO. No confundamos. Eso es muy serio, Don Latino. ¡Yo soy teósofo![191]

DON LATINO. ¡Yo no sé lo que soy![192]

DON FILIBERTO. Lo creo.

DORIO. Un golfo madrileño.

DON LATINO. Dorio, no malgastes el ingenio, que todo se acaba. Entre amigos basta con sacar la petaca, se queda mejor. ¡Vaya, dame un pito!

DORIO. No fumo.

DON FILIBERTO. ¡Otro vicio tendrá usted!

DORIO. Estupro criadas.

DON FILIBERTO. ¿Es agradable?

DORIO. Tiene sus encantos, Don Filiberto.

DON FILIBERTO. ¿Será usted padre innúmero?

DORIO. I don't aspire so high.[185]

CLARINITO. Dorio, don't make schoolboy jokes.

DON PHILBERT. Dorio my friend, I'm accustomed to such charges and thrusts of wit. These are the jousts of journalism. I don't mean the journalism of today. I exchanged repartee with the politician Silvela[186] at a banquet, and I won the prize in the Floral Games of Malaga the Beautiful. Narciso Díaz[187] in fact recalled that joust a little afterwards in his report to the *Herald.* A delightful account like most of his reports and he pointed out that I didn't play my part badly. He quoted my definition of journalism. Are you familiar with it? In any case, I'll repeat it for you. A newspaper man is the pinioned parliamentarian. Congress is a large editorial office and each editorial office, a small Congress. Journalism is mischief and travesty, just like politics. They are the same circle, only in different spheres. I could explain all of this theosophically if you had been initiated into the noble doctrine of Karma.[188]

DORIO. We've never been initiated ourselves, but the one who gets the drift a little is Don Latino.

DON LATINO. More than a little, my boy, more than just a little. You probably don't know the Cabalistic sense of my pseudonym:[189] I am Latin because of the waters of baptism; I am Latin for being born in Baetic, that is, Andalusian Spain; and Latin for having yowled in the Latin Quarter of Paris. In Cabalistic lingo, Latino is transmuted into one of the magical words: *Onital.*[190] And you Don Philbert, you seem to play a little with Magic and the Cabala.

DON PHILBERT. Let's not confuse things. This is too serious, Don Latino; I really am a theosophist![191]

DON LATINO. I don't know what I am![192]

DON PHILBERT. I can quite believe that.

DORIO. A Madrid tramp.

DON LATINO. Dorio, don't squander your wit, for everything is exhaustible. Between friends it's better to offer a cigarette. Come on, give me a fag.

DORIO. I don't smoke.

DON PHILBERT. You must have some vices!

DORIO. I rape servant girls.

DON PHILBERT. Is it fun?

DORIO. It has its charms, Don Philbert.

DON PHILBERT. You must be a father many times over.

DORIO. Las hago abortar.

DON FILIBERTO. ¡También infanticida!

PÉREZ. Un cajón de sastre.

DORIO. ¡Pérez, no metas la pata! Don Filiberto, un servidor es neomaltusiano.[193]

DON FILIBERTO. ¿Lo pone usted en las tarjetas?

DORIO. Y tengo un anuncio luminoso en casa.

DON LATINO. Y así, revertiéndonos la olla vacía, los españoles nos consolamos del hambre y de los malos gobernantes.

DORIO. Y de los malos cómicos, y de las malas comedias, y del servicio de tranvías, y del adoquinado.

PÉREZ. ¡Eres un iconoclasta!

DORIO. Pérez, escucha respetuosamente y calla.

DON FILIBERTO. En España podrá faltar el pan, pero el ingenio y el buen humor no se acaban.

DORIO. ¿Sabe usted quién es nuestro primer humorista, Don Filiberto?

DON FILIBERTO. Ustedes los iconoclastas dirán, quizá, que Don Miguel de Unamuno.[194]

DORIO. ¡No, señor! El primer humorista es Don Alfonso XIII.[195]

DON FILIBERTO. Tiene la viveza madrileña y borbónica.[196]

DORIO. El primer humorista, Don Filiberto. ¡El primero! Don Alfonso ha batido el récord haciendo presidente del Consejo a García Prieto.[197]

DON FILIBERTO. Aquí, joven amigo, no se pueden proferir blasfemias. Nuestro periódico sale inspirado por Don Manuel García Prieto. Reconozco que no es un hombre brillante, que no es un orador, pero es un político serio. En fin, volvamos al caso de nuestro amigo Mala-Estrella. Yo podría telefonear a la secretaría particular del Ministro. Está en ella un muchacho que hizo aquí tribunales. Voy a pedir comunicación. ¡Válgame un santo de palo! Mala-Estrella es uno de los maestros y merece alguna consideración. ¿Qué dejan esos caballeros para los chulos y los guapos? ¡La gentuza de navaja! ¿Mala-Estrella se hallaría como de costumbre? . . .

DON LATINO. Iluminado.

DON FILIBERTO. ¡Es deplorable!

DON LATINO. Hoy no pasaba de lo justo. Yo le acompañaba. ¡Cuente usted! ¡Amigos desde París! ¿Usted conoce París?

DORIO. I make them abort.

DON PHILBERT. So you're an infanticide to boot.

PÉREZ. A bag full of tricks.

DORIO. Don't you butt in, Pérez! Don Philbert, your humble servant is a Neo-Malthusian.[193]

DON PHILBERT. Do you put that on your calling cards?

DORIO. I've got a luminous advertisement at my home.

DON LATINO. So this is how it always ends; as we pass around an empty dish, we Spaniards console ourselves about hunger and bad administrators.

DORIO. And about bad actors, and bad plays, and about the tramway service and the paving of the street.

PÉREZ. You're an iconoclast!

DORIO. Listen respectfully, Pérez, and remain silent.

DON PHILBERT. Spain may lack bread, but she never runs out of wit and a good sense of humour.

DORIO. Would you, Don Philbert, guess who is our number one humorist?

DON PHILBERT. You damn iconoclasts will probably claim it's Don Miguel de Unamuno.[194]

DORIO. No Sir! Our number one humorist is the King, Don Alfonso XIII.[195]

DON PHILBERT. He's got the vivacity of the Bourbons and of the natives of Madrid.[196]

DORIO. Our number one humorist, Don Philbert. Number one! Our King Alfonso has just broken all records by making García Prieto Prime Minister.[197]

DON PHILBERT. Here, my young friend, you're not allowed to utter blasphemies. Our newspaper happens to be inspired by Don Manuel García Prieto. I know that he's not a brilliant man and that he's not a real orator, but he's a serious politician. Finally, let's get back to the case of our friend Max Ill-Star. I could telephone the Minister's private office. I know someone there who used to cover the Police beat for us. I'll ask to be put through. Holy Mackerel! Max Ill-Star is after all one of the maestros and he deserves some consideration. What do these gentlemen leave for the pimp and the bullies? The rabble with knives! Was Max perhaps in his usual condition?

DON LATINO. Illuminated.

DON PHILBERT. How deplorable!

DON LATINO. He didn't overstep the proprieties. I was with him. Imagine it! Friends since our days in Paris! Are you

Yo fui a París con la Reina Doña Isabel.[198] Escribí entonces en defensa de la Señora. Traduje algunos libros para la Casa Garnier.[199] Fui redactor financiero de *La Lira Hispano-Americana*. ¡Una gran revista! Y siempre mi seudónimo, Latino de Hispalis.

(Suena el timbre del teléfono. DON FILIBERTO, *el periodista calvo y catarroso, el hombre lógico y mítico de todas las redacciones, pide comunicación con el Ministerio de la Gobernación, Secretaría Particular. Hay un silencio. Luego murmullos, leves risas, algún chiste en voz baja.* DORIO DE GADEX *se sienta en el sillón del Director, pone sobre la mesa sus botas rotas y lanza un suspiro.)*

DORIO. Voy a escribir el artículo de fondo, glosando el discurso de nuestro jefe: «¡Todas las fuerzas vivas del país están muertas!», exclamaba aun ayer en un magnífico arranque oratorio nuestro amigo el ilustre Marqués de Alhucemas.[200] Y la Cámara, completamente subyugada, aplaudía la profundidad del concepto, no más profundo que aquel otro: «Ya se van alejando los escollos.» Todos los cuales se resumen en el supremo apóstrofe: «Santiago y abre España, a la libertad y al progreso.»[201]

*(*DON FILIBERTO *suelta la trompetilla del teléfono y viene al centro de la sala, cubriéndose la calva con las manos amarillas y entintadas. ¡Manos de esqueleto memorialista en el día bíblico del Juicio Final!)*

DON FILIBERTO. ¡Esa broma es intolerable! ¡Baje usted los pies! ¡Dónde se ha visto igual grosería!

DORIO. En el Senado Yanqui.

DON FILIBERTO. ¡Me ha llenado usted la carpeta de tierra!

DORIO. Es mi lección de filosofía. ¡Polvo eres, y en polvo te convertirás![202]

DON FILIBERTO. ¡Ni siquiera sabe usted decirlo en latín! ¡Son ustedes unos niños procaces!

CLARINITO. Don Filiberto, nosotros no hemos faltado.

DON FILIBERTO. Ustedes han celebrado la gracia, y la risa en este caso es otra procacidad. ¡La risa de lo que está muy por encima de ustedes! Para ustedes no hay nada respetable. ¡Maura es un charlatán!

familiar with Paris? I went to Paris with Queen Isabella.[198] I wrote at the time defending the great lady. I even translated some books for Garnier Publishers.[199] I was finance editor of the *Hispano-American Clarion*. A great review! And always under my pseudonym, Latino de Hispalis.

(A telephone is heard ringing. DON PHILBERT, *the rheumy and bald journalist, the mythical and logical man to be found on all editorial staffs, asks for a line to the private offices of the Ministry. There is a silence. Then whispers, light laughter, some jokes in a low tone.* DORIO DE GADEX *sits down in the Director's chair, he lifts his ragged boots onto the table and lets out a big sigh.)*

DORIO. I'm going to compose the leading article paraphrasing the speech of our leader: 'All the vital forces of our country are dead!' That is what our friend the illustrious Duke of Alhucemas[200] was exclaiming as recently as yesterday in a magnificent oratorical outburst. And the Chamber, completely enthralled, applauded such a profound concept, as equally profound as that other remark: 'The menacing reefs are slowly receding as the ship comes to port.' And all of them together are usually summed up in the one supreme rallying cry: 'Saint James, and open Spain–to liberty and progress.'[201]

*(*DON PHILBERT *lets go of the telephone receiver and comes into the middle of the room, covering his bald head with his yellowish, ink-stained hands. The hands of a skeleton secretary on the Day of the Last Judgment!)*

DON PHILBERT. I won't tolerate such a joke! Put your feet down! Where did you ever see such rudeness?

DORIO. In the Yankee Senate.

DON PHILBERT. You've covered my folder with dust!

DORIO. That's my philosophy lesson. Dust thou art and unto dust thou shalt return![202]

DON PHILBERT. You couldn't even say it in Latin! You're all impudent brats!

CLARINITO. The rest of us haven't shown any lack of respect, Don Philbert.

DON PHILBERT. But you've enjoyed the joke, and laughter in such a case is impudence. Laughing at something that's way above you! There's nothing respectable for you. Maura is only a charlatan!

DORIO. ¡El Rey del Camelo![203]

DON FILIBERTO. ¡Benlliure un santi boni barati![204]

DORIO. Dicho en valenciano.

DON FILIBERTO. Cavestany,[205] el gran poeta, un coplero.

DORIO. Profesor de guitarra por cifra.[206]

DON FILIBERTO. ¡Qué de extraño tiene que mi ilustre jefe les parezca un mamarracho!

DORIO. Un yerno más.[207]

DON FILIBERTO. Para ustedes en nuestra patria no hay nada grande, nada digno de admiración. ¡Les compadezco! ¡Son ustedes bien desgraciados! ¡Ustedes no sienten la patria!

DORIO. Es un lujo que no podemos permitirnos. Espere usted que tengamos automóvil, Don Filiberto.

DON FILIBERTO. ¡Ni siquiera pueden ustedes hablar en serio! Hay alguno de ustedes, de los que ustedes llaman maestros, que se atreve a gritar viva la bagatela.[208] ¡Y eso no en el café, no en la tertulia de amigos, sino en la tribuna de la Docta Casa![209] ¡Y eso no puede ser, caballeros! Ustedes no creen en nada: Son iconoclastas y son cínicos. Afortunadamente hay una juventud que no son ustedes, una juventud estudiosa, una juventud preocupada, una juventud llena de civismo.

DON LATINO. Protesto, si se refiere a los niños de la Acción Ciudadana. Siquiera estos modernistas, llamémosles golfos distinguidos, no han llegado a ser policías honorarios. A cada cual lo suyo. ¿Y parece ser que esta tarde mataron a uno de esos pollos de gabardina?[210] ¿Usted tendrá noticias?

DON FILIBERTO. Era un pollo relativo. Sesenta años.

DON LATINO. Bueno, pues que lo entierren. ¡Que haya un cadáver más, sólo importa a la funeraria![211]

(Rompe a sonar el timbre del teléfono. DON FILIBERTO *toma la trompetilla y comienza una pantomima de cabeceos, apartes y gritos. Mientras escucha con el cuello torcido y la trompetilla en la oreja, esparce la mirada por la sala, vigilando a los jóvenes modernistas. Al colgar la trompetilla tiene una expresión candorosa de conciencia honrada. Reaparece el teósofo, en su sonrisa plácida, en el marfil de sus sienes, en toda la ancha redondez de su calva.*[212]*)*

DORIO. The King of Humbug![203]

DON PHILBERT. Benlliure, a cheap saint, *un santi boni barati.*[204]

DORIO. Well spoken in Valencian.

DON PHILBERT. Cavestany,[205] the great poet, no more than a cheap rhymester.

DORIO. Gives guitar lessons with a chart.[206]

DON PHILBERT. And I wouldn't be surprised if my illustrious chief seems a shoddy dabbler to you!

DORIO. One more family connection.[207]

DON PHILBERT. As far as you're concerned, there's nothing great in our country, nothing that deserves admiration. I pity you! You're indeed silly wretches! You don't feel any patriotism!

DORIO. It's a luxury we can't afford. Wait till we all own a car, Don Philbert.

DON PHILBERT. You can't even talk in earnest for a moment. And there's one of you whom you all call teacher who dares shout, 'Hurrah for triviality'.[208] And mind you, not in the Café, not among friends, but in a meeting of the Learned Establishment![209] And that just can't go on, gentlemen! You don't believe in anything: you're nihilists and cynics. Fortunately there's another section of our youth that's not at all like you, a studious youth, a committed youth, a youth full of civic spirit.

DON LATINO. If you're referring to those little twerps in the Citizen's Committee, I object. At least these modernists, call them distinguished tramps if you like, have never sunk so low as to be honorary policemen. To each according to his merits. And by the way, is it true that one of these raincoated youngsters was killed this afternoon?[210] Have you any news?

DON PHILBERT. He was a youngster . . . relatively speaking. Sixty years old.

DON LATINO. Well, bury him. Whether there's a corpse more or less, it's only the undertaker who cares![211]

(The telephone suddenly rings. DON PHILBERT *picks up the receiver and begins a pantomime of nods, gestures and shouts. While listening with his neck twisted and the receiver to his ear, he scans the whole room, surveying carefully the modernist young men. When he hangs up, he has the candid expression of a tranquil conscience. It's the theosophist that's emerging, in his placid smile, in the ivory of his brows . . . in all the broad roundness of his baldness.*[212]*)*

DON FILIBERTO. Ya está transmitida la orden de poner en libertad a nuestro amigo Estrella. Aconséjenle ustedes que no beba. Tiene talento. Puede hacer mucho más de lo que hace. Y ahora váyanse y déjenme trabajar. Tengo que hacer solo todo el periódico.

ESCENA OCTAVA

(Secretaría particular de su excelencia.[213] *Olor de brevas habanas, malos cuadros, lujo aparente y provinciano. La estancia tiene un recuerdo partido por medio, de oficina y sala de círculo con timba. De repente el grillo del teléfono se orina en el regazo burocrático.*[214] *Y* DIEGUITO GARCÍA–DON DIEGO DEL CORRAL, *en la «Revista de Tribunales y Estrados»–pega tres brincos y se planta la trompetilla en la oreja.)*

DIEGUITO. ¿Con quién hablo?

. . .

Ya he transmitido la orden para que se le ponga en libertad.

. . .

¡De nada! ¡De nada!

. . .

¡Un alcohólico!

. . .

Sí . . . Conozco su obra.

. . .

¡Una desgracia!

. . .

No podrá ser. ¡Aquí estamos sin un cuarto!

. . .

Se lo diré. Tomo nota.

. . .

¡De nada! ¡De nada!

*(*MAX ESTRELLA *aparece en la puerta, pálido, arañado, la corbata torcida, la expresión altanera y alocada. Detrás, abotonándose los calzones, aparece* EL UJIER.[215]*)*

EL UJIER. Deténgase usted, caballero.

MAX. No me ponga usted la mano encima.

EL UJIER. Salga usted de aquí sin hacer desacato.

MAX. Anúncieme usted al Ministro.

EL UJIER. No está visible.

MAX. ¡Ah! Es usted un gran lógico. Pero estará audible.

DON PHILBERT. The order is already out to set our friend Max Estrella free. Urge him not to drink so much. He's got real talent. He can certainly do much more than what he's doing. And now please leave and let me work. I have to get the paper out all by myself.

SCENE EIGHT

(The private Secretariat of his Excellency.[213] *Smell of Havana tobacco, bad paintings, an appearance of luxury, but provincial. The room recalls in part an office and in part a room in a gambling club. Suddenly the ringing telephone urinates in the bureaucratic lap.*[214] *And* DIEGUITO GARCIA*–called* DON DIEGO DEL CORRAL *in* The Law Courts and Magistrates Journal*–takes three leaps and plants the receiver onto his ear.)*

DIEGUITO. Who's speaking?

. . .

I've already issued the order to set him free.

. . .

Not at all! Not at all!

. . .

An alcoholic!

. . .

Yes, I know his work. An unfortunate accident!

. . .

It's not possible. We don't have a cent here.

. . .

I'll tell him about it. I'll make a note now.

. . .

Not at all! Not at all!

(MAX ESTRELLA *sneaks in at the door, pale, scratched, his tie awry, his expression arrogant and somewhat deranged. Behind him, buttoning his breeches, appears the* USHER.[215])

USHER. Stop, Sir.

MAX. Don't lay your dirty hands on me.

USHER. Leave this place before you make a nuisance of yourself.

MAX. Announce me to the Minister.

USHER. He can't be seen.

MAX. Ah! You are indeed quite logical. But perhaps he can be heard.

EL UJIER. Retírese, caballero. Éstas no son horas de audiencia.

MAX. Anúncieme usted.

EL UJIER. Es la orden . . . Y no vale ponerse pelmazo, caballero.

DIEGUITO. Fernández, deje usted a ese caballero que pase.

MAX. ¡Al fin doy con un indígena civilizado!

DIEGUITO. Amigo Mala-Estrella, usted perdonará que sólo un momento me ponga a sus órdenes. Me habló por usted la Redacción de *El Popular*. Allí le quieren a usted. A usted le quieren y le admiran en todas partes. Usted me deja mandado aquí y donde sea. No me olvide . . . ¡Quién sabe! . . . Yo tengo la nostalgia del periodismo . . . Pienso hacer algo . . . Hace tiempo acaricio la idea de una hoja volandera, un periódico ligero,[216] festivo, espuma de champaña, fuego de virutas.[217] Cuento con usted. Adiós, maestro. ¡Deploro que la ocasión de conocernos haya venido de suceso tan desagradable!

MAX. De eso vengo a protestar. ¡Tienen ustedes una policía reclutada entre la canalla más canalla!

DIEGUITO. Hay de todo, maestro.

MAX. No discutamos. Quiero que el Ministro me oiga, y al mismo tiempo darle las gracias por mi libertad.

DIEGUITO. El Señor Ministro no sabe nada.

MAX. Lo sabrá por mí.

DIEGUITO. El Señor Ministro ahora trabaja. Sin embargo, voy a entrar.

MAX. Y yo con usted.

DIEGUITO. ¡Imposible!

MAX. ¡Daré un escándalo!

DIEGUITO. ¡Está usted loco!

MAX. Loco de verme desconocido y negado. El Ministro es amigo mío, amigo de los tiempos heroicos. ¡Quiero oírle decir que no me conoce! ¡Paco! ¡Paco!

DIEGUITO. Le anunciaré a usted.

MAX. Yo me basto. ¡Paco! ¡Soy un espectro del pasado!

(Su Excelencia[218] abre la puerta de su despacho y asoma en mangas de camisa, la bragueta desabrochada, el chaleco suelto, y

USHER. Withdraw, Sir. These are not his hours for interviewing.

MAX. Announce me.

USHER. These are my orders, Sir . . . And it's no good making a fool of yourself over it.

DIEGUITO. Fernández, allow the gentleman to come in.

MAX. So I finally come upon a civilized native!

DIEGUITO. Friend Estrella my 'Evil Star', you must forgive me but I can only spend a few moments with you. The office of the *Gazette* called me about you. They really like you there. Of course you're liked and respected everywhere. I'm at your service now or anytime. Don't forget me . . . Who knows! I feel nostalgic about journalistic work . . . Someday I intend to create something . . . I've been for some time hatching an idea for an illustrated leaflet, a light review, festive, witty,[216] . . . foam from champagne, ephemeral sparks.[217] So I'm counting on you. And now, goodbye, maestro. I truly regret that the occasion for our meeting should arise from such a deplorable situation.

MAX. I'm here to protest about exactly that. For a police force you people have recruited the lowest scum of all the scum in Spain.

DIEGUITO. There's a little of everything, maestro.

MAX. There's nothing to discuss. I want the Minister himself to hear me, and while at it I can thank him personally for my release.

DIEGUITO. His Excellency the Minister doesn't know anything about it.

MAX. He'll find out from me.

DIEGUITO. His Excellency the Minister is working hard at the moment. However, I'll go and see him.

MAX. And I'll go with you.

DIEGUITO. Impossible!

MAX. I'll make a scene!

DIEGUITO. You're crazy!

MAX. Yes, crazy at being ignored and rebuffed. The Minister is a friend of mine, a friend from our heroic age. I want to hear him say that he doesn't know me! Paco! Paco!

DIEGUITO. I shall announce you.

MAX. I can do it myself. Paco! I'm a phantom from the past!

(His Excellency[218] *opens the office door and looks out in his shirt-sleeves, the fly of his trousers unfastened, his waist-coat loose and*

los quevedos pendientes de un cordón, como dos ojos absurdos bailándole sobre la panza.)

EL MINISTRO. ¿Qué escándalo es éste, Dieguito?

DIEGUITO. Señor Ministro, no he podido evitarlo.

EL MINISTRO. ¿Y ese hombre quién es?

MAX. ¡Un amigo de los tiempos heroicos! ¡No me reconoces, Paco! ¡Tanto me ha cambiado la vida! ¡No me reconoces! ¡Soy Máximo Estrella!

EL MINISTRO. ¡Claro! ¡Claro! ¡Claro! ¿Pero estás ciego?

MAX. Como Homero y como Belisario.[219]

EL MINISTRO. Una ceguera accidental, supongo . . .

MAX. Definitiva e irrevocable. Es el regalo de Venus.[220]

EL MINISTRO. Válgame Dios. ¿Y cómo no te has acordado de venir a verme antes de ahora? Apenas leo tu firma en los periódicos.

MAX. ¡Vivo olvidado! Tú has sido más vidente dejando las letras para hacernos felices gobernando. Paco, las letras no dan para comer. ¡Las letras son colorín, pingajo y hambre!

EL MINISTRO. Las letras, ciertamente, no tienen la consideración que debieran, pero son ya un valor que se cotiza. Amigo Max, yo voy a continuar trabajando. A este pollo le dejas una nota de lo que desees . . . Llegas ya un poco tarde.

MAX. Llego en mi hora. No vengo a pedir nada. Vengo a exigir una satisfacción y un castigo. Soy ciego, me llaman poeta, vivo de hacer versos y vivo miserablemente. Estás pensando que soy un borracho. ¡Afortunadamente! Si no fuese borracho ya me hubiera pegado un tiro. ¡Paco, tus sicarios no tienen derecho a escupirme y abofetearme, y vengo a pedir un castigo para esa turba de miserables, y un desagravio a la Diosa Minerva![221]

EL MINISTRO. Amigo Max, yo no estoy enterado de nada. ¿Qué ha pasado, Dieguito?

DIEGUITO. Como hay un poco de tumulto callejero, y no se consienten grupos, y estaba algo excitado el maestro . . .

MAX. He sido injustamente detenido, inquisitorialmente torturado. En las muñecas tengo las señales.

his pince-nez hanging from the end of a string like two absurd eyeballs dancing on his paunch.)

MINISTER. What's all the racket about, Dieguito?

DIEGUITO. Your Excellency, I couldn't stop it.

MINISTER. And who is this man?

MAX. A friend from epic times. You don't even recognize me, Paco. Life has changed me that much! So you don't recognize me! I'm Máximo Estrella!

MINISTER. But of course! Of course! Of course! But . . . are you blind?

MAX. Blind like Homer and like Belisarius.[219]

MINISTER. Blind by accident, I suppose . . .

MAX. Definitely and irreparably. It's the gift of Venus.[220]

MINISTER. God help us. And why didn't you think of coming to see me sooner? I hardly ever see your things in the newspapers any more.

MAX. I exist, a forgotten man! You were more far-sighted to abandon the arts so that you could make us happy by governing. Paco, you can't get enough to eat from literature. Art is full of bright colours, tatters and hunger!

MINISTER. The arts, to be sure, don't get the consideration they deserve. But they're still a marketable commodity. Friend Max, I must get to my work. Leave a note with this fellow here stating what you need . . . You've come a little late.

MAX. I come in my own time. I'm not here to beg. I come to demand satisfaction and punishment. I'm blind, true; they call me a poet, I make a living composing poetry and I live in misery. You think perhaps I'm an alcoholic. Fortunately! If I weren't a drunkard I'd have blown my brains out long ago. Paco, your hired assassins have no right to slap my face and spit on me, and I come to demand the punishment of your despicable mob and some satisfaction for their offence against the Goddess Justice![221]

MINISTER. My friend Max, I don't know anything about all this. What's happened, Dieguito?

DIEGUITO. Well, because there has been some rioting in the streets, groups are not allowed to congregate, and our maestro here was somewhat excited . . .

MAX. I've been arrested for no reason, and Inquisitorially tortured. Here are the marks on my wrists.

EL MINISTRO. ¿Qué parte han dado los guardias, Dieguito?

DIEGUITO. En puridad, lo que acabo de resumir al Señor Ministro.

MAX. ¡Pues es mentira! He sido detenido por la arbitrariedad de un legionario, a quien pregunté, ingenuo, si sabía los cuatro dialectos griegos.

EL MINISTRO. Real y verdaderamente la pregunta es arbitraria. ¡Suponerle a un guardia tan altas Humanidades!

MAX. Era un teniente.

EL MINISTRO. Como si fuese un Capitán General. ¡No estás sin ninguna culpa! ¡Eres siempre el mismo calvatrueno! ¡Para ti no pasan los años! ¡Ay, cómo envidio tu eterno buen humor!

MAX. ¡Para mí, siempre es de noche![222] Hace un año que estoy ciego. Dicto y mi mujer escribe, pero no es posible.

EL MINISTRO. ¿Tu mujer es francesa?

MAX. Una santa del Cielo, que escribe el español con una ortografía del Infierno. Tengo que dictarle letra por letra. Las ideas se me desvanecen. ¡Un tormento! Si hubiera pan en mi casa, maldito si me apenaba la ceguera. El ciego se entera mejor de las cosas del mundo, los ojos son unos ilusionados embusteros.[223] ¡Adiós, Paco! Conste que no he venido a pedirte ningún favor. Max Estrella no es el pobrete molesto.

EL MINISTRO. Espera, no te vayas, Máximo. Ya que has venido, hablaremos. Tú resucitas toda una época de mi vida, acaso la mejor. ¡Qué lejana! Estudiábamos juntos. Vivías en la calle del Recuerdo. Tenías una hermana. De tu hermana anduve yo enamorado. ¡Por ella hice versos!

MAX. ¡Calle del Recuerdo,
ventana de Helena,
la niña morena
que asomada vi!
¡Calle del Recuerdo
rondalla de tuna,
y escala de luna
que en ella prendí!

EL MINISTRO. ¡Qué memoria la tuya! ¡Me dejas maravillado! ¿Qué fue de tu hermana?

MINISTER. What does the Police report say, Dieguito?

DIEGUITO. No more, frankly, than what I've just summed up for your Excellency.

MAX. Well it's a lie! I was arrested arbitrarily by some legionary whom I asked, ingenuously I thought, whether he knew the four Greek dialects.

MINISTER. All joking aside, it's your question that seems arbitrary to me, Max. To expect indeed such classical erudition from a policeman!

MAX. He was a lieutenant.

MINISTER. I don't care if he was a Captain General! You're not all that blameless, Max! You're always the same old joker! The years seem to pass you by! Ah! But how I envy your inexhaustible sense of humour.

MAX. For me, it's eternal darkness.[222] I've been blind for a year. I dictate and my wife writes, but it doesn't work.

MINISTER. Your wife, is she French?

MAX. A saint from Heaven who spells our language with the orthography of Hell. I have to dictate to her letter by letter. I lose track of all my ideas. It's torture! If there were bread in my house, I'm damned if blindness would be so painful. A blind man actually knows more about the ways of the world, because the eyes are only hopeful deceivers.[223] Goodbye Paco! Just so you know that I didn't come to ask favours. Max Estrella is not yet the poor annoying wretch.

MINISTER. Wait, Máximo don't go away. Since you've come, let's chat a while. You call back a whole epoch, perhaps the best of my life. How far away it all seems! We used to study together. You used to live in Memory Lane. You had a sister. In fact, I was in love with your sister. I even composed verses for her!

MAX. Memory Lane,

Helen's window,
The girl's dark-haired
And I saw her there.
Memory Lane,
Strolling serenade,
A moon-ladder
And I climbed to her.

MINISTER. What a memory you have! I'm amazed! Whatever happened to your sister?

MAX. Entró en un convento.

EL MINISTRO. ¿Y tu hermano Alex?[224]

MAX. ¡Murió!

EL MINISTRO. ¿Y los otros? ¡Érais muchos!

MAX. ¡Creo que todos han muerto!

EL MINISTRO. ¡No has cambiado! . . . Max, yo no quiero herir tu delicadeza, pero en tanto dure aquí, puedo darte un sueldo.[225]

MAX. ¡Gracias!

EL MINISTRO. ¿Aceptas?

MAX. ¡Qué remedio!

EL MINISTRO. Tome usted nota, Dieguito. ¿Dónde vives, Max?

MAX. Dispóngase usted a escribir largo, joven maestro: —Bastardillos, veintitrés, duplicado, Escalera interior, Guardilla B—. Nota. Si en este laberinto hiciese falta un hilo para guiarse, no se le pida a la portera, porque muerde.[226]

EL MINISTRO. ¡Cómo te envidio el humor!

MAX. El mundo es mío, todo me sonríe, soy un hombre sin penas.

EL MINISTRO. ¡Te envidio!

MAX. ¡Paco, no seas majadero!

EL MINISTRO. Max, todos los meses te llevarán el haber a tu casa. ¡Ahora, adiós! ¡Dame un abrazo!

MAX. Toma un dedo, y no te enternezcas.

EL MINISTRO. ¡Adiós, Genio y Desorden!

MAX. Conste que he venido a pedir un desagravio para mi dignidad, y un castigo para unos canallas. Conste que no alcanzo ninguna de las dos cosas, y que me das dinero, y que lo acepto porque soy un canalla. No me estaba permitido irme del mundo sin haber tocado alguna vez el fondo de los Reptiles.[227] ¡Me he ganado los brazos de Su Excelencia!

*(*MÁXIMO ESTRELLA, *con los brazos abiertos en cruz, la cabeza erguida, los ojos parados, trágicos en su ciega quietud, avanza como un fantasma. Su Excelencia, tripudo, repintado, mantecoso, responde con un arranque de cómico viejo, en el buen melodrama francés. Se abrazan los dos. Su Excelencia, al separarse, tiene una lágrima detenida en los párpados. Estrecha la mano del bohemio, y deja en ella algunos billetes.)*

MAX. She entered a convent.

MINISTER. And your brother Alex?[224]

MAX. He died!

MINISTER. And the others? There were so many of you.

MAX. I think they're all dead!

MINISTER. You haven't changed a bit! Max, I don't want to wound your pride, but as long as I remain here, I could arrange some kind of pension.[225]

MAX. Thanks!

MINISTER. Do you accept then?

MAX. I've no alternative!

MINISTER. Make a note of it, Dieguito. Where do you live, Max?

MAX. Be ready to write at length, young maestro. Little Bastards 23, a, Inside Staircase, Skylight B. Footnote: if in this labyrinth you need a thread to guide you, don't ask the concierge: she bites.[226]

MINISTER. How I envy your sense of humour!

MAX. The world is mine, everything smiles at me, I am certainly a man with no worries.

MINISTER. I really envy you!

MAX. Paco, don't be an ass.

MINISTER. Max, each month they'll take your payment to your house. And now, goodbye! Give me a hug!

MAX. Here, take a little finger and don't act so sentimental.

MINISTER. Goodbye, Genius and Anarchy!

MAX. Just so you know that I came to demand redress for my dignity and punishment for some riffraff. Just so you know that I didn't accomplish either of my objectives, and that you give me money, and that I accept it because I myself am riffraff. I was not meant to leave this world without at least once scratching the bottom of the snake pit.[227] I have indeed earned the embrace of your Excellency!

(MÁXIMO ESTRELLA *with his arms spread in a cross, his head raised, his eyes staring intensely, tragic in their blind tranquility, moves forward like an apparition. His Excellency, pot-bellied, overpainted, blubbery, responds with the sudden gesture of an old character actor in the good old French melodramas. The two embrace. When they pull apart, a tear trembles on his Excellency's eyelash. He shakes the old Bohemian's hand and presses some banknotes into it.*)

EL MINISTRO. ¡Adiós! ¡Adiós! Créeme que no olvidaré este momento.

MAX. ¡Adiós, Paco! ¡Gracias en nombre de dos pobres mujeres!

(Su Excelencia toca un timbre. El ujier acude soñoliento. MÁXIMO ESTRELLA, *tanteando con el palo, va derecho hacia el fondo de la estancia, donde hay un balcón.)*

EL MINISTRO. Fernández, acompañe usted a ese caballero, y déjele en un coche.

MAX. Seguramente que me espera en la puerta mi perro.

EL UJIER. Quien le espera a usted es un sujeto de edad, en la antesala.

MAX. Don Latino de Hispalis: mi perro.[228]

*(*EL UJIER *toma de la manga al bohemio. Con aire torpón le saca del despacho, y guipa al soslayo el gesto de Su Excelencia. Aquel gesto manido de actor de carácter en la gran escena del reconocimiento.*[229]*)*

EL MINISTRO. Querido Dieguito, ahí tiene usted un hombre a quien le ha faltado el resorte de la voluntad! Lo tuvo todo: Figura, palabra, gracejo. Su charla cambiaba de colores como las llamas de un ponche.

DIEGUITO. ¡Qué imagen soberbia!

EL MINISTRO. ¡Sin duda, era el que más valía entre los de mi tiempo![230]

DIEGUITO. Pues véalo usted ahora en medio del arroyo, oliendo a aguardiente, y saludando en francés a las proxenetas.

EL MINISTRO. ¡Veinte años! ¡Una vida! ¡E, inopinadamente, reaparece ese espectro de la bohemia! Yo me salvé del desastre renunciando al goce de hacer versos. Dieguito, usted de esto no sabe nada, porque no ha nacido poeta.

DIEGUITO. ¡Lagarto! ¡Lagarto![231]

EL MINISTRO. ¡Ay, Dieguito, usted no alcanzará nunca lo que son ilusión y bohemia![232] Usted ha nacido institucionista,[233] usted no es un renegado del mundo del ensueño. ¡Yo, sí!

DIEGUITO. ¿Lo lamenta usted, Don Francisco?

EL MINISTRO. Creo que lo lamento.

DIEGUITO. ¿El Excelentísimo Señor Ministro de la Gobernación, se cambiaría por el poeta Mala-Estrella?

EL MINISTRO. ¡Ya se ha puesto la toga y los vuelillos el Señor Licenciado Don Diego del Corral! Suspenda un momento el

MINISTER. Adieu! Adieu! You must know that I'll not forget this moment.

MAX. Goodbye, Paco! I thank you in the name of two wretched women!

(His Excellency presses a button. The USHER *comes in sleepy-eyed.* MÁXIMO ESTRELLA, *groping with his stick, goes directly to the end of the room near a balcony.)*

MINISTER. Fernández, accompany the gentleman and put him in a cab.

MAX. Surely my dog must be waiting for me at the door.

USHER. The one waiting for you is an old fellow in the ante-chamber.

MAX. Don Latino de Hispalis: my dog.[228]

(The USHER *takes the old Bohemian by his sleeve. With a slow gait he leads him out of the office and peeps sideways at the gesture of his Excellency. That worn-out gesture of an old character actor playing the father in the sublime scene of recognition.*[229]*)*

MINISTER. My dear Dieguito, here you have a man who lacked only strength of will! He had everything: demeanor, eloquence, wit. His casual conversation sparkled with brilliant colours, like the flaming sparks from a welder's torch.

DIEGUITO. What a superb image!

MINISTER. No question about it, he was worth more than anyone else of my generation.[230]

DIEGUITO. Well, look at him now deep in the gutter, reeking of alcohol and greeting all the old bawds in French.

MINISTER. Twenty years! A whole life! And quite unexpectedly, there appears this phantom of Bohemia! I was rescued from disaster by giving up the pleasure of writing poetry. Dieguito, you know nothing of this sort of life because you were not born a poet.

DIEGUITO. Touch wood![231]

MINISTER. Ah, Dieguito, you'll never understand what it means to be part of the illusory world of Bohemia![232] You were born a bureaucrat,[233] you're not a renegade from the world of dreams. But I am!

DIEGUITO. And do you now regret it, Don Francisco?

MINISTER. Yes, I believe I do.

DIEGUITO. Why, would His Excellency the Minister of the Interior exchange places with the ill-starred poet Max?

MINISTER. Well, just look at our law graduate, Don Diego del Corral, who's already parading in his lace-cuffed Judge's

interrogatorio su señoría, y vaya pensando cómo se justifican las pesetas que hemos de darle a Máximo Estrella.

DIEGUITO. Las tomaremos de los fondos de Policía.[234]

EL MINISTRO. ¡ Eironeia ![235]

(Su Excelencia se hunde en una poltrona, ante la chimenea que aventa sobre la alfombra una claridad trémula. Enciende un cigarro con sortija, y pide La Gaceta.[236] *Cabálgase los lentes, le pasa la vista, se hace un gorro, y se duerme.)*

ESCENA NOVENA

(Un café que prolongan empañados espejos. Mesas de mármol. Divanes rojos. El mostrador en el fondo, y detrás un vejete rubiales, destacado el busto sobre la diversa botillería. El Café tiene piano y violín. Las sombras y la música flotan en el vaho de humo, y en el lívido temblor de los arcos voltaicos. Los espejos multiplicadores están llenos de un interés folletinesco. En un fondo, con una geometría absurda, estravaga el Café.[237] *El compás canalla de la música, las luces en el fondo de los espejos, el baho de humo penetrado del temblor de los arcos voltaicos cifran su diversidad en una sola expresión. Entran extraños, y son de repente transfigurados en aquel triple ritmo,* MALA-ESTRELLA *y* DON LATINO.*)*

MAX. ¿ Qué tierra pisamos ?

DON LATINO. El Café Colón.

MAX. Mira si está Rubén. Suele ponerse enfrente de los músicos.

DON LATINO. Allá está como un cerdo triste.

MAX. Vamos a su lado, Latino. Muerto yo, el cetro de la poesía pasa a ese negro.

DON LATINO. No me encargues de ser tu testamentario.

MAX. ¡ Es un gran poeta !

DON LATINO. Yo no lo entiendo.

MAX. ¡ Merecías ser el barbero de Maura ![238]

(Por entre sillas y mármoles llegan al rincón donde está sentado y silencioso RUBÉN DARÍO.[239] *Ante aquella aparición, el poeta siente la amargura de la vida, y con gesto egoísta de niño enfadado, cierra los ojos, y bebe un sorbo de su copa de ajenjo. Finalmente, su máscara de ídolo se anima con una sonrisa cargada de hume-*

robes. I beg your honour to suspend interrogation for a moment and instead think of a way to justify the pesetas we're going to give our poet Max Estrella.

DIEGUITO. We'll take them from the Police secret funds.[234]

MINISTER. Ironic touch![235]

(His Excellency sinks into an armchair in front of the fireplace which flickers a trembling light on the carpet. He lights a banded cigar and asks for the Gazette.[236] *He puts on his glasses, scans the newspaper, places it over his head, and falls asleep.)*

SCENE NINE

(A café prolonged by tarnished mirrors. Marble-topped tables. Red tables. Red couches. At the back, the bar and, behind it, the bust of a light-haired little old man stands out above the varied array of bottles. It is a café with a piano and violin. The shadows and the music float among the smoky vapours and the livid tremor of the electric arc-lamps. The multiplying mirrors are filled with magazine-story interest. In the background, with an absurd geometry, the café goes awry.[237] *The vulgar beat of the music, the lights in the depths of the mirrors, the pall of smoke pierced by the trembling of the electric arc-lights commingle their diversity in a single expression. Enter* ILL-STARRED *and* DON LATINO, *strangers, but they are suddenly transfigured in this triple rhythm.)*

MAX. On what ground do we tread?

DON LATINO. The café Columbus.

MAX. See if Rubén's here. He usually sits in front of the musicians.

DON LATINO. There he is, like a sad pig.

MAX. Let's go up to him, Latino. When I'm dead, the sceptre of poetry will pass to this negro.

DON LATINO. Don't ask me to be executor of your estate.

MAX. He's a great poet!

DON LATINO. I don't understand him.

MAX. You deserve to be Maura's barber![238]

(Through the chairs and marble-tops, they reach the corner where Rubén Darío sits, silent.[239] *Faced by that apparition, the poet feels the bitterness of life and, with the egoistic gesture of an angry child, closes his eyes, and swallows a mouthful from his glass of absinth. Finally, his idol's mask is animated by a smile heavy*

dad. El ciego se detiene ante la mesa y levanta su brazo, con magno ademán de estatua cesárea.)

MAX. ¡Salud, hermano, si menor en años, mayor en prez!

RUBÉN. ¡Admirable! ¡Cuánto tiempo sin vernos, Max! ¿Qué haces?

MAX. ¡Nada!

RUBÉN. ¡Admirable![240] ¿Nunca vienes por aquí?

MAX. El café es un lujo muy caro, y me dedico a la taberna, mientras llega la muerte.

RUBÉN. Max, amemos la vida, y mientras podamos, olvidemos a la Dama de Luto.

MAX. ¿Por qué?

RUBÉN. ¡No hablemos de Ella![241]

MAX. ¡Tú la temes, y yo la cortejo! ¡Rubén, te llevaré el mensaje que te plazca darme para la otra ribera de la Estigia.[242] Vengo aquí para estrecharte por última vez la mano, guiado por el ilustre camello Don Latino de Hispalis. ¡Un hombre que desprecia tu poesía, como si fuese Académico![243]

DON LATINO. ¡Querido Max, no te pongas estupendo!

RUBÉN. ¿El señor es Don Latino de Hispalis?

DON LATINO. ¡Si nos conocemos de antiguo, maestro! ¡Han pasado muchos años! Hemos hecho periodismo en *La Lira Hispano-Americana.*

RUBÉN. Tengo poca memoria, Don Latino.

DON LATINO. Yo era el redactor financiero. En París nos tuteábamos, Rubén.

RUBÉN. Lo había olvidado.

MAX. ¡Si no has estado nunca en París!

DON LATINO. Querido Max, vuelvo a decirte que no te pongas estupendo. Siéntate e invítanos a cenar. ¡ Rubén, hoy este gran poeta, nuestro amigo, se llama Estrella Resplandeciente!

RUBÉN. ¡Admirable! ¡Max, es preciso huir de la bohemia![244]

DON LATINO. ¡Está opulento! ¡Guarda dos pápiros de piel de contribuyente![245]

MAX. ¡Esta tarde tuve que empeñar la capa, y esta noche te convido a cenar! ¡A cenar con el rubio Champaña, Rubén!

RUBÉN. ¡Admirable! Como Martín de Tours,[246] partes conmigo la capa, transmudada en cena. ¡Admirable!

DON LATINO. ¡Mozo, la carta! Me parece un poco exagerado pedir vinos franceses. ¡Hay que pensar en el mañana, caballeros!

with dampness. The blind man stops before the table and raises his arm, with the grand gesture of a statue of Caesar.)

MAX. Hail, brother, though less in years, greater in worth.

RUBÉN. Exquisite! How long has it been since we last saw each other, Max! What are you doing?

MAX. Nothing!

RUBÉN. Exquisite![240] Don't you ever drop in here?

MAX. The café is a very expensive luxury, and as death approaches, I'm dedicating myself to the tavern.

RUBÉN. Max, let's love life, and while we can, forget the Dark Lady.

MAX. Why?

RUBÉN. Let's not speak of Her![241]

MAX. You fear Her, and I court Her. Rubén, I'll carry whatever message it pleases you to give me for the other bank of the Styx.[242] I come here to shake your hand for the last time, guided by the illustrious camel Don Latino de Hispalis. A man who despises your poetry as if he were an Academician![243]

DON LATINO. Dear Max, don't exaggerate.

RUBÉN. Sir, you are Don Latino de Hispalis?

DON LATINO. Why we've known each other for ages, maestro! Many years have flown by! We were journalists together on the *Hispanic-American Clarion.*

RUBÉN. I have a poor memory, Don Latino.

DON LATINO. I was the financial editor. In Paris we were on intimate terms, Rubén.

RUBÉN. I had forgotten.

MAX. But you've never been in Paris!

DON LATINO. Dear Max, I'm telling you once again, not to exaggerate. Sit down and invite us to dinner. Rubén, today this great poet, our friend, is called Resplendent Star!

RUBÉN. Exquisite! Max, we must flee from Bohemia.[244]

DON LATINO. He's flush. He's got two pieces of folding money made of taxpayers' hides.[245]

MAX. This afternoon I had to hock my cloak, and tonight I invite you to dinner. Dinner with golden champagne, Rubén.

RUBÉN. Exquisite! Like St Martin of Tours,[246] you share your cloak with me, transmuted into dinner. Exquisite!

DON LATINO. Waiter, the menu! It strikes me as a little exaggerated to order French wines. Gentlemen, one has to think of tomorrow.

MAX. ¡No pensemos!

DON LATINO. Compartiría tu opinión si con el café, la copa y el puro nos tomásemos un veneno.

MAX. ¡Miserable burgués!

DON LATINO. Querido Max, hagamos un trato. Yo me bebo modestamente, un chica de cerveza, y tú me apoquinas en pasta lo que me había de costar la bebecua.

RUBÉN. No te apartes de los buenos ejemplos, Don Latino.

DON LATINO. Servidor no es un poeta. Yo me gano la vida con más trabajo que haciendo versos.[247]

RUBÉN. Yo también estudio las matemáticas celestes.[248]

DON LATINO. ¡Perdón entonces! Pues sí, señor, aun cuando me veo reducido al extremo de vender entregas, soy un adepto de la Gnosis[249] y la Magia.

RUBÉN. ¡Yo lo mismo!

DON LATINO. Recuerdo que alguna cosa alcanzabas.

RUBÉN. Yo he sentido que los Elementos son Conciencias.[250]

DON LATINO. ¡Indudable! ¡Indudable! ¡Indudable! ¡Conciencias, Voluntades y Potestades!

RUBÉN. Mar y Tierra, Fuego y Viento, divinos monstruos. ¡Posiblemente Divinos porque son Eternidades![251]

MAX. Eterna la Nada.[252]

DON LATINO. Y el fruto de la Nada: los cuatro Elementales, simbolizados en los cuatro Evangelios.[253] La Creación, que es pluralidad, solamente comienza en el Cuatrivio.[254] Pero de la Trina Unidad, se desprende el Número. ¡Por eso el Número es Sagrado![255]

MAX. ¡Calla, Pitágoras![256] Todo eso lo has aprendido en tus intimidades con la vieja Blavatsky.[257]

DON LATINO. ¡Max, esas bromas no son tolerables! ¡Eres un espíritu profundamente irreligioso y volteriano![258] Madama Blavatsky ha sido una mujer extraordinaria, y no debes profanar con burlas el culto de su memoria. Pudieras verte castigado por alguna camarrupa de su karma.[259] ¡Y no sería el primer caso!

RUBÉN. ¡Se obran prodigios! Afortunadamente no los vemos ni los entendemos. Sin esta ignorancia, la vida sería un enorme sobrecogimiento.[260]

MAX. ¿Tú eres creyente, Rubén?

RUBÉN. ¡Yo creo!

MAX. Let's not.

DON LATINO. I would second your opinion if, along with the coffee, the drink, and the cigar, we also took poison.

MAX. Miserable bourgeois!

DON LATINO. My dear Max, let's make a deal. I'll drink modestly, a small beer, and you, you'll hand over in real dough what my imbibing would have cost you.

RUBÉN. Don't forget your good manners, Don Latino.

DON LATINO. Your humble servant is no poet. I earn my living by harder labour than writing poetry.[247]

RUBÉN. I am also a student of celestial mathematics.[248]

DON LATINO. In that case, your pardon. Because indeed, sir, even if I see myself reduced to the sad extremity of selling mere instalments, I am an adept of Gnosis[249] and Magic.

RUBÉN. So am I.

DON LATINO. I recall that you were acquiring some knowledge in that field.

RUBÉN. I have sensed that the Elements are Consciences.[250]

DON LATINO. Indubitably! Indubitably! Indubitably! Consciences, Wills and Powers!

RUBÉN. Sea and Earth, Fire and Wind, divine monsters. Possibly divine because they are Eternities.[251]

MAX. Only nothingness is eternal.[252]

DON LATINO. And the fruit of Nothingness: the four Elementals symbolized in the four Gospels.[253] The Creation, which is plurality, only begins in the Quaternary.[254] But from the Trini-Unity, Number issues. That's why Number is Sacred.[255]

MAX. Shut up, Pythagoras![256] All this is stuff you've learned during your intimate moments with old Madame Blavatsky.[257]

DON LATINO. Max, these jokes are intolerable. You're a profoundly irreligious, Voltairean spirit![258] Madame Blavatsky was an extraordinary woman, and you have no right to profane the veneration of her memory with wisecracks. You might find yourself punished by some malefice from her *karma*.[259] And it wouldn't be the first time it's happened!

RUBÉN. Prodigies are wrought! Fortunately, we neither see nor comprehend them. But for this ignorance, life would be one enormous quiver of apprehension.[260]

MAX. Are you a believer, Rubén?

RUBÉN. I believe!

MAX. ¿En Dios?

RUBÉN. ¡Y en Cristo!

MAX. ¿Y en las llamas del Infierno?

RUBÉN. ¡Y más todavía en las músicas del Cielo![261]

MAX. ¡Eres un farsante, Rubén!

RUBÉN. ¡Seré un ingenuo!

MAX. ¿No estás posando?

RUBÉN. ¡No!

MAX. Para mí, no hay nada tras la última mueca. Si hay algo, vendré a decírtelo.

RUBÉN. ¡Calla, Max, no quebrantemos los humanos sellos!

MAX. Rubén, acuérdate de esta cena. Y ahora, mezclemos el vino con las rosas de tus versos. Te escuchamos.

*(*RUBÉN *se recoge estremecido, el gesto de ídolo, evocador de terrores y misterios.* MAX ESTRELLA, *un poco enfático, le alarga la mano. Llena los vasos* DON LATINO. RUBÉN *sale de su meditación con la tristeza vasta y enorme esculpida en los ídolos aztecas.*[262]*)*

RUBÉN. Veré si recuerdo una peregrinación a Compostela[263] . . . Son mis últimos versos.

MAX. ¿Se han publicado? Si se han publicado, me los habrán leído, pero en tu boca serán nuevos.

RUBÉN. Posiblemente no me acordaré.

(Un joven que escribe en la mesa vecina, y al parecer traduce, pues tiene ante los ojos un libro abierto y cuartillas en rimero, se inclina tímidamente hacia RUBÉN DARÍO.*)*

EL JOVEN. Maestro, donde usted no recuerde, yo podría apuntarle.

RUBÉN. ¡Admirable!

MAX. ¿Dónde se han publicado?

EL JOVEN. Yo los he leído manuscritos. Iban a ser publicados en una revista que murió antes de nacer.

MAX. ¿Sería una revista de Paco Villaespesa?[264]

EL JOVEN. Yo he sido su secretario.

DON LATINO. Un gran puesto.

MAX. Tú no tienes nada que envidiar, Latino.

EL JOVEN. ¿Se acuerda usted, maestro?

*(*RUBÉN *asiente con un gesto sacerdotal, y tras de humedecer los labios en la copa, recita lento y cadencioso, como en sopor, y destaca su esfuerzo por distinguir de eses y cedas.*[265]*)*

MAX. In God?
RUBÉN. And in Christ!
MAX. And in the flames of Hell?
RUBÉN. And even more in the sounds of Heaven![261]
MAX. Rubén, you're a fraud.
RUBÉN. Maybe naive.
MAX. You're not posing?
RUBÉN. No!
MAX. For me, there's nothing beyond the final grimace. If there is anything, I'll come back and tell you.
RUBÉN. Quiet, Max, let's not break the seals of our humanity!
MAX. Rubén, remember this meal. And now, let's mix the wine with the roses of your verse. We're listening.

*(*RUBÉN, *pulls himself together with a shudder, his gesture that of an idol evoking terrors and mysteries.* MAX ESTRELLA, *somewhat emphatically, extends his hand to him.* DON LATINO *fills their glasses.* RUBÉN *emerges from his meditation with the vast and enormous sadness that is sculptured into the Aztec idols.*[262]*)*

RUBÉN. I'll see if I can remember a 'Pilgrimage to Compostella'[263] . . . This is my latest poem.
MAX. Has it been published? If it has been published, I will have heard it read, but in your mouth it will sound new.
RUBÉN. It's possible I may not remember.

(A young man who is writing at the adjacent table, and apparently translating since he has before his eyes an open book and a stack of paper, leans shyly towards RUBÉN DARÍO.*)*

THE YOUTH. Maestro, wherever you might not remember, I could prompt you.
RUBÉN. Exquisite!
MAX. Where has it been published?
THE YOUTH. I read it in manuscript. It was going to be published in a review that died before it was born.
MAX. Could that be Paco Villaespesa's[264] review?
THE YOUTH. I was his secretary.
DON LATINO. A fine post.
MAX. You have nothing to be jealous of, Latino.
THE YOUTH. Do you remember, maestro?

*(*RUBÉN *assents with a sacerdotal gesture, and after moistening his lips in his glass, recites in slow cadences, as if asleep, and emphasizes his effort to distinguish the s's and z's.*[265]*)*

RUBÉN. ¡¡¡La ruta tocaba a su fin,
en el rincón de un quicio oscuro,
nos repartimos un pan duro
con el Marqués de Bradomín!!![266]

EL JOVEN. Es el final, maestro.

RUBÉN. Es la ocasión para beber por nuestro estelar amigo.

MAX. ¡Ha desaparecido del mundo!

RUBÉN. Se prepara a la muerte en su aldea, y su carta de despedida fue la ocasión de estos versos. ¡Bebamos a la salud de un exquisito pecador!

MAX. ¡Bebamos!

(Levanta su copa, y gustando el aroma del ajenjo, suspira y evoca el cielo lejano de París. Piano y violín atacan un aire de opereta, y la parroquia del café lleva el compás con las cucharillas en los vasos. Después de beber, los tres desterrados confunden sus voces hablando en francés. Recuerdan y proyectan las luces de la fiesta divina y mortal. ¡París![267] ¡Cabarets! ¡Ilusión! Y en el ritmo de las frases, desfila, con su pata coja, PAPÁ VERLAINE.[268]*)*

ESCENA DÉCIMA

(Paseo con jardines.[269] El cielo raso y remoto. La luna lunera.[270] Patrullas de caballería. Silencioso y luminoso, rueda un auto. En la sombra clandestina de los ramajes, merodean mozuelas pingonas y viejas pintadas como caretas. Repartidos por las sillas del paseo, yacen algunos bultos durmientes. MAX ESTRELLA *y* DON LATINO *caminan bajo las sombras del paseo. El perfume primaveral de las lilas embalsama la humedad de la noche.)*

UNA VIEJA PINTADA. ¡Morenos! ¡Chis! . . . ¡Morenos! ¿Queréis venir un ratito?

DON LATINO. Cuando te pongas los dientes.

LA VIEJA PINTADA. ¡No me dejáis siquiera un pitillo!

DON LATINO. Te daré *La Corres*, para que te ilustres; publica una carta de Maura.[271]

LA VIEJA PINTADA. Que le den morcilla.[272]

DON LATINO. Se la prohibe el rito judaico.[273]

LA VIEJA PINTADA. ¡Mira el camelista! Esperaros, que llamo a una amiguita. ¡Lunares! ¡Lunares!

RUBÉN. The road was reaching its end,
and in the obscure corner of a door hinge,
we were dividing a stale loaf
with the Marquis of Bradomín.[266]

THE YOUTH. That's the ending, maestro.

RUBÉN. It's the occasion to drink to our sidereal friend.

MAX. He has vanished from this world.

RUBÉN. He is preparing for death in his village, and his farewell letter occasioned these lines. Let's drink to the health of an exquisite sinner!

MAX. Let's drink!

(He raises his glass, and savouring the aroma of absinth, sighs and evokes the distant sky of Paris. Piano and violin attack an air from an operetta, and the café's clientele keeps the beat with the spoons on their glasses. After drinking, the voices of the three exiles are heard together speaking in French. They recall and project the lights of the divine and mortal feast. Paris![267] *Cabarets! Illusion! And to the rhythm of the phrases, there parades with his club foot,* PAPA VERLAINE.[268]*)*

SCENE TEN

(A path among flower beds in a park.[269] *The sky, clear and remote. The moon, 'moonish'.*[270] *Cavalry patrols. A motor-car rolls silently and luminously by. Ragged young broads and old hags painted like masks prowl about searching for customers in the clandestine shadows of the foliage. Some sleeping shapes are scattered here and there on the park benches.* MAX ESTRELLA *and* DON LATINO *walk in the shadows of the drive. The spring-like perfume of lilacs invades the night's humidity.)*

OLD HAG. Eh, dark and handsome! Psst! Handsome! Would you like to come here for a while?

DON LATINO. When you put some teeth in.

OLD HAG. Can't you at least spare a cigarette?

DON LATINO. I'll give you the *Messenger* instead so you can educate yourself; it carries a letter by Maura.[271]

OLD HAG. Screw him with a sausage.[272]

DON LATINO. The Judaic rite forbids it.[273]

OLD HAG. Listen to the flirt! Wait a minute and I'll call a friend, Beauty Spot! Beauty Spot!

(Surge LA LUNARES, *una mozuela pingona, medias blancas, delantal, toquilla y alpargatas. Con risa desvergonzada se detiene en la sombra del jardinillo.)*

LA LUNARES. ¡Ay, qué pollos más elegantes! Vosotros me sacáis esta noche de la calle.

LA VIEJA PINTADA. Nos ponen piso.

LA LUNARES. Dejadme una perra, y me completáis una peseta para la cama.

LA VIEJA PINTADA. ¡Roñas, siquiera un pitillo!

MAX. Toma un habano.

LA VIEJA PINTADA. ¡Guasíbilis![274]

LA LUNARES. Apáñalo, panoli.[275]

LA VIEJA PINTADA. ¡Sí que lo apaño! ¡Y es de sortija![276]

LA LUNARES. Ya me permitirás alguna chupada.

LA VIEJA PINTADA. Éste me lo guardo.

LA LUNARES. Para el Rey de Portugal.[277]

LA VIEJA PINTADA. ¡Infeliz! ¡Para el de la Higiene![278]

LA LUNARES. ¿Y vosotros, astrónomos,[279] no hacéis una calaverada?

(Las dos prójimas han evolucionado sutiles y clandestinas, bajo las sombras del paseo. LA VIEJA PINTADA *está a la vera de* DON LATINO DE HISPALIS. LA LUNARES, *a la vera de* MALA ESTRELLA.*)*

LA LUNARES. ¡Mira qué limpios llevo los bajos!

MAX. Soy ciego.

LA LUNARES. ¡Algo verás!

MAX. ¡Nada!

LA LUNARES. Tócame. Estoy muy dura.

MAX. ¡Un mármol!

(La mozuela, con una risa procaz, toma la mano del poeta, y la hace tantear sobre sus hombros, y la oprime sobre los senos. La vieja sórdida, bajo la máscara de albayalde, descubre las encías sin dientes, y tienta capciosa a DON LATINO.*)*

LA VIEJA PINTADA. Hermoso, vente conmigo, que ya tu compañero se entiende con la Lunares. No te receles. ¡Ven! Si se acerca algún guindilla, lo apartamos con el puro habanero.

(Se lo lleva sonriendo, blanca y fantasmal. Cuchicheos. Se pierden entre los árboles del jardín. Parodia grotesca del Jardín de Armida.[280] MALA ESTRELLA *y la otra prójima quedan aislados sobre la orilla del paseo.)*

(Out comes BEAUTY SPOT, *a young tart in rags, white stockings, apron, old shawl and hemp sandals. She stops in the shadow of the small garden and laughs brazenly.)*

BEAUTY SPOT. My, what elegant peacocks! You'll rescue me from the streets tonight.

OLD HAG. They'll furnish our house.

BEAUTY SPOT. A few coins for me and all's done if you pay for the bed.

OLD HAG. Misers, not even a puff!

MAX. Here, have a cigar.

OLD HAG. Joker![274]

BEAUTY SPOT. Get hold of it, silly.[275]

OLD HAG. I'll pick it up alright! It's got a band on it![276]

BEAUTY SPOT. You'll let me have a puff, won't you?

OLD HAG. I'm holding on to this one.

BEAUTY SPOT. For the King of Portugal.[277]

OLD HAG. You dummy! For the Health Inspector.[278]

BEAUTY SPOT. And you my star-gazers,[279] aren't you in the mood for something reckless?

(Subtly and clandestinely, the two harlots have evolved out of the shadows of the path. The OLD HAG *stands next to* DON LATINO DE HISPALIS; BEAUTY SPOT, *beside* ILL-STAR.*)*

BEAUTY SPOT. See how clean my petticoat is!

MAX. I'm blind.

BEAUTY SPOT. You must see something!

MAX. Nothing.

BEAUTY SPOT. Feel me. I'm real hard.

MAX. Like marble.

(The young tart, with licentious laughter, takes the poet's hand, slides it over her shoulders and presses it hard against her breast. The OLD HAG *shows her toothless gums under her whitewashed mask, and craftily tempts* DON LATINO.*)*

OLD HAG. Handsome, come along with me; your pal is getting along fine with Beauty Spot. Don't be shy! Come along! If a copper comes along, we'll get rid of him with this Havana cigar.

(She takes him away smiling, white and ghostly, whispering. They are lost among the garden trees. A grotesque parody of the 'Garden of Armida'.[280] MAX ILL-STAR *and the other prostitute are left isolated at the edge of the public walk.)*

LA LUNARES. Pálpame el pecho . . . No tengas reparo . . . ¡Tú eres un poeta!

MAX. ¿En qué lo has conocido?

LA LUNARES. En la peluca de Nazareno.[281] ¿Me engaño?

MAX. No te engañas.

LA LUNARES. Si cuadrase que yo te pusiese al tanto de mi vida, sacabas una historia de las primeras. Responde: ¿Cómo me encuentras?

MAX. ¡Una ninfa!

LA LUNARES. ¡Tienes el hablar muy dilustrado![282] Tu acompañante ya se concertó con la Cotillona. Ven. Entrégame la mano. Vamos a situarnos en un lugar más oscuro. Verás cómo te cachondeo.

MAX. Llévame a un banco para esperar a ese cerdo hispalense.

LA LUNARES. No chanelo.[283]

MAX. Hispalis es Sevilla.

LA LUNARES. Lo será en cañí. Yo soy chamberilera.[284]

MAX. ¿Cuántos años tienes?

LA LUNARES. Pues no sé los que tengo.

MAX. ¿Y es siempre aquí tu parada nocturna?

LA LUNARES. Las más de las veces.

MAX. ¡Te ganas honradamente la vida!

LA LUNARES. Tú no sabes con cuántos trabajos. Yo miro mucho lo que hago. La Cotillona me habló para llevarme a una casa. ¡Una casa de mucho postín! No quise ir . . . Acostarme no me acuesto . . . Yo guardo el pan de higos para el gachó que me sepa camelar.[285] ¿Por qué no lo pretendes?

MAX. Me falta tiempo.

LA LUNARES. Inténtalo para ver lo que sacas. Te advierto que me estás gustando.

MAX. Te advierto que soy un poeta sin dinero.

LA LUNARES. ¿Serías tú, por un casual, el que sacó las coplas de Joselito?[286]

MAX. ¡Ése soy!

LA LUNARES. ¿De verdad?

MAX. De verdad.

LA LUNARES. Dilas . . .

MAX. No las recuerdo.

BEAUTY SPOT. Feel my breasts . . . go on . . . don't be bashful . . . You're a poet!

MAX. How did you find out?

BEAUTY SPOT. By your Nazarene wig.[281] Am I wrong?

MAX. You're not wrong.

BEAUTY SPOT. If I'd only bother to give you the inside dope on my life, you'd get a first rate story. Answer me: how do you find me?

MAX. A nymph!

BEAUTY SPOT. You've got a very educated[282] speech! Your pal has already got off with the Gossiper. Come on. Give me your hand. Let's find a darker place. You'll see how I'll work you up.

MAX. Take me to a bench where I can wait for that Hispalic swine.

BEAUTY SPOT. I don't get what you mean.[283]

MAX. Hispalis, that's Seville.

BEAUTY SPOT. In gypsy gobbledegook maybe. I'm from the cheap side of town.[284]

MAX. How old are you?

BEAUTY SPOT. I don't know how old.

MAX. And is this here always your night beat?

BEAUTY SPOT. Most of the time.

MAX. You at least earn your living honourably.

BEAUTY SPOT. You can't imagine how hard I work. And I keep an eye on what I do. A madam wanted to take me into her house. A very chic brothel! I refused to go . . . This lying flat on my back, nothing doing . . . I always save my best cake for the fellow who knows how to sweet-talk me.[285] Why don't you have a try?

MAX. I haven't time.

BEAUTY SPOT. Try just to see what you can do. I'm telling you that I like you more and more.

MAX. And I tell you that I'm a penniless poet.

BEAUTY SPOT. Would you by chance be the guy who wrote the song about the bullfighter Joselito?[286]

MAX. I'm the one!

BEAUTY SPOT. Did you really?

MAX. Really.

BEAUTY SPOT. Recite it . . .

MAX. I don't remember it.

LA LUNARES. Porque no las sacaste de tu sombrerera. Sin mentira, ¿cuáles son las tuyas?

MAX. Las del Espartero.

LA LUNARES. ¿Y las recuerdas?

MAX. Y las canto como un flamenco.[287]

LA LUNARES. ¡Que no eres capaz!

MAX. ¡Tuviera yo una guitarra!

LA LUNARES. ¿La entiendes?

MAX. Para algo soy ciego.

LA LUNARES. ¡Me estás gustando!

MAX. No tengo dinero.

LA LUNARES. Con pagar la cama concluyes. Si quedas contento y quieres convidarme a un café con churros, tampoco me niego.

*(*MÁXIMO ESTRELLA, *con tacto de ciego, le pasa la mano por el óvalo del rostro, la garganta y los hombros. La pindonga ríe con dejo sensual de cosquillas. Quítase del moño un peinecillo gitano, y con él peinando los tufos, redobla la risa y se desmadeja.)*

LA LUNARES. ¿Quieres saber cómo soy? ¡Soy muy negra y muy fea!

MAX. ¡No lo pareces! Debes tener quince años.

LA LUNARES. Esos mismos tendré. Ya pasa de tres que me visita el nuncio.[288] No lo pienses más y vamos. Aquí cerca hay una casa muy decente.

MAX. ¿Y cumplirás tu palabra?

LA LUNARES. ¿Cuála? ¿Dejar que te comas el pan de higos? ¡No me pareces bastante flamenco![289] ¡Qué mano tienes! No me palpes más la cara. Pálpame el cuerpo.

MAX. ¿Eres pelinegra?

LA LUNARES. ¡Lo soy!

MAX. Hueles a nardos.

LA LUNARES. Porque los he vendido.

MAX. ¿Cómo tienes los ojos?

LA LUNARES. ¿No lo adivinas?

MAX. ¿Verdes?

LA LUNARES. Como la Pastora Imperio.[290] Toda yo parezco una gitana.

BEAUTY SPOT. Because you didn't pull it out of your own hat-box. All kidding apart, which songs are yours?

MAX. The lines about Espartero.

BEAUTY SPOT. Do you remember them?

MAX. And I sing them like a flamenco.[287]

BEAUTY SPOT. I bet you can't!

MAX. If I only had a guitar!

BEAUTY SPOT. Can you handle it?

MAX. I'm not blind for nothing.

BEAUTY SPOT. I'm really getting to like you!

MAX. I've got no money.

BEAUTY SPOT. Just pay for the bed, and that'll be all. If you're satisfied with me and you like to treat me to a coffee with doughnuts, I won't refuse you either.

(MÁXIMO ESTRELLA, *with the special fingering of a blind man, moves his hand over her round face, her neck and shoulders. The little tart laughs with an abandon of ticklish sensuality. She removes a gypsy comb from her bun and while combing her hair, she quickens her laughter and grows languorous.)*

BEAUTY SPOT. Would you like to know how old I am? I'm very black and very ugly!

MAX. You don't seem to be. You must be fifteen years old.

BEAUTY SPOT. That's exactly my age. It's been only three years since I had my annunciation.[288] Stop thinking about it and let's go. There's a very decent house nearby.

MAX. And you're going to keep your word?

BEAUTY SPOT. Which one? Let you taste my cake? You don't seem flamenco enough to me.[289] But what a hand you have! Stop feeling my face. Feel my body.

MAX. Is your hair black?

BEAUTY SPOT. It is!

MAX. You smell of orange-blossoms.

BEAUTY SPOT. Because I was selling them.

MAX. What kind of eyes do you have?

BEAUTY SPOT. Can't you guess?

MAX. Green?

BEAUTY SPOT. Like those of Pastora Imperio the dancer.[290] Every bit of me is like a gypsy.

(De la oscuridad surge la brasa de un cigarro y la tos asmática de DON LATINO. *Remotamente, sobre el asfalto sonoro, se acompaña el trote de una patrulla de Caballería. Los focos de un auto. El farol de un sereno. El quicio de una verja. Una sombra clandestina. El rostro albayalde de otra vieja peripatética.*[291] *Diferentes sombras.)*

ESCENA UNDÉCIMA[292]

(Una calle del Madrid austríaco.[293] *Las tapias de un convento. Un casón de nobles. Las luces de una taberna. Un grupo consternado de vecinas, en la acera. Una mujer, despechugada y ronca, tiene en los brazos a su niño muerto, la sien traspasada por el agujero de una bala.*[294] MAX ESTRELLA *y* DON LATINO *hacen un alto.)*

MAX. También aquí se pisan cristales rotos.[295]
DON LATINO. ¡La zurra ha sido buena!
MAX. ¡Canallas! . . . ¡Todos! . . . ¡Y los primeros nosotros, los poetas!
DON LATINO. ¡Se vive de milagro!
LA MADRE DEL NIÑO. ¡Maricas, cobardes! ¡El fuego del Infierno os abrase las negras entrañas! ¡Maricas, cobardes!
MAX. ¿Qué sucede, Latino? ¿Quién llora? ¿Quién grita con tal rabia?
DON LATINO. Una verdulera, que tiene a su chico muerto en los brazos.
MAX. ¡Me ha estremecido esa voz trágica!
LA MADRE. ¡Sicarios! ¡Asesinos de criaturas!
EL EMPEÑISTA. Está con algún trastorno, y no mide palabras.
EL GUARDIA. La Autoridad también se hace el cargo.
EL TABERNERO. Son desgracias para el restablecimiento del orden.
EL EMPEÑISTA. Las turbas anárquicas me han destrozado el escaparate.
LA PORTERA. ¿Cómo no anduvo usted más vivo en echar los cierres?
EL EMPEÑISTA. Me tomó el tumulto fuera de casa. Supongo que se acordará el pago de daños a la propiedad privada.
EL TABERNERO. El pueblo que roba en los establecimientos

(The red amber of a cigarette and the asthmatic cough of DON LATINO *emerge from the darkness. The trot of the Cavalry patrol is heard distinctly on the echoing asphalt. Lights of a car, the lantern of a night-watchman. The hinge of an iron gate. A clandestine shadow. The whitish face of another, peripatetic old hag.*[291] *Various shadowy forms.)*

SCENE ELEVEN[292]

(A street of Austrian Madrid.[293] *The garden walls of a convent. An aristocrat's residence. The lights of a tavern. On the pavement, a distressed group of women from the area. A woman, her breast bare and her voice hoarse, holds in her arms a dead child, its temple riddled with a bullet-hole.*[294] MAX ESTRELLA *and* DON LATINO *come to a sudden stop.)*

MAX. Here too we're stepping on broken glass.[295]

DON LATINO. It must've been a good scuffle!

MAX. Scum! All of them! . . . We the poets more than anybody.

DON LATINO. One lives on miracles!

MOTHER. Queers, cowards! May the fire of Hell burn out your black entrails! Queers, cowards!

MAX. What's going on, Latino? Who's crying? Who's yelling in such a raging passion?

DON LATINO. A vegetable vendor holding a dead child in her arms.

MAX. That tragic voice has shattered me.

MOTHER. Hired assassins! Killers of children!

PAWNBROKER. She's a little upset and doesn't know what she's saying.

THE POLICEMAN. The authorities take all this into account.

BAR OWNER. These are unfortunate accidents in the efforts to re-establish law and order.

PAWNBROKER. Those damned anarchist mobs destroyed my shop-window.

CONCIERGE. How was it you didn't lower the metal shutters sooner?

PAWNBROKER. I was away from home when the scuffle began. I suppose that they'll agree to pay for damages to private property.

BAR OWNER. People who loot public establishments, which

públicos donde se le abastece es un pueblo sin ideales patrios.

LA MADRE. ¡Verdugos del hijo de mis entrañas!

UN ALBAÑIL. El pueblo tiene hambre.

EL EMPEÑISTA. Y mucha soberbia.

LA MADRE. ¡Maricas, cobardes!

UNA VIEJA. ¡Ten prudencia, Romualda!

LA MADRE. ¡Que me maten como a este rosal de mayo!

LA TRAPERA. ¡Un inocente sin culpa! ¡Hay que considerarlo!

EL TABERNERO. Siempre saldréis diciendo que no hubo toques de Ordenanza.

EL RETIRADO. Yo los he oído.

LA MADRE. ¡Mentira!

EL RETIRADO. Mi palabra es sagrada.

EL EMPEÑISTA. El dolor te enloquece, Romualda.

LA MADRE. ¡Asesinos! ¡Veros es ver al verdugo!

EL RETIRADO. El principio de Autoridad es inexorable.

EL ALBAÑIL. Con los pobres. Se ha matado, por defender al comercio, que nos chupa la sangre.

EL TABERNERO. Y que paga sus contribuciones, no hay que olvidarlo.

EL EMPEÑISTA. El comercio honrado no chupa la sangre de nadie.

LA PORTERA. ¡Nos quejamos de vicio!

EL ALBAÑIL. La vida del proletario no representa nada para el Gobierno.

MAX. Latino, sácame de este círculo infernal.

(Llega un tableteo de fusilada. El grupo se mueve en confusa y medrosa alerta. Descuella el grito ronco de la mujer, que al ruido de las descargas aprieta a su niño muerto en los brazos.)

LA MADRE. ¡Negros fusiles, matadme también con vuestros plomos!

MAX. Esa voz me traspasa.

LA MADRE. ¡Que tan fría, boca de nardo!

MAX. ¡Jamás oí voz con esa cólera trágica!

DON LATINO. Hay mucho de teatro.

MAX. ¡Imbécil!

(El farol, el chuzo, la caperuza del sereno, bajan con un trote de madreñas por la acera.)

are there only to serve others, are people with no patriotic feeling.

MOTHER. Butchers of the darling of my heart!

MASON. The common people are hungry.

PAWNBROKER. And very arrogant.

MOTHER. Queers, cowards!

OLD WOMAN. Be prudent, Romualda!

MOTHER. Let them kill me as they killed this little rosebud of May!

RAG-WOMAN. Innocent like a lamb! Must take that into account.

BAR OWNER. I suppose you'll now claim that there were no alarm warnings.

RETIRED OFFICER. I myself heard them.

MOTHER. It's a lie!

RETIRED OFFICER. My word is sacred!

PAWNBROKER. Grief is driving you stark crazy, Romualda.

MOTHER. Murderers! To look at you is to look at hangmen!

RETIRED OFFICER. The principle of Authority is unrelenting.

MASON. Against the poor. We're getting killed to protect the merchants who keep on sucking our blood.

BAR OWNER. And who happen to pay their taxes. Take that into account too.

PAWNBROKER. Honest merchants don't suck the blood of anyone.

CONCIERGE. We obviously have no cause to complain!

MASON. A worker's life means nothing to the Government.

MAX. Latino, get me out of this circle of Hell.

(A rattling tac, tac, tac of shots is heard. The group moves about warily, confused and frightened. The hoarse cries of the mother rise higher as, on hearing the shooting, she presses her dead child against her breast.)

MOTHER. Come, you black rifles, kill me too with your lead bullets!

Max. That voice pierces me like a knife.

MOTHER. How cold you feel, rose lips!

MAX. I've never heard a voice with such tragic fury.

DON LATINO. I'll admit it's a good performance.

MAX. Imbecile!

(Coming down the pavement, accompanied by the trot of wooden shoes, appear the night watchman's lantern, pike and pointed hood.)

EL EMPEÑISTA. ¿Qué ha sido, sereno?
EL SERENO. Un preso que ha intentado fugarse.[296]
MAX. Latino, ya no puedo gritar . . . ¡Me muero de rabia! . . . Estoy mascando ortigas. Ese muerto sabía su fin . . . No le asustaba, pero temía el tormento . . . La Leyenda Negra, en estos días menguados, es la Historia de España. Nuestra vida es un círculo dantesco. Rabia y vergüenza. Me muero de hambre, satisfecho de no haber llevado una triste velilla en la trágica mojiganga.[297] ¿Has oído los comentarios de esa gente, viejo canalla? Tú eres como ellos. Peor que ellos, porque no tienes una peseta y propagas la mala literatura por entregas. Latino, vil corredor de aventuras insulsas,[298] llévame al Viaducto.[299] Te invito a regenerarte con un vuelo.
DON LATINO. ¡Max, no te pongas estupendo!

ESCENA DUODÉCIMA

(Rinconada en costanilla y una iglesia barroca por fondo. Sobre las campanas negras, la luna clara. DON LATINO *y* MAX ESTRELLA *filosofan sentados en el quicio de una puerta. A lo largo de su coloquio, se torna lívido el cielo. En el alero de la iglesia pían algunos pájaros. Remotos albores de amanecida. Ya se han ido los serenos, pero aún están las puertas cerradas. Despiertan las porteras.)*

MAX. ¿Debe estar amaneciendo?
DON LATINO. Así es.
MAX. ¡Y qué frío!
DON LATINO. Vamos a dar unos paseos.
MAX. Ayúdame, que no puedo levantarme. ¡Estoy aterido!
DON LATINO. ¡Mira que haber empeñado la capa!
MAX. Préstame tu carrik, Latino.
DON LATINO. ¡Max, eres fantástico!
MAX. Ayúdame a ponerme en pie.
DON LATINO. ¡Arriba, carcunda![300]
MAX. ¡No me tengo!

PAWNBROKER. What's happened, watchman?

WATCHMAN. It was a prisoner attempting to escape.[296] Some Catalonian fellow.

MAX. Latino, I can't even scream anymore . . . I'm bursting with rage! I'm chewing nails. This dead man knew his fate . . . Death didn't even frighten him, but he was afraid of torture . . . In these wretched times, the 'Black Legend' is the only history of Spain. Our life is Dante's *Inferno*. I die hungry but content that I didn't bring any tiny votive candle to this tragic clowning.[297] Did you hear the comments of these people here, you old bastard? You're just like them. Worse than they are because you don't have a penny and yet you propagate and peddle lousy literature by instalments. Latino, miserable errand boy of insipid adventures,[298] lead me to the Viaduct.[299] I'm inviting you to be reborn in one spectacular plunge.

DON LATINO. Don't get too excited, Max!

SCENE TWELVE

(Corner on a steep, sloping street and a baroque church for background. Clear moon over the dark hills. DON LATINO *and* MAX ESTRELLA *philosophize, sitting on the steps of a doorway. During the course of their conversation, the sky becomes lighter. On the rooftop of the church, some birds are chirping. Distant glimmerings of day-break. The night watchmen have already left but the doors are still closed. The concierges are beginning to wake up.)*

MAX. Dawn must be breaking.

DON LATINO. It's just beginning to.

MAX. And how cold it is!

DON LATINO. Let's take a few steps.

MAX. Help me, I can't get up. I'm really numb.

DON LATINO. Well, this is what you get for pawning your cloak!

MAX. Lend me your overcoat, Latino.

DON LATINO. Max, you are incredibly fantastic.

MAX. Help me get on my feet.

DON LATINO. Up with you, you phony reactionary.[300]

MAX. I can't bend my legs.

DON LATINO. ¡Qué tuno eres!

MAX. ¡Idiota!

DON LATINO. ¡La verdad es que tienes una fisonomía algo rara!

MAX. ¡Don Latino de Hispalis, grotesco personaje, te inmortalizaré en una novela!

DON LATINO. Una tragedia, Max.

MAX. La tragedia nuestra no es tragedia.[301]

DON LATINO. ¡Pues algo será!

MAX. El Esperpento.

DON LATINO. No tuerzas la boca, Max.

MAX. ¡Me estoy helando!

DON LATINO. Levántate. Vamos a caminar.

MAX. No puedo.

DON LATINO. Deja esa farsa. Vamos a caminar.

MAX. Échame el aliento. ¿Adónde te has ido, Latino?

DON LATINO. Estoy a tu lado.

MAX. Como te han convertido en buey, no podía reconocerte. Échame el aliento, ilustre buey del pesebre belenita. ¡Muge, Latino! Tú eres el cabestro, y si muges vendrá el Buey Apis. Le torearemos.[302]

DON LATINO. Me estás asustando. Debías dejar esa broma.

MAX. Los ultraístas son unos farsantes.[303] El esperpentismo lo ha inventado Goya.[304] Los héroes clásicos han ido a pasearse en el callejón del Gato.[305]

DON LATINO. ¡Estás completamente curda!

MAX. Los héroes clásicos reflejados en los espejos cóncavos dan el Esperpento. El sentido trágico de la vida española[306] sólo puede darse con una estética sistemáticamente deformada.

DON LATINO. ¡Miau! ¡Te estás contagiando!

MAX. España es una deformación grotesca de la civilización europea.

DON LATINO. ¡Pudiera! Yo me inhibo.

MAX. Las imágenes más bellas en un espejo cóncavo son absurdas.

DON LATINO. Conforme. Pero a mí me divierte mirarme en los espejos de la calle del Gato.

MAX. Y a mí. La deformación deja de serlo cuando está sujeta a una matemática perfecta.[307] Mi estética actual es transformar con matemática de espejo cóncavo las normas clásicas.

DON LATINO. How well you fake.

MAX. Idiot!

DON LATINO. I admit that your face has a rather peculiar look.

MAX. Don Latino de Hispalis, grotesque figure, I shall make you immortal in a novel!

DON LATINO. In a tragedy, Max.

MAX. Our tragedy is no longer a tragedy.[301]

DON LATINO. But it's got to be something!

MAX. *Esperpento.*

DON LATINO. Don't twist your mouth, Max.

MAX. I'm freezing to death!

DON LATINO. Come on, get up. Let's start walking.

MAX. I can't, I tell you.

DON LATINO. Stop this farce. Let's take a walk.

MAX. Breathe hard on me. Where have you gone, Latino?

DON LATINO. I'm at your side.

MAX. Since you've been transformed into an Ox, I can't recognize you. Breathe on me, Illustrious Ox from Bethlehem's stable. Bellow, Latino! You are the bell-ox, and if you bellow hard, the Sacred Bull will appear. We'll play torero with him.[302]

DON LATINO. You're beginning to frighten me. You should drop that joke.

MAX. The avant-garde are humbugs.[303] It was Goya who invented the Grotesque.[304] The classical heroes have gone to take a stroll in Cat Alley.[305]

DON LATINO. You're completely balmy.

MAX. Classical heroes reflected in concave mirrors yield the Grotesque. The tragic sense of Spanish life[306] can be rendered only through an aesthetic that is systematically deformed.

DON LATINO. Catshit! You're about to catch that disease yourself!

MAX. Spain is a grotesque deformation of European civilization.

DON LATINO. Perhaps! I'm staying out of all this!

MAX. In a concave mirror, even the most beautiful images are absurd.

DON LATINO. Agreed. But I enjoy looking at myself in the mirrors in Cat-Alley.

MAX. Me too. Deformation stops being deformation when subjected to a perfect mathematic.[307] My present aesthetic approach is to transform all classical norms with the mathematics of the concave mirror.

DON LATINO. ¿Y dónde está el espejo?

MAX. En el fondo del vaso.[308]

DON LATINO. ¡Eres genial! ¡Me quito el cráneo!

MAX. Latino, deformemos la expresión en el mismo espejo que nos deforma las caras y toda la vida miserable de España.

DON LATINO. Nos mudaremos al callejón del Gato.

MAX. Vamos a ver qué palacio está desalquilado. Arrímame a la pared. ¡Sacúdeme!

DON LATINO. No tuerzas la boca.

MAX. Es nervioso. ¡Ni me entero!

DON LATINO. ¡Te traes una guasa![309]

MAX. Préstame tu carrik.

DON LATINO. ¡Mira cómo me he quedado de un aire!

MAX. No me siento las manos y me duelen las uñas. ¡Estoy muy malo!

DON LATINO. Quieres conmoverme, para luego tomarme la coleta.

MAX. Idiota, llévame a la puerta de mi casa y déjame morir en paz.

DON LATINO. La verdad sea dicha, no madrugan en nuestro barrio.

MAX. Llama.

*(*DON LATINO DE HISPALIS, *volviéndose de espaldas, comienza a cocear en la puerta. El eco de los golpes tolondrea por el ámbito lívido de la costanilla, y como en respuesta a una provocación, el reloj de la iglesia da cinco campanadas bajo el gallo de la veleta.)*

MAX. ¡Latino!

DON LATINO. ¿Qué antojas? ¡Deja la mueca!

MAX. ¡Si Collet estuviese despierta! . . . Ponme en pie para darle una voz.

DON LATINO. No llega tu voz a ese quinto cielo.[310]

MAX. ¡Collet! ¡Me estoy aburriendo!

DON LATINO. No olvides al compañero.

MAX. Latino, me parece que recobro la vista. ¿Pero cómo hemos venido a este entierro? ¡Esa apoteosis es de París! ¡Estamos en el entierro de Víctor Hugo![311] ¿Oye, Latino, pero cómo vamos nosotros presidiendo?

DON LATINO. And where is this mirror to be found?

MAX. At the bottom of the drinking glass.[308]

DON LATINO. You are ingenious! I take my head off to you.

MAX. Latino, let's deform style in the same mirror that distorts our faces and contorts the whole miserable life of Spain.

DON LATINO. We'll just get installed in Cat-Alley.

MAX. Let's go and see what sort of palace we can rent. Come, prop me against the wall. Shake me up.

DON LATINO. Don't twist your mouth.

MAX. It's a nervous twitch. I'm not even aware I do it.

DON LATINO. It's a poor joke to pull on me.[309]

MAX. Lend me your overcoat.

DON LATINO. And look how I'm left numb, standing in the cold.

MAX. I can't feel my hands any more and my finger tips hurt. I'm very sick.

DON LATINO. You're just trying to fool me so you can have my overcoat.

MAX. Idiot, take me to the door of my house and let me die in peace.

DON LATINO. You know well that people don't get up early around these parts.

MAX. Shout.

(DON LATINO DE HISPALIS, *turning his back on* MAX, *begins to kick and pound at the door. The echo of the blows rebounds in the ghostly enclosure of the steep, sloping street, and as if responding to some sort of provocation, the church clock strikes five times under the weathercock.*)

MAX. Latino!

DON LATINO. What's your fancy now? Stop making faces.

MAX. If Collet were only awake! Help me on to my feet so I can call her.

DON LATINO. Your voice'll never carry as far as that fifth heaven you live in.[310]

MAX. Collet! I am bored stiff!

DON LATINO. Don't forget your old pal by your side.

MAX. Latino, I think I'm recovering my sight. But how is it that you and I came to this funeral? Such an apotheosis belongs only in Paris! Ah, I get it, we're at the funeral of Victor Hugo![311] Listen, Latino . . . yet how come it's we who're presiding over this affair?

DON LATINO. No te alucines, Max.

MAX. Es incomprensible cómo veo.

DON LATINO. Ya sabes que has tenido esa misma ilusión otras veces.

MAX. ¿A quién enterramos, Latino?

DON LATINO. Es un secreto que debemos ignorar.

MAX. ¡Cómo brilla el sol en las carrozas!

DON LATINO. Max, si todo cuanto dices no fuese una broma, tendría una significación teosófica . . .[312] En un entierro presidido por mí, yo debo ser el muerto. Pero por esas coronas, me inclino a pensar que el muerto eres tú.

MAX. Voy a complacerte. Para quitarle el miedo del augurio, me acuesto a la espera. ¡Yo soy el muerto![313] ¿Qué dirá mañana esa canalla de los periódicos, se preguntaba el paria catalán?[314]

(MÁXIMO ESTRELLA *se tiende en el umbral de la puerta. Cruza la costanilla un perro golfo que corre en zigzag. En el centro, encoge la pata y se orina. El ojo legañoso, como un poeta, levantado al azul de la última estrella.)*

MAX. Latino, entona el gori-gori.[315]

DON LATINO. Si continúas con esa broma macabra, te abandono.

MAX. Yo soy el que se va para siempre.

DON LATINO. Incorpórate, Max. Vamos a caminar.

MAX. Estoy muerto.

DON LATINO. ¡Que me estás asustando! Max, vamos a caminar. Incorpórate, ¡no tuerzas la boca, condenado! ¡Max, Max! ¡Condenado, responde!

MAX. Los muertos no hablan.

DON LATINO. Definitivamente, te dejo.

MAX. ¡Buenas noches![316]

(DON LATINO DE HISPALIS *se sopla los dedos arrecidos y camina unos pasos incorporándose bajo su carrik pingón, orlado de cascarrias. Con una tos gruñona retorna al lado de* MAX ESTRELLA. *Procura incorporarle hablándole a la oreja.)*

DON LATINO. Max, estás completamente borracho y sería un crimen dejarte la cartera encima, para que te la roben. Max, me llevo tu cartera y te la devolveré mañana.

DON LATINO. Don't be hallucinated, Max.

MAX. Why, it's incredible how well I see.

DON LATINO. You know, this is not the first time you've had this vision.

MAX. Who is it we are burying, Latino?

DON LATINO. It's a secret we should keep to ourselves.

MAX. How bright the sun shines on the funeral hearse.

DON LATINO. Max, if what you are babbling were not a big joke, it would have a theosophical significance . . .[312] In a funeral presided over by me, I should be the dead one. But all these wreaths incline me to suspect that the dead one must be you.

MAX. I'll do the honours. Just to calm you a little for the fright my foreboding gave you, here I lie down in wait. Indeed, I am the dead one![313] And what will those scum newspapers report tomorrow? That's what the Catalan Outcast was asking himself.[314]

*(*MÁXIMO ESTRELLA *lies down on the threshold of the door. A stray dog running in a zig-zag, crosses the sloping street. Stopping right in the middle, he lifts his hind leg and urinates. His bleary eyes, like a poet's, raised towards the sky's last star.)*

MAX. Latino, intone the *Dies irae*.[315]

DON LATINO. If you continue with this macabre joke, I'm going.

MAX. I'm the one who's going forever.

DON LATINO. Get on your feet, Max. And let's move on.

MAX. I'm dead.

DON LATINO. You're beginning to frighten me! Max, let's walk on. Stand up and don't twist your mouth, damn you! Max, Max! Damned wretch! Answer me!

MAX. Dead people don't talk.

DON LATINO. I'm leaving you for sure.

MAX. Good night.[316]

*(*DON LATINO DE HISPALIS *blows on his benumbed fingers and takes a few steps, straightening up under his tattered jacket which is splattered with spots of dry mud. With a grumpy cough, he comes back to* MAX ESTRELLA*'s side. He tries to prop him up a little, all the while talking in his ear.)*

DON LATINO. Max, you're dead drunk and it'd be a crime to leave this wallet on you and let someone rob you. Max, I'll hold your wallet till tomorrow.

(Finalmente se eleva tras de la puerta la voz achulada de una vecina. Resuenan pasos dentro del zaguán. DON LATINO *se cuela por un callejón.)*

LA VOZ DE LA VECINA. ¡Señá Flora! ¡Señá Flora![317] Se le han apegado a usted las mantas de la cama.

LA VOZ DE LA PORTERA. ¿Quién es? Esperarse que encuentre la caja de mixtos.

LA VECINA. ¡Señá Flora!

LA PORTERA. Ahora salgo. ¿Quién es?

LA VECINA. ¡Está usted marmota! ¿Quién será? ¡La Cuca, que se camina al lavadero!

LA PORTERA. ¡Ay, qué centella de mixtos! ¿Son horas?

LA VECINA. ¡Son horas y pasan de serlo!

(Se oye el paso cansino de una mujer en chanclas. Sigue el murmullo de las voces. Rechina la cerradura, y aparecen en el hueco de la puerta dos mujeres: La una, canosa, viva y agalgada, con un saco de ropa cargado sobre la cadera. La otra, jamona, refajo colorado, pañuelo pingón sobre los hombros, greñas y chancletas. El cuerpo del bohemio resbala y queda acostado sobre el umbral al abrirse la puerta.)

LA VECINA. ¡Santísimo Cristo, un hombre muerto!

LA PORTERA. Es Don Max el poeta, que la ha pescado.[318]

LA VECINA. ¡Está del color de la cera!

LA PORTERA. Cuca, por tu alma, quédate a la mira un instante, mientras subo el aviso a Madama Collet.

*(*LA PORTERA *sube la escalera chancleando. Se la oye renegar.* LA CUCA, *viéndose sola, con aire medroso, toca las manos del bohemio y luego se inclina a minarle los ojos entreabiertos bajo la frente lívida.)*

LA VECINA. ¡Santísimo Señor! ¡Esto no lo dimana la bebida! ¡La muerte talmente representada! ¡Señá Flora! ¡Señá Flora! ¡Que no puedo demorarme! ¡Ya se me voló un cuarto de día! Que se queda esto a la vindicta pública, señá Flora! ¡Propia la muerte!

(Finally from behind the door the rough voice of a tenant is heard. The echo of steps within the hall. DON LATINO *trails off down an alley.)*

TENANT'S VOICE. Seña Flora, Ma'm! Seña Flora, Ma'm![317] You're certainly nailed to your bed!

CONCIERGE'S VOICE. Who is it? Wait till I get the box of matches.

TENANT. Seña Flora, Ma'm!

CONCIERGE. I'm coming out right now. Who is it?

TENANT. What a sluggard you are . . . who else can it be? Cuca, on my way to the laundry.

CONCIERGE. Ah! These cursed matches! But is it time already?

TENANT. It's time all right, and long past it.

(The tired steps of a woman in slippers are heard. There follows a murmur of voices. The lock grates, and in the hollow space of the door, two women emerge: the one, whitehaired, lively and as skinny as a greyhound, with a bag of clothes propped on her hip. The other one, chubby and middle-aged with frayed reddish skirt, ragged shawl around her shoulders, tangled mop of hair and slippers. The Bohemian's body slides over and remains still on the threshold as the door opens.)

TENANT. Blessed Jesus! A dead man!

CONCIERGE. It's Don Máximo the poet who's been dragged here drunk.[318]

TENANT. He has a waxen look!

CONCIERGE. Listen, Cuca, for the good of your soul, keep an eye on things for a minute. I'll run up and tell Madame Collet.

(The CONCIERGE *goes up the street stairs with her slippers clacking. One can hear her cursing.* CUCA, *left alone, somewhat afraid, touches the Bohemian's hands and then leans over to peer at his half-open eyes under his livid forehead.)*

TENANT. Good Lord! Such a thing doesn't come from drinking! It's death alright, painted true to life! Seña Flora, Ma'm! Seña Flora, Ma'm! I simply can't wait around anymore. I've already lost half a day! Let the public authorities take care of it! And to put such a horror on display! Seña Flora, Ma'm! It's Death itself!

ESCENA DECIMOTERCIA[319]

(Velorio en un sotabanco. MADAMA COLLET *y* CLAUDINITA, *desgreñadas y macilentas, lloran al muerto, ya tendido en la angostura de la caja, amortajado con una sábana, entre cuatro velas. Astillando una tabla, el brillo de un clavo aguza su punta sobre la sien inerme.*[320] *La caja, embetunada de luto por fuera, y por dentro, de tablas de pino sin labrar ni pintar, tiene una sórdida esterilla que amarillea. Está posada sobre las baldosas, de esquina a esquina, y las dos mujeres, que lloran en los ángulos, tienen en las manos cruzadas el reflejo de las velas.* DORIO DE GADEX, CLARINITO *y* PÉREZ, *arrimados a la pared, son tres fúnebres fantoches en hilera. Repentinamente, entrometiéndose en el duelo, cloquea un rajado repique, la campanilla de la escalera.)*

DORIO. A las cuatro viene la funeraria.

CLARINITO. No puede ser esa hora.

DORIO. ¿Usted no tendrá reloj, Madama Collet?

MADAMA COLLET. ¡Que no me lo lleven todavía! ¡Que no me lo lleven!

PÉREZ. No puede ser la funeraria.

DORIO. ¡Ninguno tiene reloj! ¡No hay duda de que somos unos potentados!

*(*CLAUDINITA, *con andar cansado, trompicando, ha salido para abrir la puerta. Se oye rumor de voces y la tos de* DON LATINO DE HISPALIS. *La tos clásica del tabaco y del aguardiente.)*

DON LATINO. ¡Ha muerto el Genio! ¡No llores, hija mía! ¡Ha muerto y no ha muerto!... ¡El Genio es inmortal!... ¡Consuélate, Claudinita, porque eres la hija del primer poeta español! ¡Que te sirva de consuelo saber que eres la hija de Víctor Hugo! ¡Una huérfana ilustre! ¡Déjame que te abrace!

CLAUDINITA. ¡Usted está borracho!

DON LATINO. Lo parezco. Sin duda lo parezco. ¡Es el dolor!

CLAUDINITA. ¡Si tumba el vaho de aguardiente!

DON LATINO. ¡Es el dolor! ¡Un efecto del dolor, estudiado científicamente por los alemanes!

*(*DON LATINO *tambaléase en la puerta, con el cartapacio de las revistas en banderola y el perrillo sin rabo y sin orejas, entre las*

SCENE THIRTEEN[319]

(A funeral gathering in a garret. MADAME COLLET *and* CLAUDINITA, *dishevelled and wan, weep for the deceased who is already stretched in the narrowness of the coffin, shrouded in a sheet, between four candles. Splintering a board, the shiny tip of a nail points at the deceased's inanimate temple.*[320] *The casket is covered on the outside with black as if in mourning while the rough, unpainted pine boards inside are covered by a sordid yellowing mat. The casket is set on the tiled floor while the two women who are weeping at the two corners receive the reflection of the candles on their crossed hands.* DORIO DE GADEX, CLARINITO *and* PEREZ, *leaning against the wall, are three funeral puppets lined up one after the other. Suddenly, all mourning is interrupted by the rippling sound of the door bell's tinkle.)*

DORIO. The undertaker is coming at four.

CLARINITO. It can't be that time already.

DORIO. Do you happen to have a watch, Madame Collet?

Mme COLLET. Don't let them take him away from me yet! Don't let them carry him off!

PEREZ. It can't possibly be the undertaker.

DORIO. No one has a watch! No doubt about it: we're a fine lot of potentates!

(CLAUDINITA, *with a slow, tired walk, stumbling a little, has left to answer the door. There is a buzz of voices and the cough of* DON LATINO DE HISPANIA. *The classic cough of tobacco and brandy.)*

DON LATINO. The Genius is dead! Don't cry, my dear child! He has died and he has not died! . . . Genius is immortal! . . . Console yourself Claudinita because you're lucky to be the daughter of Spain's leading poet! You should be consoled knowing that you're the daughter of Victor Hugo! An illustrious orphan! Let me embrace you!

CLAUDINITA. You're drunk!

DON LATINO. It only looks like that. Undoubtedly I seem drunk. It's my grief!

CLAUDINITA. Why your breath reeks with brandy.

DON LATINO. It's my grief! The effect of profound sorrow, a phenomenon corroborated scientifically by the Germans.

(DON LATINO *staggers toward the door carrying a satchel full of magazines slung across his back and his little tailless and*

cañotas. Trae los espejuelos alzados sobre la frente y se limpia los ojos chispones con un pañuelo mugriento.)

CLAUDINITA. Viene a dos velas.[321]

DORIO. Para el funeral. ¡Siempre correcto!

DON LATINO. Max, hermano mío, si menor en años...

DORIO. Mayor en prez. Nos adivinamos.

DON LATINO. ¡Justamente! Tú lo has dicho, bellaco.

DORIO. Antes lo había dicho el maestro.

DON LATINO. ¡Madama Collet, es usted una viuda ilustre, y en medio de su intenso dolor debe usted sentirse orgullosa de haber sido la compañera del primer poeta español! ¡Murió pobre, como debe morir el Genio! ¡Max, ya no tienes una palabra para tu perro fiel! ¡Max, hermano mío, si menor en años, mayor en...

DORIO. ...prez!

DON LATINO. Ya podías haberme dejado terminar, majadero. ¡Jóvenes modernistas, ha muerto el maestro, y os llamáis todos de tú en el Parnaso Hispano-Americano! ¡Yo tenía apostado con este cadáver frío sobre cuál de los dos emprendería primero el viaje, y me ha vencido en esto como en todo! ¡Cuántas veces cruzamos la misma apuesta! ¿Te acuerdas, hermano? ¡Te has muerto de hambre, como yo voy a morir, como moriremos todos los españoles dignos! ¡Te habían cerrado todas las puertas, y te has vengado muriéndote de hambre![322] ¡Bien hecho! ¡Que caiga esa vergüenza sobre los cabrones de la Academia![323] ¡En España es un delito el talento!

(DON LATINO *se dobla y besa la frente del muerto. El perrillo, a los pies de la caja, entre el reflejo inquietante de las velas, agita el muñón del rabo.* MADAMA COLLET *levanta la cabeza con un gesto doloroso dirigido a los tres fantoches en hilera.)*

MADAMA COLLET. ¡Por Dios, llévenselo ustedes al pasillo!

DORIO. Habrá que darle amoniaco. ¡La trae de alivio![324]

CLAUDINITA. ¡Pues que la duerma![325] ¡Le tengo una hincha!

DON LATINO. ¡Claudinita! ¡Flor temprana!

CLAUDINITA. ¡Si papá no sale ayer tarde, está vivo!

DON LATINO. ¡Claudinita, me acusas injustamente! ¡Estás ofuscada por el dolor!

CLAUDINITA. ¡Golfo! ¡Siempre estorbando!

DON LATINO. ¡Yo sé que tú me quieres!

DORIO. Vamos a dar unas vueltas en el corredor, Don Latino.

earless dog between his skinny legs. He has his glasses raised on his forehead and wipes his bleary eyes with a filthy handkerchief.)

CLAUDINITA. He's lit up like a candle.[321]

DORIO. All for the funeral. Always sure to do the right thing.

DON LATINO. Max my brother, though less in years . . .

DORIO. Greater in worth. We anticipated each other.

DON LATINO. Exactly. You said it, you cad.

DORIO. The maestro has said it before you.

DON LATINO. Madame Collet, you're an illustrious widow, and in the midst of your intense pain you should feel proud to have been the companion of Spain's leading poet! He died poor, as Genius ought to die! Max, you no longer say a word to your loyal dog! Max, my brother, though less in years, greater in . . .

DORIO. . . . worth!

DON LATINO. You could at least have let me finish, buffoon! Young Modernists, the maestro is dead, and you address one another familiarly in the Hispano-American Parnassus! I took a bet with this cold stiff as to which one between us would be the first to undertake this final journey, and he won the bet as always! How many times did we make the same bet. Do you remember, brother? You died of hunger, as I shall, just as all we worthy Spaniards shall die of hunger! They slammed all doors in your face and you took your revenge by starving to death![322] Well done! Let this shame fall on the cuckolds of the Academy![323] In Spain, talent is a crime.

(DON LATINO *bends over and kisses the forehead of the dead man. At the foot of the coffin between the restless glimmering of the candles, the little dog shakes his stumpy tail.* MADAME COLLET *lifts her head with a painful gesture directed at the three puppets lined up in a row.)*

Mme COLLET. For heaven's sake, take him into the passageway.

DORIO. We'll have to give him smelling salts. He's been on a real spree![324]

CLAUDINITA. Well let him sleep it off![325] I loathe him.

DON LATINO. Claudinita, you accuse me unjustly. You're muddled from too much grief!

CLAUDINITA. Tramp! Always butting in!

DON LATINO. I know that you really love me!

DORIO. Let's stroll around the corridor, Don Latino.

DON LATINO. ¡Vamos! ¡Esta escena es demasiado dolorosa!

DORIO. Pues no la prolonguemos.

*(*DORIO DE GADEX *empuja al encurdado vejete y le va llevando hacia la puerta. El perrillo salta por encima de la caja y los sigue, dejando en el salto torcida una vela.*[326] *En la fila de fantoches pegados a la pared queda un hueco lleno de sugestiones.)*

DON LATINO. Te convido a unas tintas. ¿Qué dices?

DORIO. Ya sabe usted que soy un hombre complaciente, Don Latino.

(Desaparecen en la rojiza penumbra del corredor, largo y triste, con el gato al pie del botijo y el reflejo almagreño de los baldosines. CLAUDINITA *los ve salir encendidos de ira los ojos. Después se hinca a llorar con una crisis nerviosa y muerde el pañuelo que estruja entre las manos.)*

CLAUDINITA. ¡Me crispa! ¡No puedo verlo! ¡Ese hombre es el asesino de papá!

MADAMA COLLET. ¡Por Dios, hija, no digas demencias!

CLAUDINITA. El único asesino. ¡Le aborrezco!

MADAMA COLLET. Era fatal que llegase este momento, y sabes que lo esperábamos . . . Le mató la tristeza de verse ciego . . . No podía trabajar, y descansa.

CLARINITO. Verá usted cómo ahora todos reconocen su talento.

PÉREZ. Ya no proyecta sombra.

MADAMA COLLET. Sin el aplauso de ustedes, los jóvenes que luchan pasando mil miserias, hubiera estado solo estos últimos tiempos.

CLAUDINITA. ¡Más solo que estaba!

PÉREZ. El maestro era un rebelde como nosotros.[327]

MADAMA COLLET. ¡Max, pobre amigo, tú solo te mataste! ¡Tú solamente, sin acordarte de estas pobres mujeres! ¡Y toda la vida has trabajado para matarte!

CLAUDINITA. ¡Papá era muy bueno!

MADAMA COLLET. ¡Sólo fue malo para sí!

(Aparece en la puerta un hombre alto, abotonado, escueto, grandes barbas rojas de judío anarquista y ojos envidiosos, bajo el testud

DON LATINO. Let's go! This scene is simply too painful!

DORIO. Let's not prolong it then.

*(*DORIO DE GADEX *shoves the slightly drunk old fellow and leads him slowly toward the door. The little dog jumps over the coffin and follows them, knocking down one of the candles.*[326] *In the row of puppets stuck to the wall there is left a hollow space full of suggestions.)*

DON LATINO. I'll treat you to a few glasses of red. What do you say?

DORIO. You know well I'm an easy man to please, Don Latino.

(They disappear in the reddish penumbra of the long and sad corridor, with the cat at the foot of the jug and the blood-orange reflection on the tiles. CLAUDINITA *sees them going away, her eyes burning with anger. Then, hysterically, she breaks out in sobs and bites the handkerchief she's been squeezing in her hands.)*

CLAUDINITA. He makes me shudder! I can't stand looking at him. That man is father's murderer!

Mme COLLET. For God's sake child, don't say crazy things.

CLAUDINITA. The only murderer. I hate him!

Mme COLLET. This fatal moment had to come; it was inevitable and you know we were expecting it . . . The sadness of being helplessly blind, that's what killed him . . . He couldn't work, and now he rests.

CLARINITO. You'll see now how everyone will start recognizing his talent.

PÉREZ. He no longer casts a shadow.

Mme COLLET. Without the acclamation of all you young men who also struggle through a thousand miseries, he would have been alone in his final days on earth.

CLAUDINITA. Even more alone than before!

PÉREZ. The maestro was a rebel, like us.[327]

Mme COLLET. Max, my poor companion, you alone killed yourself! You did it alone, not remembering these two poor women! And all your life you've worked hard to kill yourself!

CLAUDINITA. Papa was so good!

Mme COLLET. He was only bad to himself!

(There appears at the door a tall man buttoned-up, austere, with the long, red beard of a rabbinical anarchist and envious eyes under the skull of an obstinate buffalo. He is a rascally German

de bisonte obstinado. Es un fripón periodista alemán, fichado en los registros policíacos como anarquista ruso y conocido por el falso nombre de BASILIO SOULINAKE.[328]*)*

BASILIO. ¡Paz a todos!

MADAMA COLLET. ¡Perdone usted, Basilio! ¡No tenemos siquiera una silla que ofrecerle!

BASILIO. ¡Oh! No se preocupe usted de mi persona. De ninguna manera. No lo consiento, Madama Collet. Y me dispense usted a mí[329] si llego con algún retraso, como la guardia valona[330] que dicen ustedes siempre los españoles. En la taberna donde comemos algunos emigrados eslavos, acabo de tener la referencia de que había muerto mi amigo Máximo Estrella. Me ha dado el periódico el chico de Pica Lagartos. ¿La muerte vino de improviso?

MADAMA COLLET. ¡Un colapso! No se cuidaba.

BASILIO. ¿Quién certificó la defunción? En España son muy buenos los médicos y como los mejores de otros países. Sin embargo, una autoridad completamente mundial les falta a los españoles. No es como sucede en Alemania.[331] Yo tengo estudiado durante diez años medicina y no soy doctor. Mi primera impresión al entrar aquí ha sido la de hallarme en presencia de un hombre dormido, nunca de un muerto. Y en esa primera impresión me empecino, como dicen los españoles.[332] Madama Collet, tiene usted una gran responsabilidad. ¡Mi amigo Max Estrella no está muerto! Presenta todos los caracteres de un interesante caso de catalepsia.[333]

*(*MADAMA COLLET *y* CLAUDINITA *se abrazan con un gran grito, repentinamente aguzados los ojos, manos crispadas, revolantes sobre la frente las sortijillas del pelo.* SEÑÁ FLORA, *la portera, llega acezando. La pregona el resuello y sus chancletas.)*

LA PORTERA. ¡Ahí está la carroza! ¿Son ustedes suficientes para bajar el cuerpo del finado difunto? Si no lo son, subirá mi esposo.

CLAUDINITA.[334] Gracias, nosotros nos bastamos.

BASILIO. Señora portera, usted debe comunicarle al conductor del coche fúnebre que se aplace el sepelio. Y que se vaya con viento fresco. ¿No es así como dicen ustedes los españoles?

MADAMA COLLET. ¡Que espere!... Puede usted equivocarse, Basilio.

LA PORTERA. ¡Hay bombines y javiques en la calle, y si no me engaño, un coche de galones! ¡Cuidado lo que es el mundo,

journalist, listed in police registers as a Russian anarchist, and known by the false name of BASILIO SOULINAKE.[328] *)*

BASILIO. Peace to all!

Mme COLLET. Pardon us, Basilio! We don't even have a chair to offer you!

BASILIO. Oh! Don't worry about my person. In no manner at all. I won't consent to it, Madame Collet. And you must please forgive me[329] if I come with some delay, just like the Walloon Cavalry,[330] which is what you Spaniards usually say. In the tavern where some of us immigrant Slavs eat, I've just received the communiqué that my dear friend Máximo Estrella has died. Lizard-Chopper's bar gave me the newspaper. Did his death come unexpectedly?

Mme COLLET. A sudden collapse! He didn't take good care of himself!

BASILIO. Who verified the passing away? Doctors are very good in Spain, as good as the best in other countries. Spaniards, nonetheless, lack an authority that's internationally recognized. This is not the case in Germany.[331] I've studied medicine for ten years and am not a doctor. Now my first impression when I entered here was that I was in the presence of a man asleep, not at all before a dead man. And about this first impression, I'm obstinate, as the Spaniards say.[332] Madame Collet, you have a big responsibility. My friend Max Estrella is *not* dead! He exhibits all the characteristics of an interesting case of catalepsy.[333]

*(*MADAME COLLET and CLAUDINITA *embrace each other with a big shriek, their eyes suddenly vivid, their hands contracted, and their curls fluttering on their forehead.* SEÑA FLORA, *the concierge, arrives panting. Her gasps and her old slippers announce her.)*

CONCIERGE. The coach is down there! Are there enough of you to carry down the body of the late deceased? If not, my husband can come up.

CLAUDINITA.[334] Thanks, we can handle it.

BASILIO. My dear concierge, please inform the hearse driver that the burial is postponed. And may he have a fair wind. Isn't that the way you Spaniards put it?

Mme COLLET. Have him wait! . . . You could be making a mistake, Basilio.

CONCIERGE. There are bowler hats and even frock-coats on the pavement and unless I'm mistaken, an ornate funeral

parece el entierro de un concejal! ¡No me pensaba yo que tanto representaba el finado! Madama Collet, ¿qué razón le doy al gachó de la carroza? ¡Porque ese tío no se espera! Dice que tiene otro viaje en la calle de Carlos Rubio.

MADAMA COLLET. ¡Válgame Dios! Yo estoy incierta.

LA PORTERA. ¡Cuatro Caminos![335] ¡Hay que ver, más de una legua, y no le queda tarde!

CLAUDINITA. ¡Que se vaya! ¡Que no vuelva!

MADAMA COLLET. Si no puede esperar . . . Sin duda . . .

LA PORTERA. Le cuesta a usted el doble, total por tener el fiambre unas horas más en casa. ¡Deje usted que se lo lleven, Madama Collet!

MADAMA COLLET. ¡Y si no estuviese muerto!

LA PORTERA. ¿Que no está muerto? Ustedes sin salir de este aire no perciben la corrupción que tiene.

BASILIO. ¿Podría usted decirme, señora portera, si tiene usted hechos estudios universitarios acerca de medicina? Si usted los tiene, yo me callo y no hablo más. Pero si usted no los tiene, me permitirá de no darle beligerancia, cuando yo soy a decirle que no está muerto, sino cataléptico.

LA PORTERA. ¡Que no está muerto! ¡Muerto y corrupto!

BASILIO. Usted, sin estudios universitarios, no puede tener conmigo controversia. La democracia no excluye las categorías técnicas, ya usted lo sabe, señora portera.

LA PORTERA. ¡Un rato largo! ¿Conque no está muerto? ¡Habría usted de estar como él! Madama Collet, ¿tiene usted un espejo? Se lo aplicamos a la boca, y verán ustedes como no lo alienta.

BASILIO. ¡Ésa es una comprobación anticientífica! Como dicen siempre ustedes los españoles: Un me alegro mucho de verte bueno. ¿No es así como dicen?

LA PORTERA. Usted ha venido aquí a dar un mitin y a soliviantar con alicantinas a estas pobres mujeres, que harto tienen con sus penas y sus deudas.

BASILIO. Puede usted seguir hablando, señora portera. Ya ve usted que yo no la interrumpo.[336]

(Aparece en el marco de la puerta el cochero de la carroza fúnebre: narices de borrachón, chisterón viejo con escarapela, casaca de un luto raído, peluca de estopa y canillejas negras.)

coach! What a funny world it is: you'd think it was the funeral of a Councillor! I never thought the deceased man so important! Madame Collet, what explanation can I give the coachman? Because that character will not wait! He says that he's got to make another round in Carlos Rubio street.

Mme COLLET. So help me God! I can't decide what . . .

CONCIERGE. Cuatro Caminos![335] Just think of it, it's miles away and the afternoon is almost over.

CLAUDINITA. Let him go away! We don't want him back!

Mme COLLET. If he can't wait . . . no doubt we can't . . .

CONCIERGE. It'll cost you double, and all just to keep the cold stiff in the house a few hours more. Madame Collet, let them take him away!

Mme COLLET. And if he's not dead?

CONCIERGE. Not dead? You haven't left this room so you don't notice the stench it has.

BASILIO. Could you kindly tell me, madame, if you've ever studied medicine in a University? If you have, I'll keep silent and add nothing more. But if you haven't, you will permit me not to enter into an argument with you when I tell you that he's not dead but only cataleptic.

CONCIERGE. Not dead? Why, dead and stinking!

BASILIO. You, madame, not having studied in a University, cannot dispute about such things with me. Democracy does not exclude technical categories, you at least know *that*, Madame Concierge.

CONCIERGE. Just watch this! You say he's not dead, right? You should be like him! Madame Collet, do you have a mirror? Put it in front of his mouth and you'll see how he's *not* breathing.

BASILIO. I object. Such proof is not scientific! As you Spaniards always say, it's an 'I'm very glad to see you well'. Isn't that how you put it?

CONCIERGE. You came here to hold a meeting and upset these two poor women with a hoax. They've quite enough to worry about with their sorrow and debts.

BASILIO. You can keep on talking Madame Concierge. You can see that I'm not interrupting you.[336]

(The COACHMAN *of the hearse appears at the edge of the door: nose of a drunkard, old silk hat with cockade, threadbare mourning coat, stuffed wig, and black breeches.)*

EL COCHERO. ¡Que son las cuatro, y tengo otro parroquiano en la calle de Carlos Rubio!

BASILIO. Madama Collet, yo me hago responsable, porque he visto y estudiado casos de catalepsia en los hospitales de Alemania. ¡Su esposo de usted, mi amigo y compañero Max Estrella, no está muerto!

LA PORTERA. ¿Quiere usted no armar escándalo, caballero? Madama Collet, ¿dónde tiene usted un espejo?

BASILIO. ¡Es una prueba anticientífica!

EL COCHERO. Póngale usted un mixto encendido en el dedo pulgar de la mano. Si se consume hasta el final, está fiambre como mi abuelo. ¡Y perdonen ustedes si he faltado!

(EL COCHERO *fúnebre arrima la fusta a la pared y rasca una cerilla. Acucándose ante el ataúd, desenlaza las manos del muerto y una vuelve por la palma amarillenta. En la yema del pulgar le pone la cerilla luciente, que sigue ardiendo y agonizando.* CLAUDINITA, *con un grito estridente, tuerce los ojos y comienza a batir la cabeza contra el suelo.*)

CLAUDINITA. ¡Mi padre! ¡Mi padre! ¡Mi padre querido!

ESCENA DECIMOCUARTA

(*Un patio en el cementerio del Este. La tarde, fría. El viento, adusto. La luz de la tarde, sobre los muros de lápidas, tiene una aridez agresiva. Dos sepultureros apisonan la tierra de una fosa. Un momento suspenden la tarea. Sacan lumbre del yesquero y las colillas de tras la oreja. Fuman sentados al pie del hoyo.*)

UN SEPULTURERO. Ese sujeto era un hombre de pluma.

OTRO SEPULTURERO. ¡Pobre entierro ha tenido!

UN SEPULTURERO. Los papeles lo ponen por hombre de mérito.

OTRO SEPULTURERO. En España el mérito no se premia. Se premia el robar y el ser sinvergüenza. En España se premia todo lo malo.

UN SEPULTURERO. ¡No hay que poner las cosas tan negras!

OTRO SEPULTURERO. ¡Ahí tienes al Pollo del Arete![337]

COACHMAN. It's already four o'clock and I've got another customer on Rubio Street!

BASILIO. Madame Collet, I'll assume the responsibility, because I've seen and studied cases of catalepsy in German hospitals. Your husband, my friend and companion Max Estrella, is *not* dead!

CONCIERGE. Will you please try not to make a scene, my dear gentleman? Madame Collet, where do you keep the mirror?

BASILIO. It's an anti-scientific experiment!

COACHMAN. Just put a lighted match to his thumb. If it burns to the end the stiff is as gone as my grandpa. And forgive me if I've been indiscreet!

(The COACHMAN *props his whip against the wall and strikes a wax match. Crouching before the coffin, he loosens the dead man's hands, and turns up one of the yellowish palms. On the finger tip, he puts the lighted match which keeps on burning and then slowly expires.* CLAUDINITA *lets out a strident shriek, rolls her eyes and begins to beat her head against the floor.)*

CLAUDINITA. My father! My father! My beloved father!

SCENE FOURTEEN

(A patio in the cemetery of East Madrid. The evening, cold; the wind, sharp. The evening light on the rows of gravestones has an aggressive aridity. Two gravediggers are packing down the earth of a grave. They stop working for a moment. They strike a light with their tinderbox for the cigarette butts from behind their ears. They smoke sitting at the foot of the grave.)

FIRST GRAVEDIGGER. This fellow was a man of letters.

SECOND GRAVEDIGGER. Rotten funeral he had!

FIRST GRAVEDIGGER. The papers put him down as a man of great worth.

SECOND GRAVEDIGGER. In Spain, merit is never rewarded. What's rewarded is corruption and rascality. Everything bad is rewarded in Spain.

FIRST GRAVEDIGGER. You don't have to paint things so black!

SECOND GRAVEDIGGER. Well, take Cock-Earring over there![337]

UN SEPULTURERO. ¿Y ése, qué ha sacado?

OTRO SEPULTURERO. Pasarlo como un rey siendo un malasangre. Míralo, disfrutando a la viuda de un concejal.

UN SEPULTURERO. Di un ladrón del Ayuntamiento.

OTRO SEPULTURERO. Ponlo por dicho. ¿Te parece que una mujer de posición se chifle así por un tal sujeto?

UN SEPULTURERO. Cegueras. Es propio del sexo.

OTRO SEPULTURERO. ¡Ahí tienes el mérito que triunfa! ¡Y para todo la misma ley!

UN SEPULTURERO. ¿Tú conoces a la sujeta? ¿Es buena mujer?

OTRO SEPULTURERO. Una mujer en carnes. ¡Al andar, unas nalgas que le tiemblan! ¡Buena!

UN SEPULTURERO. ¡Releche con la suerte de ese gatera![338] (*Por una calle de lápidas y cruces vienen paseando y dialogando dos sombras rezagadas, dos amigos en el cortejo fúnebre de* MÁXIMO ESTRELLA. *Hablan en voz baja y caminan lentos, parecen almas inbuidas del respeto religioso de la muerte. El uno, viejo caballero con la barba toda de nieve y capa española sobre los hombros, es el céltico* MARQUÉS DE BRADOMÍN.[339] *El otro es el índico y profundo* RUBÉN DARÍO.)

RUBÉN. ¡Es pavorosamente significativo que al cabo de tantos años nos hayamos encontrado en un cementerio!

EL MARQUÉS. En el Camposanto. Bajo ese nombre adquiere una significación distinta nuestro encuentro, querido Rubén.

RUBÉN. Es verdad. Ni cementerio ni necrópolis. Son nombres de una frialdad triste y horrible, como estudiar Gramática. Marqués, ¿qué emoción tiene para usted necrópolis?

EL MARQUÉS. La de una pedantería académica.

RUBÉN. Necrópolis, para mí es como el fin de todo, dice lo irreparable y lo horrible, el perecer sin esperanza en el cuarto de un Hotel. ¿Y Camposanto? Camposanto tiene una lámpara.

EL MARQUÉS. Tiene una cúpula dorada. Bajo ella resuena religiosamente el terrible clarín extraordinario, querido Rubén.

RUBÉN. Marqués, la muerte muchas veces sería amable si no existiese el terror de lo incierto. ¡Yo hubiera sido feliz hace tres mil años en Atenas![340]

FIRST GRAVEDIGGER. And what did he get out of it?

SECOND GRAVEDIGGER. Living like a king though he was a snake in the grass. Look at him frolicking with the widow of the Councillor.

FIRST GRAVEDIGGER. You mean a city-council thief.

SECOND GRAVEDIGGER. You said it. Did you think a woman of her position would get moon-struck with such a character?

FIRST GRAVEDIGGER. Blindness! Just like females!

SECOND GRAVEDIGGER. That's how virtue triumphs! And the same holds everywhere.

FIRST GRAVEDIGGER. Do you know this bird? Is she a real dish?

SECOND GRAVEDIGGER. Succulent meat. When she walks her bottom jiggles. Great stuff!

FIRST GRAVEDIGGER. What blasted luck that tomcat has![338] *(Through a pathway of gravestones and crosses, two shadows that have lagged appear walking slowly and chatting: two friends from the funeral cortege of* MAX ESTRELLA. *They talk in a low voice and walk slowly; giving the impression of two souls imbued by religious respect for death. One of them, an old gentleman with a snow white beard and a Spanish cape around his shoulders, is the Celtic* MARQUIS OF BRADOMÍN.[339] *The other is the Aztec-like and profound* RUBÉN DARÍO.*)*

RUBÉN. It's frighteningly significant that after so many years you and I should meet in a cemetery!

THE MARQUIS. On Consecrated Ground. If you call it that, my dear Rubén, our meeting acquires a different significance.

RUBÉN. That's true. Neither cemetery nor necropolis. They're names denoting a sad and terrible chillness–like studying grammar. Marquis, what does necropolis evoke for you?

THE MARQUIS. Academic pedantry.

RUBÉN. Necropolis is for me like the end of everything, I mean the irreparable and horrible . . . perishing without hope in a hotel room. Consecrated Ground? Consecrated Ground harbours a light.

THE MARQUIS. It has a golden dome. And under it, my dear Rubén, there resounds religiously the extraordinary and terrible trumpet.

RUBÉN. Marquis, death could even be lovable if it were not for the terror of the unknown. I would have been happy three thousand years ago in ancient Athens.[340]

EL MARQUÉS. Yo no cambio mi bautismo de cristiano por la sonrisa de un cínico griego. Yo espero ser eterno por mis pecados.[341]

RUBÉN. ¡Admirable!

EL MARQUÉS. En Grecia quizá fuese la vida más serena que la vida nuestra . . .

RUBÉN. ¡Solamente aquellos hombres han sabido divinizarla!

EL MARQUÉS. Nosotros divinizamos la muerte. No es más que un instante la vida, la única verdad es la muerte . . .[342] Y de las muertes, yo prefiero la muerte cristiana.

RUBÉN. ¡Admirable filosofía de hidalgo español! ¡Admirable! ¡Marqués, no hablemos más de Ella![343]

(Callan y caminan en silencio. LOS SEPULTUREROS, *acabada de apisonar la tierra, uno tras otro beben a chorro de un mismo botijo. Sobre el muro de lápidas blancas, las dos figuras acentúan su contorno negro.* RUBÉN DARÍO *y* EL MARQUÉS DE BRADOMÍN *se detienen ante la mancha oscura de la tierra removida.)*

RUBÉN. Marqués, ¿cómo ha llegado usted a ser amigo de Máximo Estrella?

EL MARQUÉS. Max era hijo de un capitán carlista que murió a mi lado en la guerra.[344] ¿Él contaba otra cosa?

RUBÉN. Contaba que ustedes se habían batido juntos en una revolución, allá en Méjico.[345]

EL MARQUÉS. ¡Qué fantasía! Max nació treinta años después de mi viaje a Méjico. ¿Sabe usted la edad que yo tengo? Me falta muy poco para llevar un siglo a cuestas. Pronto acabaré, querido poeta.

RUBÉN. ¿Usted es eterno, Marqués?

EL MARQUÉS. ¡Eso me temo, pero paciencia!

(Las sombras negras de LOS SEPULTUREROS*—al hombro las azadas lucientes—se acercan por la calle de tumbas. Se acercan.)*

EL MARQUÉS. ¿Serán filósofos, como los de Ofelia?[346]

RUBÉN. ¿Ha conocido usted alguna Ofelia, Marqués?

THE MARQUIS. I'll not exchange my Christian baptism for the smile of a cynical Greek. I expect to be eternal because of my sins.[341]

RUBÉN. Exquisite!

THE MARQUIS. Perhaps life in Greece was more serene than ours . . .

RUBÉN. Those were the only men who know how to sanctify life.

THE MARQUIS. We sanctify death. Life is no more than an instant; Death is the only truth.[342] And of all deaths, I prefer the Christian death.

RUBÉN. Exquisite philosophy of a Spanish nobleman! Exquisite! Marquis, let's speak no more of Her.[343]

(They stop talking and walk silently. The GRAVEDIGGERS *have finished packing the earth and take turns drinking lustily from the same wineskin. Against the row of white gravestones the black contours of the two figures are accentuated.* RUBÉN DARÍO *and the* MARQUIS OF BRADOMÍN *halt before the dark blemish of the grave mound.)*

RUBÉN. Marquis, how did you come to be a friend of Máximo Estrella?

THE MARQUIS. Max was the son of a Carlist captain who died at my side during the war.[344] Why, did he tell you something else?

RUBÉN. He told how the two of you had fought together in a revolution, over there in Mexico.[345]

THE MARQUIS. What imagination! Max was born thirty years after my trip to Mexico. Do you know what age I've reached? Only a little more and I shall be carrying a whole century on my back. Well, my dear poet, I shall soon render my account.

RUBÉN. Are you eternal, Marquis?

THE MARQUIS. I'm afraid so . . . but, patience!

(The black shadows of the GRAVEDIGGERS*–their shining spades on their shoulders–are approaching through the pathway of tombs. They keep on approaching.)*

THE MARQUIS. Could they be philosophers, like those at Ophelia's grave?[346]

RUBÉN. Marquis, have you ever known an Ophelia?

EL MARQUÉS. En la edad del pavo todas las niñas son Ofelias. Era muy pava aquella criatura, querido Rubén. ¡Y el príncipe, como todos los príncipes, un babieca![347]

RUBÉN. ¿No ama usted al divino William?

EL MARQUÉS. En el tiempo de mis veleidades literarias, lo elegí por maestro. ¡Es admirable! Con un filósofo tímido y una niña boba en fuerza de inocencia, ha realizado el prodigio de crear la más bella tragedia. Querido Rubén, Hamlet y Ofelia, en nuestra dramática española, serían dos tipos regocijados. ¡Un tímido y una niña boba! ¡Lo que hubieran hecho los gloriosos hermanos Quintero![348]

RUBÉN. Todos tenemos algo de Hamletos.

EL MARQUÉS. Usted, que aún galantea. Yo, con mi carga de años, estoy más próximo a ser la calavera de Yorik.[349]

UN SEPULTURERO. Caballeros, si ustedes buscan la salida, vengan con nosotros. Se va a cerrar.

EL MARQUÉS. Rubén, ¿qué le parece a usted quedarnos dentro?

RUBÉN. ¡Horrible!

EL MARQUÉS. Pues entonces sigamos a estos dos.

RUBÉN. Marqués, ¿quiere usted que mañana volvamos para poner una cruz sobre la sepultura de nuestro amigo?

EL MARQUÉS. ¡Mañana! Mañana habremos los dos olvidado ese cristiano propósito.

RUBÉN. ¡Acaso!

(En silencio y retardándose, siguen por el camino de LOS SEPULTUREROS, *que, al revolver los ángulos de las calles de tumbas, se detienen a esperarlos.)*

EL MARQUÉS. Los años no me permiten caminar más de prisa.

UN SEPULTURERO. No se excuse usted, caballero.

EL MARQUÉS. Pocos me faltan para el siglo.

OTRO SEPULTURERO. ¡Ya habrá usted visto entierros!

EL MARQUÉS. Si no sois muy antiguos en el oficio, probablemente más que vosotros. ¿Y se muere mucha gente esta temporada?

UN SEPULTURERO. No falta faena. Niños y viejos.

THE MARQUIS. In the 'age of the peacock', all maidens are Ophelias. That creature was quite a 'peahen', my dear Rubén. And the Prince, of course, like all princes, a simpleton.[347]

RUBÉN. Don't you like the divine William?

THE MARQUIS. In the period of my literary flightiness, I chose William for my teacher. He's splendid. With just a timid philosopher and a silly girl in all her naiveté, he worked the miracle of creating the most beautiful tragedy. In our Spanish theatre, my dear Rubén, Hamlet and Ophelia would become two highly amusing characters: a timid youth and a silly girl! Think what our glorious Quintero Brothers would have done with them![348]

RUBÉN. We all have something of Hamlet in us.

THE MARQUIS. Maybe you, who are still courting women. As for me, burdened by years, I am nearer to being the skull of Yorick.[349]

FIRST GRAVEDIGGER. If you're looking for the exit, gentlemen, just come with us. The place is closing.

THE MARQUIS. Rubén, how would you enjoy it if we stayed inside?

RUBÉN. Horrible!

THE MARQUIS. Well then let's follow these two.

RUBÉN. Marquis, would you like to come back tomorrow and place a crucifix on our friend's sepulchre?

THE MARQUIS. Tomorrow! By tomorrow you and I will have forgotten this Christian intention.

RUBÉN. Perhaps!

(Silently and lingering somewhat, they follow behind the GRAVEDIGGERS *who, turning the corner of the lanes of tombs, stop to wait for them.)*

THE MARQUIS. My years no longer permit me to walk any faster.

FIRST GRAVEDIGGER. You don't have to apologize, Sir.

THE MARQUIS. I need but few years to complete a century.

SECOND GRAVEDIGGER. You must really have seen funeral after funeral!

THE MARQUIS. Unless you've been at this trade a long time, probably more than you. And, are there many people dying this season?

FIRST GRAVEDIGGER. There's no shortage of work. Young and old.

OTRO SEPULTURERO. La caída de la hoja siempre trae lo suyo.

EL MARQUÉS. ¿A vosotros os pagan por entierro?

UN SEPULTURERO. Nos pagan un jornal de tres pesetas, caiga lo que caiga. Hoy, a como está la vida, ni para mal comer. Alguna otra cosa se saca. Total, miseria.

OTRO SEPULTURERO. En todo va la suerte. Eso lo primero.

UN SEPULTURERO. Hay familias que al perder un miembro, por cuidarle de la sepultura, pagan uno o dos o medio. Hay quien ofrece y no paga. Las más de las familias pagan los primeros meses. Y lo que es el año, de ciento, una. ¡Dura poco la pena!

EL MARQUÉS. ¿No habéis conocido ninguna viuda inconsolable?

UN SEPULTURERO. ¡Ninguna! Pero pudiera haberla.

EL MARQUÉS. ¿Ni siquiera habéis oído hablar de Artemisa y Mausoleo?[350]

UN SEPULTURERO. Por mi parte, ni la menor cosa.

OTRO SEPULTURERO. Vienen a ser tantas las parentelas que concurren a estos lugares, que no es fácil conocerlas a todas. *(Caminan muy despacio.* RUBÉN, *meditabundo, escribe alguna palabra en el sobre de una carta. Llegan a la puerta, rechina la verja negra.* EL MARQUÉS, *benevolente, saca de la capa su mano de marfil y reparte entre los enterradores algún dinero.)*

EL MARQUÉS. No sabéis mitología, pero sois dos filósofos estoicos.[351] Que sigáis viendo muchos entierros.

UN SEPULTURERO. Lo que usted ordene. ¡Muy agradecido!

OTRO SEPULTURERO. Igualmente. Para servir a usted, caballero.

(Quitándose las gorras, saludan y se alejan. EL MARQUÉS DE BRADOMÍN, *con una sonrisa, se arrebuja en la capa.* RUBÉN DARÍO *conserva siempre en la mano el sobre de la carta donde ha escrito escasos renglones. Y dejando el socaire de unas bardas, se acerca a la puerta del cementerio el coche del viejo* MARQUÉS.*)*

EL MARQUÉS. ¿Son versos, Rubén? ¿Quiere usted leérmelos?

SECOND GRAVEDIGGER. The leaf's fall brings autumn's harvest.

THE MARQUIS. And so they pay you by the funeral?

FIRST GRAVEDIGGER. They give us a daily wage of three pesetas, come what may. With the cost of living nowadays, it's not enough to eat even poorly. We pick up a little extra here and there. In short, poverty.

SECOND GRAVEDIGGER. Everything depends on luck. That's the main thing.

FIRST GRAVEDIGGER. Some families, when they lose one of their number, pay us one or two pesetas, or a half, to take care of the grave. There are always those who promise and don't pay. Most families pay for the first few months. But for the whole year, out of a hundred, maybe one. Sorrow doesn't last long.

THE MARQUIS. Haven't you known even one unconsolable widow?

FIRST GRAVEDIGGER. Not one! But perhaps there is one.

THE MARQUIS. Haven't you even heard of Artemisia and Mausolus?[350]

FIRST GRAVEDIGGER. As far as I'm concerned, nothing at all!

SECOND GRAVEDIGGER. There are so many women relatives that come to this spot that it's difficult to know them all. *(They walk slowly.* RUBÉN, *meditative, scribbles something on an envelope. They arrive at the door, and the black iron gate creaks.* THE MARQUIS *benevolently takes his ivory hand from under his cape and distributes some money to the gravediggers.)*

THE MARQUIS. You don't know mythology but you *are* two stoic philosophers.[351] May you yet witness many a funeral!

FIRST GRAVEDIGGER. At your service! Thank you very much!

SECOND GRAVEDIGGER. Same here. We're here to serve you, Sir.

(Taking off their caps, they salute and move away. THE MARQUIS OF BRADOMÍN *with a smile wraps himself up in his cape.* RUBÉN DARÍO *still holds in his hand the envelope on which he has scribbled a few lines. And abandoning the shelter of some foliage, the old Marquis's coach approaches the cemetery gate.)*

THE MARQUIS. Is that a poem, Rubén? Do you wish to read it to me?

RUBÉN. Cuando los haya depurado. Todavía son un monstruo.

EL MARQUÉS. Querido Rubén, los versos debieran publicarse con todo su proceso, desde lo que usted llama monstruo hasta la manera definitiva. Tendrían entonces un valor como las pruebas de aguafuerte. ¿Pero usted no quiere leérmelos?

RUBÉN. Mañana, Marqués.

EL MARQUÉS. Ante mis años y a la puerta de un cementerio, no debe pronunciar la palabra mañana. En fin, montemos en el coche, que aún hemos de visitar a un bandolero. Quiero que usted me ayude a venderle a un editor el manuscrito de mis Memorias.[352] Necesito dinero. Estoy completamente arruinado desde que tuve la mala idea de recogerme a mi Pazo de Bradomín. ¡No me han arruinado las mujeres, con haberlas amado tanto, y me arruina la agricultura![353]

RUBÉN. ¡Admirable!

EL MARQUÉS. Mis Memorias se publicarán después de mi muerte. Voy a venderlas como si vendiese el esqueleto. Ayudémonos.

ESCENA ÚLTIMA

(La taberna de PICA LAGARTOS. *Lobreguez con un temblor de acetileno.* DON LATINO DE HISPALIS, *ante el mostrador, insiste y tartajea convidando al* POLLO DEL PAY-PAY.[354] *Entre traspiés y traspiés, da la pelma.)*

DON LATINO. ¡Beba usted, amigo! ¡Usted no sabe la pena que rebosa mi corazón! ¡Beba usted! ¡Yo bebo sin dejar cortinas![355]

EL POLLO. Porque usted no es castizo.

DON LATINO. ¡Hoy hemos enterrado al primer poeta de España! ¡Cuatro amigos en el cementerio! ¡Acabóse! ¡Ni una cabrona representación de la Docta Casa![356] ¿Qué te parece, Venancio?

PICA LAGARTOS. Lo que usted guste, Don Latí.

DON LATINO. ¡El Genio brilla con luz propia! ¿Que no, Pollo?

EL POLLO. Que sí, Don Latino.

RUBÉN. When I have polished it. It's still a monstrosity.

THE MARQUIS. My dear Rubén, poems ought to be published in all their stages, from what you call monstrous up to their definitive form. In that way they would acquire the same value as the proofs of etchings. But are you sure you don't wish to read it to me?

RUBÉN. Tomorrow, Marquis.

THE MARQUIS. In the presence of a man my age and before the gate of a cemetery, the word 'tomorrow' should not be uttered. In any case, let's climb into the coach for we've still got to visit a bandit. I want you to help me sell the manuscript of my *Memoirs* to a publisher.[352] I need the money, I'm completely ruined ever since I got the unfortunate idea of retiring to my Castle of Bradomín. Women haven't ruined me, despite my loving them so much. What's ruined me is agriculture![353]

RUBÉN. Exquisite!

THE MARQUIS. My memoirs will be published after my death. I'm going to sell them as if I were selling my skeleton. Let's help each other.

SCENE FIFTEEN

(The tavern of LIZARD-CHOPPER. *Gloom with a flickering of an acetylene burner.* DON LATINO DE HISPALIS *stands before the counter, insisting and stuttering as he invites a* FOP, FAN-FAN,[354] *to drink. He stumbles, slips and becomes a nuisance.)*

DON LATINO. Drink up, my friend! You can't imagine the sorrow that overflows in my heart! Drink up! I drink to the dregs.[355]

FOP. That's because you're not a well-bred drinker.

DON LATINO. Today we've buried Spain's number one poet! Only four friends in the cemetery! That was all! Not even one bastard representing the Learned Establishment![356] What do you think of that, Venancio?

LIZARD-CHOPPER. Whatever you say, Don Latí.

DON LATINO. Genius shines with its own light! Isn't that right, young fellow?

FOP. Indeed it is, Don Latino.

DON LATINO. ¡Yo he tomado sobre mis hombros publicar sus escritos! ¡La honrosa tarea! ¡Soy un fideicomisario! Nos lega una novela social que está a la altura de *Los Miserables*.[357] ¡Soy un fideicomisario! Y el producto íntegro de todas las obras, para la familia. ¡Y no me importa arruinarme publicándolas! ¡Son deberes de la amistad! ¡Semejante al nocturno peregrino, mi esperanza inmortal no mira al suelo! ¡Señores, ni una representación de la Docta Casa! ¡Eso, sí: los cuatro amigos, cuatro personalidades! El Ministro de la Gobernación, Bradomín, Rubén y este ciudadano. ¿Que no, Pollo?

EL POLLO. Por mí, ya puede usted contar que estuvo la Infanta.[358]

PICA LAGARTOS. Me parece mucho decir que se halló la Política representada en el entierro de Don Max. Y si usted lo divulga, hasta podrá tener para usted malas resultas.

DON LATINO. ¡Yo no miento! ¡Estuvo en el cementerio el Ministro de la Gobernación! ¡Nos hemos saludado!

EL CHICO. ¡Sería Fantomas![359]

DON LATINO. Calla tú, mamarracho. ¡Don Antonio Maura estuvo a dar el pésame en la casa del *Gallo!*

EL POLLO. José Gómez, *Gallito*,[360] era un astro, y murió en la plaza, toreando muy requetebién, porque ha sido el rey de la tuaromaquia.

PICA LAGARTOS. ¿Y *Terremoto*, u séase Juan Belmonte?[361]

EL POLLO. ¡Un intelectual!

DON LATINO. Niño, otra ronda. ¡Hoy es el día más triste de mi vida! ¡Perdí un amigo fraternal y un maestro! Por eso bebo, Venancio.

PICA LAGARTOS. ¡Que ya sube una barbaridad la cuenta, Don Latí! Tantéese usted, a ver el dinero que tiene. ¡No sea caso!

DON LATINO. Tengo dinero para comprarte a ti, con tu tabernáculo.[362]

(Saca de las profundidades del carrik un manojo de billetes y lo arroja sobre el mostrador, bajo la mirada torcida del chulo y el gesto atónito de Venancio. EL CHICO DE LA TABERNA *se*

DON LATINO. I've taken the big job of publishing his writings. A glorious task! I'm the literary executor! He has bequeathed us a social novel with the stature of Hugo's *Les Misérables.*[357] I'm a trustee. And the money from the sale of his works will go every bit of it to the family. And I don't care if I'm ruined publishing them! Such are the duties of friendship! Like the nocturnal pilgrim, my immortal hope is not earthbound! Gentlemen, not one representative from the Learned Establishment! But at least this much: four true friends, four real personalities! The Minister of the Interior, Old Bradomín, the poet Rubén, and your humble servant. Isn't that true, young fellow?

FOP. For all I care you can tell us that the Infanta herself was there.[358]

LIZARD-CHOPPER. I think you go too far in claiming that the Government was represented at the funeral of Don Max. And if you let that get around, you're going to find yourself in the soup.

DON LATINO. I'm not lying! The Minister of the Interior was at the cemetery in person! We even exchanged greetings.

BAR BOY. It must've been the Phantom.[359]

DON LATINO. Shut up, you milksop. Didn't President Maura himself go to express his sympathy for the family of Gallo the bullfighter?

FOP. José Gómez, Gallito the Matador,[360] was a star, and he died in the arena fighting the bull brilliantly, because he was king of the bullring.

LIZARD-CHOPPER. And how about the 'earthquake' torero? I mean Juan Belmonte?[361]

FOP. An intellectual!

DON LATINO. Boy, another round. This is the saddest day of my life! I have lost a fraternal friend and my maestro! Venancio, that's why I am drinking.

LIZARD-CHOPPER. Your bill is rocketing sky-high, Don Latí! Feel your pockets and see if you've got any money. Just in case!

DON LATINO. I've got enough money to buy you and your whole tabernacle.[362]

(He pulls out a handful of notes from the recesses of his overcoat and throws them on the counter, under the scrutinizing sideglance of the young dandy and Venancio's gesture of stupefaction. The

agacha por alcanzar entre las zancas barrosas del curda un billete revolante. La niña PISA-BIEN, *amurriada en un rincón de la tasca, se retira el pañuelo de la frente, y espabilándose fisga hacia el mostrador.)*

EL CHICO. ¿Ha heredado usted, Don Latí?

DON LATINO. Me debían unas pocas pesetas, y me las han pagado.

PICA LAGARTOS. No son unas pocas.

LA PISA-BIEN. ¡Diez mil del ala![363]

DON LATINO. ¿Te deben algo?

LA PISA-BIEN. ¡Naturaca! Usted ha cobrado un décimo que yo he vendido.

DON LATINO. No es verdad.

LA PISA-BIEN. El 5775.

EL CHICO. ¡Ese mismo número llevaba Don Max!

LA PISA-BIEN. A fin de cuentas no lo quiso, y se lo llevó don Latí. Y el tío roña aún no ha sido para darme la propi.[364]

DON LATINO. ¡Se me había olvidado!

LA PISA-BIEN. Mala memoria que usted se gasta.

DON LATINO. Te la daré.

LA PISA-BIEN. Usted verá lo que hace.

DON LATINO. Confía en mi generosidad ilimitada.

*(*EL CHICO DE LA TABERNA *se desliza tras el patrón, y a hurto, con una seña disimulada, le tira del mandil.* PICA LAGARTOS *echa la llave al cajón y se junta con el chaval en la oscuridad donde están amontonadas las corambres. Hablan expresivos y secretos, pero atentos al mostrador con el ojo y la oreja.* LA PISA-BIEN *le guiña a* DON LATINO.*)*

LA PISA-BIEN. Don Latí, ¡me dotará usted con esos diez mil del ala!

DON LATINO. Te pondré piso.

LA PISA-BIEN. ¡Olé los hombres!

DON LATINO. Crispín, hijo mío, una copa de anisete a esta madama.

EL CHICO. ¡Va, Don Latí!

DON LATINO. ¿Te estás confesando?

LA PISA-BIEN. Don Latí, ¡está usted la mar de simpático! ¡Es usted un flamenco! ¡Amos, deje de pellizcarme![365]

EL POLLO. Don Latino, pupila, que le hacen guiños a esos capitales.

BAR BOY *squats to pick up a note dropped on the muddy legs of the old sot. The young* TREAD-WELL, *hitherto downcast in a corner of the joint, removes the handkerchief from her forehead and, brightening up a little, keeps her eye on the counter.)*

BAR BOY. Have you come into a fortune, Don Latí?

DON LATINO. Someone owed me a few pesetas and finally produced them.

LIZARD-CHOPPER. They're not so few!

TREAD-WELL. Ten thousand beads of wampum![363]

DON LATINO. Do I owe you anything?

TREAD-WELL. You damn well do! You cashed in on that lottery ticket I sold.

DON LATINO. It's not true.

TREAD-WELL. Number 5775.

THE BAR BOY. That's exactly the number Don Max had!

TREAD-WELL. In the end he didn't want it and Don Latí picked it up. And the old miser hasn't come around to deliver my cut.[364]

DON LATINO. It never even crossed my mind!

TREAD-WELL. You've got a bad memory.

DON LATINO. I'll give you your share.

TREAD-WELL. You know what's right.

DON LATINO. You can count on my unlimited generosity.

(The BAR BOY *slips behind his boss and stealthily, pretending to do something else, pulls him by the apron.* LIZARD-CHOPPER *locks his cash register and goes with the lad to a dark spot where the wine skins are heaped up. They whisper and gesture keeping all the while a sharp eye and ear on the goings-on at the counter.* HENRIETTA TREAD-WELL *winks at* DON LATINO.*)*

TREAD-WELL. Don Latí, you could set up a dowry for me with all that loot.

DON LATINO. I'll furnish a flat for you.

TREAD-WELL. Hooray for men!

DON LATINO. Crispín my boy, a glass of anisette for the lady.

BAR BOY. Coming, Don Latí!

DON LATINO. Are you going to confession?

TREAD-WELL. Don Latí, you're a hell of a nice chap! A real flamenco type! Hey, com'on, stop pinching me![365]

FOP. Look out Don Latino, everybody's flirting with your money.

LA PISA-BIEN. ¡Si llevábamos el décimo por mitad! Don Latí, una cincuenta, y esta servidora de ustedes, seis reales.

DON LATINO. ¡Es un atraco, Enriqueta!

LA PISA-BIEN. ¡Deje usted las espantás para el calvorota![366] ¡Vuelta a pellizcarme! ¡Parece usted un chivo loco!

EL POLLO. No le conviene a usted esa gachí.

LA PISA-BIEN. En una semana lo enterraba.

DON LATINO. Ya se vería.

EL POLLO. A usted le conviene una mujer con los calores extinguidos.

LA PISA-BIEN. A usted le conviene mi mamá. Pero mi mamá es una viuda decente, y para sacar algo, hay que llevarla a la calle de la Pasa.[367]

DON LATINO. Yo soy un apóstol del amor libre.

LA PISA-BIEN. Usted se junta con mi mamá y conmigo, para ser el caballero formal que se anuncia en *La Corres*.[368] Precisamente se cansó de dar la pelma un huésped que teníamos, y dejó una alcoba, para usted la propia. ¿Adónde va usted, Don Latí?

DON LATINO. A cambiar el agua de las aceitunas.[369] Vuelvo. No te apures, rica. Espérame.

LA PISA-BIEN. Don Latí, soy una mujer celosa. Yo le acompaño.

*(*PICA LAGARTOS *deja secretos con el chaval, y en dos trancos cruza el vano de la tasca. Por el cuello del carrik detiene al curda en el umbral de la puerta.* DON LATINO *guiña el ojo, tuerce la jeta, y desmaya los brazos como un pelele.)*

DON LATINO. ¡No seas vándalo!

PICA LAGARTOS. Tenemos que hablar. Aquí el difunto ha dejado una pella que pasa de los tres mil reales–ya se verán las cuentas–y considero que debe usted abonarla.

DON LATINO. ¿Por qué razón?

PICA LAGARTOS. Porque es usted un vivales, y no hablemos más.

*(*EL POLLO DEL PAY-PAY *se acerca ondulante. A intento deja ver que está empalmado, tose y se rasca ladeando la gorra.* ENRIQUETA *tercia el mantón y ocultamente abre una navajilla.)*

TREAD-WELL. Why, we had split the lucky ticket fifty-fifty! Don Latí paid one peseta fifty and yours truly matched it.

DON LATINO. This is armed robbery, Henrietta!

TREAD-WELL. Leave the cold feet for 'Baldy' the bull-fighter![366] There you go pinching me again! I swear you're an old lecher.

FOP. That broad is not the thing for you.

TREAD-WELL. I'd wear him down to his grave in a week.

DON LATINO. We'll see about that.

FOP. What you need is a dame whose ardours have been dampened.

TREAD-WELL. My mother would suit you better. But Ma is a decent widow, and to get something out of her, you'd have to take her to the Registry Office.[367]

DON LATINO. I'm an apostle of free love.

TREAD-WELL. Come and live with me and my Ma and you'll be the respectable gentleman lodger advertised for in the papers.[368] In fact, just now a lodger of ours got tired of kicking around and left a guest room that would do you beautifully. Where are you off to, Don Latí?

DON LATINO. To see a man about a horse.[369] Be right back. Don't worry, darling. Wait here for me.

TREAD-WELL. Don Latí, I'm a very jealous woman. I'm going with you.

*(*LIZARD-CHOPPER *stops his secret session with the lad and in two long strides crosses over to the counter. Grabbing the old sot by the collar of his overcoat he stops him in the doorway.* DON LATINO *blinks his eyes, twists his mouth, and droops his arms like a puppet.)*

DON LATINO. Don't be such a brute!

LIZARD-CHOPPER. You and I have something to discuss. The dead man left a debt here that runs into hundreds. You can check the bills later, but I suggest you take care of the debt now.

DON LATINO. What for?

LIZARD-CHOPPER. Because you're a sly dog and we both know it.

*(*THE FOP, FAN-FAN, *approaches them swaying a bit. He deliberately lets the others see that he is hiding a knife in his hand. He coughs and scratches his head tilting his cap.* HENRIETTA *wraps herself in a shawl and secretly opens a small knife.)*

EL POLLO. Aquí todos estamos con la pupila dilatada, y tenemos opción a darle un vistazo a ese kilo de billetaje.

LA PISA-BIEN. Don Latí se va a la calle de ganchete con mangue.

EL POLLO. ¡Fantasía!

PICA LAGARTOS. Tú, pelmazo, guarda la herramienta y no busques camorra.

EL POLLO. ¡Don Latí, usted ha dado un golpe en el Banco!

DON LATINO. Naturalmente.

LA PISA-BIEN. ¡Que te frían un huevo, Nicanor![370] A Don Latí le ha caído la lotería en un décimo del 5775. ¡Yo se lo he vendido!

PICA LAGARTOS. El muchacho y un servidor lo hemos presenciado. ¿Es verdad, muchacho?

EL CHICO. ¡Así es!

EL POLLO. ¡Miau!

(PACONA, *una vieja que hace celestinazgo*[371] *y vende periódicos, entra en la taberna con su hatillo de papel impreso, y deja sobre el mostrador un número de* El Heraldo. *Sale como entró, fisgona y callada. Solamente en la puerta, mirando a las estrellas, vuelve a gritar su pregón.*)

LA PERIODISTA. *¡Heraldo de Madrid! ¡Corres! ¡Heraldo!* ¡Muerte misteriosa de dos señoras en la calle de Bastardillos! *¡Corres! ¡Heraldo!*

(DON LATINO *rompe el grupo y se acerca al mostrador, huraño y enigmático. En el círculo luminoso de la lámpara, con el periódico abierto a dos manos, tartamudea la lectura de los títulos con que adereza el reportero el suceso de la calle de Bastardillos. Y le miran los otros con extrañeza burlona, como a un viejo chiflado.*)

LECTURA DE DON LATINO. El tufo de un brasero. Dos señoras asfixiadas.[372] Lo que dice una vecina. Doña Vicenta no sabe nada. ¿Crimen o suicidio? ¡Misterio!

EL CHICO. Mire usted si el papel trae los nombres de las gachís, Don Latí.

DON LATINO. Voy a verlo.

EL POLLO. ¡No se cargue usted la cabezota, tío lila!

LA PISA-BIEN. Don Latí, vámonos.

EL CHICO. ¡Aventuro que esas dos sujetas son la esposa y la hija de Don Máximo!

DON LATINO. ¡Absurdo! ¿Por qué habían de matarse?

FOP. Here we are, all sharp-eyed, and we have priority in taking a good look at this wad of money.

TREAD-WELL. Don Latí's stepping out of here leaning on my arm.

FOP. Delirium!

LIZARD-CHOPPER. Hey you blighter, keep that gadget low and don't go looking for trouble.

FOP. Don Latí, you've pulled a job at the bank!

DON LATINO. Naturally.

TREAD-WELL. Go fry an egg, you nincompoop.[370] Don Latí hit the jackpot with his lottery ticket 5775. I sold it to him myself!

LIZARD-CHOPPER. The boy and I were witnesses. Isn't that right, lad?

BAR BOY. That's right!

FOP. Baloney!

*(*PACONA, *an old procuress,*[371] *also a newsvendor, enters the tavern with her small pack of papers and leaves a copy of the* Herald *on the counter. She leaves as she entered, inquisitive and silent. Only at the door, while looking at the stars, does she utter her cry again.)*

NEWSPAPER WOMAN. The Madrid *Herald*! The *Herald*! Mysterious death of two women on Bastardillos Street. Read all about it! The *Herald*!

*(*DON LATINO *breaks away from the group and approaches the counter, suspicious and enigmatic. In the luminous spot of the lamp, he holds the open newspaper in his two hands, stammers through the headlines with which the reporter announces the events at Bastardillos street. The others look at him with mocking surprise as if he were a daft old sot.)*

DON LATINO. 'Coal fumes. Two women asphyxiated.[372] Found by a neighbour. Doña Vicenta knows nothing. Crime or suicide? Mystery!'

BAR BOY. See if the paper gives the names of the two females, Don Latí.

DON LATINO. Let me see.

FOP. Don't rack your brains, you old fool.

TREAD-WELL. Let's go, Don Latí.

BAR BOY. I bet you the dead females are the wife and daughter of Don Máximo!

DON LATINO. That's absurd! Why should they kill themselves?

PICA LAGARTOS. ¡Pasaban muchas fatigas!

DON LATINO. Estaban acostumbradas. Solamente tendría una explicación. ¡El dolor por la pérdida de aquel astro!

PICA LAGARTOS. Ahora usted hubiera podido socorrerlas.

DON LATINO. ¡Naturalmente! ¡Y con el corazón que yo tengo, Venancio!

PICA LAGARTOS. ¡El mundo es una controversia!

DON LATINO. ¡Un esperpento!

EL BORRACHO. ¡Cráneo privilegiado!

LIZARD-CHOPPER. They were facing hard times!

DON LATINO. They were used to that. There could be only one explanation. Grief at the loss of that luminous star!

LIZARD-CHOPPER. And just when you'd have been able to help them out.

DON LATINO. Of course! And I've got a heart of gold, Venancio!

LIZARD-CHOPPER. The world is topsy-turvy!

DON LATINO. A carnival nightmare!

THE DRUNK. Phenomenal brain-pan!

NOTES

1 The title is literal, symbolic and aesthetic: first *Bohemian Lights* is about night life in the Bohemian section of Madrid among artists who led an unconventional and non-conforming way of life. The night wanderers are a group of late nineteenth and early twentieth-century Bohemian artists who held that art was superior to nature, that the finest beauty was that of dying or decaying things, and who, both in their lives and art, acted with a disregard for accepted moral or social standards of behaviour. The Madrid Bohemia of 1900 to 1920 had a distinctly literary flavour, was full of decadents, most of them followers of Paul Verlaine, Charles Baudelaire and Rubén Darío among others. Secondly, the play is also a symbolic representation about those few who see light in the darkness, that is, who are lucid enough to break through the confused shadows often symbolized by Bohemia. This is especially true of the blind hero, whose name *Estrella* is a play on 'Starry Light' and 'Dark Fate' and who has, as he says, 'eyes that few people have'. Thirdly, the entire setting of the action offers a highly stylized contrast between night and city lights, between obscurity and illumination. Finally, the complete title of 1924 is a deliberate, meaningful pun on darkness and light: *Luces de Bohemia: Esperpento sacado a luz por Don Ramón del Valle-Inclán, i.e., Lights of Bohemia: an Esperpento Brought to Life* (or illuminated) *by Don Ramón del Valle-Inclán.*

2 The new dramatic genre was christened *esperpento* by Valle-Inclán because the term indicated a grotesque and ridiculous aspect of reality. See note 301.

3 Almost all the characters, with the possible exception of the blind protagonist Max, represent Spanish types and, together, sum up the salient characteristics of the social, political and artistic groups of contemporary Spain. Valle-Inclán deliberately portrays each character with values and attitudes peculiar to his social class.

4 This is an exact description of the urban setting and life style as represented in this play: life was chaotic and senseless because of constant strikes and repressions; it was verbally brilliant in that everyone was ingenious in making sport or wit out of the situation; and, given the economic hard times, the needy artists or poor workers were often desperate and hungry (especially since, where lockouts were in force, people could be seen on the streets begging for a few pennies). 'Absurd, brilliant and hungry'

is also a fitting description of the life of the blind protagonist.

5 A model for the blind poet was probably Valle-Inclán's old friend Alejandro Sawa (1862–1909), Andalusian, Bohemian writer and journalist who had lived in Paris, had met the French writers in the Cafés of the Rive Gauche but who ended in Madrid, dying, blind and crazy. Sawa was considered a brilliant wit and an eccentric, and was well remembered for his hyperbolic and theatrical gestures. Sawa's posthumous work, a miscellaneous collection of autobiographical pieces called *Iluminaciones en la sombra* (*Illuminations in the Darkness*) is a fitting title for a blind man who sees things, and it obviously influenced the content and title of *Bohemian Lights*.

6 Sawa's wife was also a Frenchwoman, Jeanne Poirier. They had spent much time in Paris, were later living in a small apartment in Madrid and had a young daughter.

7 An allusion to the bull-headed god of ancient Egypt, regarded as an incarnation of Osiris. Max refers to an unidentified powerful editor and politician, a Mr 'Big-Shot' to whom everyone must bow. See note 302.

8 Valle-Inclán wrote in a letter to Rubén Darío (see notes 109, 181) how their friend Sawa had received notice that the publication, *El Liberal*, would stop paying him the 60 pesetas for his contributions. The bad news drove Sawa mad in his last days: 'A desperate madness. He wanted to kill himself. His end was like that of a king in a tragedy: mad, blind and furious'. See note 5.

9 A reference to the fumes of the glowing charcoal in an open brazier which can cause slow asphyxiation (see note 372). *Perra* was a copper coin: *perra gorda* = 10 centimes; *perra chica* = 5 centimes.

10 Max's classic looks are compared to the sculptured pieces of blind, bearded messengers of Greek antiquity called the *Hermes* or *Hermae*. The similarity also stresses, however, the uncanny contrast between antiquity and modern times and focuses, ironically, on the absurd aspect of classic or tragic heroes in modern dress. Valle-Inclán explained the premises of his newly conceived, grotesque dramaturgy by pointing out that while the great, tragic roles of life were once played by noble, god-like heroes, the situation is different in our times: man's destiny may be the same now and so are his fatality, his greatness, his haughtiness, his pain . . . *but* the people who act out the tragic roles have changed radically. Actions, anxieties, power, pride are the

same roles of the past and will not change. Man is now different, however, he is too tiny and unimportant to be able to sustain the weight of such heavy responsibilities. The heavy roles of life are too much for modern actors. Hence the contrast, the disparity, the absurd sense of man's performance in life. Blindness, for example, was a beautiful and noble role in Homer. Yet in *Bohemian Lights*, this same blindness is sad, pitiful and pathetic because we are dealing only with a Bohemian poet.

11 The Moncloa Walk with its palace and gardens is at the Northwest corner of Madrid near University City; the style was eighteenth-century French and in the early 1920s the section was one of the most picturesque.

12 *Hispalis* is the old Latin name for Seville; here it is the pseudonym of an old parasite running errands for writers. Max's companion is not identified but typifies the cynical, opportunistic hanger-on of genuine Bohemians.

13 Do not awaken him! 'Cradled by Hypnos' or 'in the arms of Morpheus' were the sort of bookish, affected expressions used by Modernist writers and imitated by pedants. Valle-Inclán records much of the pretentious, stilted and cliché-ridden talk of Bohemians and others.

14 *Apoquinar* is Madrid slang for 'coughing up' the money. Almost every character uses colloquial expressions.

15 The original is also a play on *pipi*, *pipiolo*, colloquial for 'novice', i.e., 'I blundered like a novice', or 'I was taken like a kid.'

16 The *duro* is worth five pesetas.

17 *Faena* is either a 'chore' or a 'pass' with a cape in a bullfight, i.e., 'we'll put on quite a good show for the crowd'. Spaniards are fond of bullfighting expressions and Valle-Inclán reproduces most of them in his later works.

18 Indirect allusion to Virgil guiding Dante through the circles of Hell. The allusive *Latino* is obvious, while the disparity between the two guides or between Dante's journey and Max's modern descent into the Hell of Madrid (called Dante's *Inferno* and Dantesque circle in Scene XI) will become elaborated as the blind poet's night wanderings, with Latino's guidance, continue.

19 The entire Scene II was interpolated in the 1924 edition. See Introduction.

20 Playful parody of Nietzsche's 'Superman' and Plato's 'cave'. The bookseller's nickname alludes to the mythical Persian prophet Zoroaster popularized by Nietzsche's *Thus Spake Zarathustra* (1883–91). The character somewhat

resembles Gregorio Pueyo, an old complaining bookseller who also edited some Modernist works and whose small, dingy cubbyhole was in the same location. Valle-Inclán's Zarathustra represents, of course, a degeneration of the Persian's virtue of telling the truth and aiming straight.

21 A small street off Calle Mayor toward the picturesque section of Old Madrid to the south of the centre. The route which Max takes from his house to Old Madrid and back again may be easily traced by the streets, buildings and parks. His journey is a veritable itinerary of Old Madrid.

22 Such weekly issues devoted to Gothic-like melodramas were published on inferior paper with loud, glossy sensational pictures. Pulp magazines used to print separate episodes of sensational stories about crimes, scandals and love. Very popular and usually superficial and in bad taste.

23 Max's majestic greeting is an adaptation from Calderón de la Barca's *Life is a Dream* (*La vida es sueño*), Act 1, Scene 1, 17–19: 'How rudely, Poland, you receive/a stranger, for you write down with blood/her entry into your domain.' There are several allusions, most of them ironic, to known literary passages in *Lights*. Bohemians, deeply versed in literature as they were, often made it a point to quote from literary works. See notes 61, 67, 109, 222.

24 *Intendente* is also an 'administrator of property'; since Max owns nothing, he is sarcastic and self-disparaging. Self-irony becomes the key to his final outlook on life and art.

25 A rather light striped cotton duck worn by Spanish soldiers in the hot climate of Cuba. Valle-Inclán constantly refers to most Spanish campaigns abroad and the Cuban debacle becomes central in his esperpentic trilogy, *Martes de Carnaval* (*Shrove Tuesday Carnival*), 1930.

26 This character is patterned after the picturesque jack-of-all-genres and errant man of letters Ciro Bayo (1850–1939), known as the Spanish Lazarillo because of his many wanderings. He was author of *The Spanish Lazarillo* (1911), *The Amusing Pilgrim* (1910) and various travel experiences. Valle-Inclán later based much of his famous novel *Tirano Banderas* (1925) on Bayo's Mexican chronicle of *The Marañones*.

27 The Latin expression was the ancient Roman way of beginning letters, meaning 'I wish you well being' or 'I hope you are well'.

28 An imaginary sixteenth-century chivalresque novel, part

of the famous cycle of *Palmerines*. The third of these, *Palmerín de Inglaterra*, survives in only one copy, which is in the British Museum. It was edited by A. Bonilla y San Martín in Vol. XI of the *Nueva Biblioteca de Autores Españoles*. Bayo was an expert in old manuscripts and had done extensive editorial work.

29 Don Gay suggests wittily that he did not see the Royal Family because they did not accord him the honour of coming to see him off at the pier when his ship left port. Most of the characters try to be witty and Valle-Inclán is obviously ironic.

30 This vignette of the prisoner led away is the nucleus of two other new scenes, VI and XI, which like II were added in 1924 and which reflect the violent political crises of 1917 to 1920: arbitrary arrests, beatings, shootings in the back, skirmishes, roaming mobs, patrols. The added material involving this prisoner becomes integrated to the night odyssey of the blind hero.

31 The Catholics' basic conception of Protestantism was the opposition to the use of images in worship.

32 Various religious philosophical trends in the early twentieth century set out to strengthen the hold of authentic religious feeling in people, called for a new, more human attitude to the Christian Gospel and preached religious reform. Don Gay implies that if the aim of life is to seek a union of Man and God then a social organization must be founded on religious practices. His generalizations are a mixed bag of theosophy, neo-mysticism and primitivism, all in the air at the time.

33 The leader of the Bolshevik revolution in Russia was very much in the news at the time. The Spaniards were more impressed with Lenin as a bold, decisive man of action ready to go to extremes than as a Marxist ideologue.

34 The Escorial is one of the most remarkable buildings in Spain, comprising at once a convent, a church, a palace and a royal mausoleum. Near Madrid on the western slopes of the Guadarrama plain, it was built in the sixteenth century by the religious King Philip II and is known, somewhat ironically, as Philip's 'convent-palace'.

35 Max refers to the supplies of granite-like stone, the Spanish *berroqueña*, with which the Escorial was built.

36 First of several remarks about contemporary 'Theosophical Societies', i.e., sects which incorporated elements of Buddhism (China-Japan) and Brahmanism (form of esoteric speculation of India) and which proposed to go

beyond religious institutions by establishing direct, mystical contacts with divine principles. Rather than prayer or devotion, theosophers stressed contemplation and revelation. Theosophy was widely debated among contemporary artists and intellectuals. The sect is treated somewhat ironically in *Lights* because much of the doctrine about pantheistic evolution or reincarnation was obscure and at times led to intellectual charlatanism. See notes 188, 191, 257.

37 Belief in and practice of a purer, more primitive way of Christian life-style, a sort of Christian socialism, was identified with Leo Tolstoy's attempt to lead what he called the pure, simple kind of life that Christ himself or his apostles had led. It was a move away from ecclesiastical rules or from excessive Church practice and a return to the basic tenets of love, good work and simple desires. Some Spanish anarchists, with whom Max is often identified, preached the same ideas.

38 Much of Max's sarcastic tirade is a burlesque version of Spanish catechism and a parody of Sunday sermons, especially the vulgar simplicity of certain notorious lay preachers and their sensational fear-mongering.

39 Well-known parochial organizations of young, unmarried women who collaborated with the churches in charitable works.

40 The borderline between religious faith and religious superstition had always fascinated Valle-Inclán and he dramatized the problem in *Divine Words: A Village Tragicomedy* which appeared in 1920, a few months before *Lights*.

41 Women could not vote at the time and in England some were taking a militant stand about their political rights. In Spain, the news about suffragettes was treated as another foreign eccentricity and a joke.

42 Don Gay's description of a poor man's hostel is in fact a paraphrase of a tourist guide. By coincidence, Ciro Bayo (see note 26) used to publish cheap tourist pamphlets advising Spanish holidaymakers where to go and what to do.

43 Playful allusion to the national myth that the geographical environment (climate, soil, sun etc.) is a key factor in the quick temper or irascible nature of the Spanish people.

44 A novel of sensational occurrences, disappearances and returns, dealing with loyalty, vengeance and love, published in weekly parts so that the solution of the dilemma, the unmasking of the perpetrator or the identification of

the mysterious stranger are not revealed until the last instalments. It was a way of exploiting suspense economically – hence Zarathustra's real motives for not divulging the mystery.

45 A character in another *esperpento, The Horns of Don Friolera* (1921). For the reappearance of characters in Valle-Inclán's works, see note 339.

46 The beginning of a long line of ironic allusions to absurd government practices: here a mocking reference to the system of 'royal decrees' propagated by Antonio Maura's government in 1907–09 (see note 119). Such decrees became obsolete procedures because of the incredibly slow-moving Parliament. One newspaper commented sarcastically: 'Maura's Ideal: a Spain of Royal Decrees'.

47 Busy street starting at the Puerta del Sol (see note 124), at the time full of cabarets and bookstalls. The times were changing early in the twentieth century and life in Old Madrid had drifted away from the more commercial Plaza Mayor and adopted the more picturesque Puerta del Sol, bordered with taverns and populated at night by journalists, students, hustlers, actors, Bohemians, workers, anarchists, and all sorts of artists. Max's journey is a good itinerary of the section of Old Madrid, then the heart of nightlife.

48 *Mus* is a card game based on kings and threes and lends itself to light gambling with small stakes.

49 These were called *quinces* because each wineglass cost about 15 centimes.

50 *Marquesa del Tango* is a burlesque nickname for a woman of easy virtue. The Argentine tango caused a sensation in Madrid around 1919–20. *Lights* is full of such indirect allusions to contemporary fashions, news and events.

51 Max is sarcastic in calling the little tart 'lady' because of her nickname *Marquesa* and thus puns on the second meaning of *dama*, 'mistress' or 'concubine'.

52 The boy tries to be clever by alluding to the serialized melodramas (see note 44) which Don Latino sells (see notes 22, 298).

53 The Spanish *mala sombra* is colloquial, a reaction to a bad pun: 'What a stupid joke!' or the colloquial 'wise guy'. Reference to the boy's redundancy of *finado difunto* ('deceased dead person').

54 Graphic image for 'twitching her lips'.

55 Tread-Well (because she runs around) is probably modelled after a one-eyed flower girl who also sold lottery

tickets and was known to many by the nickname of *ojo de plata* ('silver eye').

56 *De su parte, caballero* is an idiomatic response, usually polite, acknowledging greetings for someone. (To 'my best to the family' one responds, *de su parte*, i.e., 'thank you', 'I won't forget'.)

57 *Décimo* refers to one ticket from a block of ten, which usually receives ten percent of the prize.

58 Like *7557*. From *cap y cúa* in Catalan.

59 Reference to a 'client', a widower. *Cabrito* is a derogatory diminutive for cuckold.

60 Emilio Castelar (1832–99) was a successful politician and famous flowery orator. He represented an oratorical mode of speaking and writing that was fostered by the spectacular parliamentary debates at the end of the nineteenth century. See note 72.

61 A pet phrase of Francisco (Paco) Villaespesa (see note 264). Possible reminiscence of St John of the Cross' first strophe of *Spiritual Canticle* ('Like the stag you have fled, /having wounded me'). Such literary expressions were commonplace among Bohemians and Valle is often ironic about their use. See note 23.

62 Sawa (note 5) wrote in *Illuminations* about himself: 'I am, on the inside, a man radically different from what I'd like to be and, on the outside, that is, in my external behaviour, a not very graceful caricature of myself'.

63 Euphemism for being hungry but unable to do anything about eating.

64 An aniseed-flavoured brandy made in the small, old Andalusian town of Rute.

65 A humorous parallel to marriages between royalty and commoners. Tread-Well contrasts her ordinary background, a concubine at best, to that of her husband, the King of Portugal, which is really the nickname for a pander. See note 70.

66 Reference to the face pustules which come from smallpox; the tramp's silly smile brings his pock-marked face grotesquely into bold relief. A good example of Valle-Inclán's manner with literary caricature. See also note 212.

67 Burlesque reference to Góngora's *romance* 'Hermana Marica', ('My sister Marica') which ends, 'hacemos yo y ella/las bellaquerías /detrás de la puerta' ('She and I do/ lots of roguish acts/behind doors').

68 *Manolo*, a familiar form of Manuel, the name of the dethroned Portuguese king, is also a low class resident of

Madrid, dressing loud and living fast; a 'sharpie', what today would be called a 'cool' fellow.

69 Tread-Well jokes on her man's nickname: 'Are you afraid that [by entering a low joint and demeaning your category as king] you may lose your crown? So enter as if you were not a king, you big oaf.' *So* in Spanish is slang for *you* before derogatory epithets: e.g., '*so* granuja' for 'you damn rascal'. This is an indirect satirical allusion to the situation of the Spanish Monarchy and the various pretenders to the throne. See note 76.

70 Literally: 'Since she went to Lisbon and found out the value of money'. Tread-Well's husband objects to his nickname because since Portugal, and in particular Lisbon, were often associated with prostitution, his alias can mean 'king of pimps'; i.e., he rules over the commerce of sexual relations. See note 65. (In the *Esperpento of the Regalia of the Deceased* 1926 (*Las galas del difunto*), Lisbon is considered superior to Barcelona for brothels.)

71 *Pica Lagartos* is a pejorative nickname meaning sharpie or sly thief and obviously refers to his trade as tavern-keeper.

72 Because of Castelar's use of verbal exaggeration and rhetorical display. See note 60.

73 That is, his father was influential enough to help buy votes and thus help elect him to parliament. Valle-Inclán refers to a known, accepted fact that there had not been a single honest or genuine election to the Cortes in the past forty years.

74 Don Manuel Camo was a local, political boss (*cacique*) from Huesca, a small city of Aragón, in whose honour a statue was erected. *Caciquismo* (political bossism), among other things, had to do with rigging elections.

75 A well-known order of Brothers devoted to good education, founded in Rome at the end of the sixteenth century by San José de Calasanz.

76 Don Jaime de Borbón y Parma was Carlist pretender to the throne (see note 344) who travelled extensively and was often the object of ironic jibes. For the joke on *incognito*, see note 69.

77 The clashes in the streets here refer to the national strikes and political disturbances of 1917–19. The labour crisis was aggravated, contending mobs roamed the streets, one side was provoking the other, and this fluid situation often led to violence and bloodshed.

78 Probably the general strike that was called by the Socialist

Labour Union (U.G.T.) early in August of 1917 and which the anarchists joined. Valle-Inclán, of course, makes a synthesis of all proletarian and strike activities in the first two decades of the twentieth century, starting with the infamous repression of the 1909 'Tragic Week' to the bloodshed of 1917–19.

79 The Workers' House of the Socialist labour union U.G.T. in Madrid (Unión General de Trabajadores) was also an assembly hall where big union meetings were held. The Socialist *Casas del Pueblo*, with their primitive libraries and lecture courses, were replacing the old casino as a centre for the cultural diffusion of the proletariat.

80 *Acción Ciudadana* was a Citizen's Council Organization made up of business men or property owners and considered conservative, if not reactionary. See note 103.

81 The tavernkeeper's comments on employers is historically accurate. Labour agitation had induced a more and more pronounced defensive psychosis among the small employers who began organizing precisely during the 1910–20 decade. A Spanish Employer's Confederation was established in 1911 and a solid front of small and big management began opposing the unity of wage workers.

82 Tread-Well mocks the Red Cross organization for recruiting women to do hospital work.

83 The *New York Times* reported on 20 February 1919, that 'All the stores and cafés have been closed'.

84 On 2 May 1808 the popular uprising against the French which took place in the Puerta del Sol (see note 124) started the War of Independence.

85 See note 50.

86 Main streets were sprinkled with sand or gravel in order to safeguard patrolling army and police on horseback from slipping and falling.

87 See note 83.

88 An example of the Modernist cult of sensorial effect, especially through the combination of light and colour.

89 Reference to emergency policemen who wore round, Roman-like safety helmets. During the strikes of 1917–19 extra enforcements were frequently mobilized to suppress the strikers. Emergency policemen used clubs and also carried guns.

90 A shop selling *buñuelos* (a kind of doughnut) and frequented by Modernists and Bohemians. Such places were common and kept very late hours, serving coffee, fritters, *aguardiente*, brandy, hot chocolate, etc. The *Buñolería* was

one of the last stops before returning home late, sometime after midnight.

91 Ironic comparison of the two Bohemians to the ancient Greek philosophers, followers of Aristotle, when teaching and discussion usually took place during walks. An ironic contrast: the Madrid Bohemians are extravagant, would-be thinkers and represent the degeneration of the classic Athenians, the serious disciples of Aristotle, who taught and discussed during their walks. See note 10.

92 The result of violent skirmishes between strikers and police. (See note 296.) The *New York Times* reported that 'The labour situation in Madrid and Barcelona has undergone no improvement, the situation in Madrid becoming more serious. Strikes are spreading all over' (Dec. 25).

93 The original is a learned expression, intended humorously, for *¿Qué camino seguimos?*. 'Which way are we heading?'. See note 146.

94 Sawa in his *Illuminations*: 'The torture of living in the café and roaming the streets—why was I not condemned to other places of exile?'

95 *De recuelo* referred to a cheap coffee made from left-over grounds, served in most *Buñolerías*.

96 The technique of the stage direction here is cinematic: there's darkness, the light moves and suddenly focuses on a new character, as if the camera following the eyes of those searching surprised Tread-Well in her position. There is an instantaneous transfer from one scene to the next as if there were a blur between them. Valle-Inclán experimented with the use of cinema, especially cuts and montage, in his stage descriptions.

97 That is, three poor wretches; poor and miserable like brute cave-dwellers. In the original the repetition of the sound *tr* is a tongue-twister similar to the traditional 'en un plato de *tr*igo, *tr*es *tr*istes *t*igres *tr*igo comieron'.

98 A sarcastic comment and cruel joke since Max cannot see. The representation of such lack of sensitivity is a fundamental aspect of the *esperpento*. Indifference to the blind poet will be intensified in each scene. See note 138.

99 The original is a slang expression referring to the three pesetas Max was trying to borrow from the tavern-keeper (Scene III).

100 Count Romanones (1864–1950) was one of Spain's wealthiest politicians with a reputation among the people for being greedy and stingy—hence Max's allusion.

101 The Bolshevik revolution had by 1920 established itself and

was acting as a powerful magnet on many workers, intellectuals or anarchists.

102 The Cibeles is the square in the centre of Madrid, a hubbub of activity and at the time the scene of many protest strikes.

103 Literally, 'Honorary Cops'. These were the voluntary policemen of *Acción Ciudadana* (see note 80). They were hated by the labour unions and were often the targets of syndicalist gunmen. See note 210.

104 *Amarillos* was the disparaging term for strike-breakers. That is, the striking workers attacked those who refused to join or act with the labour union and especially when 'scabs' or 'blacklegs' took the place of strikers. Also probably an allusion to members of the *Sindicatos Libres* (Free Unions), founded in October 1919 with the collusion of the employers' federation.

105 In the late nineteenth century the Modernists had stood for a stylistic revolution in poetry and prose, but by 1920 their period had ended, their poetry had deteriorated considerably and their defence of 'pure poetry' or 'art for art's sake' was no longer very convincing to most writers.

106 These figures are now readily identifiable because they were among the many second and third-rate young poets mentioned in contemporary reviews. Of them, Rafael Gálvez wrote sonnets that were well received. The others were the perennial hangers-on, the arty Bohemians during the end of an era.

107 Dorio de Gadex was the pseudonym of Eduardo de Ory from Cádiz, a Modernist prose writer. Two of his novels are *Truce* (*Tregua*), 1908 and *A Coward* (*Un cobarde*) 1909. He was known as a facile writer, a vagabond and an irritating snob and know-all. He had been savagely ridiculed earlier for his crude plagiarisms from Anatole France in 1910.

108 The original *ceceoso como un cañí* is a colloquial reference to those (mainly Andalusians) who pronounce *s* as *z* (a heavy *th*); here a special reference to Gad*ex* and Cádi*z* where such lisping is extreme. Since Valle-Inclán also lisped heavily, there may be some self-irony here.

109 From the opening lines of Rubén Darío's 'Responso a Verlaine' ('Anthem for the Death of Paul Verlaine'), 1896: 'Father and Master of Magic, Celestial Lyre-bearer, / to the Olympic organ and the rustic pipe,/you gave your enchanting music.' Darío (1867–1916), the influential Nicaraguan poet and leader of the Modernist movement,

was a close friend of Sawa and Valle-Inclán. He exerted a big influence on Valle-Inclán and on almost all the Modernists. Fragments of his poems were quoted constantly. He appears in person twice, in Scenes IX, XIV. The anachronism in the play is obvious: *Lights* takes place around 1917–1920; Darío died in 1916 and Sawa in 1909.

110 Though the Modernist youths proclaim him their leader, Max is openly negative about them and about their aloofness from the common people; he finds their poetry uninteresting and their wit stale. Besides, they are uncommitted socially and politically when the national situation calls for commitment. See note 327.

111 The original (*traje de luces*) is an allusion to the bullfighters' glittering costume. See note 17.

112 Dorio de Gadex refers pretentiously to Ibsen's late symbolist play *When We Dead Awaken* (1899), where the mountain becomes a symbol of what brings man nearer and nearer to a confrontation with eternal truths. These are the fine truths which, according to the snobbish Dorio, are not accessible to the common people who remain at the foot of the mountain. An elitist interpretation of Ibsen.

113 Max's apparent desertion of Modernist aesthetics for a more radical and sociological attitude toward art may parallel Valle-Inclán's change from the decadent refinements of his earlier *Sonatas* to the disconcerting realities of the *esperpentos*. Though Max is certainly not Valle, the blind poet often resembles his author in opinions concerning art and society. On 3 September 1920, for example, precisely at the time when *Lights* came out, Valle answered a reporter's question 'what are we writers supposed to do?' with ideas similar to those uttered by Max: 'Not art. We must not cultivate art at this time, because it is immoral and miserable to go on playing in these times. The first thing to do is bring about social justice' (*El Sol*).

114 Max hints strongly that the Modernists' language is affected and their style artificial. He obviously distinguishes between the pretentious poets who stress art for art's sake and another brand of modernism which consciously takes a stand on social issues. He is against evasion, at least here. Modernist talk, once elegant, euphemistic and symbolic, has in writers like Dorio de Gadex degenerated into bookish clichés.

115 The Spanish Royal Academy was founded in 1713 to give and preserve certain rules to the Spanish language and to immortalize Spain's great writers. The success with which

great writers have been recognized or new members were selected by the Academy has been a moot point. Between 1900–20 the Academy came under heavy attacks and savage ridicule both by young writers and by the press.

116 This is a free rendering. The original 'one has to please all the Segismundos' is an allusion to lines 1338–39 in Act II of Calderón's *Life is a Dream* (see note 23). Valle-Inclán's satirical darts against the stuffiness of the Academy members are proverbial.

117 See note 7.

118 Valle-Inclán throughout his career attacked the Royal Academy as intellectually reactionary and mocked it as aesthetically stuffy and banal. He devotes an entire irreverent section in *The Pipe of Kif* (1919).

119 Antonio Maura (1853–1925), several times Prime Minister, conservative leader and also director of the Spanish Academy—hence Max's negative reaction to him as politician and academic. Maura was a dominating and controversial figure for the first two decades of the century, giving rise to *Maurismo* (revolution from the top) and to the polemical slogan 'Maura sí, Maura no'. He is constantly mentioned in *Lights* in a derogatory manner. See notes 46, 129, 149.

120 Allusion to the recent death of the great novelist, Benito Pérez Galdós (1843–1920). Valle-Inclán admired Galdós but the Modernists considered his style commonplace and prosaic; hence the reference to the 'chick-pea' (*garbanzo*), a key ingredient for the stew *cocido*, popular with the middle classes, that is, Galdós is called a mediocre writer of the middle class. Also, the protagonist of Galdós' *El amigo Manso* is a gentle philosopher whose weakness is a love of chick-peas—hence the famous nickname for Galdós.

121 Reference to Francisco Basallo Becerra, a war prisoner in the Moroccan disaster of 1921 who was then thrust into the national scene, honoured as a national hero and even made to write his *Memoirs* (1923). Max is sarcastic at the Academy's poor taste, opportunism and above all at its false and unjust recognition of authentic talent. The 'sad plight of the Academy' was a favourite topic among the majority of artists, writers and intellectuals. See note 115.

122 *El Enano de la Venta* is a proverbial expression referring to a folklore midget whose head is bigger than his body, that is, it refers to those whose bark is bigger than their bite. The expression stands for empty boasting, while the

'New Couplets' ('Joys', *Gozos*, in the original) satirize some contemporary musical hits. The Spaniards have been masters of short popular genres like musical comedies (*zarzuela*) and one-act farces (*sainetes*). A good part of the content of the *esperpentos* comes from popular genres.

123 The original is a literal translation from the French *chef d'œuvre* and a deliberate Gallicism typical of Modernist style. The consciously mannered language of the Modernists is parodied in *Lights*. See note 176.

124 The major traffic hub bordered with shops and taverns, the centre of Old Madrid. By World War I, night life had drifted away from the Plaza Mayor and shifted deeper into Old Madrid. See notes 47, 125.

125 *Retén* refers to a special detachment of reserve police in the Ministry of Interior, located in the Puerta del Sol (see note 124), used for putting down disorders.

126 Rafael el Gallo was a famous bullfighter known for his brilliant, daring passes. See note 286, 360.

127 See note 122. The Dwarf obviously alludes to some boasting politician much in the news.

128 The original is pronounced *jarca*. The young Modernists are mocking the Hispanic-Moroccan military unit under a Spanish commander in Africa between 1917 and 1923. Significantly the phrase *Quiere gobernar la jarca* was interpolated in the second 1924 edition, that is, after the overseas disaster (see note 171) which made military boasts and Spain's confused policy appear ludicrous. The *Enano* 'Dwarf' here may be Antonio Maura himself whose pretentious calls to nationalism did sound like empty boasts to many.

129 The religious hypocrite, protagonist of *Tartuffe*, refers here to some contemporary politician, perhaps Maura (see note 119). *Malsín* means a malicious gossip or troublemaker.

130 *¡Chola!* is an onomatopeic reference to an empty head, something like the colloquial 'noodle'.

131 These are, of course, free renderings of the rhymes of the original.

132 The use of the Latin *équites* is ironic. It was used by Modernists and often satirized in popular farces. Typical scene of the times: 'Martial law has been declared in Madrid, and troops are patrolling the streets' (*NYT*, March 1919).

133 St John Chrysostom was the most persuasive preacher of patristic times and his name in Greek means 'golden mouth'.

134 By comparing the captain sarcastically to a commanding officer of ancient Rome, Max can only provoke him because the intellectuals, who were notoriously antimilitarist, used to dub the cavalry with the pejorative 'Roman soldiers' (see note 89).

135 The captain uses a very colloquial form *delega* for *Delegaciónde Orden Público*. He thus treats Max scornfully.

136 Here Max responds cynically to the Captain's slang (*borrachín* and *delega*), telling him that he, a poet, can do as well as any other when it comes to the vulgar street parlance of the city slickers (*chulos*). *Más chulo que un ocho* for *Más erguido o altanero que un ocho* is very idiomatic, standing for *yo no soy menos que tú*, that is, 'I can match you every step', or 'and damn proud of it'.

137 Many nightwatchmen in Madrid were from rural areas like Asturias, hence the sarcastic *trogloditas* and *domesticar* ('taming brute animals'). *Serenos* were considered reactionary collaborators of the Police and the Army.

138 Max compares the *sereno* to the Patron Saint of the Blind but the nightwatchman does not understand the blind poet's sarcasm. In the original there is a play on light/darkness (*luz, lucía, estrella, sereno*).

139 A typical grouping on the part of the authorities of all sorts of radicals, or political, cultural and social outcasts.

140 *Punto* is strongly pejorative for 'jerk', or 'fool'.

141 Reference to the Police station attached to the Ministry of Interior and located in the Puerta del Sol. See note 124.

142 *La duerma* refers to *dormir la mona*, 'to sleep off the effects of drunkenness'.

143 *Sus* for *os*, is an imitation of the Asturian dialect.

144 Don Mariano de Cavia (1855–1919) was a famous journalist and reputed alcoholic, said to be drinking like a poet who learned his Latin in Horace and Bacchus. A member of the Academy (note 115) he was openly scorned by Valle-Inclán and other writers.

145 Dorio uses a superstitious expression to suggest indignation: 'God forbid that we poets should be vulgar newspapermen.' (See note 231.)

146 Latino imitates Max's literary question. See note 93 for the original.

147 See note 125.

148 Maura as a 'hypocrite' makes him the most likely butt of the *Enano* parody. See note 122.

149 Allusion to claims or rumours that Maura was a *chueta*, i.e., a *converso* (Christianized Jew) from Mallorca. The

implications of Maura's 'impurity of blood' were ironically drawn even in Parliament. See note 119.

150 A free translation: the original is a euphemism for a scatological oath.

151 A pejorative nickname, *bonito* being an effeminate epithet for the Police Inspector's foppishness.

152 *Mala Estrella* is *mala suerte* ('bad luck') or *mal hado*, that is, Max Estrella is branded by a tragic fate. Max is beginning to mock the tragic role he has been playing.

153 See note 118 for Max's sarcasm about the Royal Academy.

154 Max is ironic about the politically loaded term, *cesante*, which meant being dismissed from the civil service and left without a job. Each change of administration involved firing and making new appointments and inevitably the *cesante*, who symbolized the insecurity of bureaucratic appointments, was often the object of ridicule. Being 'in' or 'out' for government employees was the inevitable accompaniment of every political change. Max uses the term metaphorically, sarcastically alluding to his dismissal as a newspaper contributor by the all-powerful editor Buey Apis. See note 7.

155 San Cosme was a small street near Calle de Atocha, that is, on the edge of Old Madrid near the railroad station.

156 The French Romantic poet, dramatist and novelist Victor Hugo (1802–85) was a hero of the Modernists because of his great stylistic range and his striking images. Comparison with Hugo became conventional praise.

157 Here a reference to arbitrary imprisonment, to tortures and to the harsh suppression of nonconformists.

158 This entire scene was added in 1924 and develops the episode of the handcuffed man led to prison in Scene II. See note 30.

159 Allusion to the strikes and repressions in Catalonia from 1917 to 1919, which led to national political turmoil. Barcelona had a revolutionary atmosphere and became the refuge of *agents provocateurs*, gunmen and other adventurers who intervened in labour disputes and offered their services for hire. Violence and assassinations were the result.

160 In accepting his lot as a worker rejected by the Spanish establishment, the prisoner becomes an aggressive outcast, an anarchist, for whom the state is to blame if a man becomes lawless. The outcast must resist the government even by terrorism.

161 A rash recommendation to revive the 'Reign of Terror'

during the French Revolution, when revolutionary courts condemned thousands of suspects to death. Many executions were public, hence Max's suggestion of setting up a modern, push-button guillotine in a busy thoroughfare for all to witness.

162 Most anarchists were sympathetic to the Bolshevik revolution, and Lenin's success often served as a stimulus for strikes, uprisings, sabotage, and assassinations.

163 A peculiar mixture of Bakunin and Lenin: the prisoner, like other Spanish anarchists, aimed at creating by violence a state from which even the mildest form of ownership—and hence compulsion—was excluded. The wicked owners who had for so long oppressed others were to be eliminated. Anarchist workers believed that there could be no social harmony unless the idea of property were eradicated. Bakunin's theory that the chief oppressor of man is the state (in *Statehood and Anarchy*) was influential in Spain.

164 Around 1924 Valle-Inclán said in a letter that the *gachupines* (Spanish settlers in America) represented the very essence of Iberian savagery, that they owned 70% of the land and that in their hands land had become the most pernicious kind of property. He suggested expelling them unless, of course, they could be put to the sword. Valle-Inclán developed the prisoner's political views in his novel *Tyrant Banderas*, which followed the second edition of *Lights* in 1924.

165 Allusion to the frequent terrorist attempts in Barcelona and to the bloody reprisals and counter reprisals between syndicalists and the establishment. Ever since the infamous 'tragic week' of 1909, when a general strike degenerated into a riot and brought military suppression, there were assassinations and a wide-spread fear held Catalan employers in its clutches. That is what Max alludes to.

166 Probably a reference to Mateo Morral, the young Catalan anarchist who in Madrid threw a bomb at King Alfonso XIII and Queen Victoria Eugenia on their wedding day.

167 Spanish anarchists were for the most part embittered and poverty-stricken workmen who felt that they had to resort to direct violent action against the employers and the government. Rather than prepare for an organized revolution they tended to plunge headlong into action—hence the sabotage and murder. Such a mystique of violence brought anarchists, in general, closer to Bakunin than to Lenin.

168 Barcelona was the commercial centre of Spain. The anarchists often proclaimed a connection between mercantilism and the myth of the Jewish commercial temperament.

169 For the anarchists Carthage and Jerusalem, cities which suffered destruction at the hands of Rome, were examples of materialism and commercial interests.

170 Caesar's famous remark 'The die is cast!'

171 Probably an allusion to the failure of the Socialist-oriented general strike of 1917, and to the fact that several anarchists in Barcelona refused to be drafted for the Moroccan colonial war, a war that was going from bad to worse. See note 128. Valle-Inclán reassembles several seemingly disparate events, making them fit into a composite picture of the disturbing national situation.

172 *Ley de fugas* was a well-known practice during the period 1915–22; the police arrested syndicalists and shot them as they were being conducted to or from the Police station. They were reported as shot while trying to escape. The striker's fate here closely parallels what happened to others under the repressive measures of General S. Martínez Anido (1862–1938), whose cynical reaction to the repression in 1920 was that the strikers had not improved enough and that 'tougher measures' had to be taken against them.

173 'The Black Legend' was a term coined by Spaniards to refer to the prejudiced belief of foreigners, disseminated in the sixteenth century by the powers hostile to Spain and fostered by the French Encyclopaedists of the eighteenth century, that Spain had always been an obscurantist, backward and cruel country.

174 In the original, the ring of the bell is expressed in an avant-garde metaphor: the bell chirps like a cricket.

175 Sarcastic use of *capitalista* in calling plutocrats those who live by sponging on others.

176 In the original, *journal* is a pretentious Gallicism for *periódico*. See note 123.

177 Charles II was known as *el Hechizado* ('the Bewitched') and his reign (1665–1700) was the last of the Hapsburg dynasty. Dorio refers to the age of autocracy, the Inquisition and monarchical ineffectiveness. He responds to Latino's *Desgobernación* ('Misgovernment').

178 The original ('So help me a wooden saint') is a witty version of *válgame un santo que está en los altares* ('So help me a saint who is on the altars', meaning 'raised to the altars',

i.e., canonized). The statues of saints on the altars are of course carved in wood.

179 The prisoner and Max had discussed in Scene VI how the papers report only what they are told in connection with disturbances.

180 Philip II (1556–98) was a symbol of autocratic intransigence. Dorio here responds to Latino's comment about the 'violation of individual rights'.

181 The Modernist poet Rubén Darío. See note 109.

182 A quotation from the famous 'Autumn Song in Spring' ('Canción de otoño en primavera'): 'Juventud, divino tesoro,/¡ ya te vas para no volver!' is the recurring refrain lamenting lost youth. See note 109.

183 Dorio de Gadex is here portrayed as a pretentious writer with affected manners. His notoriety for bad taste is portrayed in the provocative way he talks and acts. See note 107.

184 Ironic reference to the ring-like marks of dandruff or hair-grease on the coat collar; Dorio means that 'we so overflow with cleverness that it shows in our dandruff'. There is a constant exchange of witticisms in this scene.

185 Dorio interprets Filiberto's words literally, and deliberately makes an obscene reference to the tongue (*lengua*). An example of degenerated wit.

186 Francisco Silvela (1845–1905) was a conservative politician, famous orator and academician. Dubbed *la daga florentina* ('the Florentine dagger') for his sharp tongue, he wrote, among many other things, on the Parliamentary system, hence Filiberto's later comment, *el plumífero parlamentario*.

187 Narciso Díaz de Escobar (1860–1935) won many prizes for his journalistic pieces; he wrote, significantly, 'Floral games', *Apuntes históricos sobre los juegos florales* (Málaga 1900) and other works on prizes and debates. He was often parodied by younger writers.

188 The theosophical movement launched by Mme Blavatsky (see notes 36, 191) in 1875 claimed to have attained the ultimate truth concerning the nature of man and God. *Karma* meant 'action', 'deed' or 'fate', and taught how the nature and circumstances of man's future re-incarnation were to be determined. Filiberto suggests that the same law of cause and effect, the same unmitigated law of retribution, applies to journalism, to politics, to games as to all human activity. Any action is only a part in the cycle of the Wheel of Life.

189 'Cabalistic sense', i.e., the hidden meaning of Latino's pen-name. Much of this discussion reflects a favourite topic of the time, but made pretentious in order to satirize pseudo-intellectuals. Fascinating ideas are bandied about by frivolous thinkers; in an *esperpento* such overblown discussion signifies sophistry.

190 Latino, as usual, is giving himself airs, and the magical transmutation is merely his name spelt backwards.

191 See note 188. Filiberto's baldness and his 'theosophical' explanation of things may be a deliberate reference to Roso de Luna (1872–1931), who was strikingly bald, and also the best known of the Spanish theosophists. He was President of the 'Ateneo teosófico', and founded the theosophic review *Hesperia*. He wrote a series of articles expounding the theosophical implications of archaeology, published in *Simbología arcaica* (1921). See note 20.

192 Mocking version of the Spanish commonplace of honour and pride; 'yo sé quién soy' ('I know who I am').

193 The English economist Thomas Malthus (1766–1834) held that unless an increase in population were checked, whether by prudent restraint or by wars and epidemics, poverty and famine would be inevitable. Dorio's connection of abortion with Malthus is, for Valle-Inclán, a degeneration of wit, covering over a vacancy of thought.

194 Unamuno (1864–1936), the Spanish thinker and writer famed for his serious preoccupation with the tragic sense of human life. Don Philbert's ironic 'guess' points to a deliberate contrast between the irreverent Modernists and the stern members of the 'generation of 1898' who, like Unamuno, saw Spanish problems ethically rather than aesthetically, and who were concerned with the permanent causes of Spanish backwardness and political disorders.

195 Alfonso XIII, who abdicated in 1931, was the last Spanish king. He had meddled continually in the process of government.

196 Filiberto suggests that the king is both urbane and conservative. The Bourbon dynasty ruled in Spain from 1700 to 1931 and came to be identified with political and social reaction. King Alfonso's political interference led to constant ministerial instability. From 1902–23 some 33 prime ministers passed in and out of office, their average term being seven and a half months. Governmental changes and Alfonso's equivocal intentions were the 'jokes' of the time.

197 Manuel García Prieto (1859–1938), leader of the Liberal-Democratic party was appointed Prime Minister in

September 1917, in November 1918 after Maura's fall and finally, in 1923 on the eve of Primo de Rivera's *coup d'état*. The king's sense of humour stems from selecting a mediocre, windbag of a politician (called in Madrid by some 'Manolito el Tonto'). See notes 200, 201.

198 Queen Isabella II, daughter of Fernando VII. Politically and morally suspect (she was reputed to be promiscuous) she was compelled to abdicate in 1868 and lived afterwards in Paris. Valle-Inclán published in 1920 a picturesque satire about her, *Farce and Promiscuity of the Pure Spanish Queen* (*Farsa y licencia de la reina castiza*). See Chronology.

199 This French publishing house published in Spanish several original works and translations. Some Spanish writers worked for them, including Darío, the Machado brothers and Sawa.

200 García Prieto (see note 197) was given this title after signing, as Foreign Minister, the Hispano-Moroccan treaty of 1911–12.

201 *Santiago y abre España* plays on the famous war cry of medieval Spaniards in their battles against the Moors, *Santiago y cierra España* ('St James, and charge [also close] Spain'). Valle-Inclán, through Dorio, is parodying several of Prieto's cliché-ridden speeches in parliament.

202 A quotation from the Roman liturgy of Ash Wednesday: 'Memento homo quia pulvis es et in pulverem reverteris'.

203 'King of doubletalk'; a reference to Maura's flowery oratory in which he promised much but, according to his detractors, was never able to fulfil his pledges. Maura was often reproached in the press for his rhetoric. See notes 46, 119.

204 Benlliure, a Valencian sculptor who erected many statues, including Castelar's, in Madrid and was considered 'conventional' by Modernists. The Italian-sounding *santi boni barati* (for *santos buenos baratos*) was a street advertisement for wooden or plaster marionettes and figurines of religious figures usually made in Italy. The expression here deflates Benlliure's art as common, cheap and mass-produced.

205 Cavestany (1861–1924), poet and playwright, was a member of the Academy and, for many, a sign of that Institution's mediocrity. See notes 115, 144.

206 *Por cifra* means rendering musical notation positions by numbers. It signifies a prosaic way of learning, and hence one who plays or teaches mechanically. Cavestany was the object of ridicule for the 'padding' of his style: in

contemporary reviews 'los ripios de Cavestany' became proverbial.

207 *Un yerno más* alludes to the form of nepotism called *yernocracia*, i.e., 'government by and for sons-in-law'. A cynical comment made the rounds in the press that when Spaniards changed politics or parties they were only exchanging relatives. *Yernocracia* is the title of one of Clarín's stories. The theme was a great stand-by for music-hall jokes. It was known that both Maura and García Prieto (see notes 119, 197), one a conservative, the other a liberal, had launched their political careers after marrying daughters of influential and wealthy families.

208 *Bagatela* is a key term in the cultural history of Spain in the early twentieth century because writers like Azorín, Baroja and Valle-Inclán, had on occasion used the expression to launch an attack against established ideas. *Bagatela* was a way of being anti-traditional and modern, it represented a light and, hence, scornful treatment of something profound. At the end of Valle-Inclán's *Winter Sonata* (1905) the 'ugly, Catholic and sentimental' lover-hero, the Marquis of Bradomín (see notes 266, 339), admitted that all his doctrine was contained in the phrase *Viva la bagatela*. Here Don Philbert means that young Modernists are irreverent, while many of the modern writers and intellectuals do not believe in anything and that their purpose is to destroy the traditional values of Spain. The cult of 'trifling matters' and the literary elaboration of *peu de chose* are important for a better understanding of the development of Valle-Inclán as a writer, especially since he had been accused, by no less a person than Ortega y Gasset, of wasting his talents on frivolous subjects. Here we have a confrontation of the new and the old Valle-Inclán: as a light and scornful treatment of stuffy, pretentious realities, the *bagatela* is related to the aesthetic of the *esperpento* (see Introduction), but the *bagatela* is simultaneously parodied as wantonly used by Modernists, who treat important human values as if they were trivial. Valle-Inclán is never nihilistic in the *esperpentos*, but some of his characters are.

209 Allusion to the prestigious Ateneo of Madrid, which since the Restoration had been a famous literary and political society, with a very large library, where intellectuals met for lectures and discussions. Founded in 1835 as a literary club, it was at the time of our play regarded as a stronghold of liberalism. It had included all the more distin-

guished figures of Spanish life among its members. The Ateneo has been regarded as exemplifying both the worst and the best in Spanish intellectual life; hence Valle-Inclán's ambivalent position, negative early on, favourable at the end.

210 Reference to one of many political assassinations which between 1919 and 1923 totalled over a thousand. Murders increased on both sides because the syndicalists, as seems suggested here, exacted strict reprisals for the killings by *pistoleros* and for the 'protectionist' activity of the Honorary Policemen. The 'raincoated' victim was obviously an 'honorary policeman'. See note 103.

211 The cynic Latino repeats a burlesque version of the Romantic poet Espronceda's 'Que haya un cadáver más, ¿qué importa al mundo?' ('What does the world care if there's one more corpse to bury') which had been also parodied in the *género chico*, 'c'haiga un cadáver más, ¿qué importa al mundo?' Cf. A. Zamora Vicente, p.23.

212 The physical appearance of the theosophist Don Philbert emerges in four stages and is a good example of Valle-Inclán's art of grotesque caricature: we first see 'a *bald* man' writing and, next, the '*bald* newspaperman', or 'Don Philbert, the rheumy and *bald* journalist', i.e., the adjective becomes a fixed epithet. Then the character begins to be submerged in his baldness as we see him 'covering his *bald head* with his yellowish, ink-stained hands'. Finally, he reappears smiling 'in all the *broad roundness* of his *baldness*'. The theosophist is not seen merely as a bald man at the end but, rather, as a personality hidden under his baldness and unable to escape his one dominant physical characteristic. As with all the characters, the grotesque physical image predominates completely and weighs heavily upon the human personality. See also note 66.

213 The Minister's office at the Puerta del Sol was next to the Police station where Max was imprisoned. See notes 124, 125.

214 Extravagant image typical of avantgarde writing. Valle-Inclán often parodies such imagery. See note 174.

215 Once released, Max simply found his way next door. See notes 124, 125.

216 Ironical reference to the ephemeral little avantgarde magazines (*Madrid Cómico, Vida Nueva, Helios, Arte Joven*) which had their heyday between 1908 and 1924; they had a small circulation, very limited capital and usually short lives.

217 *Fuego de virutas* means 'burning wood shavings' whose blaze lasts for a moment; it is a further parody of the style of Maura (note 119) who in 1903 had used the phrase *fogatas de virutas* ('fires of shavings').

218 Although there is no complete identification his Excellency resembles somewhat the journalist and later Minister of Public Education, Don Julio Burell, a friend of Valle-Inclán who often helped him.

219 Reminiscent of a line from Victor Hugo. Max Sawa is blind and a Mediterranean poet, like Homer; Belisarius (died 565) was Justinian's general who, blinded, wandered as a beggar to Constantinople.

220 A euphemism for venereal disease.

221 By alluding to the goddess of justice and wisdom, Minerva, Max appeals to the literary pretentions of his old school friend.

222 The original recalls the refrain to one of St John of the Cross's poems '*aunque es de noche*' ('For I well know the fountain that wells up and flows,/although it is night').

223 The traditional idea of the 'seeing blind man', or of 'wisdom in blindness', as in the case of Teiresias or Oedipus, provides one of the meanings of the title *Bohemian Lights* and prepares for the definition of the *esperpento*, since the grotesque representation of reality will be formulated in the blind poet's own vision.

224 Possibly an inner duplication of character since Alejandro Sawa signed letters as Alex. See note 5.

225 The Minister's proviso 'as long as' reflects the instability of governments at the time, a period dubbed by historians as the *vals de los ministerios* ('The Waltz of Cabinets'). Burrell himself, for example, was Minister in 1917 (April–June) under Dato and again, fleetingly, in November 1918.

226 A grotesque image transforming cantankerous door-keepers into the Minotaur of the Cretan Labyrinth of apartment buildings.

227 Max 'touches' rock bottom, in that, he reaches the lowest depths of human indignity, but he simultaneously 'taps' the 'Madrid snakepit', which was slang for the secret funds used by the Ministry of the Interior to bribe informers. *El fondo de los reptiles* was also used to buy witnesses against radicals, anarchists and strikers. Max claims, sarcastically, that he has reached the limit of degradation because he is paid like any other police lackey (*canalla*).

228 Max had previously (in Scene 1) called Latino a 'cynic' which, etymologically, means 'like a dog'.

229 *Actor de carácter* is a theatrical term for the actor who usually takes the part of an elderly man.

230 The 'authentic Bohemian' or the 'Emperor of Bohemia' was the way Alejandro Sawa had been described by Rubén Darío and others because of his brilliant wit. In the prologue to the posthumous *Illuminations in the Darkness* (see note 5) Darío contrasts Sawa's great gestures and pride with his lack of will in his later dark and tragic days.

231 See note 145. That is, 'God forbid that I should be a poet'.

232 Pío Baroja, among others, described the paradox of Bohemian life in the early twentieth century as rough, rebellious, lazy, slanderous, iconoclastic; 'illusion' and 'rebellion' eventually led to alcoholism, and to the erratic behaviour or animated conversations of the perennial tenants of the shabby night cafés. The man of letters was identified with the Bohemian: the two were thought to be nonconformist, original and eccentric.

233 There is a double meaning here. An *institucionista* was also a product of the *Institución Libre de Enseñanza* (Free Institute of Education), the liberal and progressive school founded by the jurist and pedagogue Francisco Giner de los Ríos (1839–1913). The Institución played a big part in Spanish life after 1900 and the allusion here is to the fact that young men, like Dieguito, gained good positions due to their particular education.

234 See note 227. Max had guessed correctly about the source of his stipend and thus his self-deprecation was justified.

235 The original is, phonetically, the classical Greek pronunciation of 'irony': Max did not get justice but he received bribe-money like a common informer for denouncing the policeman who beat him up.

236 A band indicates a good brand of cigar; *La Gaceta* was the official publication reporting governmental activity and legislation.

237 This striking sentence recalls the early Cubist-like distortions of space, especially interiors; the objects of the café are reduced to elementary geometrical bodies and the total picture is a synthetic, bizarre schematization of furnishings, noises and people.

238 See note 119.

239 See notes 109, 181.

240 *Admirable* was the pet phrase of Rubén Darío, and many others kept on repeating it. It became the prestigious expression of the era, while *imbécil* stood for the opposite, for what was low and scornful. *Admirable* and *imbécil*

were the two commonplaces of Modernist criticism: Rubén Darío was *admirable*, for example, while the Nobel Prize winner Echegaray was *imbécil*.

241 'Her' alludes to *La Dama de Luto*, 'Dark Lady' or 'Lady of Mourning'. The Darío of 'Cantos de vida y esperanza' ('Songs of Life and Hope'), 1905, who loves life, fears death and is sentimental about old age, often referred to death in his poetry as *Ella*. Here it is probably a reference to 'Nocturno' (1905), where the poet looks at life as a sad dream from which only *Ella* (Death) awakens us. Max admires Darío as a poet but mocks his sentimental view of life and death.

242 The mythological river which at death the soul must cross on its passage to the netherworld.

243 See notes 115, 121, 205.

244 A perennial topic of all Bohemians was the need to escape, but the impossibility of escaping from the waste of that life-style.

245 *Pápiros* is slang for *billetes de banco*, i.e., 'banknotes made of taxpayers' hides' because they came from government funds. See notes 227, 234.

246 St Martin (c. 319–397), bishop of Tours, gave, when a soldier, half his military cloak to a beggar. This became a symbol of charity.

247 A contrast is intended here between the noble type of Bohemian who has the genius or temperament of the artist and the tramp-like Bohemian who lives parasitically in the shadow of real artists.

248 Darío here claims initiation in those esoteric cults that desired communion with the harmony of the 'Great Whole' by seeking, like mathematicians, the occult meaning of creation.

249 *Gnosis* means mystical knowledge of spiritual mysteries. Though Latino is again being pretentious, Valle-Inclán was interested in the aesthetic implications of gnosticism.

250 In other words, Rubén offers a subjective, mystical interpretation of the forces that constitute nature or the universe; basic constituent realities exist only insofar as man has an intuitive awareness of their existence.

251 In traditional cosmology the world was regarded as being composed of the four substances, earth, air, fire and water which were hostile to one another, constantly battling and regrouping. For Darío the forces of the atmosphere are the first basic principles and their rudimentary nature is so mysterious that, like the Universe or man's place in it, they

are incomprehensible to man and thus have a religious meaning. Rubén Darío had astonished Spaniards with his mixture of agnosticism, superstition and Christianity, and with his peculiar beliefs in witches or evil spirits as well as more refined religious concepts.

252 Max's terse rejection of Darío's explanations may be one of the early twentieth-century foreshadowings of later existentialist thought about the inescapable reality of nothingness, and the consequent belief that since man comes from and goes into nothing, his existence precedes his essence. Many of these ideas came from Nietzsche and were a part of the avantgarde vision. Valle-Inclán plays with existentialist ideas in almost all his works.

253 One more of the fashionable attempts by theosophists to marry nature, philosophy, the concept of numbers and Christianity.

254 The 'Quaternary' is a combination of fours used by mathematicians and mystics, a favourite Pythagorean concept among the theosophists and found in their occult terminology. Latino is rehashing their jargon about physical, astral or mental bodies. See notes 189, 190.

255 The concept 'Number' was once the object of various mystical speculations by Plato and Pythagoras and was revived by theosophists.

256 The ancient Greek philosopher and mathematician Pythagoras was interested in the harmony of the spheres and the transmutation of the soul. The merging of religion and science was popular with theosophists, hence Max's sarcastic epithet.

257 Madame Helena Petrova Blavatsky (1831–1891) founded the Theosophical Society, 'Universal Brotherhood', in 1875 and published a *Glossary of Theosophical Terms* and *The Key to Theosophy*. Valle-Inclán read her book *Isis Unveiled*, a new interpretation of the Egyptian mysteries about death and resurrection. Though admired for her energy and enthusiasm, her so-called 'psychic powers', very much in the news at the end of the nineteenth century, were considered a fraud. Her 'Secret Doctrine' was seen to be a crude compilation of vague, contradictory and garbled extracts from various sources.

258 *Volteriano* (from Voltaire) is a common term in Spanish for a sceptic or cynic.

259 *Camarruma* is the Sanskrit *Kama Rupa*, a term used in esoteric theosophy to designate an inner, astral form which lives on after the death of the body; *Karma* is a

Sanskrit term for retribution. Latino's threat stems from a belief propagated by Mme Blavatsky (note 257), whom Max has just insulted, that evil exists and that the Godhead can punish irreverence. There is retribution (*karma*) in reincarnation because reincarnation depends on man's good or evil acts. These terms are found in Roso de Luna's writings. See note 191.

260 Darío's ideas are a mixture of Christianity, oriental teachings, occultism, theosophy and pagan mysticism: he defends poetically the existence of mysterious other-world forces with which some people can always hope to establish contact. Like theosophists or oriental thinkers, he is most at his ease when moving within the circle of the so-called Divine Essence of which he claims not knowledge but insight.

261 A Pythagorean idea, revived by and incorporated in many occult sects, that a certain quantitative interval is the basis of musical notes and harmony and that there must be a cosmic 'harmony of the spheres'.

262 The description is fairly accurate: Darío's tall figure, usually clad in a frock coat, and his strange mask-like face with its fixed concentration of the eyebrows—a face that had more Indian than Spanish blood in the veins—always attracted attention.

263 The famous shrine of pilgrimage in Galicia, Santiago de Compostela. Valle-Inclán often pitted the serenity of the Galician Compostela against the harsh severity of the Castilian Toledo.

264 Paco Villaespesa (1877–1936) was poet, dramatist, founder of many reviews, and a pillar of Modernism and the avantgarde.

265 As a Latin American, Darío normally made no differentiation between *s* and *z* (th). He was a master in the art of writing and reciting flowing, musical verse. He composed several poems on Valle-Inclán, in the most famous of which each stanza ends with the perfect, sonorous endecasyllabic refrain, 'Don Ramón María del Valle-Inclán'.

266 The Marqués de Bradomín is the Galician, Don Juan-like hero of Valle-Inclán's four *Sonatas*. Darío's verses come from a very late poem, 'Peregrinaciones' ('Pilgrimages'), which was not collected in book form. Darío also wrote 'Soneto autumnal al marqués de Bradomín'.

267 Darío, Sawa and most Modernists had recognized Paris as their spiritual home.

268 The lame Paul Verlaine (1844–96), famous French sym-

bolist poet, was a major influence on the Modernists and especially Rubén Darío. Sawa was a close friend of his when he was living as a Bohemian in Paris, and was instrumental, like Darío, in acclimatizing aspects of Verlaine's musical and symbolist style in Spain. 'Verlaine, limping, reigned supreme', wrote Darío in the prologue to Sawa's *Illuminations in the Darkness* (see note 5). The stage direction here effectively recreates the Bohemia of late nineteenth-century Paris, relived momentarily in the inebriated minds of the old decadent Bohemians, Darío and Estrella, in the Bohemia of early twentieth-century Madrid.

269 Either the largest park of Madrid, the *Retiro*, or the Botanical Gardens on the south side of the Prado Museum. Max and Latino have left the Bohemian section of Old Madrid, crossed over to the more central Cibeles (see note 102) and are slowly walking through one of these parks on their way to Atocha and Max's garret (see note 155).

270 The original *la luna lunera* is a popular expression surviving in lullabies ('luna lunera/cascabelera/ojitos azules/carita morena'), and in popular songs ('Ya salió la luna/luna lunera'), and has been used by many poets, including García Lorca. The meaning is vague, something like 'Harvest Moon' or 'Moonish Moon'. Here it suggests playfully the absurd mating of something Lunar (the prostitute) and Astral (Max).

271 *La Corres* is an abbreviation for the newspaper *La Correspondencia de España*. Maura (see note 119) was not only a politician but also an active journalist who continually published short and long items in this and other papers, including his own. He wrote so much, in fact, that his pronouncements were labelled 'catechisms' and considered banal by his detractors.

272 *Que le den morcilla* is an idiom equivalent to 'to hell with him'. *Morcilla* is a black pudding, made from pig's blood.

273 By taking *morcilla* literally, Latino makes a joke on Maura's alleged Jewish origins. See notes 149, 272.

274 *Guasíbilis!* comes from *guasón* ('joker', 'witty') and is an elongation typical of Madrid speech. A common example is *fresquíbilis*. It is as if we could say in English that a woman 'is a beautifulis'.

275 The cigar is given an obscene connotation.

276 Probably one of the Minister's good cigars given to Max. See note 236.

277 An obvious reference to a professional pander, probably to Tread-Well's husband. See note 65.

278 In order to bribe him. In the large Spanish cities there were many expedients for keeping illegal prostitution thriving.

279 *Astrónomos* alludes to Max's and Latino's extravagant appearance—the Bohemian attire and the arty manner—which made them seem to be up in the clouds. See note 1.

280 Armida, in Tasso's *Gerusalemme liberata*, was the captivating witch whose magic palace was decorated with pictures of the Triumph of Love and whose gardens had a sensuous, 'Arabian Nights' quality. A feature of the *esperpento* is the burlesque imitation of classical situations by making contemporary, ridiculous people act out the old classical scenes (see note 10). It is similar to the technique of Cervantes in Don Quixote, which Valle-Inclán had studied carefully. See Introduction.

281 The Prostitute is describing the long, loose hair of Bohemians, something like that of Christ. Also, what follows is a parody of two relationships: Christ with Mary Magdalene; and Don Quixote with Maritornes.

282 *Dilustrado* is a contraction of *de ilustrado*, i.e., 'the speech of a very educated man'.

283 *Chanelar* is underworld slang.

284 That is, she comes from Chamberí, then a colourful district of Madrid to the northwest of Cibeles. It was mainly working-class and the inhabitants had a picturesque and racy manner of speech which La Lunares exemplifies.

285 *Gachó* (or *gachí*) is slang for a lover.

286 Famous bullfighter nicknamed 'el Gallito'. (See note 360). Some of the most popular songs and ballads in Spain are about bullfighters.

287 That is, like an Andalusian. Andalusia is the home of *Cante jondo* or the flamenco type of singing.

288 *Que me visita el nuncio*, 'a visit from the apostolic nuncio', is a colloquial euphemism for a girl's first menstruation.

289 Here *flamenco* is colloquial for manly, virile.

290 A famous cabaret gypsy dancer with striking green eyes, who caused a sensation as a young girl when she danced in tights. A legend in her day, her green eyes are said to have captivated her audiences, creating almost ecstatic reactions and a sort of frenzy.

291 *Peripatética* is a euphemism for a street walker looking for clients. (Cf. note 91).

292 The whole of this scene was added in the 1924 edition and its content (the Catalan prisoner and the strikes) is a logical climax of the other two added scenes, II and VI. Valle-Inclán's elaboration of the political disturbances

offers a grotesque reflection of historical events that are so far from the human ideal as to be already grotesque *per se*.

293 The Madrid of the time of the Hapsburgs (sixteenth and seventeenth centuries). This is the southern section of old Madrid from the Plaza Mayor to Atocha. Max and Latino have left the parks, have probably crossed over Atocha Street and are slowly approaching home.

294 This is typical of Valle-Inclán's 'esperpentic' vision of Spain: one more anonymous, innocent victim of the violent clashes during the police suppression of the strikes. The scene may allude to a real event: in mid-August 1920, an eleven-year-old boy was shot accidentally by the police during the quelling of a riot at Cuatro Caminos.

295 This scene has accurately reflected the clashes between anarcho-syndicalists and the authorities, due to the labour crisis of 1917 which produced riots and assassinations in several Spanish cities and, in Barcelona in particular, a reign of terror. The reactions of the employers to the revolutionary strikes were violent and hastened the alliance between the middle class and the traditional Spanish Right. All this is reflected in the comments of the retired officer, bar-owner and the Pawnbroker. The revolutionary slogans are evident in the retorts of the mason, the old woman and the concierge. Fearing a revolution like that of the Bolsheviks, or the occupation of factories as in Italy, the employers, assured of the backing of government and army, refused to satisfy many of the claims of the workers and fought the unions in a series of lock-outs. This is the historical background of this scene but, as part of an *esperpento*—i.e., as a grotesque version of a historical situation—political argument becomes pure bickering in the midst of a profound social and personal tragedy and degenerates into outlandish gesticulation (the *esperpento* is Dante's descent into the *Inferno*); all rational norms, any personal or political actions appear absurd. The essential ingredients of this *genre* are depicted in victimized innocence, consequent calamity, wasted tragic concern, callousness, moronic cynicism, and out-and-out disgust. In a theatrical production, the spectator is made to face simultaneously an unspeakable tragedy, a disturbing apathy and an incredible idiocy. The staccato of Max's reaction, *imbécil* (see note 240), dramatically pinpoints the histrionic display of senseless disaster.

296 The cellmate of Max in Scene VI, who had predicted that policemen would shoot him in the back and then would

cynically report that he had attempted to escape (see note 172). The arrest, beatings and assassinations of various strikers were commonplace and the whole calamity is a well-documented story.

297 The paradoxical phrase *trágica mojiganga* is a key definition of the *esperpento*, which captures the tragic dimensions of farce or the farcical aspects of a tragedy. The paradox is found in contemporary journalism: in the same magazine where *Lights* appeared one can read descriptions of the national chaos as *la tragedia bufa* ('tragic buffoonery' or 'clownish tragedy'), *un plano convulsivo de tragedia* ('an uproarious level of tragedy'), or *farsa de fusilamiento* ('the farce of executions'), etc.

298 See notes 22, 44 and 52.

299 Max recommends ending it all from Madrid's favourite suicide spot, the Viaduct carrying Segovia Street in the southwestern district of Old Madrid. *Dar un salto en el Viaducto* ('take a leap from the Viaduct') is Madrid slang for committing suicide.

300 *Carcunda* (from *carca*) is a disparaging term for Carlist (see note 344). Latino alludes to Max's early political leanings, and especially to Max's father who was a captain in the Carlist army, according to the Marqués de Bradomín in Scene XIV.

301 Max rejects tragedy as a literary genre because its manner of depicting morally significant struggles ending in ruin or profound unhappiness cannot in modern times accurately represent the situation of Spaniards. Their tragic situation, he suggests, is too calamitously absurd to have the nobility of traditional tragedies. The word *esperpento* normally refers to an ugly person or thing, or to an absurdity. This is the first time it is used to denote a particular category of literary composition, one in which events are characterized by ludicrous or incongruous distortion. According to Rubia Barcia, Valle-Inclán may have first seen the term *esperpento* applied to a literary work in Mexico. A Mexican dictionary of 1905, for example, relates *esperpento*, like the local *culebrón*, to theatrical pieces of burlesque nonsensical and macabre action.

302 This speech and Max's preceding 'breathe hard on me' refer to the opening scene of play when he was 'left out in the cold' without employment by Buey Apis, the arrogant editor who rejected his newspaper articles (see note 7). Max constructs a series of complicated analogies: here he is freezing to death and needs someone's breathing

(*aliento*), like that of the ox in the manger of Bethlehem. Latino, at his side, is thus transformed into this ox. Max next suggests that his guide-dog, Latino, should be the leading ox (*cabestro*) that carries the bell, and if he bellows the other oxen will follow, among them perhaps the Sacred Bull, that is, the Buey Apis who took his livelihood away. Finally, since Mr Big Shot is only a bull, Max suggests teasing him (*torear*), and thus becoming a bullfighter showing off before a crowd.

303 'Avantgarde' translates *ultraístas*. *Ultraísmo* was the most advanced literary movement around 1918, related to the Imagism, Cubism and Dadaism of other countries.

304 The Spanish painter Goya (1746–1828) was famous, among other things, for his grotesque *Caprichos* and *Disparates*, in which he systematically deformed reality. Valle-Inclán was particularly influenced by such *Caprichos* as the one in which a mirror distorts a man's face and converts it into that of a monkey or a serpent.

305 Álvarez Gato is the name of a real alley off the Plaza de Santa Ana, next to the Puerta del Sol. In front of a hardware store there were, in the 1920s, some distorting mirrors, like those found in fairs and carnivals, and the passers-by would stop and amuse themselves by being reflected: a concave mirror elongates the figure while a convex one shortens and broadens it. The heroes of tragedy are deformed in an *esperpento* in the same way as the onlookers who stopped before the mirrors in the alley of Álvarez Gato.

306 Allusion to Unamuno's famous work *Del sentimiento trágico de la vida en los hombres y en los pueblos* (1913). Valle-Inclán's systematic deformation entails a revision, or even inversion, of the values of the Generation of 1898; the tragic attitude toward Spain should be rejected as a falsification.

307 The *esperpento* does not catch reality according to classical norms, but as in a concave mirror that distorts and ridicules appearances. In the imaginative reflection of the artist's mind, human deformations, like disparate numbers arranged systematically in a mathematical formula, acquire their own order and become, aesthetically speaking, 'beautiful'.

308 *En el fondo del vaso*, is a euphemism for 'being drunk', since it denotes draining the full glass. Intoxication was, of course, traditionally related to artistic inspiration and imagination.

309 *Traerse una guasa* (from the colloquial *guasón*, 'joker'), means to make sport of somebody or something.

310 A reference to the garret where Max lives. See the opening stage direction.

311 Victor Hugo had one of the most spectacular funerals in the history of Paris, the classical funeral of the Romantic poet.

312 That is, Max's vision of funerals could be a religious speculation about the mystical apprehension of God. See notes 36, 188, 191.

313 Witnessing one's own death and funeral was a commonplace of Romantic literature, favourite macabre motif among some Modernist writers.

314 The allusion to the prisoner's bitter realization (at the end of Scene VI) about how the press would report his murder was interpolated in the 1924 edition. Thus Max's explanation of the *esperpento* in the final edition is related in a more direct way to the historical crises of 1917–20. Max's recollection of the murdered striker grafts the entire political background into the central narrative of the blind poet's last hours.

315 *Gori-gori* is a humorous colloquialism for the Latin prayers mumbled by priests at funerals.

316 It is difficult to distinguish in the blind poet's death the tragic from the farcical. This precarious borderline between solemnity and playful absurdity is the scaffold round which Valle-Inclán builds almost all the climactic situations of his *esperpentos*. Max can jest while dying because he now views his 'tragedy' from a detached, alienated position; laughter, ironically, becomes a release from the grotesque deformation of tragedy.

317 *Señá* is a colloquial contraction of *señora*.

318 In the phrase *la ha pescado*, the object pronoun refers to *la borrachera* ('drunkenness'). Obviously it was common knowledge in the neighbourhood that Max was habitually drunk.

319 While scenes I–XIII take place in about 10–12 hours, from dusk to dawn, and deal with the last hours of the blind poet, scenes XIII-XV which deal with the wake, funeral and aftermath occur about one to two days later. The bizarre circumstances of Sawa's death and wake were evoked earlier by Pío Baroja's version of the death of Villasús in part VI, Chapter 8 of *El árbol de la ciencia* ('The Tree of Knowledge', 1911). Valle-Inclán's presentation is, however, different.

320 This chilling description of the splinter on the temple is a detail recorded also in Sawa's funeral; it was even mentioned that the splinter caused a trickle of blood on the corpse's skin. Cf. A. Zamora Vicente, p.126. (See note 333).

321 *A dos velas* is Madrid slang for drunk.

322 A contemporary of Sawa, Eduardo Zamacois, said similar things: 'I'll never forget the painful scenes that I witnessed in this tragedy of Sawa's real life. And I'll never forget either my country's cruel indifference toward this one Spaniard, a devotee of foreign culture, whom Spain condemned to die of hunger' (quoted by Zamora Vicente, p.126).

323 See notes 115, 121, 205.

324 In *¡La trae de alivio!* the *la* refers to *borrachera* ('drunkenness'): i.e., 'he has such a bad case of intoxication that he really needs some relief!'.

325 The object pronoun *la* again has the same meaning, but with *dormir* the noun understood would be *la mona.*

326 This bizarre detail is not an attempt at realism or naturalism, but is totally anti-sentimental; the art of the grotesque undercuts the tragic sense of sombre realities like funerals, which are not allowed to retain any dignity. The effect is direct and yet nightmarish.

327 Casinos Assens observed in 1916 that what Angel Ganivet had meant to the preoccupied intellectuals of the generation of 1898 is what Alejandro Sawa (see note 5) meant for the young artists of the 1900s (*Las escuelas literarias*, p.274). Sawa was legendary in his lifetime, living on the outskirts of a literary aesthetic revival and in some ways a precursor of later literary movements: he made young Spaniards think not of moral writers like Taine or Montaigne, but of aesthetes like Verlaine and Mallarmé. It is important to note, however, that in Valle-Inclán's version of Sawa, the blind poet ends by rejecting these same youths who were calling him 'maestro' (see note 110) and had criticized their movement as a farce (see note 303).

328 Basilio Soulinake was the assumed name of one Ernesto Bark, Russian emigré writer, known Bohemian and anarchist in the early twenties. He was author of a short work *La santa Bohemia* (*Holy Bohemia*), 1913, in which he includes, among several portraits that of his close friend Sawa. He appeared as an adept of Gnosis in Valle-Inclán's *La lámpara maravillosa: Ejercicios espirituales* (*The Wondrous Lamp: Spiritual Exercises*, 1916).

329 '*Me dispense usted a mi*' is a flowery and slightly inaccurate way of apologizing. These qualities characterize this foreigner's use of Spanish throughout his appearance.

330 Spanish kings had a Walloon Guard.

331 Soulinake's praise of German doctors may echo the petition signed in 1919 by several Spanish intellectuals requesting help for German scientists who were hampered in the continuation of their research by their country's defeat in the First World War.

332 This persistence degenerates into grotesquerie: Sawa wrote in his *Illuminations* (see note 5) that Soulinake-Bark was 'extremist', 'stubborn' and a 'radical anarchist'.

333 It is possible that in order to make Soulinake suspect muscular rigidity Valle-Inclán had stressed the disturbing detail of the splinter at Max's temple. See note 320.

334 In the 1920 edition it is Clarinito who responds; this is more appropriate within the context than Claudinita.

335 Carlos Rubio Street is near the Glorieta de Cuatro Caminos, then a distant suburb on the outskirts of northwest Madrid.

336 The ridiculous argument between Soulinake and the Concierge converts the traditional funeral scene into something outlandish. The comic note, with Max lying dead and his widow and daughter perplexed and grief-stricken, detaches the spectator from the scene. A shift from sympathy to estrangement is a characteristic of the *esperpento*. Tragedy creates catharsis while the *esperpento* causes estrangement: the grotesque funeral intermingles laughter and grief, thus precluding the unequivocal response that we associate with traditional comedy or tragedy. The same effect of uneasy laughter or amused consternation is found in most of the crowd scenes of the *esperpento*—e.g. Scenes II, V, VII, XI.

337 *Arete* is an earring; hence it is a nickname for the young fellow (*pollo*) who accompanies the Councillor's wife.

338 With this connotation, *gatera* (literally 'cat-flap') is Madrid slang.

339 Bradomín (note 266) was, like Valle-Inclán himself, from Galicia, the Celtic part of Spain. This character reappears or is mentioned in some twelve works. He is often Valle-Inclán's *alter ego*, sometimes straightforwardly, sometimes ironically. Here he is different from what he was in 1903–1907 and these changes may reflect Valle-Inclán's own development. Bradomín is no longer a Modernist and here returns to steal the thunder of Rubén Darío. Like Balzac,

Zola and Galdós before him, Valle-Inclán has various of his characters reappear from work to work, thus constructing a fictional microcosm.

340 Darío implies a contrast between the Christians who urge man to be constantly aware of the mystery of an after-life and the ancient Greek pagans who were concerned with this life more than the next.

341 An ironical yet orthodox statement of Christian belief: man cannot escape eternity, whether in Heaven or Hell.

342 Ironically, Bradomín is here paraphrasing Darío's own lines from 'Nocturno'. See note 241.

343 See note 241.

344 Carlists were the supporters of the pretenders, the first being Don Carlos de Borbón, brother of Ferdinand VII, who had challenged Isabella II's right to the throne. The reference here is to the two civil wars (1833–40 and 1873–76) in which the conservative Carlist faction fought persistently but ultimately lost. Bradomín appears fighting as a Carlist in *Sonata de invierno* (*Winter Sonata*) and in the trilogy *La guerra carlista* (*The Carlist War*). The reference to Max's early Carlist leanings, along with his present anarchist ideas, are to some extent autobiographical, since Valle-Inclán had once flirted with Carlism, and felt some sympathy for many anarchist ideals. Such a paradox can be explained only within modern Spanish history which is remarkably well reflected in *Lights*. Despite radical differences and open enmity, the Spanish Carlists of the Northern Provinces and the anarchists of Catalonia, Andalusia and Madrid had certain fundamental principles in common, namely a hate for middle class mentality, a scorn for bourgeois ethical values, an urge for violence against the establishment, an inner nostalgia for the past (for the anarchists, a yearning for the communes in the revolt against Charles V), a faith in the sound instincts of the Spanish peasant; the emphasis on faith and passion as against reason, and a strong sense of righteousness and justice.

345 Bradomín's erotic adventures in *Sonata de estío* (*Summer Sonata*) take place in Mexico. Valle-Inclán's visits to Mexico had a strong influence on his writings.

346 The influence of *Hamlet*, evident in Valle-Inclán's own gravediggers' scene, is now acknowledged.

347 *La edad del pavo* not only refers to early adolescence but is a euphemism for the awakening of sexual desire in young girls. Bradomín had an encounter with such an 'Ophelia'

in *Sonata de invierno* (*Winter Sonata*). Hamlet was a 'simpleton' according to Bradomín, because he was not aware of Ophelia's sexual leanings; he was not responsive to the tempting young girl.

348 Ironical reference to the Brothers Quintero, Serafín (1871–1938) and Joaquín (1873–1944), two established, popular playwrights responsible for over 150 plays, mostly light comedies and sentimental dramas. No doubt here as elsewhere Bradomín's sarcasm reflects Valle-Inclán's view of the sterility of the Spanish stage, whose representatives like Echegaray, Benavente or the Brothers Quintero gave only a Spanish variety of banal bourgeois morality and predictable, facile characterization.

349 The first clown gravedigger in Hamlet identifies a skull as that of Yorick, who had been the king's jester, and Hamlet starts his famous speech, 'Alas! poor Yorick. I knew him . . .'

350 Artemisia, widow of Mausolus, King of Caria, erected to his memory the costly monument called the Mausoleum. This legend became the classical symbol of a widow's devotion to her dead husband.

351 Bradomín calls the gravediggers stoics because of their ability to remain unaffected by the grief of death; they are realistic about the dead, the relatives' mourning, or their own profession, and they are not moved by the pain or pretence of others.

352 Valle-Inclán's four *Sonatas* (1092–05) were written in the form of 'memoirs' and were subtitled *Memorias del Marqués de Bradomín.*

353 When Valle-Inclán temporarily abandoned literature and tried his hand at agriculture in 1913, by renting and cultivating the farm 'La Merced', he failed miserably as a small farmer and, like Bradomín here, had to sell some of his writings because he needed the money. Bradomín's failure further reflects to some extent Galicia's unsuccessful efforts to emerge from a primitive economy; it was thought that the special interests of Galician agriculture were neglected in Madrid.

354 *Pay-pay* is here a nickname but it comes from the Philippine expression for 'straw fan'.

355 *Beber sin dejar cortinas* ('to drink without leaving curtains') means drinking beer without leaving foam on the glass.

356 The Ateneo. See note 209.

357 Valle-Inclán wrote to Darío about Sawa: 'Alejandro has

left an unpublished book. The best that he has written'. This was *Illuminations in the Darkness*. See note 5.

358 Reference to the popular Princess Isabella, who used to be present at many public functions, among them the première of some of Valle-Inclán's own plays.

359 Allusion to a mysterious, attractive thief who appeared in popular, French detective novels and in films in the period around 1910–20. He was a proverbial figure because of his unexpected appearances in unlikely places.

360 Reference to Joselito, 'el Gallito' (see note 286). His death in the bullring of Talavera, and Maura's visit to his wake and funeral were special news items in the press of 19 May 1920.

361 Nickname for the famous bullfighter Juan Belmonte, a favourite among artists, Bohemians and intellectuals. There were many debates about the merits and demerits of famous bullfighters. Many arguments centred precisely on the vivid, colourful Joselito vs. the more classical, 'intellectual' Belmonte.

362 An ironical use of etymology, for 'tabernacle' was originally a little *taberna*.

363 *¡Diez mil del ala!* is a Madrid idiom for 10,000 pesetas safely stored away (i.e., literally tucked 'under the wing').

364 *Propi* is a colloquial contraction of *propina*, like *Lati* for *Latino*. See note 317.

365 *Amos* is a colloquial form of *Vamos*.

366 Reference to the notorious moments of frights in the bullring shown by Rafael Gómez el Gallo (brother of el Gallito, see notes 286 and 360), who was bald. These moments of fright are the *espantás*, a colloquial pronunciation of *espantadas*. Many a Sunday was marred by some accident in the bullring, followed by the bickerings of devotees whether the accident was due to cowardice or daring. See notes 17, 361.

367 *Calle de la Pasa* is Raisin Street. The obvious pun produced the Madrid proverb 'El que no pasa por la calle de la Pasa, no se casa' ('He who does not pass through the Raisin Street will never marry').

368 See note 271.

369 The literal meaning of the original is 'to change the water of the olives'.

370 In Spanish slang this phrase has an obscene connotation.

371 *Hacer celestinazgo* ('to act like a Celestina') derives from the old go-between in the famous *La Celestina*, or *Tragicomedia de Calisto y Melibea* (1499) by Fernando de Rojas.

372 This was Max's plan for his family's collective suicide in the opening scene (see note 9). Unlike most of the rest of the plot, this ending, which provides the final touch of irony to the play, has no basis in reality. Valle-Inclán and Darío kept on sending money to Sawa's widow who responded with grateful acknowledgements. See note 6.

APPENDIX. *Chronology of Valle-Inclán's Plays*

1899 CENIZAS (*Ashes* or *Human Remains*), 'drama in three acts'. His first play was performed with little success, then published in book form. It was revised in 1908 as EL YERMO DE LAS ALMAS. It's a sentimental version of adultery among the bourgeois: a tubercular married woman, trapped between her lover and her home, attempts to regain social respectability and spiritual peace.

1903 TRAGEDIA DE ENSUEÑO (*Tragedy of Reverie*), short narrative in dramatic form, included in the collection of short stories *Jardín Umbrío* (*Shadowy Garden*).

1905 COMEDIA DE ENSUEÑO (*Comedy of Reverie*), short narrative in dramatic form, included in the collection of short stories *Jardín Novelesco* (*Fictional Garden*).

1906 EL MARQUÉS DE BRADOMÍN (*The Marquis of Bradomín*, 'Romantic conversations'), had its première. Valle-Inclán's first major attempt at drama is a theatrical adaptation of his famous quartet of novels, SONATAS, especially SONATA DE OTOÑO (*Autumn Sonata*). The title hero, Bradomín, is an 'ugly, catholic and sentimental' Don Juan, a monarchist (a supporter of the pretender, Don Carlos) for 'aesthetic' reasons. The action takes place in the gardens and palaces of Galicia.

1907 ÁGUILA DE BLASÓN, 'Comedia bárbara' (*Heraldic Eagle*, 'Barbaric Comedy'), published in book form. The dramatic use of dialogue and manipulation of crowds through shapes and gestures characterize the first of three 'Barbaric Comedies' and foreshadow his later grotesque style.

1907–08 ROMANCE DE LOBOS, 'Comedia bárbara dividida en cinco jornadas' (*Ballad of the Wolves*, 'Barbaric Comedy divided into five acts'), first serialized and later in book form. Here Valle-Inclán created his first important archetype, Montenegro, a tyrannical yet loving nobleman, hospitable and cruel, proud and humble, feared by the aristocracy and loved by the peasants, both envied and resented by his sons. Together with CARA DE PLATA (the only good son of Montenegro) of 1922, the 'Barbaric Comedies' form a violent triptych about Galician feudalism.

1908 EL YERMO DE LAS ALMAS, 'episodios de la vida íntima' (*The Waste Land of the Spirit*, 'Episodes of Intimate Life'), a reworking of the first play, *Cenizas*, appeared in book form. The major change is in the elaborate stage directions.

1910 FARSA INFANTIL DE LA CABEZA DEL DRAGÓN (*The Infantile Farce of the Dragon's Head*), farcical drama in verse, performed. Published in 1914. The never-never land of Disney-like knights and ladies here contains the broadest kind of incongruous farce and harsh social criticism. It also contains considerable puppet-like material, later utilized for farces and *esperpentos*.

1910 CUENTO DE ABRIL, 'escenas rimadas en manera extravagante' (*April Fairy Tale*, 'Episodes rhymed in an extravagant style'), poetic drama, produced and published as a book. The setting is a garden of Provençe in the Middle Ages and deals with the choice a beautiful princess finally makes between a sensitive troubadour and a brute warrior from Castile.

1911 VOCES DE GESTA, 'tragedia pastoril' (*Epic Cries*, 'A Pastoral Tragedy'), verse play, appeared in book form. It was staged in 1912. The locale is the forested regions of Old Castile during the civil wars of the nineteenth century between the Carlist faction and government forces. It deals with legendary epic themes of loyalty, sacrifice, faith, cruelty, heroism and bloody vengeance.

1912 LA MARQUESA ROSALINDA, 'farsa sentimental y grotesca' (*The Marchioness Rosalinda*, 'A sentimental and grotesque farce'), in verse, had its première. The verse-play borrows much from Mozart and from the *commedia dell'arte*; it mingles irony and farce with courtly glamour and sentimentality. The fusion of theatrical extremes takes shape in this play. The play satirizes several Modernist themes.

1913 EL EMBRUJADO, 'tragedia de tierras de Salnés' (*The One Bewitched*, 'A tragedy of the Lands of Salnés'), was finished in late 1912, then read at the Ateneo of Madrid (see note 209). The play had been rejected by the artistic director of the Teatro Español, the famous novelist and playwright, Benito Pérez Galdós. It's a drama about how rural people are spellbound by avarice, lust and death. In 1927, it became the centre piece of the puppet-show quintet listed below.

1919 LA PIPA DE KIF, 'versos' (*The Pipe of Kif*, 'poetry'). Here Valle-Inclán develops the grotesque vision of the world in verse stage directions. The carnival atmosphere is visualized like a spectacle and *Kif* reads, in part, like closet drama. Sections of *Kif* have been adapted for the stage both in Spain and the USA. *Kif* is a poetic dramatization of the Circus, influenced by the paintings of early Picasso, Solana and other modern artists.

1920 FARSA ITALIANA DE LA ENAMORADA DEL REY (*The Italian Farce of the Girl in Love with the King*), farce in verse, appeared as a book. It had its best production in 1967–8 under the direction of José Luis Alonso. The farce takes place in the eighteenth century and deals with the quixotic love of a beautiful innkeeper's daughter for the ugly, senile king Charles III. It presents a fusion of various techniques—puppets, burlesque, lyricism, impressionism—with a satire of academic literature.

1920 DIVINAS PALABRAS, 'Tragicomedia de Aldea' (*Divine Words: A Village Tragicomedy*), a grotesque tragicomedy, appeared first in a magazine serial and then as a book. All the elements of the 'aesthetic of systematic distortion' of the *esperpentos* are here in a new, gruesomely spectacular version of adultery in Galicia. It is the play of Valle-Inclán's that is most often performed. The role of the indomitable Mari-Gaila offers an outstanding opportunity for a great actress.

1920 LUCES DE BOHEMIA, 'Esperpento sacado a luz por Ramón Mª del Valle-Inclán' (*Bohemian Lights*), a new genre dealing with the grotesque, called *esperpento*, in 12 scenes, appeared first in serial form in a magazine. A later version with 15 scenes in book form appeared in 1924. It is the key *esperpento*, both in theory and practice.

1920 FARSA Y LICENCIA DE LA REINA CASTIZA, 'befa de muñecos' (*The Farce and Promiscuity of the Pure Spanish Queen*), a grotesque farce and 'scoffing by Puppets' in verse, appeared in serial form in a review. Contempt for Alfonso XIII's reign and the Monarchy in general lie behind the burlesque treatment of Isabel II's court. It is the most satirical of the farces, one in which men act hilariously like puppets in absurd situations. The deformed and hence comic view of Spanish reality is like that of the *esperpentos*.

1921 ESPERPENTO DE LOS CUERNOS DE DON FRIOLERA (*Esperpento of the Horns of Don Friolera*), the second *esperpento*, appeared in the review *La Pluma* and was later (1925) published in book form. *Don Friolera* has never passed the censorship in Spain and has not been performed except by clandestine student groups. It is an honour play of the old Spanish type, but done in modern dress. It contains Valle-Inclán's clearest exposition of theatrical 'distance' and artistic 'estrangement'. *Don Friolera* became in 1930 the central piece of the trilogy MARTES DE CARNAVAL.

1922 CARA DE PLATA, 'Comedia bárbara' (*Silver Face*, 'Barbaric Comedy'), appeared in the review *La Pluma*. It dramatizes the conflict between Montenegro and his only son, Cara de Plata, and forms the first part of the trilogy of the *Comedias bárbaras*: CARA DE PLATA (1922), ÁGUILA DE BLASÓN (1907), ROMANCE DE LOBOS (1907–08).

1924 LA ROSA DE PAPEL, 'novela macabra' (*Paper Rose*), a one-act play subtitled 'macabre story' in a review of 1924, but later 'melodrama para marionetas' ('melodrama for marionettes'). It's a tale of unnatural passion, necrophilia, set in a proletarian home of Galicia. A parody of bourgeois drama.

1924 LA CABEZA DEL BAUTISTA, 'novela macabra' (*The Head of John the Baptist*, 'a macabre story') was staged. Like *Rosa de Papel* it was later subtitled 'melodrama para marionetas'. It's a sensationalist version of the settlement of old accounts, based on the biblical theme of Salome, with a gruesome love scene as the finale.

1924 Definitive 15-scene version of the *esperpento* of LUCES DE BOHEMIA.

1926 TABLADO DE MARIONETAS PARA EDUCACIÓN DE PRÍNCIPES (*Puppet Stage for the Education of Princes*), a trilogy of farces published earlier, LA ENAMORADA DEL REY (1920), LA CABEZA DEL DRAGÓN (1910) and LA REINA CASTIZA (1920).

1926 LIGAZÓN, 'auto para siluetas' (*The Bond*, 'a morality play for silhouettes') was performed. Lighting is used expressionistically to project actors as dark shapes or contours against a light background. A violent love intrigue involving procurement and a secret blood pact.

1926 EL TERNO DE DIFUNTO, 'novela' (*The Dead Man's Suit*), a grotesque story, appeared as a book. It was later labelled *esperpento* with the title LAS GALAS DEL DIFUNTO (*The Regalia of the Deceased*). This *esperpento* has not passed the official censors. It deals with an ex-soldier's theft of a dead man's clothes and his relations with a prostitute. A cynical, grotesque view of patriotism.

1927 RETABLO DE LA AVARICIA, LA LUJURIA Y LA MUERTE (*Puppet-Show of Avarice, Lust and Death*) a collection in book form of five plays: *The Bond* and *Paper*

Rose both one-act melodramas for marionettes, *The Bewitched,* a 3-act tragedy first read in 1913; *The Head of John the Baptist* and SACRILEGIO (*Sacrilege*) both one-act pieces for silhouettes. *Sacrilege*, the only new piece, is about a prisoner's confession of incest before his execution by bandits. The group consists of morality plays in modern dress, with a mixture of the real and the uncanny, in which actors must act as both persons and as puppets.

1927 ESPERPENTO DE LA HIJA DEL CAPITÁN (*Esperpento of the Captain's Daughter*), a grotesque play, appeared in a monthly issue of sensational stories and was immediately removed and censored, supposedly for its implicit attack on the government of the dictator Primo de Rivera. It has never been performed. It deals with a series of military and political scandals involving prostitution, gambling, murder and blackmail, which lead to an absurd but real coup d'état by the army.

1930 MARTES DE CARNAVAL, 'esperpentos' (*Shrove Tuesday Carnival*). The title is a pun: *Marte* meaning either Tuesday or Mars. The book is a collection of three revised *esperpentos:* LAS GALAS DEL DIFUNTO, LOS CUERNOS DE DON FRIOLERA and LA HIJA DEL CAPITÁN. The three plays portray three aspects of militarism in Spain from the disaster of 1898 to the military coup d'état of 1923.